Comrade Charlie

COMRADE CHARLIE

Brian Freemantle

St. Martin's Press
New York

Library of Congress Cataloging-in-Publication Data
Freemantle, Brian.
    Comrade Charlie : a Charlie Muffin spy story / Brian Freemantle.
        p.   cm.
    "A Thomas Dunne book."
    ISBN 0-312-08166-9
    I. Title.
PR6056.R43C6   1992
813'.914—dc20   92-26157
                                                                        CIP

First published in Great Britain by Century Hutchinson Ltd.

First U.S. Edition: December 1992
10 9 8 7 6 5 4 3 2 1

*To John Garfield, an extraordinary
surgeon to whom I owe so much. With
sincere gratitude.*

Yet each man kills the thing he loves
By each let this be heard.
Some do it with a bitter look,
Some with a flattering word.
The coward does it with a kiss,
The brave man with a sword.

The Ballad of Reading Gaol
Oscar Wilde

Comrade Charlie

1

Charlie Muffin was surprised to feel as uncomfortable as he did. The need for self-preservation normally overcame all scruples and Charlie was convinced he needed all the self-protection he could get, or manipulate from wherever he could get it. Since when had he been bothered by scruples anyway? He reckoned he'd lost them around the same time as he'd lost his tonsils, when he was about eleven. Too late to back off now: he was committed. Necessarily committed.

'Lovely place,' said Laura.

'Got a great write-up in one of the Sunday food sections,' smiled Charlie. How much had the proprietor slipped the lying bugger to write that this was the most exciting eatery in London? On the standard so far he'd probably had to throw his virgin sister in, to swing it. It was a place of pinewood, checked tablecloths and waiters who wore earrings, jammed with yelling, table-swopping people all of whom seemed to know each other but be unable to speak at any sound level less than a hundred decibels. And the food was crap: Charlie was currently undecided whether his salmon had died from decaying old age or from botulism with a distinctive mercury flavour. The botulism was favourite.

'I read it,' said the girl. 'Never guessed I'd get here. Or be with you when I did.'

Charlie searched for a gallant reply. 'I'm glad you're enjoying it,' he said, which wasn't it. She didn't seem to notice. If they waited for the wine waiter to do his job they'd both die from dehydration, providing the fish didn't get them first. Charlie finished off the bottle of Puligny Montrachet between them and returned the bottle neck-down in the cooler, as a hopeful distress signal. Maybe he should have attached a white flag.

'Do you want to know a secret?'

'If you like,' accepted Charlie. It was to hear any secrets she might have – and to feed back as much disinformation as he could plant in her mind – that Charlie was spending an arm and a leg on a disgusting meal in a place where he could hardly hear himself think. He pushed the fish away, half-eaten. Definitely mercury-tasting botulism. He remembered hearing from someone in the Technical Sections where they actually invented assassination methods that the most virulent killer toxins were still made from fish.

'The girls at the office were jealous when I told them where we were going!' announced Laura.

He knew he was expected to flatter her back, like he would be expected to do others things, later. Survival time, sunshine, he told himself: everything's allowed, to survive. He said: 'I can't understand why they should be!' and thought: Oh Christ! It sounded like he was enjoying it and wanted more: like he was an absolute prick, in fact.

'Can't you?' she said, even more coquettish. 'No one seems to understand you, Charlie. And there are stories! Intriguing ones.'

Like what the hell was he doing in intelligence at all, the uninvited interloper who wouldn't take the hint that he wasn't wanted. It had been all right under a couple of Directors General but since Sir Alistair Wilson's collapse he didn't have the protection at the top any more. Rather, he had the complete reverse. Charlie paraded the rehearsed response, even to someone who worked in the department and was a signatory to the Official Secrets Act, although

10

he hoped Laura wouldn't let that get in the way too much tonight. He said: 'Fairy-tale stuff. We're all just clerks.'

She grinned knowingly. 'Clerks don't break spy rings and go in and out of the Eastern bloc on false passports and have a biography in Records labelled "Director General Eyes Only".'

The turn in Charlie's stomach might just have been the fish but he didn't think so. Encouragingly he said: 'Sounds as if you've been checking.'

'Maybe someone has,' said Laura. She was secretary to Richard Harkness, who hated his guts more than the lousy fish appeared to do and who'd been acting Director General since Wilson's illness.

'How many guesses do I get?'

'I don't think you'd need a lot,' said the girl. 'Why does Harkness shit on you so much?'

'Face doesn't fit, I guess,' said Charlie, casually, not wanting her to guess what the evening was all about because that would be cruel. He said: 'You think that's what he does, shits on me?'

'Come *on*, darling!' said Laura. 'You've been assigned nothing but Dog Watch stuff since Harkness has been in charge! I frankly don't know how you've put up with it like you have!'

Charlie noted he had become darling to Laura. He said: 'Someone's got to do the menial jobs.'

Laura cocked her head to one side, smiling quizzically. 'I'm not buying that, Charlie Muffin. That's not your style.'

'Maybe that's the problem,' said Charlie. 'I haven't got any style.'

'I think he's trying to make life so unpleasant that you'll quit,' declared Laura. 'Either that or get you fired.'

Then Harkness would need to try a bloody sight harder, thought Charlie. He'd endured four months

11

so far: four months as nothing more than the clerk
he'd just told Laura he was, checking long-ago and
out-of-date records for revelations the trained analysts might have missed, poring over airport and port
immigrant entries for false passport trails that would
have been cold anyway, reading the translations –
when translations had been necessary – of Eastern
bloc publications to detect policy changes which the
Foreign Office had an entire division to work on.
Charlie felt he was atrophying, gradually turning
into a fossil, like something in a natural history
museum, a frozen-in-stone example of something
that had roamed the earth a million years before.
But if it meant defeating Richard St John Harkness,
Charlie knew he'd go on for another four months
or four years or for ever: he'd been fucked over
by experts and Harkness certainly wasn't an expert.
Charlie said: 'I guess there might be a way but I don't
think Harkness knows where to find it.'

'What's that mean?'

'That I'm not going to make it easy for him.'

'You know how many new Conduct Rules and
Regulations he's introduced since he's been in
charge? Every one of which I've had to write up and
get legally phrased!' demanded Laura, outraged.

'No,' said Charlie, who'd memorized every one because failure to observe some bloody absurd dictum
or other was precisely the sort of thing that Harkness
would try to invoke against him.

'Fifteen!' said Laura. 'The man should have been
a lawyer!'

'He is,' disclosed Charlie, whose personal rules insisted that he always know everything about his en-
emies. 'He studied finance law at Oxford: that's why
he's so good at cutting expenses.'

'Which you don't get any more,' reminded Laura,
painfully.

'It'll pass,' said Charlie unconvincingly.

'Would it really hurt so much to show some respect, to his face at least?' urged Laura. 'He *is* the Director General now.'

'*Acting*,' qualified Charlie instantly. And it *would* hurt to show respect to an asshole like Harkness: hurt like hell.

'He's out to get you, Charlie. He's going to invent so much red tape he'll strangle you with it.'

'Or himself.'

'He's the *boss*, for Christ's sake! He can *make* the rules. Change the goalposts whenever he wants to.'

The metaphors were becoming mixed, Charlie decided. He said: 'I've got one or two things in mind.' He looked desperately around for their waiter. The man was several tables away but looking in their direction. Charlie grabbed the dead bottle and waved it at the man. The waiter twiddled his fingers in an answering wave. One thing he'd never lacked before was bar-presence, reflected Charlie; he seemed to be losing everything these days.

'Try to do something,' said Laura. 'I don't like to see you being constantly bullied.'

Was that what was happening to him? Charlie supposed it was but he'd never thought of it as being bullied. 'I'll live,' he said flippantly. There'd been quite a few occasions, too many, when he hadn't believed he would: at least now he was safe from physical harm.

The waiter arrived with another bottle of Montrachet and said: 'Bet you thought I hadn't understood!'

'I had every faith,' assured Charlie. 'You've got that way of inspiring confidence.'

'The coffee mousse with coulis is the house speciality and it's divine,' recommended the man, collecting up the discarded fish.

'I've got to think of my figure!' said Laura clumsily.

'Let me do that,' parroted Charlie on cue. There! He'd done it! Casanova wouldn't have been much impressed but it was his best shot so far and Laura seemed to appreciate it. She was a very pretty girl, with good legs and tits where they should have been and innocent-wide eyes and striking red hair that moved when she did, constantly shifting about her shoulders. Altogether too nice to be tricked, like he was tricking her. Or was he? She was a grown-up girl, he tried to reassure himself. He'd done far worse — cheated and tricked and manipulated — in the past and knew damned well, if the need arose, that he'd do it all over again in the future. So why the hell didn't he stop all this conscience-stirred posturing? It didn't suit him.

'What's it going to be, folks?' asked the returning waiter.

'Mousse for the lady,' said Charlie. 'I don't want to spoil the experience of the fish.'

'Unusual, wasn't it?' said the unsuspecting waiter.

'Unique!' said Charlie. 'Positively unique!'

'You are a bastard!' Laura giggled when the man had gone.

'Never ever!' denied Charlie in mock outrage. To avoid the purpose of the evening becoming too obvious he led the conversation on to Laura herself. The account was the role model for department entry at female personal assistant rank: private school education, finished off in Switzerland, Daddy with an army chum who'd moved on into the government, a word here, a word there and wasn't it super, look where she was now!

'Super,' agreed Charlie.

The waiter swooped up in an exaggerated glide, pudding dishes balanced along his arm like a conjuring display, and plopped Laura's mousse in front of her. It really looked like something that had plopped down from the sky and Charlie was glad he hadn't ordered it. Time to get back to the business in hand, he decided. He said: 'Is there much gossip about personnel among you girls?'

'This and that,' conceded Laura.

'What's this and that?'

She smiled, passingly embarrassed. 'Comparing people. . .imagining what some are like, against others. . .would be like. . .' She paused, biting her lower lip, half provocative, half uncertain. 'That surprise you. . .shock you?'

'Not particularly,' said Charlie. Edith had always said he wouldn't believe what was written on the walls of ladies' lavatories. 'You don't have to access Records for that, do you?'

'Harkness tried to call your biog up a couple of weeks ago: that's how I knew. Raised a fuss because it wasn't released to him as he was only *acting* Director General,' disclosed the girl.

He'd done this sort of thing once before, a long time ago, remembered Charlie. Cultivated a relationship with a personal secretary as well placed as Laura and for the same reason, to find out just where the knives were coming from. He tried to remember the other girl's name but couldn't. Better, he thought: how it should be. He was too old to develop a conscience now. Charlie said: 'What's happened about it?'

'There are memos going back and forth about temporary authority and confirmed authority,' further disclosed the girl. 'Nothing's been resolved yet.'

Charlie was resolving a number of things, though. The most important was that for the moment at least Sir Alistair Wilson was expected to return and not be forced into permanent retirement by the heart attack, otherwise the access restrictions would not

15

still be in force. But just how long would the Joint Intelligence Committee and the Prime Minister wait? Equally clearly Harkness' role could not continue for any length of time on such a temporary basis. Why, with Charlie being relegated to duties a monkey could be trained to perform, had Harkness wanted his personnel history? Charlie had often wished he could get hold of it himself. *If* Harkness got access and *if* Charlie romanced Laura then perhaps he could persuade her to... No, stopped Charlie. Tempting though it was he wouldn't do that. Gossip was gossip, although still sufficient to get her dumped from the department. Photocopying personnel records, even for the man about whom they were compiled, was Official Secrets trials, the dock at the Old Bailey and ten years in those women's prisons where the girls got up to all sorts of hanky-panky. Bastard he might be but not that much of one, not yet: just close.

The waiter glided back and asked Laura: 'How was the mousse?'

'Wonderful,' she said.

'Some coffee and brandy?' suggested Charlie.

'I thought we might have that back at my place,' invited Laura.

Why hadn't he had offers like this from girls like this when he was eighteen and keen? Where would all those cinema usherettes and bus conductresses be now? 'That would be nice,' Charlie accepted.

The bill clearly stated that a fifteen per cent service charge had been added but the waiter frowned at the exact money Charlie counted out.

'Some people like to leave additional gratuities, you know!' the man sniffed.

'Life's a bitch and then you're dead,' said Charlie. He'd seen it inscribed on a T-shirt and thought it was rather good: he'd been waiting for an opportunity to

16

use it. Upon reflection he was not sure that this had been the occasion.

The bistro was sufficiently trendy for taxis to queue outside, so they didn't have to wait. Laura snuggled very close to him in the back and said: 'That really was lovely.'

Charlie's stomach moved, as a reminder of what had been inflicted upon it, and his feet were aching but then they usually did this late at night, so he was used to that. He said: 'A little overrated, I thought.'

'Disappointing that there was no one famous there,' said Laura. 'They all go there, you know? Famous people?'

'I didn't know,' said Charlie. He really didn't want to go through the bed routine: that really would be tricking her. He said: 'You could always lie to the girls tomorrow: make somebody up. They wouldn't know, would they?'

'I don't suppose they would,' seized Laura eagerly.

She lived in the rich part of Chelsea, in a terraced house in a cobbled mews about which housing agents used words like exquisite and sought-after. She'd already gone ahead, leaving the door ajar, by the time Charlie turned around from paying the cab. Stairs inside led up to a first-floor, low-lighted drawing room. When he entered Laura was standing stone-faced but flushed by a telephone answering machine at the far side, beside the drinks tray.

'I don't believe it!' she said. 'I just don't bloody well believe it!'

'Believe what?' asked Charlie, bewildered.

Laura gestured towards the machine which Charlie realized was on rewind, after relaying its messages. 'Paul's on his way in from the airport. He wasn't due home for three or four days yet.'

'Paul?'

Laura made another impatient hand movement,

this time towards a studied portrait photograph of a pleasant-faced, kindly looking man. 'My husband. He's in Venezuela. . .*was* in Venezuela. *Shit!*'

Charlie thought again of the T-shirt slogan and decided that sometimes, very rarely, life wasn't a bitch after all. Pitching the false regret perfectly in his voice, he said: 'I see. That's. . . I'm sorry about that.'

Laura held out her hands to him and said: 'Darling, I'm sorry. I really am *sorry*.'

'So am I,' said Charlie, soft-voiced now. Careful, smart-ass, he thought: you're working towards an escape, not an Oscar nomination. 'If he's on his way in from the airport I'd better be going, hadn't I?'

'You'd better,' she agreed.

Laura came close, expecting to be kissed: she smelled very nice, perfumed and clean. Charlie kissed her, lightly, feeling backwards with a painful foot for the beginning of the stairway down into the mews.

'Charlie?' she said.

'What?'

'I didn't get what I wanted,' said the woman. 'You got what you wanted, though, didn't you?'

Charlie laughed, glad that Laura did too. He said: 'You've made me feel a lot better.'

'I've still got to wait for the same feeling,' she said.

The mews was sealed off at one end but at the other still had the canopied brick entrance from when it had all been stables and artisans' cottages, although the original huge gate had long since been removed. As Charlie emerged he saw someone paying off a taxi and hurried to get it before it drove off. When he reached it he recognized the passenger as the man in Laura's photograph.

'Night!' said Charlie brightly.

The man was momentarily surprised at such friendliness from a stranger in the middle of London. 'Goodnight,' he said.

Charlie got to the Pheasant with twenty minutes to spare before closing time. He downed the first Islay malt in one because that wasn't a drink at all: that was medicinal, to gaff the fish that still felt as if it were swimming upstream. He took most of the second the same way. He began to relax on the third, deciding that as evenings go the encounter with Laura had gone very successfully indeed. If she tittle-tattled back to Harkness the enigmatic remarks about the man looking in the wrong place for embarrassments it might be perfect. He might even be able to stuff the red tape right back down the man's throat.

The barman approached, mopping the counter, looking inquiringly at Charlie's glass. 'It's been the quietest night for a long time,' he said. 'Quiet all day.'

'They're the best sort though, sometimes,' insisted Charlie. 'Days when nothing at all happens.'

It was, however, far from being a day when nothing happened. It was the day when the US Defense Committee met at the Pentagon and approved the construction of the missile intended to form the nucleus of America's Strategic Defense Initiative, more commonly known as its Star Wars programme.

The approval session – and the identity of those Defense-approved contractors to whom development of the prototype missile was to be awarded – carried the highest security classification. But Washington DC is a porous place where rumours, even over something so sensitive, are balanced for their political advantage. After so many concessions from a Moscow and a Soviet hierarchy different from any they had known or dealt with before, the State Department saw no harm in the smallest of leaks, hopefully to influence the continuing Conventional Arms Limitation discussions in Geneva.

That most influential of aeronautical magazines, *Aviation Weekly*, was the first to publish an indication of the Star Wars decision, quickly followed by other monitoring publications and other monitoring commentators.

It was also monitored in Moscow, which was the State Department intention, although not at all in the way that they had expected.

2

No established order of Soviet society has suffered a greater upheaval by the ascent to power of Mikhail Gorbachev than the KGB, which is the most established of all orders of Soviet society. From the moment of its inception, within a month of the 1917 revolution, the Russian intelligence apparatus, through all its name changes, developed into *the* essential core of government yet insularly aloof from it. An elaborate spider's web of internal directorates and sections and departments, each enveloping strand interlocking with another enveloping strand to control the Soviet people, was spun to maintain the power of successive leaders and their Politburo. And those leaders were always made gratefully aware of the fact. In 1953 Nikita Krushchev – the man later responsible for its last name change to the KGB – successfully challenged the autonomy of the organization by defeating the bid of its then chairman, Lavrenti Beria, to succeed Stalin. Krushchev's mistake was introducing at the same time the edict that the Politburo approve every major international espionage activity before its commencement.

The KGB has always been chameleon-like in its ability to adjust its appearance to merge into its current surroundings. For a while, even after Krushchev's demise, the system of control appeared to operate, although those within the organization continued as they had since 1917, a people apart from other Russian people, with access to concessions and luxuries and privilege, untouched by the perpetual shortages and deprivations suffered by the rest. The adjustment to circumstances and surroundings took

21

place at the very top: if the KGB had instinctively to know the attitudes of the Politburo, ran the persuasion, then its chairmen needed to be members of that ultimate controlling, policy-forming body. So the successive appointments were made, which put the KGB where it always sought to be, at the absolute heart and mind of things. Making the organization, in fact, stronger and more powerful than it had ever been before.

Then came Mikhail Gorbachev. And *glasnost*. And *perestroika*. And after freedom and openness came the most unimaginable change of all. The KGB was demoted, by every definition of the word. Chairman Viktor Chebrikov was transferred to another ministry and his successor, Colonel-General Vladimir Kryuchkev, was denied that all-important elevation to the ruling Politburo. The republics of Estonia and Latvia and Lithuania were allowed publicly to vote against Moscow's central control and thousands paraded in the streets in support of autonomy. Yet bigger demonstrations were permitted – and even more incredibly, *seen* on Soviet television to be permitted! – between Azerbaijan and Armenia.

The chameleon changes colour when it's frightened but this time the frightened KGB didn't know which hue to adopt: internal and external directorates and divisions instead scuttled around in disarray, seeking concealment and disguise.

There were two KGB executives, intimate friends yet pragmatic even in friendship, for whom the American Star Wars revelations destroyed any chance of the hoped-for, regroup-and-think concealment. One was General Valeri Kalenin, a slightly built Georgian and First Deputy of a service to which he had devoted his life to the exclusion of all else, even marriage. The other was his immediate subordinate, Alexei Berenkov, also a general, and head of the KGB's First Chief Directorate, its overseas espionage arm.

It was a mark of their friendship that Kalenin had alerted Berenkov at the moment of the Kremlin summons, bringing the man from the First Chief Directorate on the Moscow ring road to the KGB headquarters in Dzerzhinsky Square.

The chief executive offices of the KGB are on the seventh floor of the original pre-revolutionary building, quite separate from the wartime, prison-laboured extension added by Stalin. Berenkov waited for Kalenin's return at a window overlooking the square, with its beard-tufted statue of Feliks Dzerzhinsky, the service's founder, and at the lights pricking on against the evening's dusk in the GUM department store beyond, wondering how many others had stood at windows in the building as he was now, mourning the passing of previous traditions. A lot, he guessed: just as a lot more would, in the future, whatever that future was for their organization.

Berenkov was a giant of a man, big in every way, booming-voiced and flamboyant-gestured. He was rarely affected by personal doubt, even during a period of imprisonment in Britain and thought that the current apprehension was unnecessary, supremely confident of his own ability to survive government policy changes. Which made Berenkov an unusual person. But then he was already unusual at his level within the KGB, someone with practical, gut-churning experience of what it was like to be an espionage officer in the field. From a London base he had operated clandestinely for more than ten years. Apart from rare snatched reunions under KGB guard in the hideaway places, he'd endured for all those years the separation from Valentina, the wife whom he adored. And still remained a getting-to-know stranger to Georgi, the son whose growing

23

up from a child into a near-adult teenager he'd never known. Now Berenkov, a florid-faced man still heavy from the indulgence of being a Europe-wandering wine importer, which had been his London cover, enjoyed his equally indulgent and elitist existence in Moscow. He justifiably considered he had earned it all; the city centre apartment and the summer dacha in the Lenin Hills and the favoured Black Sea holidays and the Chaika limousine and the concessionary store facilities.

The door into Kalenin's office was electronically secured and Berenkov turned from the window at the faint sound of it being disengaged. Kalenin, a bearded man who did not often smile, appeared more serious than usual: he wore his full uniform, which indicated the formality of the encounter from which he had returned. He unbuttoned the tunic as he crossed the room, slumping into the high-backed chair.

'Well,' he said, resigned. 'We've been set our challenge by the new order!'

Berenkov walked closer, finding a chair of his own. 'The Directorate? Or ourselves?'

'It's one and the same, isn't it?' said Kalenin, whose primary function was chief tactician of the KGB's overseas activity.

'So what is it?'

'The Strategic Defense Initiative,' announced Kalenin, shortly. 'We will not only match but beat the American development.'

'What!' said Berenkov, temporarily off-balanced.

'Those were the words,' elaborated Kalenin wearily. 'We are to identify the builders. We are to discover every detail of their technology and manufacture. Having obtained it we are to turn it over to our space technicians who will construct whatever the Americans are developing but in advance of that

American development. And we will launch ahead of the Americans, proving yet again that the Soviet Union are leaders in space exploration.'

'Have they any conception of what they're asking?' said Berenkov bitterly.

'They're not asking,' corrected Kalenin. 'They're demanding.'

There was no other man whom Berenkov regarded as a closer or better ally than Kalenin. They had attended spy academy together and Kalenin had been the supporter at his wedding to Valentina and was Georgi's guardian in the event of their deaths. Kalenin had played a considerable personal part in freeing him from imprisonment in Britain and protected him greatly on one particular occasion after his repatriation.'The order names me personally?' he anticipated.

'Yes,' confirmed Kalenin reluctantly. 'You can have whatever facilities you require: manpower, resources, money...anything.'

'Luck,' said Berenkov. 'I'll need a lot of luck.'

Which he got and was not unduly surprised at because Berenkov believed himself an inherently lucky man. But in the beginning a great deal was achieved through basic intelligence procedures.

The KGB maintains its biggest external espionage system in the world within the United States, despite the public displays of relaxation between Washington and Moscow. In Washington itself the *rezidentura* operates from the Russian embassy on 16th Street, less than a mile from the White House. But by far the greater concentration of intelligence officers work from the United Nations in New York: estimates vary but American counter-intelligence guess there are two hundred agents installed supposedly as international civil servants in the green-glassed skyscraper overlooking the East River. And as international civil servants they are not subject to the travel restrictions that apply to the Washington embassy or to the other spy centre, the Soviet consulate at 2790 Green Street, in Pacific Heights district of San Francisco.

Following the Dzerzhinsky Square meeting, Alexei Berenkov activated every one, ordering all other intelligence-gathering activity suspended and drafting ten officers immediately from New York to Washington. *Aviation Weekly* really is the foremost and best-informed aeronautical publication, and three of the New York operatives were deputed to read through the previous year's magazines for all references to Star Wars technology. Others from New York focused upon every government department even remotely likely to be involved in such development. The overall government budgets and then its financial breakdown between those various departments – all public documents – were pored over in the Senate and House libraries in the search for an allocation to any company awarded space technology contracts. The Congressional libraries also provided the previous year's record of every hearing of every committee of the two chambers involved in space exploration.

A chart was created from budget details and newspaper and magazine listings of all Pentagon-approved defence contractors, the logic being that bureaucracy moves on straight and well-regulated lines and that the development was likely to be awarded to a corporation which had already undergone a full security clearance and proved itself reliable in the past.

The dictionary-recorded word lobbying was invented in Washington, to describe favour-seekers who waylaid a nineteenth-century US President in the lobby of the Willard Hotel. Since that time lobbying has progressed into an accepted and recognized profession in the American capital, with the majority of national industries and companies paying substantial retainers to people specializing in their subjects to influence Congressmen and purchasing authorities into directing business their way. The KGB make full use of innocent lobbyists, retaining them through American-incorporated front companies to learn as much as possible about all scientific and technological advances that become known on Capitol Hill. Every Soviet-retained lobbyist in space or space component development was canvassed.

On the West Coast of America lobbyists are called consultants and their function varies slightly. They monitor and keep abreast of trends in that crucible of American high-tech concentrated in California's Santa Clara County and known as Silicon Valley. Their utilization by the KGB is, however, exactly the same: unknowingly retained through Russian front companies but for convenience usually controlled through the consulate in San Francisco.

The information that Berenkov sought was built up fragmented and piecemeal. Several lobbyists and two consultants tried to earn a fee by regurgitating the *Aviation Weekly* article but two Washington-based specialists confirmed inquiries from other, genuine US aeronautical component manufacturers. From those earlier inquiries the lobbyists were able to provide the names of companies that had *not* tendered for the Star Wars work, narrowing the list of those who might have done. The possible identity was further narrowed by filleting from Congressional inquiry hearings the names of five corporations who had been barred from future government work for overcharging on some previously awarded contracts.

A breakthrough pointing to the West Coast came from a four-line reference to private-but-approved contractor use of existing shuttle landing facilities

27

in the Mojave Desert in an Appropriations Committee report. There were three potential West Coast manufacturers remaining on the reducing list of possibilities. From Moscow Berenkov ordered that all three companies and their senior executives should be targeted.

The KGB head at the San Francisco consultate, Alexandr Petrin, took over the investigation of a company which a man named Emil Krogh was chairman.

Petrin, a darkly handsome native of Turkmenitya, which made it easy for him to pass as someone of Mediterranean birth, came to regard it as the best intelligence assignment of his KGB career.

Richard St John Harkness was a person elevated by a combination of convenient circumstance and personal good fortune to the fullest extreme of his abilities, although he would never have conceded it because the judgement had never occurred to him. The most recent example of that combination was the illness of Sir Alistair Wilson. The Director Generalship was being held open but Harkness believed that merely to be a temporary and cosmetic gesture, a reassurance to avoid causing the man any further, dangerous worry. And that his own promotion to ultimate control was inevitable. It was a role he craved desperately and was implacably determined to get. And when he did he intended restoring the department to one of proper order and respect. Sir Alistair and some Directors before him had been far too unconventional, tolerating riffraff and adventurers. It was all going to change when his position was confirmed. The riffraff, one in particular, was going to be weeded out and dispensed with: Harkness was impatient with the continuing delay.

3

Charlie Muffin was aware he had to tread warily, which with his feet he always did anyway. The more he thought about it the more he came to believe the hundred quid he'd spent risking food poisoning with Laura Nolan was money well spent in the war with Harkness. *I think he's trying to make life so unpleasant that you'll quit.* An all-important disclosure because Laura was around the pompous old fart all the time, picking up the inner feelings, overhearing all the chance remarks. Charlie hadn't realized Harkness' campaign was as positive as that. At worst he'd believed the bloody man was showing off, during a brief opportunity of power: that all he had to do was keep his head down, shovel the shit without complaint and await the return of Sir Alistair Wilson. But with more time to think about it Charlie recognized that the dispute over the Records access could be viewed two ways, not confined to the simple view he'd first taken. Sure the continued restriction could be interpreted as indicating that Sir Alistair would be coming back. But the immediate challenge from Harkness, a form-filling bureaucrat piss-pants scared of challenging anything, could equally indicate the Director General was *never* returning, which made Harkness confident enough to launch the purge he'd had wet dreams about for so long.

The Director General's summons light was blinking demandingly when Charlie got to Westminster Bridge Road and what he regarded as a box but which government requisition documents described as office space, single occupancy for the use of, Grade III desk, chair, two highest security filing cabinets and polyester carpet square, two foot by two foot. Avocado was the official colour description: Charlie thought it closer to puke green.

With a new resolve not to provide Harkness with any gratuitous ammunition, Charlie went straight up to the ninth floor. The lift opened on to a sealed-off, protected area where he had to identify himself, although he knew the security guards by their christian names as they knew him by his. Beyond the check were carpets soft under soundless if awkward feet, the richly dark panelling, interspersed with original oil portraits of frock-coated or uniformed men in wigs, reassuringly old. Men may come and men may go but the British Establishment lasts for ever, thought Charlie. He wondered if there would ever be a formal picture of Richard St John Harkness staring down reprovingly. Some of the far-away looking men Charlie was passing were captured against globes of the world or with navigational compasses in their hands, tools of their trade. Charlie supposed that if Harkness were ever painted he'd be shown with an expenses sheet in one hand and an erasing pen in the other.

Laura was waiting at the door of the outer office, her pretty face twisted with concern. She said: 'Remember what I said about showing respect!'

'Engraved on my heart,' said Charlie. 'How's Paul?'

'This isn't the time or the place to talk about Paul,' refused the girl cursorily. Denying herself at once she said: 'As a matter of fact he's red raw with prickly heat.'

'Sure it's prickly heat?' said Charlie. 'You can catch some terrible things from toilet seats in South America.'

'I don't need to worry,' said Laura enigmatically.

Richard Harkness, who'd moved into the Director General's office on the same day that Wilson suffered his heart attack, was sitting personally immaculate behind an impeccably clean desk that unfortunately appeared too big for him. He was pink-faced, grey hair fantailed over his ears, and faultlessly tailored in a foppish kind of a way, the black suit broad chalk-striped and the pastel yellow shirt set off against a matching yellow tie and pocket handkerchief. Charlie couldn't see because the man's feet were hidden beneath the desk, but he guessed the socks would be some sort of coordinated yellow: Harkness tried hard to finish everything off.

There were no chairs conveniently near to the desk, which meant Charlie had to stand: Prick, he thought, smiling towards the man. Harkness looked back blank-faced.

'You've no outstanding assignment, have you?' Harkness asked expectantly.

'Holding myself in readiness,' said Charlie. He believed the cocky, Jack-the-lad routine got up Harkness' nose, which was why he did it.

'There's a request from the Other Place,' announced Harkness, using the inter-departmental jargon for MI5, Britain's counter-intelligence service. 'They've got a bit of a staff shortage and have asked for some temporary secondment for embassy observation.'

Which was roughly equivalent to parking meter warden or leaf sweeper in public parks, Charlie assessed: freezing your ass off in a supposed secure house overlooking communist embassies, monitoring and photographing the comings and goings of one day and comparing them to the comings and goings of the previous day. Spot-the-Spy, the latest quiz game the entire family can play, brought to you courtesy of Her Majesty's Secret Service. He said: 'Sorry to hear that: must be a problem for them.'

'I'm transferring you, until further notice,' announced Harkness with self-satisfied contentment.

No you're not, asshole, thought Charlie. He said: 'Oh dear!'

'Is there a problem?' asked Harkness, smiling at last at his own personal joke.

'I hope not,' said Charlie. 'You can call upon other people, can't you?'

Cold silence came down upon the room. Harkness did not speak for several moments and Charlie was unsure whether there was a nervous tug pulling at the corner of the man's left eye. Harkness said: ' Other people?'

'Well, I can't go across, can I?' said Charlie. 'These new Orders of Conduct you've issued: they specifically state that all active operatives attend assessment courses every six months. I've got my instructions to go at the end of the week. Sorry about that.'

Laura Nolan looked up, smiling hopefully, when Charlie emerged. 'What happened?' she said.

'The dick-head tripped over his own red tape,' reported Charlie.

The girl frowned. 'You did show him the proper respect, didn't you?'

Charlie snapped his fingers, an exaggerated gesture. 'Shit!' he said. 'I knew there was something!'

4

Emil Krogh came awake first and was glad because it gave him time to compose himself, get some life into his face and pull the lines up. Not that it was a real problem. Kept himself in shape in the exercise room at home and the lift-and-tuck job he'd had before he met Cindy had worked just fine, taken off ten years at least. Like the moderate but discreetly maintained tinting, allowing just the right amount of mature greying at the temples but literally not a hair's breadth more; if a President could do it, why couldn't he? No, it wasn't the waking moment Krogh was uneasy about; it was the sleeping ones. And something Peggy, who knew about the face-lift, had said about five months earlier: *Almost time for another one, honey: asleep your face drops in those old relax lines and we don't want that, do we?* Not that his wife really cared what he looked like. All she cared about was the kids and baby-minding the grandchildren, which was fine by Krogh because of the time and freedom it gave him in addition to what he manipulated for himself, which was a lot. But he was grateful for the warning. Which was why he was glad he'd awakened first. Goddamn miracle that he had, after what he and Cindy had done last night; he should feel exhausted but he didn't. Felt fine. Another, perhaps the best, indication that he was in great shape.

There was only a sheet covering them and that hardly at all, and Krogh eased it further away, better to see Cindy's nakedness. Christ, what a body! Tight and firm, not the slightest droop to those fantastic tits even lying like she was, the powder puff between her legs turned towards him, like the invitation he was definitely going to accept. Krogh wondered if he could get out of bed without disturbing her, to clean his teeth: he knew he was dragon-breathed after all that Mexican shit they'd eaten with those tequila drinks the previous night. But only clean his teeth, not shave. Cindy preferred him unshaven when he went down on her; said it was more exciting. Krogh checked his watch as he slipped off the bed. Plenty of time for that. A lot more, too. Still only eight a.m. and he'd been vague when he spoke to Peggy about what time he'd get home, just some time that evening and not to bother waiting dinner.

Krogh scrubbed his teeth, able from the condo window to see the ocean nudging in against the beach. It was a grey, clouds-against-the-water sort of day that visitors didn't expect at Malibu and felt cheated to find. There were the usual joggers and exercise freaks and owners walking dogs and scuffing sand over their crap instead of collecting it up, like they were supposed to. On balance Krogh decided the outlook from Barbara's apartment in San Francisco was better, the bay and the Golden Gate Bridge and the higgledy-piggledy buildings clutching to the side of Nob Hill. He rinsed his mouth and found some mouthwash in the bathroom cabinet and tried that, too, smiling to himself through tight-together lips as the thought came to him. He'd set the day aside for Cindy. But they'd already been together for two celebratory days because of the customary time allowance he'd built in to the East Coast trip and the meetings in Washington DC and at the Pentagon, signing the formal, committing contracts. So why didn't he move on, to celebrate some more? He could fly up to San Francisco in less than an hour: meet Barbara for lunch and spend the afternoon in the sack with another equally attractive and inventive girl. He'd done it before, quite a few

34

times, going straight from one to the other, always managing to make it happen for both of them, proving himself. He'd need to phone Barbara, of course. Let her know he was coming. But not from here, because the number would be recorded on the bill and it would be a dumb thing to do even though he looked after all the bills, the telephone and the condo payments and all the charges, just like he did for Barbara. Have to make it before ten: Barbara left for art classes promptly at ten and it was difficult to get her to a telephone if she were posing. Eight fifteen, Krogh saw: still plenty of time.

Cindy was awake when he went back into the bedroom. She'd pushed the sheet further off herself and brought one leg up so he could see better, and had her hand there although she wasn't doing anything.

'I almost started without you,' she said. She was blonde, naturally so and able to prove it lying like that, and brown-eyed and utterly uninhibited, enough to worry him sometimes with some of the things she wanted to do. They'd met a year before in San Diego, at a convention where she'd been one of the promotional girls for an aircraft interior accessory firm. He'd balled her that first night and set her up in the Malibu condominium a month later.

'It was good of you to wait.'

'I thought you'd like me to.'

Krogh guessed she'd only just managed to hold back. Cindy devoured him, literally, not allowing him to lead in anything and he let her, doing what she guided him to do after she'd done what she wanted. He was finding it difficult to match her but she pulled away just at the right moment, cutting the lines on the little marble slab from the bedside drawer and taking two herself before offering him the chance. Krogh was frightened, although

35

he was confident he was strong enough never to become addicted and so he'd done it with her a few times and he did it now, needing the help. It was good stuff and hit immediately and all their tiredness went and they did it all again, but longer this time.

'Jesus!' gasped Krogh, when they finally parted. 'Sweet Jesus!'

'You're guaranteed the gold when fucking becomes an Olympic event,' said Cindy. Always tell the guy it was the best it had ever been, she thought: worked every time. Actually it had been pretty terrific.

'At the moment I couldn't get up on the rostrum to collect it,' said Krogh.

'When are you leaving?'

It was gone ten, he saw; too late for Barbara now. He was down from the coke and felt absolutely drained, like he'd been wrung out to dry, and didn't think he could have managed it with Barbara anyway. He said: 'Afternoon somewhen: no particular hurry.' The contract signing confirmed everything, which made it pretty fantastic, but his father-in-law was never at the plant in the afternoon and he was the only person it was really necessary to impress.

'So we've got lots of time?'

Krogh looked nervously across the bed. 'What for?'

She giggled. 'Shopping. Just shopping. Well. . . looking, too.'

'I thought we'd shopped already,' said Krogh. That's all they had done, apart from screw, ever since he'd arrived in Los Angeles: he reckoned he'd parted with enough to pay the taxes on Rodeo Drive and Wiltshire Boulevard for a year.

'Honey!' she said, in the pouting, little-girl voice

she had for asking special favours.

'I didn't say we couldn't,' assured Krogh quickly. He liked being the big spender, the whatever-you-want-you-get man. He could afford it, after all.

She came closer to him, nuzzling against him. 'Now?'

'Sure. Now, if that's what you want.'

'You're very good to me. And I love you for it. I still like the car, of course. Love it like I did when you bought it for me.'

The sudden jump confused him. 'What?'

'My car. I still like it.'

'Good.' It was red, the colour she'd wanted: a Honda sports. Krogh liked to treat them both the same so he'd bought one for Barbara, as well. Barbara had chosen blue.

'It's just that I've seen this convertible: a Volkswagen GTI, all white. White upholstery, white top, white wheel trim,' recited Cindy, as if she were reading from the sales brochure. 'It's the prettiest thing I've ever seen in my life and I love it to death and want to show it to you. Not to buy. Just to show you, so you can look. That OK?'

'Sure that's OK,' said Krogh. The price of a new car would be swallowed without a ripple in the profits coming to him from the Pentagon deal. He wished he'd thought of it as a gift instead of her having to ask. He could still make it a surprise for Barbara.

'I really do love you,' repeated the girl. 'Don't you ever leave me, will you?'

'You're the one who'll want it all to end one day,' said Krogh realistically.

'I won't!' insisted Cindy. 'I won't ever want that!'

'Let's not talk about it.'

'I said noon. It's a quarter off eleven already.'

Again Krogh was confused. 'Noon?'

'To meet the salesman who'd got the dinkie little VW. I knew you'd say yes because you're so wonderful so I made an appointment to see him. You don't mind, do you?'

'No,' sighed Krogh. 'We'd better get cleaned up.'

The salesroom was on Sunset, just short of where it ceases being smart movie-magazine Hollywood and gives way to the tacky I-could-have-been-a-star cocktail places. The car was on the front, glistening from a polish job, the Sold sticker already on the windscreen. Cindy said the man must have misunderstood. They went through the hood-lifting, ass-in-the-seat-for-comfort routine and the salesman said he'd take the Honda sports off their hands at a price they would not get anywhere else. Krogh bought it on the spot, which he'd known in bed that morning that he would and Cindy had known in bed that morning that he would. Krogh insisted on all the paperwork being in his name – in owning the car, in fact – just like he owned the condo on Malibu and the apartment and the car in San Francisco. Krogh knew exactly what he was doing and with whom he was doing it and when the girls moved on or he moved on he didn't intend losing out on real estate that was appreciating in value all the time or on automobiles that still had some equity in them. As they parted with handshakes the salesman said: 'Your daughter's never going to want another car after this one, Mr Krogh. I hope she knows what a truly lucky girl she is.'

'Asshole!' said Cindy as they went back towards the ocean.

'If he's an asshole why'd you take the card he slipped you?'

'He didn't *slip* me anything!' said the girl indignantly. 'He gave me his card in case anything came up with the car I wanted to talk to him about.'

Krogh hoped to Christ she was careful: he had a very real fear of catching something from either Cindy or Barbara. They went to eat at Gladstones, on the beach. There were a lot of halter tops and cut-off jeans and bare flesh and yells and shouts of young recognition and Krogh felt very old. Krogh didn't finish his steak and their waiter, who wore a ponytail tied with a spotted ribbon and knew Cindy by her christian name, fashioned a take-home tinfoil doggy bag in the shape of a long-necked swan.

'You coming back so I can thank you properly for my car?'

'I should get back,' said Krogh. He *would* go into the plant. His father-in-law would hear about it even if the man weren't there: things like that – his dedication to work – were important. He was as safe as hell and up to his ass in stock options but his father-in-law retained the title of President and controlled the stockholders' votes. Krogh enjoyed impressing the old man, like he enjoyed facing down the critics who'd sneered at the shopfloor draughtsman who'd gone for the main chance and married the boss's daughter. It was going to be difficult to criticize now, after the Star Wars deal.

Cindy ran him to the airport and Krogh promised to call. There were no delays on the flight nor hindrance on the road after landing in San Francisco and Krogh was at the plant by four, making sure he was seen going through the office level to the executive suites. He tried Barbara's number, just to talk, but got the answering machine and rang off without leaving any message. Peggy picked up the call at home and when he told her he was at the plant said: 'You work too hard. You don't allow any time for yourself.'

'I will,' said Krogh easily.

'Busy trip?'
'I'm worn out.'

It was the sort of club that could exist only in Los Angeles or New York, a flowered place for the butterfly people to flutter and briefly settle before moving on. Cindy's sort of place.

She cruised the jostled bar and the fast and slow disco, sure of herself and in no hurry to prove anything. She refused two quick approaches, hello goodbye, hello goodbye, already aware of the man at the bar, like he was aware of her: a hunk and knowing it, very dark-haired, chisel-faced, smiling at her but not doing anything else. In the end Cindy made the move, detouring on her way back from the powder room. When she got to him she said: 'I just checked for my second head: I couldn't find it.'

'The one you've got is fine.'

'Glad to hear it. At last.'

He bought her kir royale, champagne and cassis, without asking what she wanted, and stayed with vodka, neat, for himself, and danced like a dream. When he suggested dinner at Spago she said he'd never get a table and he did, without her seeing any money change hands, and they both knew he was coming back to Malibu without their even talking about it.

'I like the car,' he said, outside the restaurant.

'My daddy bought it for me,' said Cindy.

'You must have a very generous daddy,' said Alexandr Petrin.

5

There had been occasions, quite a few in fact, when Charlie had regarded the assessments sessions to be a holiday: sitting in the sun, hat-over-the-eyes stuff. But not this time. He derided Harkness for behaving like a prissy schoolmaster – perhaps school *mistress* was more accurate – but that was exactly what this was going to be, just like being at school with all the report marked up in credit and debit columns. And Charlie was bloody sure – absolutely convinced – that if he didn't get well over passmark in every course Harkness would have him. All the reasons could be manufactured, to bury him in some clerical division: failure to reach minimal but required standards, lack of concentration, inability to cope with the demands of the job, etcetera, etcetera.

So Charlie tried. He couldn't recall trying so hard in a practice environment because before he'd always considered war-games to be just that, kids' games, bang, bang, you're dead. Now it was different. Now it wasn't playing pretend. It was him against Harkness, although it wasn't quite a physical contest. Near enough, though. Important for him to win: always for him to win.

There was a week of practical fieldwork, mostly around London. The second surveillance exercise was much cleverer and more difficult for him to isolate, although he did. And his target failed to pick Charlie up at all when the situations were turned around and he became the Watcher. He got four Dead Letter boxes, which was the maximum, observing genuine message caches used by the Czechoslovak and Cuban consulates and broke a sample code for which he was allowed two hours in just under one hour. Marksmanship was a real pain, in every meaning of the word. Charlie didn't like or trust guns because they went off with a hell of a noise and attracted too much attention in a genuine situation, they made his wrist hurt and his ears ache, despite the protectors, and he could never stop his eyes from blinking at the moment of pressing the trigger, when they should have been open. He made a real effort and got five points above the pass level, which with anything else would have worried him but didn't here. The department had a section composed of men who were experts with guns: funny blokes who didn't smile much and who always looked behind doors and wore jackets with lots of room in the shoulders. Charlie had his own method of responding to armed confrontation: turn the other way and run like buggery, even with feet as difficult as his.

The second week was spent in Herefordshire, on a totally secure army base where Charlie lived in barracks and didn't have a single drink and was disappointed that he didn't feel any better than he normally did when he woke up in the mornings. Charlie was confident about the language examinations, both written and oral, and felt he'd done well in the three papers of political analysis he was set. He didn't enjoy the medicals. He had to pee in a lot of bottles and had fingers jabbed up his bum and panted on treadmills and had enough blood drawn for a vampires' Christmas party. His eyes and ears and nose and throat were peered and poked into and he was attached to machines that blipped and told doctors things from their jumping wavy lines. There were also psychiatric and psychological tests where in the past Charlie had mucked about, quite sure the examiners were dafter than he'd ever be, but now he remained serious and didn't try to make jokes to risk offending them.

Charlie felt quite sad in the middle of the third week when the assessment drew to a close and he realized that even being away from the same surroundings as Harkness was practically a holiday. It was an unsettling, sobering reflection because Charlie, who was always scrupulously honest with himself if rarely with anyone else, recognized at once that really *was* how he felt. Which meant Harkness was getting to him far more insidiously than he'd realized. And that had to stop, right away. He was buggered if he'd let the prick make his life that much of a misery.

The final session was with someone with whom he'd concluded such visits before, a balding, heavily moustached man named Shearer. He was the Director of the spy school and Charlie was always curious why the man wore a white coat, as if he were a member of the medical section. The time before last they'd played a few games of chess together when all the tests of the day were over, and the man had even kept it on then. Perhaps Shearer didn't like his role and felt the protective clothing prevented his becoming contaminated.

'Quite a turn-up for the books in every subject this time,' announced Shearer. 'You've excelled yourself.' He'd cut himself that morning shaving and it had stained the collar of his check shirt.

Although he was sure he'd done well it was still good to hear it for a fact. Charlie said: 'You know me: always try my best.'

'I *do* know you, so cut the bullshit,' stopped Shearer. 'You usually treat all this as a great big joke. Why the sudden seriousness?'

'I've always passed,' insisted Charlie.

'Because you don't find it as difficult as most because you're a born cheat and a liar and that's what good intelligence officers mostly are, born cheats and liars,' said the Director. 'And that's not an answer to my question. I asked why the sudden seriousness?'

'No reason,' avoided Charlie. Was he a cheat and a liar? Only when he had to be: circumstances forced it on him, more often than not.

'Worried about lasting to collect your pension,' demanded Shearer with unknowing prescience.

Not the pension, conceded Charlie, honest again with himself. It was the other bit: the staying on. It was, he supposed, all part of the loneliness. He filled his spare time well enough, at the Festival Hall and the Old Vic and the Barbican. And he went to movies and he read books. But *filled* was the operative word. There was almost a conscious anxiety completely to occupy one off-duty period until he could go the next morning to Westminster Bridge Road. Charlie thought he was like a pit pony that had spent all its life down an old-fashioned coal mine until it went blind and couldn't find its way around in any other environment: all he'd ever known, all his working life, was espionage. He wouldn't know what to do without it. Stirring himself to reply, Charlie said: 'Never thought of what I do as a pensionable occupation.'

Shearer moved through the papers assembled on the desk before him and Charlie wondered if he were genuinely reading them or doing it for effect. The Director looked up abruptly and said: 'One of the blood tests is good for measuring residual alcohol content. You know that?'

'No,' admitted Charlie uncomfortably.

'You're a good friend to the whisky distillers.'

'I take a drink or two sometimes,' said Charlie.

'You take more than a drink or two a lot of the time,' disputed the man responsible for presenting the final report upon him. 'You think it's a problem for you?'

'Definitely not,' said Charlie, as forcefully as possible. Harkness was a teetotaller: it was the sort of thing he would seize upon. Medical progress was a bloody nuisance.

'Why so sure?'

'Drunks get swept up. Caught. I haven't been swept up. I won't be.'

'It's only got to happen once.'

'It won't,' insisted Charlie.

'Liver shows no fatty tissue, which it would if the body regarded the intake as excessive,' mused Shearer. 'In fact, considering how you abuse yourself, you're remarkably fit.'

Something else that was good to know: when he was a kid the teachers said abusing yourself when they meant masturbation. Charlie decided against trying to make a joke of it. 'I feel fine,' he said.

Shearer half raised himself from his chair, so he could look unnecessarily over his desk, then sat down again. 'Still scuffing about in those preposterous shoes?'

Charlie gazed down at the Hush Puppies that had expanded and shaped themselves to his feet over months of wear. He wished he hadn't had to thread new laces: it made them look odd. He guessed it wouldn't take long for them to age in. He said: 'Got bad feet.'

'You've got flat feet, with a slight bone deformity in the left one, so slight it required an X-ray to show it up,' corrected Shearer. 'What you need are the opposite to what you're wearing. You need proper leather, built up to create a support.'

'Tried it,' said Charlie, 'didn't work.'

'Surveillance people commented about them,' disclosed Shearer. 'About the ramshackle way you dressed: said rather than making you fade into the background it marked you out.'

Charlie became immediately attentive. 'If that's so, if I make it so easy, how come they lost me as completely as they did?' he demanded. He wasn't having the disgruntled bastards score off him like that.

'*Touché!*' acknowledged Shearer.

'And I was able to describe how every one of the people tracking me was dressed!' reminded Charlie.

'It's all here,' accepted Shearer, patting the files. 'No one is saying you didn't do well. I already told you that.'

Charlie recognized, discomfited, that there had been a petulance in his voice, and hoped the other man hadn't discerned it. He said: 'Now all I've got to do is maintain the standard.'

'Things OK between you and Harkness, now he's acting Director General?'

'Why shouldn't they be?' sidestepped Charlie. He'd forgotten how complete the knowledge of the assessors, and particularly the spy school Director, had to be. If one of these people defected the rest of them might as well shut up shop and go home.

'Don't answer my question with another question,' rebuked Shearer sharply.

The whole bloody lot of them were a bunch of schoolmasters, thought Charlie. He said: 'There's an adequate working relationship.'

Shearer nodded, as if he understood more than Charlie had said. 'He's requested an assessment be marked for him personally, as well as one going through the normal channels.'

Charlie stared steadily across the desk at the Director. *Not* a fussy schoolmaster, he corrected. Why was Shearer telling him? A private Charlie Muffin rule:

Never stop anyone being indiscreet if that's the way the mood takes them. He said: 'That all?'

'He's asked for your case history file, as well.'

The same case history file the prat couldn't get out of the computer. Which had to mean it was still being denied the man. Why *was* Shearer telling him? Did Harkness *want* him to know, to be unsettled by the interest? Charlie said: 'Such a file is in Records, at Westminster Bridge Road.'

'I know,' said Shearer. 'There's a procedure for my making it available but because of the medical details it contains there's a requirement that the subject's permission be obtained.'

Thank you Lord for doctors' confidentiality and Whitehall bureaucracy, thought Charlie: much more of this and he'd have to start observing the regulations himself. He said: 'The requirement specifically governing this place?'

'Yes,' confirmed Shearer.

So it wouldn't have been in the Westminster Bridge Road rule book, so Harkness wouldn't know it! Got you again, shithead, decided Charlie. He said: 'So I could refuse?'

'You have the right,' agreed the Director.

'And Harkness would have to be told I'd refused?'
'Yes.'

So what did the file contain? His illegitimacy, but Charlie didn't give a sod about anyone knowing that, any more than his mum had: he'd done very well as a kid from all those uncles passing briefly through the house. School records and the fact that he didn't go to university, which Harkness might regard as indicative of some failing or other but something else Charlie couldn't give a stuff about. Probably the details of that petrol sale episode during his army service in the fuel supply depot. But the investigation had been inconclusive. And there hadn't been a

47

formal charge so there was no ammunition there and it was far too long ago anyway. The case histories themselves, every assignment upon which he'd worked. No problem there. Harkness knew, because that was how the man had come to be appointed, how he screwed the previous Director and deputy Director for trying to sacrifice him: he'd been forgiven and re-admitted to the department so there was no mileage for Harkness in stirring those long-dead embers. Charlie said: 'What about the reverse? What if I give my permission now? Would Harkness be told?'

Shearer shrugged. 'It's not essential: we'd just supply the information, as requested.'

'But you *could*,' stressed Charlie. 'I mean you could, as required by regulations, attach some sort of notification that I'd approved the release of the details? So that he'd know?'

Shearer looked down at his disordered desk so Charlie was not able to see if the man were smiling. The Director was certainly serious-faced when he looked up again. 'I could do that,' the man agreed.

'I don't see any reason whatsoever why I should object,' said Charlie.

'You think the changes apparently going on in Russia are important?' asked Shearer abruptly.

'That's what I said in one of the political papers,' reminded Charlie. 'It's quite a second revolution.'

'I mean at our level,' elaborated the school's Director. 'You imagine any real difference affecting us and what we do?'

'Not for a considerable time,' judged Charlie. 'The most compelling reason for the Soviet change of course is that their economy is up the spout. They're practically skint. To become anywhere near efficient they need Western technology and they can't afford to buy it. So they'll steal it. Or try to. Which means that the KGB remains as important as it ever was.'

'That's what I think,' said Shearer. 'I'm glad you believe that, too.'

'Glad?' queried Charlie, guessing there had been a purpose to the exchange he hadn't yet discerned.

'They're the people we should be watching out for: regarding as the opposition,' said Shearer. 'There shouldn't be constant in-fighting, within our own service.'

Charlie realized at last why Shearer had shown the confiding friendliness. He said: 'You will see my agreement to the acting Director General's request is included, won't you?'

'Good luck, whatever's going on,' said the other man.

Henry Blackstone considered he had a good life – a bloody good life – apart from that one major problem. Money. He'd been trying to think of something for a while now but hadn't managed to come up with anything. Thank Christ the horses were running good for him. Bloody silly to imagine that he could rely on the luck lasting, though. He needed desperately to come up with something permanent. If he could, then things would be perfect. He had a job he enjoyed in a part of the country where he liked living, and a loving and gentle wife in Ann. And in Ruth, too. Not so gentle, so placid, maybe, but just as loving. He was a fortunate man.

Apart from the money Blackstone had never had any trouble adjusting to bigamy, not from the very first day of taking a second wife in addition to the first. He loved Ann. And he loved Ruth. Equally and sincerely: well, as sincerely as he ever could.

So, unable to choose, he'd married both, one within eight months of the other.

Blackstone, who was a man of wide emotional

swings, from overweening confidence to deep depressions to confidence again, truly believed his way of life made sense: this way everyone was happy. And they *were* happy. There were times – his super-confident times – when he'd even imagined they would all be able to live in complete harmony under the same roof, one big family. Not that he really thought of suggesting it, letting one know about the other. He knew he would be able to do it, but he wasn't sure the women would be able to adjust as well. So why risk upsetting an arrangement that was already near perfect, apart from the money?

Blackstone caught the first available car ferry from Portsmouth to the Isle of Wight, the one he normally got after a weekend on the mainland with Ruth. It would get him to the factory early but that didn't matter. There was an experimental flexible-hours scheme running at the moment, so he would be able to get home to Ann correspondingly early. He was missing her, after the long weekend.

6

The thought occurred to Emil Krogh at the start of the stockholders' meeting that this was the moment for which he'd waited for years. They'd cleared with the Pentagon and with NASA what could publicly be said about the Star Wars contract, which was limited but still enough, and Peggy's father claimed his presidential right to make the official announcement. Peggy was there, of course. And Joey and Peter, so the whole family heard the praise of Krogh's negotiating skills and the prestige of the award to the company, all cleverly made by the old man with pauses for the applause which always came on schedule. Krogh sat modestly on the raised directors' dais, head bent most of the time over the table. Coming of age time, he thought, warmed by the reception. He'd earned his appointment as chairman a dozen times, sticking the middle finger to all the snide boss's son-in-law cracks. But this was the best: the multi-million government award that confirmed the company at the top of Washington's approval list, guaranteeing jobs and profits for years. And they had to acknowledge it, these directors and top managers and passed-over executives: acknowledge it and applaud and smile and nod to each other and say things like 'Christ, what a deal!' and 'I always knew he could do it' and 'What a guy to have as chairman!'

Krogh caught Peggy's eye when he looked up one time. She was flushed and smiling but her face was slightly broken up, as if she were going to cry. Pride, he knew. Like Joey and Peter were looking proudly at him, although not near tears. It was a fantastic feeling.

He kept his own speech fittingly modest and got the loudest applause when he declared that year's eight per cent dividend increase with the forecast that it would double if not go higher in the immediately succeeding years. A man named Freidham, whom Krogh knew to be one of his strongest critics, had to give the speech of congratulations, which was a particularly good moment.

The national media had been invited, even international magazines like *Time* and *Newsweek* and the television majors like CBS and NBC and ABC, so a press conference was convened. His father-in-law was a bad performer in front of cameras and lights so Krogh led here, carefully remaining within the Washington-imposed limits but going along with self-answering questions like 'new American era in space' and 'nothing like it since Kennedy said reach for the stars'.

The stockholders' meeting had been held in one of the conference rooms at the Fairmont and a private room reserved for the celebration lunch afterwards. Peggy sat next to him and whispered how marvellous it all was and there were toasts in imported champagne. Krogh let himself relax but remained sober because he had an insecure person's fear of ever losing control. He played his own private, little kid's game by constantly smiling at Freidham and his coterie, so that they had to smile back as if they admired him.

Krogh announced that he intended going back to the plant, which gave him an hour for Barbara to prove how grateful she was for the new car, blue again, and Peter agreed to drive his mother home to the Monterey estate. Krogh promised to get back early for the family dinner that Peggy wanted to give him with both sons and daughters-in-law and the grandchildren, as well.

He stood in the looped forecourt of the hotel, gesturing them off ahead of him, and was turning to call for his own limousine when he became conscious of someone close beside him.

'Mr Krogh?' said a voice politely.

'Yes.'

'I wonder if I might talk with you?'

One of the journalists, Krogh guessed: a patient guy who'd hung around all this time to try to improve upon his story. 'Sure,' said Krogh, staying modest. 'What about?'

'Cindy,' said Alexandr Petrin. 'And Barbara.'

Petrin insisted they sit in the huge lobby, a cavern of a place, full of people some of whom recognized him from all the fuss of the morning and smiled and Krogh had to smile back and try to appear unconcerned when what he really wanted to do was throw up and maybe the other thing or even both. Not that there would have been anything there because a huge hand had reached in and scooped out his guts so all that was left was a numb emptiness. He wanted a drink, just liquid, not necessarily booze, but he didn't think he could get anything here in the lobby: he was too frightened to try, anyway.

'They're nice girls,' said Petrin conversationally. 'Lucky, too. You're very generous.' He slid across the table between them a manila packet he took from his pocket.

Krogh stared down at the envelope, making no attempt to pick it up. 'What is it?'

'Photographs,' identified Petrin. 'Photographs of the sales contract in your name for the condo at Malibu and the apartment just over the hill here, in San Francisco. Copies, too, of the purchase agreements for the two VW cars and of the registration details, both in your name. Pictures of Cindy and

53

Barbara, too. With the cars and with you. Quite a few of Barbara without clothes on, posing like she does. Fantastic tits, hasn't she? And the charge card facilities, in your name, at Saks and Nieman Marcus.'

Krogh swallowed, trying to get his head in order. Jesus, didn't they have him! The ever-producing milch cow who'd have to go on delivering as long as they kept milking. He said: 'You with both of the blackmailing bitches or just one?'

'I'm with neither of them,' said Petrin. 'And neither of them has the slightest idea that I know about you.'

'We've got to discuss this!' said Krogh urgently. 'What sort of money are we talking about here?'

'No money at all,' said Petrin simply.

Krogh stared across the small table, not speaking, and Petrin gazed back, not speaking either. Then the American said: 'So what do you want?'

'The best, for both of us,' said Petrin. 'Which for you means getting the cover story in *Newsweek* and staying just as you are now, the admired and respected chairman and a happily married man with a couple of swingers you can go on nailing whenever you feel like it.'

'And in return?'

'I want access to all – and copies of – every part of the Star Wars vehicle that you're making. Everything, you understand? Every bolt, screw, wire and clip. Drawings, specifications, plans. . .the lot.'

'Jesus!' said Krogh in sagged awareness. 'Oh Jesus!'

'It'll work just fine, believe me.'

'No,' refused Krogh, striving to sound strong. 'I won't. . .can't. . .'

'You need to think about it,' said Petrin, unworried by the refusal. He pushed the envelope further towards Krogh. 'Take these, please. I've got lots more copies. Look at it all and think about the

alternatives. . .the humiliation and the scandal. . .'
The Russian took from his pocket a card bearing
a single telephone number. He said: 'You call that
when you've had your think.'

Reluctantly Krogh picked up both the card and the
envelope but then suddenly sniggered. He said: 'It's
not going to work, you know!'

'Why not, Mr Krogh?'

'We don't have all the contract. One of the most essential parts of the missile body shell, the reinforced
resin carbon fibre, is being moulded quite separately
in England!'

Charlie had set his own burglar alarm system, like
he always did, leaving just inside the flat doors carefully arranged letters any intruder would have disarranged – which they weren't. He still checked the
other precautions, doors apparently left ajar, things
placed in remembered positions in cupboards and
drawers, before finally deciding there'd been no entry while he'd been away.

The place smelled stale, a locked-up-and-left
smell, and he opened windows and squirted an air
freshener here and there.

There was quite a lot of mail in addition to his
burglar precautions. There were two separate in-
vitations to have his windows double glazed and a
communication from *Reader's Digest* assuring him
he'd been chosen over millions of others not so lucky
for a chance to win £100,000: there was a mystery gift
simply for replying.

His mother's letter was last, the writing spiky and
in places impossible to read, cramped on a sheet
torn from a lined exercise book. He tried the parts
that did appear intelligible but quickly gave up, because they didn't really make sense. The matron
must have guessed he would have difficulty because

she'd enclosed a typewritten note saying she knew
he would be pleased to know that after so long his
mother was showing protracted periods of lucidity
and that the old lady would appreciate a visit. The
last had been three months before, she reminded
him unnecessarily: his mother frequently asked for
him by name. And there could be some changes
to his mother's State pension he might like to hear
about.

Charlie doubted if the recovery were as good as
the matron indicated but it would have been nice
to think his mother was emerging at last from her
closed-off, shuttered world. There was the whole
weekend to find out.

There could, of course, be no question of Harkness
disclosing his confident expectation of permanent
promotion to anyone, because Harkness was a protectively reserved man, although he was sure he
could have trusted Hubert Witherspoon with the
secret. Witherspoon was a good and loyal colleague,
which was only to be expected. They'd both gradu-
ated from Balliol, although at different times: by
coincidence they were today both wearing their Oxford school ties. He said: 'They're sure?'

Witherspoon was a languid, superior man who
hadn't conducted the interview but debriefed the
men afterwards. He said: 'It wasn't easy to make
sense of a lot of what she said, apparently. But she
definitely didn't know anything about what he did in
Moscow.'

'A pity,' said Harkness. 'A great pity.'

7

There is a part of the Test valley, near Stockbridge in Hampshire, where the river winds back upon itself, as if it's lost and can't find its way, the water sluggish and uncertain. The banks and then the cow meadows are tiered away towards the higher levels, where the trees grow like sparse hair. Near the very top there is a cleft formed by a whim of nature, like a giant footprint, a protected, wrapped-around place to look down upon the view set out for approval below. The nursing home was safe and cosy there, forgotten about like most of the people in it. There were stories that on a clear day it was possible to look across the valley and pick out the distant spire of Salisbury Cathedral proving how tall it was, but Charlie had never seen it and he'd visited his mother on quite a few very clear days. He tried this time and failed: perhaps he wasn't standing in the right spot.

He'd telephoned ahead and arranged the most convenient time, so the matron was expecting him. Her name was Hewlett: her signature made it impossible to identify the christian name, apart from the initial letter E, but then she was not a person to be addressed familiarly. She was not particularly tall but very wide. The large and tightly corseted bust was more a prow than a bosom, parting the waves before her, and she always walked with thrust-forward urgency, as if she were late. She invariably wore, like now, a blue uniform of her own design with a crimped and starched headpiece and an expression of fierce severity.

'You said ten,' she accused at once, loud-voiced. It was fifteen minutes past.

57

'Bad traffic,' apologized Charlie, unoffended. She was one of those brusque-mannered women of inordinate love and kindness towards all the old people for whom she cared.

'Your mother is a great deal better, as I told you in my note,' said the matron at once. 'She still drifts a little but she's much more aware than she's been for a long time.'

'You trying some new treatment or drug?'

The formidable woman shook her head. 'It happens. We've just got to hope it lasts. I'm glad you were able to come as quickly as you did.'

So was he, thought Charlie. For more than two years now his mother's senility had locked her away in a dream world no one could enter. 'Does she know I'm coming?'

The matron nodded. 'She's had her hair washed. Don't forget to tell her it looks nice.'

'Any limit on how long I can stay?'

'As long as you like,' said the woman. 'Not a lot of relatives come: some of the others will enjoy a different face, as well.'

Charlie followed the woman, tender to battleship, in a surge through the nursing home. It was a conversion from the long-ago status symbol of a wool millionaire when men became millionaires in the wool trade. There had been the minimum of alteration, little more than stairway lifts and door widening for wheelchairs. All the panelling and flooring was the original wood and the huge floor-to-ceiling verandah doors were retained in the drawing rooms, so that the occupants could easily get outside when it was warm enough, which it was today. The place smelled of polish and fresh air, with no trace of old-people, decay or clinical antiseptic anywhere.

His mother was just outside the furthest room, raised into a sitting position by a back support in a bed equipped with large wheels to make it easier to manoeuvre. Her pure white hair was rigidly waved and she'd arranged the pillows to end at her shoulders so that it did not become disarranged. There was the faintest touch of rouge, giving her cheeks some colour, and a very light lipstick as well. She wore a crocheted bed jacket over a floral-print nightdress and was sitting in calm patience with her hands, black-corded with veins, on the bed before her. She was wearing a wedding ring she'd bought herself when he was about eighteen but which he couldn't remember her using for quite a while.

'Hello Mum,' greeted Charlie.

'Hello Charlie,' she said, in immediate recognition. It was the first occasion for a long time that she'd known him. He kissed her, aware of a furtive audience on the verandah and further away, from groups on the lawns.

Charlie offered the box he carried and said: 'Chocolates. Plain. The sort you like.'

'Hard centres? I do like hard centres.'

'At least half,' promised Charlie. He'd forgotten about that.

'I'll give the soft ones away to the silly old buggers who haven't got any teeth.'

His mother didn't have many herself but she was proud of what there were. There was a chair considerately near the bed. Charlie pulled it closer and as he sat she extended her hand, to be held. Again it was in full view of everyone. Charlie said: 'How are you, then?'

'Going into Salisbury on the bus on Friday,' said his mother, who had been bedridden for almost a year. 'Do some shopping.'

'That'll be nice,' said Charlie easily.

'With George.'

'George?'

His mother made a vague gesture towards a group of mostly men near a grey fir, on a far lawn. 'George,' she said. 'Only just arrived. He likes me.'

'Careful you don't get into trouble,' warned Charlie.

'I need company, with your father gone and all.'

'Sure you do,' said Charlie. The skin of his mother's hand felt thin, like paper.

'He was very fond of you, your dad. Remember when he used to take you fishing, on that river down there? And to football matches?'

'Of course I do,' said Charlie, to whom none of it had ever happened.

'William,' said the old lady, producing a name like a rabbit out of a hat. 'Always William: never Bill. Nice man. Worked on the railways.' She began to pick with her free hand at the cellophane wrapping of the chocolate box and Charlie helped her, opening it fully. She touched several with a wavering finger, as if she were counting, before finally making her choice. 'Those others didn't bring any chocolates,' she said.

Charlie looked out at a group of old people by the drooping fir tree, curious if there really were anyone called George. He said: 'Matron says she's very pleased with you. How you're getting on.'

'Tells lies,' his mother insisted at once. 'She doesn't like me. Hits me for not eating cake with nuts in and you know I don't like cake with nuts in. Told you in my letter.'

'I don't remember that bit,' said Charlie.

'They said they'd tell her but I don't think they did. How's Edith?'

'Edith's dead, Mum.'

She chose another chocolate, nodding in recollection. 'I remember now,' she said. 'Never knew anyone die of flu before.'

'Flu that became pneumonia,' said Charlie. He

was surprised she recalled the explanation he'd produced, instead of the numbing truth: that Edith had been blasted apart in mistake for him by a trigger-happy mob from the CIA avenging their Director he'd disgraced, along with his own, for being prepared to sacrifice him on a border crossing during the Berenkov pursuit. Charlie said: 'Quite a while ago now.'

'Liked Edith. Posh but she never had any side to her. Never looked down on me. Often wondered what she saw in a scruffy bugger like you.'

So had he, since she'd been dead, reflected Charlie. He knew a lot had in the department before that and certainly when they'd got married. *Inconceivable, old boy. I mean, lovely girl like Edith! General's daughter, would you believe! Double First at Cambridge, head of Research. And that threadbare little oik who shouldn't have been allowed office space in the first place. I mean! Inconceivable!* Charlie said, with deep feeling: 'I miss her.' He missed Natalia, too. Maybe more so because he believed Natalia was still alive in Moscow, although he didn't know absolutely. And never would know.

'The men asked about her,' said the woman. 'I tell you some thing! Edith wouldn't have let you go around like that. Look at you! Bloody tramp. You never wore shoes like that when I was responsible for you. John wouldn't have allowed it. Heart of gold, your dad. Very proud of you, John was. Good to me, too.'

Muddled about some things. What about others? He stroked her hand and said: 'What men, Mum?'

'Told you,' she said with ancient belligerence. 'Didn't bring any chocolates. I didn't like them. Kept asking me questions...' She plucked out a chocolate shaped in a half moon and said: 'I can't find that on the chart that tells you what they are. Is it a hard or a soft one?'

61

'It's soft,' said Charlie. 'That square shape is a hard one.' Charlie had the impression of a distant warning, a far-away bell almost too muted properly to distinguish. He smoothed his mother's hand some more and said coaxingly: 'These men: was that the new man who likes you? And a friend of his, perhaps?'

The woman splayed her hand with the wedding ring Charlie had noticed when he first arrived. 'George gave me that,' she said. 'That is how I know he likes me. Calls me Judith. I don't know why but that's what he calls me. Judith.' Her name was Mary.

'Was it, Mum? Was George one of them?'

'What are you talking about?' she demanded suspiciously.

'I want to know about these men who didn't bring you chocolates or complain to matron about the cake with nuts.'

She looked suddenly, sharply, at him like a disturbed bird. 'Course it wasn't George, you silly sod. They were visitors, like you. . .' She smiled, showing the real teeth she possessed. 'No one's had more visitors than me, not for weeks! Matron said, so there!'

'Who were they?' said Charlie. He didn't look at her as he spoke, making it all sound casual.

'Men were always fond of me,' she said, drifting off. 'Popular. That's what I was. Always enjoyed a good laugh.'

'Have they been before?'

'Course not. They're important. Official. Told me. From a Ministry. . .something like that. . .'

The bells were louder now, easier to hear. 'What did they want?'

'All sorts of things. Asked about Edith. . .you. . . lots of things I can't think of now. . .' She suddenly tightened her fingers upon his. 'You haven't done anything wrong, have you? Been up to thieving or something like that.'

62

'No, Mum,' said Charlie gently. 'I haven't been thieving. How many were there?'

'Two,' she said at once. 'Dressed nice. Not like you, scruffy bugger. They wrote things down.'

The matron, Ms Hewlett, had written about pension changes in her letter. He was abruptly anxious to talk to the woman. He said: 'How did they speak?'

She giggled, engulfing him in chocolate breath. 'Like every else speaks, of course!'

'I mean how did they sound? Did they sound English or foreign?'

She frowned and Charlie thought how unlined his mother's face normally was, apart from this momentary effort at recall. 'Properly,' she decided. 'Not foreign.'

There were always fantasies about men who liked her but he'd never known her maintain a pretence as consistently as this before. He said: 'Did they tell you they'd come back again?'

The frown stayed. 'You haven't told me you like my hair.'

'I was going to,' said Charlie, irritated at forgetting. 'It looks good. You're very pretty.'

'Went into Salisbury yesterday to get it done.'

'On the bus?' anticipated Charlie, deciding momentarily to break the single-track questions.

'Don't need to go by bus,' she said. 'George drives me, in his car. He's got a car, you know? You can't see it, though. It's around the back of the house, in a garage. It's green and it's got a radio.'

'Did they have a car, the men who came to see you?'

The old woman nodded. 'Black. It had lots of things to make a radio work.'

Two aerials: would the second have been for a telephone or a two-way radio? 'What about them coming back?' repeated Charlie.

Once more there was the furrowed-brow effort at

recollection, then a shrug. 'I don't know. Maybe.'

'Try and help me, Mum,' pleaded Charlie. 'Try to think of something they said, the way they said it. Just one thing.'

'Is this a hard centre?'

It was an oblong shape described on the chart as a praline surprise. 'It should be,' said Charlie.

'You couldn't get chocolate during the war, you know? I could, though. I knew this American army sergeant. . .' Her face twisted. '. . .Can't remember his name right now. Hershey bars, they were called. You remember all that chocolate when you were young?'

'Yes, Mum,' said Charlie, who didn't. He looked around, trying to locate the matron.

'Not bitter chocolate, though. I like bitter chocolate best,' said the woman. She suddenly brightened. 'I might get more money!' she announced.

Charlie sighed at the new avenue to nowhere opening up in his mother's confused mind. He said: 'That'll be useful.'

'What's it called, when you get extra because you need it?' she demanded, looking directly at him.

'Extra what, Mum?'

'Pension,' she said impatiently.

'Is that what the men said, that you were going to get more pension money?' seized Charlie.

'I think that's what they meant.'

'Supplementary,' suggested Charlie.

'That was it!' said the woman. 'That was the word. It means extra money, doesn't it?'

'Yes,' said Charlie. 'That's what it means.'

'That's it then: what I'm going to get,' she said, triumphantly. 'Why didn't Edith come with you?'

'She's dead, Mum.'

'Dead? Edith? When?'

'Quite a long time ago.'

'Never knew. Why didn't you tell me?'

'I meant to,' said Charlie. 'I'm sorry.'

'Shame.' Her eyes closed. She made a tiny attempt to open them but it seemed too difficult. She tried again, even more feebly, and then stopped. Her held-away head went at last against the pillow: so lacquered was her hair that the tight waves flowed on undisturbed.

Charlie waited several minutes before easing his hand from hers, managing to stand without grating the chair. He checked as he walked, satisfying himself the matron was not in the grounds, relieved that she was in the office when he got there.

'Great improvement, isn't it?' the woman demanded at once.

'She's gone to sleep now,' said Charlie. 'She rambled a little.'

'At least she's talking!'

'About some men,' said Charlie. 'Men in a black car.'

'That's right,' agreed the matron. 'Pension people. I told you in my letter.'

Charlie nodded. 'So people *did* come. I thought you were referring to some form or notice or something.'

'Supplementary Benefit,' smiled the woman. 'They check from time to time, into everybody's financial circumstances. To see if there's any special need.'

'Have other people here been visited?'

'Quite a few, from time to time.'

'By these two particular men?'

The matron's face set in a serious expression. Instead of replying she said: 'Is something wrong?'

'I'm sure there's not,' said Charlie reassuringly. 'I'm just curious, that's all.'

Ms Hewlett did not look completely convinced. She said: 'These were inspectors I had not seen

65

before. But that has no significance. Quite often the people are different from those who have come before.'

'*Two* inspectors!' queried Charlie. 'Does it always take two inspectors?'

The woman's colour began to rise. Again there was a hesitation. 'No,' she said. 'It's not usually two.'

'They carried identification, of course?'

'They telephoned several days in advance. That's the normal procedure. Told me they were coming and why. And they quoted your mother's National Insurance number, the one that's on her pension book. No one else has access to details like that except people from the Ministry.'

Was he overreacting, Charlie asked himself. Possibly. But Charlie frequently responded to the antennae of instinct and he thought there was a message here somewhere. He said: 'Where do such inspectors come from when they carry out these checks? Towns, I mean?'

'It varies,' said the woman. 'Salisbury, Andover, Winchester. . .all over. . .'

'From what office did the two men come to see my mother?'

The subsiding colour grew again. 'They didn't say.'

'No number? Nowhere you could contact them?'

'They said when they left that she didn't qualify. That there'd be no need to talk about it again.'

'So that looks like the end of it,' said Charlie with attempted finality.

'Did they upset her?' asked the woman. 'They said they'd like to see her, and she was so much better I thought it would be a treat for her. Visitors. It's important to them, visitors. I knew they were wasting *their* time: of course I did. It was your mother I was thinking about, not them.'

Poor woman, thought Charlie: poor innocent, compassionate, unknowing woman. He said: 'I'm sure she enjoyed it.' He didn't think he'd get into cake with nuts. He added: 'Did she sign anything?'

'Oh no!' insisted the woman. 'Your mother was on the verandah, just like today. And I was outside all the time they were with her. I would have seen.'

'Like I said,' repeated Charlie. 'I'm sure it's all perfectly proper.'

'I *know* it is,' insisted the woman.

From his Vauxhall apartment, not from Westminster Bridge Road, Charlie contacted every regional and local pensions office remotely likely to have organized the visit to his mother. None had. He extended the check to the main department building in London and was once more assured there was neither interest in nor consideration of awarding his mother any supplementary pension allowance.

There was the beginning of fury – but only briefly, because Charlie didn't allow it. Fear had its benefits; released adrenaline and heightened senses. But not anger or fury. Neither. That sort of emotion was positively counter-productive: obscured the proper reasoning and the correct balances. This time, anyway, his feelings catapulted far beyond fury. Charlie was engulfed by an implacable, vindictive coldness. He'd chosen an existence of constant deceit and constant suspicion, a sinister shape to every shadow, a dangerous meaning to every word. That's what he gave and that's what he expected back. A fragile old lady with skin like paper wasn't any part of that; a fragile old lady in whose twilight life long-ago lovers stayed on as names with indistinct faces, William who became John and who might not have been a real person at all. But they'd made her part of it: sullied her with it. His own people; he was convinced of it being his own people, directed by Harkness. Wrong to move prematurely, though: he had to establish it absolutely. And there was a way: a required, procedural way that would protect him if he were wrong – if he were the target of a hostile pursuit – and raise a stink in all the embarrassing places if he were right. Harkness was going to regret this vendetta.

Ironically another vendetta was being conceived against Charlie Muffin almost four thousand miles away.

'We've got to start all over again,' announced Alexei Berenkov, who had sought the encounter with Valeri Kalenin. 'Part of the Star Wars missile is being made in England.'

Kalenin shrugged philosophically. 'We've done well enough in America,' he said. 'This can only be a setback, surely.'

Berenkov had come to Dzerzhinsky Square intending to suggest to Kalenin that the English involvement provided an opportunity for a further operation, but abruptly he changed his mind. He shouldn't involve this man who'd risked so much for him. Berenkov knew he could, on his own, evolve the retribution for all the harm that Charlie Muffin had caused and attempted to cause him. With customary confidence Berenkov decided he didn't need any help or advice in destroying Charlie Muffin, as the man had sought to destroy him. But failed. Berenkov said: 'I have the same freedom to operate in England as I have in America?'

'Of course,' confirmed Kalenin at once. 'Do whatever you consider necessary.'

Berenkov supposed that, by a fairly substantial stretch of imagination, those words might later be construed as permission for what he had in mind. He began planning that day.

It was Ann's birthday, her fortieth, so they had to

68

celebrate although Blackstone couldn't afford it. He made a reservation at a pub just outside Newport he'd heard talked about at the factory and when they arrived discovered it specialized in seafood. Blackstone couldn't run to real champagne but Ann seemed thrilled enough with a sparkling imitation. He tried to compensate by ordering quite an expensive white wine to go with their *fruits de mer*, which included lobster as well as crab and shrimp and some chewy shellfish neither had had before and didn't like: Ann was brave enough to say so first and stop eating them. The wine was sugar sweet, a dessert drink, but neither knew and both thought it was very nice.

Blackstone waited until they reached the pudding before giving Ann her present, a single-strand chain with a solitary pendant pearl. She put it on immediately and kept fingering it, to reassure herself it was there. 'It's beautiful,' she said.

Blackstone, who was in one of his ebullient moods, thought it was, too. Ann, who was dark-haired, still without any grey, had a good skin she didn't spoil with too much make-up, and the necklace was shown off perfectly against her throat. It had cost far more than he was able to afford. He said: 'The chain's eighteen-carat gold. And the man in the shop said it was a cultured pearl.'

'Beautiful,' she said again. 'You shouldn't have spent so much.'

He shouldn't, Blackstone knew. He seemed to think of nothing else these days but the expense of running two homes. And it wasn't as if Ann or Ruth didn't help. They both worked and each contributed to the housekeeping and neither complained about living in rented accommodation instead of buying their own places, which would well and truly have crippled him financially. Blackstone fought to retain his optimism: at least there was *something*. Deciding to tell her about it, he said: 'I've applied for a better job.' He liked impressing both his wives and tried to do so as often as possible. He was a senior tracer at the aerospace factory, although Ann believed him to be a quality control inspector required to tour all their installations in England, which accounted for the time he spent commuting to and from the mainland during the time he spent with Ruth, who trustingly believed the same story.

'A different one?' Ann asked.

'No,' said Blackstone. 'Some tie-up with America, a space job. It's all very hush-hush. There was just a general memorandum inviting applications to become involved.'

'I think you're ever so clever,' praised the woman admiringly. 'Would it mean you didn't have to travel around so much?'

'Oh no,' said Blackstone, quickly. 'I'd still have to do that.' The secret project carried another £1,000 a year and he reckoned he could just about manage on that.

'Go to America, you mean?'

Blackstone hesitated, recognizing the opportunity. Holidays, manoeuvring sufficient time for both, was always a problem with the dual lives he led: a supposed fortnight's business trip to the United States would be the ideal excuse. He said: 'I don't know yet. Nobody knows anything apart from the senior scientific staff. I would think it's a strong possibility I'd have to go, if I got it.' He was glad he'd started the conversation.

'When will you know?'

'Quite soon,' said Blackstone. 'There's a lot of excitement at the factory about it.'

Ann fingered the necklace again. 'I think you're the best husband anyone could have,' she said.

'And I think you're the best wife,' said Blackstone. 'Happy birthday, darling.'

The telephone was answered on the second ring but without any identification beyond the single word, 'Yes?'

'I don't want to be laughed at: to be humiliated,' said Krogh. His voice was weak and uneven, someone either on the point of tears or who had already succumbed to them.

'Of course you don't,' agreed Petrin soothingly.

'Nothing will go wrong, will it. . . ? I mean, it'll be. . . ?'

'I've worked it all out,' guaranteed Petrin.

Which he had, observing the universally accepted intelligence maxim that an entrapment achieved has to be consolidated. The Russian dictated the contents and the place of the first handover, in a restaurant in that wharf area of San Francisco converted into a tourist attraction of waterside shops, amusements and exhibitions. Their meeting – and particularly when Krogh handed over the envelope – was extensively photographed by carefully placed KGB technicians. So a record was created of a millionaire American defence contractor passing information to someone who, if renewed or additional pressure were ever needed, could be identified as a KGB operative.

8

It should have been a relaxed, contented occasion, but for Berenkov it wasn't because abruptly – and unusually – he was troubled by doubts about what he intended doing. Not, actually, in initiating the secondary British operation that hopefully was to involve Charlie Muffin but at keeping it, for the moment, from Kalenin.

Kalenin, who disdained a dacha of his own, had in the past shared a visit to the rambling, bungalow-style country home of the Berenkovs and this week-end there was a particular reason for his being there because Georgi was home from engineering college. Berenkov was inordinately proud of his stranger son and inclined to over-compensate for the long period they had been apart: the boastfulness – urging him to tell his guardian of examination marks and com-mendations from his instructors – embarrassed the boy. He was tall and thickly dark-haired, like Beren-kov, but avoided this father's girth: Georgi played centre-field in the college soccer team and had also represented the college in cross-country skiing for two seasons.

They read and walked in the woods and staged their own chess championship, with a ten-ruble prize, which Kalenin – who had played at Master level – let Georgi win.

On the Sunday Berenkov and Kalenin sat in re-clining chairs on the wood-strip verandah while Valentina and the boy cleared the midday meal. Kalenin said: 'These are good times: I enjoy them.'

Berenkov, who used the concessionary facilities to their fullest to maintain the lifestyle he had cultivated in the West, poured French brandy heavily into two goblets and left the bottle uncorked, Russian style, for each to top up as they wished. He said 'We should make more use of this place.'

'I'm glad Georgi didn't try to follow you into the service,' declared the other man. Kalenin regarded Fidel Castro as unpredictable and Cuba therefore a doubtful satellite but the cigars were an unarguable benefit: he kindled one now and exhaled against the glowing tip, threatening brief fire.

'It was never considered, by either of us,' said Berenkov. What he was planning in England amounted to deceiving this man, Berenkov thought uncomfortably.

As he sipped his brandy Kalenin twisted towards the dacha, from which they could discern the sounds of Georgi and Valentina although not what they were saying. Kalenin said: 'I envy you, Alexei. Having a complete family.'

He *was* complete, accepted Berenkov: he had everything he could possibly want, *would* ever want. With the awareness came another sink of unease, at the thought of losing it. So rare was uncertainty to the man that Berenkov became impatient with it, hurrying more brandy into his glass. He said: 'I know my good fortune.'

'Guard it carefully,' cautioned Kalenin.

It was almost as if the man suspected what he was about to do and was warning him against it. Berenkov said: 'You're attaching too much importance to the changes.'

'This is different than before,' insisted Kalenin. 'This is a genuine upheaval.'

'Any Russian leader needs two things,' Berenkov argued back. 'The support of the military and the support of the KGB. And they know it.'

'I hope you're right,' said the doubtful Kalenin.

'For both our sakes.'

There is a period between the season changes in Moscow when in the late afternoon the river valley fills up with mist, cloaking the buildings, and when they drove down from the Lenin Hills it was like going into some milky, untroubled sea where there were never any storms. At Kutuzovsky Prospekt Kalenin and Georgi embraced and Kalenin said he was a fine boy. Back in the apartment, Berenkov and Valentina helped Georgi to pack and both drove him to Kazan station and waited on the platform until the train departed.

In the car on the way back Valentina said: 'I thought Kalenin was quiet this weekend.'

'He worries too much,' dismissed Berenkov.

'What about?'

'Everything,' said Berenkov. He was glad the weekend was over: the doubts weren't with him any more, out of Kalenin's company.

'There's nothing wrong between you, is there?' asked the woman curiously.

Berenkov risked frowning across the car at her. 'Of course not,' he said. 'What could there be?'

'Just an impression,' said Valentina. 'I thought you were quiet, too.'

At the apartment they decided they did not want to eat again but Berenkov opened wine, a heavy Georgian red. He drank looking across the room at the wife from whom he had been apart for so much of their married life, thinking back to that afternoon's conversation about envy and good fortune. Valentina was still beautiful, Berenkov decided: not young-girl beautiful, flush-cheeked and pert breasted, but maturely so, settled. It was an odd word but it fitted because that was how he felt: settled and contented, a very satisfied man. He said: 'I love you very much.'

Valentina, who had always remained faithful during their parting but sometimes wondered if Berenkov, who was a sexual man, had done the same, said: 'I love you, too.'

The following day Berenkov sent in the diplomatic bag to London the entire file that had been established and maintained upon Charlie Muffin, from the moment of the Moscow episode, with instructions that the maximum effort be made to locate the man.

Natalia Nikandrova Fedova believed most of the time that she had completely recovered, as a person who has been ill convinces themselves that they are better with the passing of time; but as a convalescent still feels an occasional twist of pain so she had bad moments, like tonight.

Certainly she had escaped any material punishment, which had been her greatest fear. Charlie's, too. She'd undergone fairly intensive interrogation but she knew the ways of such interviews (if she didn't, who did?) and they hadn't caught her out, not even Kalenin himself when he'd led the questioning. And after so long they had to be satisfied. If they hadn't been satisfied she wouldn't have been allowed to continue as a KGB debriefer and most definitely not been promoted, as she had been six months earlier, to the rank of full major. Or still be permitted the single occupancy of the two-bedroom apartment, with separate bathroom and kitchen, just off Mytninskaya, particularly now that Eduard was hardly ever home any more. Eduard was another indication of their full trust, Natalia recognized, expertly: if there'd been the slightest doubt about her loyalty Eduard would not have gone unhindered along the privileged, KGB-sponsored route to the officer-grooming military academy.

So her elitist life in Moscow could go on

uninterrupted: cosseted, protected, safe. And utterly empty.

Despite her aching unhappiness Natalia knew she had done the right thing in not returning to England with Charlie Muffin. There had been a different regime then. If she'd fled when Charlie had pleaded with her to do so, become a defector, punishment would have been exacted against Eduard. That was the way it had always been; perhaps still was although she suspected it might be different under Gorbachev.

Eduard hadn't been the only reason for holding back. She'd been frightened, Natalia remembered: desperately frightened and bewildered. There'd been the discovery that Charlie wasn't the disaffected British traitor he was supposed to be: that he'd beaten her at the debriefings with which she'd been entrusted specifically to find out whether he were genuine or not. Too late, of course, when she *had* found out. By then they had become lovers, proper lovers not together for the excitement of the sex although that had been good for them both, after such a long time, but *in* love, content simply to be with each other, each knowing the other was near at hand. Comfortable. She'd seriously thought of running with him. Briefly, momentarily putting aside the effect upon Eduard. That had possibly been the most frightening moment of all, confronting the unknown. Charlie had said he would protect her: guard against any Soviet pursuit or British pressure to defect properly, to go through the debriefing procedure and name names and identify places. But she hadn't been able to lose the fear. Then it had been equal to the love; no, she decided, in immediate contradiction. Then it had been greater than the love, making the decision to stay easier, irrespective of any consideration about Eduard.

76

What about now?

Natalia greeted the recurring question like an old friend. She supposed it was easier to imagine herself now making a different decision because she was not, nor would she ever again be, faced by it. If she were to do so she wasn't sure that fear would overwhelm her other emotions, not this time. The thought had always occupied a part of her mind during the unfilled, echoing months and she'd come to recognize a truth she hadn't fully accepted before. It had not been until Charlie was gone that Natalia had known, too late, how complete and absolute her love had been.

Natalia gazed around the apartment, relaxing in the warmth of nostalgia but unsettled by it as well. They'd spent more hours here than in his flat. He'd sat in that chair over there and they'd read together, one explaining to the other the nuances of whichever language. He'd perfected his Russian here and she'd learned all the Western swearwords in his irritation at getting the phrasing and the pronunciation wrong. It was here that. . . Natalia closed the curtain in her mind, refusing to go on. There was no point, no purpose. She'd made her choice – she never thought of it as a sacrifice – and she had survived and Eduard had survived and she guessed she should be grateful. She had a life that accorded her many things, and that had to be sufficient now. There was nothing else; no chance of anything else.

The curtain flicked back, as it usually did during the bad times like tonight, and she allowed herself the final reflection. What, she wondered, would Charlie be doing now? Not professionally: she wasn't interested in that. Personally. Would there be another woman? It would be understandable, if there were. What had occurred between them had been a long time ago. There'd been no contact since that last day, when they'd parted by the Moskva River, he to flee to the British embassy on its banks, she hurrying to denounce him in the way he'd rehearsed her, to keep her safe. So yes, there would probably be another woman. A wife, even. Children. Would he be happy as, she believed, he had been happy with her? She hoped so, difficult though the generosity was for her. It would be wrong for her not to hope he was happy: go against her love with him, in fact. She'd like to think something else: that occasionally – just very occasionally – Charlie thought of her. Smiled, like she smiled, at some private, secret recollection that would only have meaning for the two of them. She'd like to think that very much indeed.

There *was* a man thinking of Natalia Nikandrova Fedova, although it was not Charlie Muffin.

Berenkov sat in his darkened office long after all the other senior executives at the First Chief Directorate had left, just burning the lamp directly behind his desk, staring down at a picture of the KGB debriefer which he had extracted from her records file. There was nothing in that file that Berenkov did not know. He had listened, too, to all the recordings of her interrogations with Charlie Muffin. And then located traces of other conversations, which at the moment formed part of no official dossier: conversations too professionally blurred by people who had suspected listening devices in the Mytninskyaya apartment. But unquestionably proof of two people living there, when he knew the boy to have been away at school.

Berenkov pulled back in his chair, out of the concentrated brightness of the light. 'You're the way, Natalia Nikandrova,' he said, unashamedly talking to himself. 'I know you're the way.'

Charlie did everything absolutely by the book,

complying with every procedural regulation. The risk of a British intelligence officer being identified and targeted by a hostile service is accorded the highest-priority investigation not only by the department's internal security but by MI5 in its official counter-intelligence role. Charlie ensured the widest circulation to both of his memoranda on his mother's interrogation. He dispatched a fuller, separate report to Harkness, completely confident there was nothing the acting Director General could do to halt a sweeping, formal inquiry being conducted.

Laura caught him just as he was leaving his cubbyhole office. 'What the hell's going on?' she demanded. 'It's chaos up there!'

'I'm being officially investigated,' said Charlie simply.

The girl looked at him, obviously at the point of leaving. 'Where are you going?'

'Until it's over I'm officially suspended,' said Charlie. 'It's all in Harkness' book of rules: paragraph twenty-five, page ten to be precise.'

9

A combination of circumstances and events enabled the KGB to suborne Henry Blackstone. There was a great deal of intelligence expertise. Some carelessness by someone who should not have been careless. Audacity verging upon recklessness from a very ambitious Soviet espionage officer named Vitali Losev. And some good fortune because they got away with the audacity and approached the impoverished and aggrieved Blackstone at a moment when he was particularly susceptible, at the depth of a depression.

The identity of the British firm participating in the Star Wars missile development, including the limited correspondence that had passed between them, was the information demanded by Alexandr Petrin at that first San Francisco meeting with the now hopelessly enmeshed Emil Krogh. From the covering letter accompanying outline drawing specifications came the name of the project engineer in England, Robert Springley.

That one name – and the comparative smallness of the Isle of Wight with its county capital at Newport – was more than sufficient for Losev, the balding, fussily neat KGB head of station at the Soviet embassy in London's Kensington Palace Gardens. Losev assigned five operatives to Newport, two to hunt the name Robert Springley through the listings at the telephone headquarters there, the other three to search the entries in the Voters' Register, which is a publicly available record of all adults qualified to vote in parliamentary elections and held at every county library. There were five Robert Springleys and it only took thirty-six hours to find them all.

By the early morning of the third day KGB observers were positioned to follow the occupants of each discovered address to their workplace. The Robert Springley they wanted turned out to be a prematurely white-haired man of forty-two who was contentedly married to a part-time teacher, with two school-age children of his own and who drove, badly, a three-year-old Rover car from a terraced Victorian house at Ryde. He also suffered from the absentminded carelessness of a scientific engineer whose thoughts were more often upon esoteric theory than upon practical reality.

The London posting was the first position of command for Losev, who was an intensely ambitious Ukrainian determined to fulfil absolutely an assignment to which, from the priority coding of his instructions, he knew Dzerzhinsky Square attached the highest importance. From that first day Springley's every move and habit were charted by unseen observers and his carelessness instantly established because such failings are the sort of advantages constantly sought by intelligence personnel. There also appeared to be a habit associated with that carelessness.

The aerospace factory was a sprawl of buildings added to the town-centre original as the company expanded with its success. The obviously fenced and permanently guarded secure area was easily isolated by Springley's daily parked Rover, the convenient marker for the man's movements. Which were invariably not straight home at the end of each day. Instead the man's routine, minutely documented by the watching Russians, was to stow his coat and briefcase and whatever else he was carrying in the locked boot of his vehicle the moment he left the protected secure section. But then to drive from that section the five hundred yards to an expansive, unrestricted car park fronting the firm's sports and social club, of which Springley was that year's honorary chairman. And into which, for the hour he customarily spent inside, he never carried the briefcase.

Losev and his team waited in readiness for two evenings but could move on neither because Springley parked his car too near and too obviously close to the clubhouse. But there was no such convenient space the third night and the locked boot of Springley's car was sprung within seconds of the man entering the building. Losev's hire car moved off at once, the *rezident* and a Soviet photographer hunched in the rear, working as it travelled. The photographer, Yevgenni Zazulin, was professionally trained and assigned to the London *rezidentura* precisely for his technical expertise. He used an ultra-fast film on a wide exposure to compensate for the poor light, with a miniature Minox camera fitted with a proxile copying lens. Losev made no attempt to sort or read the contents of the picked-open briefcase, anxious to return it to the Rover before the project chief quit the club. Losev was still cautious, however, replacing each document in the way and in the space from which he had extracted it and insisting every exposure be duplicated to provide a back-up photograph as insurance against the first being marred by the car's movement. The copying was completed in thirty minutes and the relocked case put back into the relocked boot of the Rover twenty minutes before Springley emerged, never to suspect the theft, for his delayed journey home.

Springley was not, however, so careless as to carry in his briefcase classified and therefore prohibited material. What there was proved enough, although it was not at first identified as such. At that stage the intent was still to find something manipulative about the project manager himself, so the concentration was upon the credit-card dockets and bills – some receipted, some not but none overdue – and bank statements. The only discovery was an easily manageable overdraft facility of £3,000, which certainly wasn't manipulative. Losev did not properly appreciate the significance of the one-way correspondence file until he reached the third letter. And then fell back satisfied in his chair, immediately and correctly appreciating what he held in his hand to be the internal applications from company employees seeking secondment to the Star Wars development.

And an information goldmine.

Each application necessarily itemized the qualificational background – up to and including security clearance ratings – of every applicant. Each listed the current pay scale of the writer, by so doing showing that the secret project carried a higher-than-normal salary structure and therefore hinting at a possible, money-related reason for such application. Each set out family background and circumstances, complete with home addresses. And two thirds gave their banks – again complete with addresses – with permission for them to be approached for character references.

All of which were approached, immediately, with the request for a credit guarantee by a finance company registered and provably functioning in the Channel island of Jersey, its public operation an impenetrable cover for its proper KGB purpose of probing the financial weaknesses of potential victims. From the same Jersey company requests were also made through the Central Credit Register and to all the major credit-card companies for assurances of the credit worthiness of everyone whose name emerged from Springley's briefcase.

The inquiry – specifically for finance guidance and not character assessment – threw up the first clue to Henry Blackstone's problems. There was a clearly ambiguous reply from the man's bank from which it was easy to infer that Blackstone's income only just met his outgoings and frequently failed. And from two credit-card companies came the information of applications received but refused. These alone were enough to mark Blackstone out from the rest. And then came another public record check, initially begun upon each application.

Over the course of many years in the relentless pursuit of blackmail the KGB has become expert in the use of Britain's national repository of births, death and marriages at St Catherine's House, in London's Kingsway, and it was automatic for a search to be made there upon target groups.

The marriage of Henry George Blackstone, a tracer, to Ruth Emerson, a spinster of the parish of Emsworth, in Hampshire, was recorded at Portsmouth Register Office on 6 May 1975. The marriage of Henry George Blackstone, a tracer, to Ann Crouch, a computer operator of the parish of Freshwater, Isle of Wight, was shown to have taken place at Newport Register Office on 9 January 1976. The KGB researcher had only two floors to go to complete his investigation, idly reflecting as he went from one section of the building to the other on the shortness of grief in the event of Ruth Blackstone, née Emerson, genuinely having died after such a tragically brief union. It took him less than an hour in the department listing the country's deaths to establish, however, that Ruth hadn't died. And that Blackstone was the bigamist he already suspected the man to be.

Although the evidence looked conclusive, Losev did not immediately try to use it, displaying unusual restraint by instead concentrating all the KGB surveillance solely upon Blackstone. The Russian was becoming disappointed by the discovery of a mundane existence of Monday-night cinema and Thursday-night darts at the pub nearest to Blackstone's Newport home, but on the Friday was glad that he'd waited. Because that night, instead of going from the East Cowes factory to the home he'd made with Ann, Blackstone caught the Portsmouth-bound ferry, bought a cheap spray of flowers from a street stall and was with Ruth in Anglesea Terrace by six thirty. And from there, the following Monday, began commuting to the island for the period he was allowing himself to be with his first wife.

Losev was never completely to know the fortunate coincidence of his actual approach to Blackstone: not how the fingers-crossed five-horse accumulator upon which Blackstone's weekend outing with Ruth depended had failed on the same day that the man had been officially informed he was not getting the hoped-for transfer to the better-paying Star Wars project as part of Springley's team. Losev learned soon enough about the work rejection, though: a lot of tight-lipped complaints about lack of appreciation and years of service given for bugger all and how some people didn't deserve loyalty.

Losev had manouevred the conversation on the ferry going to Portsmouth and timed the inquiry about what Blackstone did, with chosen precision, just before the ship docked. The Russian feigned perfectly the surprise at hearing that Blackstone was an industrial tracer and said wasn't that a co-incidence and wasn't the world a small place and did Blackstone know how difficult it was to find reliable industrial tracers, which the bemused Blackstone said he didn't.

Losev suggested a drink at a pub called the Keppel's Head, named after an admiral and practically on the quay against which they moored, and Blackstone looked at his watch and said all right but he only had time for one. Losev allowed Blackstone to bring the conversation back to the shortage of tracers and what, exactly, it was he wanted tracing. Losev was intentionally vague, talking generally of creating manufacturing drawings and blueprints from engineers' specification notes and Blackstone shook his head and sniggered and agreed that it *was* coincidentally a small world because that was *exactly* the sort of work he did all the time.

'Ever do any freelance work?' asked Losev ingenuously.

'Freelance work?'

'That's all I'm looking for at the moment.' said Losev. 'Someone reliable I can trust to take the load off my permanent draughtsmen and tracers; we've got so much work on we don't know which way to turn.'

'Maybe I could take something on,' said Blackstone, in what he foolishly imagined to be an opening bargaining ploy.

'You're not serious!' said the obviously delighted Losev.

'Why not?' shrugged Blackstone, not wanting to appear as desperately eager as he was. 'You want a tracer. I'm a tracer. Why don't we give it a try?'

'You wouldn't know how grateful I'd be: how much of a relief it would be.'

'We'd come to some financial arrangement, of course?'

'Of course,' agreed Losev enthusiastically. He smiled, nudging the other man. 'And a proper financial arrangement. Cash. No nonsense with income tax or anything like that. You interested?'

Blackstone was so excited he did not immediately

trust himself to speak, so he sipped his beer to cover the gap. Then he said: 'I wouldn't mind giving it a go.'

'Could we meet here again, say, tomorrow night, for me to give you the specification notes?'

'Sure,' agreed Blackstone. He had to ask, to get it finalized! He said: 'What sort of money are we talking about here?'

'This is a rush job, very important to me,' said Losev. 'You get a set of drawings back to me by the weekend and I've got a good chance of securing a contract that's going to make me a very happy man. So you do that for me and there's five hundred pounds in your pocket, no questions asked.'

Blackstone hid behind his beer glass again. Finally he managed: 'Here this time tomorrow night then?'

'I can't believe how lucky we are to have met,' said Losev.

'Neither can I,' said Blackstone, deeply sincere. 'I don't even know your name.'

'Stranger,' said Losev, reciting the Moscow-dictated legend name. 'Mr Stranger.'

Legend name for Petrin, in San Francisco, was Friend. Both had been selected by Alexei Berenkov with much forethought.

Berenkov had the summons hand-delivered to Natalia in her office three floors below him in the First Chief Directorate headquarters on the Moscow ring road, knowing she would be there to receive it because he'd made himself responsible for her movements.

Natalia sat for several moments held by the shock, the words blurring before her, then becoming clear, then bluring again. It had finally come, she decided at once: the demand she'd feared every day since Charlie's departure.

Natalia, who'd observed her religion even before the Gorbachev relaxations made church attendance easier, thought: Oh God! Dear God, please help me!

10

Berenkov stood politely as the woman entered his office and went halfway across the room to greet her, escorting her to the overly ornate visitors' chair he'd moved specially, to bring her closer to his desk, not to its front but to one side. That was the extent of the relaxation: there was a less official area of chairs and couches to one side, near the window, but Berenkov decided it would have been going too far.

'Welcome, Natalia Nikandrova,' said Berenkov. 'Welcome indeed.'

'Comrade General,' responded Natalia. Her voice was higher than it should have been but he would expect some apprehension at the personal interview. She put her hand up to the thick-rimmed spectacles before she realized she was doing it and stopped the nervous gesture; it would have seemed like a fatuous wave. Why this clumsy, artificial politeness? Where were the escorting guards and the stenographer, to note the interrogation for later production as evidence at a trial?

'There has not been the opportunity before for me to congratulate you upon your promotion.'

Nor the need, thought Natalia, further bewildered. Unable to think of anything better, she said: 'Thank you, Comrade General.' There was an approach taught like this at the training academy: the soft, beguiling beginning, lulling into a sense of misleading security. Everything was undoubtedly being recorded by hidden microphones so she supposed there was no necessity for official stenographers.

'Well deserved,' said Berenkov. Truthfully he added: 'I've spent time considering your entire career. It is extremely commendable.'

She and Charlie had tried to prepare for an encounter like this. It was imperative, Charlie had insisted, that she remain unshakable in her story of never imagining he intended to return to the West until the very day she'd denounced him. She could go as far as admitting their affair – which she had done to Kalenin – but insist it was contrived by her, without any real affection, to trick him into some indiscretion to confirm her growing suspicion of his loyalty to Moscow. *Survive*, Charlie had repeated again and again: *Think of nothing except surviving.* Cautiously, stiffly, she said: 'I am gratified you should think so, Comrade General.'

'And your son is an exemplary student at the military academy,' said Berenkov.

The alarm flared through her. The beginning of the pressure, the remainder of what she had to lose? She said: 'He appears to be doing well.'

'But away for most of the time now? No longer needing his mother's guidance?'

Which direction was this? A hint at how vulnerable Eduard was? Or the first move to take the apartment away from her? 'That is so,' she conceded. She was terrified of the moment coming but she almost wished, fatalistically, that the bloated man would stop playing with her and come out openly with the accusation.

'So there is no personal reason against your taking another job?' Definitely nervous, decided Berenkov. But controlling it well. Then again, she had been educated to control her emotions.

'I'm afraid. . .I don't quite. . .another job?' stumbled Natalia, badly. 'Forgive me,' she recovered, more forcefully. 'What job could I have different from what I already do. . .for which I have been particularly schooled?' She was now totally bewildered, too confused to anticipate or guess at anything Berenkov might say.

'Everyone and everything has to adjust to the times through which we are going,' said Berenkov. 'Ourselves included. I fully recognize that yours has until now been a specialized subject and that you might not have considered any other field. But there is one; one for which your language expertise fits you very well indeed.'

What *was* all this! Certainly not, apparently, what she'd feared. Natalia stopped the relief, before it had time properly to form. Everything was still far too uncertain, too jumbled, for her to feel relief. 'What else could I do but debrief?'

There was suspicion, gauged Berenkov. There should have been apprehension, at being called to the Director's office and there should have been surprise, at what he was nebulously offering. But suspicion didn't have a place. He wanted very much to produce Charlie Muffin's name, to observe her reaction. But he couldn't, he accepted; she always had to remain the unknowing bait, against her warning him if Charlie Muffin did respond. He said: 'You can listen. Expertly, the way you've been taught. Understand the nuances beyond the flat words.'

'Listen to whom?'

'Official ministry delegations, to the West. They are going to increase, in the coming months, under the new order at the Kremlin.' Berenkov was leaning forward on his desk, intent upon her. Pinpricks of colour came to her face, the way people become flushed when they are excited.

The West! Somewhere she'd never imagined herself ever being able to reach, somewhere where Charlie. . .Natalia stopped determinedly. Rigidly professional, she said: 'There are always interpreters...other people from our organization forming part of the support staff as well. I would have no proper or useful role.'

An intelligent objection, accepted Berenkov; the woman was fully controlled now, demure hands in the demure lap of her stern black suit, hair tightly in a bun at the back of her head, in a style he found oddly antiquated. She wore no make-up, either. As if she were dressing down or not bothering with her appearance. 'We think you would: a very useful role. Interpreters have access at all times and at all levels but as I've already told you we don't expect from you the translations of what is said. The others can provide that. From you we want the analyses, independent of the other various ministry opinions.'

'Supplied to whom?' queried Natalia. 'The ministries? Or here?'

'Here, of course,' smiled Berenkov. That had to be the way for any uncertainties in her mind to be satisfactorily allayed.

'I would be a KGB spy upon the delegations, in fact?' queried Natalia directly.

Berenkov shook his head. 'Others form part of every overseas group to ensure proper behaviour: you said so yourself, a few moments ago. All we seek is what I've asked for. Independent analysis.'

Natalia supposed that with so many changes happening in Moscow it made practical, understandable sense for the KGB to know first hand as much as possible of such overseas visits, properly to formulate their own forward policies. She wouldn't have thought it needed a change of leadership before the necessity was realized, however. She said: 'So I am being officially transferred?'

'How would you feel about such a move?' said Berenkov, conveying the impression she had a choice.

'It is too sudden. . .too unexpected. . .for me properly to be able to answer that. . .'

All the early unease had gone now, assessed Berenkov. She was a woman capable of adapting remarkably quickly. Making it obvious there hadn't really been a choice at all, Berenkov said: 'You will begin immediately.'

Recognizing the dismissal, Natalia stood and said: 'I hope I will fulfil what's required of me.'

'I hope that too,' said Berenkov, in a remark of which she was never to understand the true meaning.

Natalia had completely recovered from all the doubts by the time she left Berenkov's suite, able to think and rationalize. That initial reaction, immediately associating Charlie with the West, as if there were a chance of her seeing him again, was perhaps natural but in reality quite foolish. There would never be a chance of a reunion. How could there be?

Charlie underwent one routine interrogation and, more expert than his questioners, he guessed within minutes that they were merely going through the required motions and that the investigation had already been resolved. And if it had, in a little over a week, he knew, too, that he'd been correct about the episode at the Hampshire nursing home.

His formal notice to return to Westminster Bridge Road came during the second week but the date for that return was not until the the end of the month, giving the vague semblance of a proper inquiry. Charlie surmised the truth to be that Harkness was trying to delay the inevitable confrontation and considered making contact with Laura to find out what he could. Not fair, he dismissed at once: if he'd succeeded in escalating everything to the level he hoped, he could get Laura fired out of hand for even speaking to him. He could wait, Charlie decided: he had all the time in the world.

'What's their explanation?' demanded the outraged Harkness. In his anger his face had gone from its usual pink to bright red.

'It's most unfortunate,' said Witherspoon, unhappy at being caught in the middle. 'I briefed them thoroughly but no one expected the story of their being from the Ministry of Pensions to be checked so thoroughly.'

'The man Muffin is a confounded nuisance; an embarrassment and a nuisance,' insisted Harkness. 'Now I've got to provide an explanation. Can you imagine that!'

'A great nuisance,' agreed Witherspoon.

'This department – this service – has got to be rid of him!'

'Yes,' said Witherspoon in further agreement.

'And I want your help in achieving it.'

'Whatever I can do,' accepted Witherspoon at once. He knew Charlie Muffin laughed at him: despised him even. There would be a great satisfaction in being the one who laughed, for a change.

11

Things happened far more quickly than Natalia Fedova had expected, almost too quickly to allow her properly to think and to encompass all that the change meant to her. Although she could not easily conceive what training or preparation there could be she had still anticipated some period of instruction, but there was none. There was a memorandum from Berenkov officially confirming the decision of their meeting and telling her she would continue to operate from her existing office within the First Chief Directorate. And some Foreign Ministry circular advising her of allowances she could claim, together with a request for accreditation photographs and a personal biography form to complete. Five days after she submitted it, she was assigned her first interpreter-escort role, accompanying a Foreign Ministry delegation to Canberra.

It was fortunately a brief and comparatively simple trip, an exploratory journey to discuss and assess whether an official visit to Australia at Foreign Minister level would be acceptably worthwhile to both countries. Natalia conducted herself with absolute propriety and decorum, guessing herself to be very much on trial. Technically her rank within the KGB – and the fact that she *was* KGB – put her above the constraints of other, ordinary Soviet ministry officials towards the delegation leaders, but Natalia never took advantage of it. She was polite and considerate to everyone, even the most junior clerks, and showed the proper deference to those in charge. She identified the monitoring KGB officers before the aircraft landed in the Australian capital, a fat, borish

Armenian and a younger, confident Moscow-born man. From them there was an attitude of reserved uncertainty but on the fourth day the younger one made the inevitable approach. Natalia's tempted reaction was to use her rank. Instead she rejected the man without humiliating or embarrassing him. The official interpreter was a man whom Natalia suspected of having KGB links too, because such advantageously placed officials customarily did. She anticipated resentment but there wasn't any, which she took as further proof of the man's Dzerzhinsky Square connections and of his having been told how to behave towards her.

Natalia found herself enjoying her role. The official meetings were not difficult to interpret, either verbally or by intention, and after shutting herself away in the Mytninskaya apartment for so long the sudden social change was pleasant, as well. She liked the cocktail parties and the receptions and the dinners. There were limited but interesting tourist outings and three press conferences, each with photocalls from which Natalia instinctively and protectively recoiled until pressured into forming part of the groups.

When she returned to Moscow she was surprised to see the photographs published in *Pravda* and *Izvestia*, both with her name printed in full.

Dutifully fulfilling her imagined function, Natalia wrote a comprehensive and annotated report of the visit, with a single-sheet summary in which she judged that although the Australians had been welcoming and friendly she did not believe an official invitation would be forthcoming so close to a general election within the country. It proved to be an accurate assessment.

The North American tour was longer and with a different government group, a perennial Trade

Ministry quest for grain sales to supplement another failed Russian harvest. This time there was advanced publicity, a group photograph published in *Pravda* and again with everyone identified by name.

Natalia conducted herself as carefully as before. This time the sexual advance came from a deputy minister who accepted her refusal philosophically and switched his attention at once to one of the accompanying female stenographers who was equally unoffended but still said no. There were eight days in Ottawa, again concluding with press conferences and photographs, and from Canada they flew south to Washington. The scheduled American visit lasted a week and ended with a joint conference with US agricultural and trade officials who disclosed tentative agreement to supply the full amount needed to make up the Russian shortfalls.

In her assessment upon her Moscow return Natalia warned against their becoming over-reliant upon American supplies that could be used as a bargaining lever in some quite separate, later negotiation between the two countries.

Berenkov responded by return, congratulating her upon her analyses – as he had after her correct interpretation in Australia – and assured Natalia her transfer was being regarded even beyond the First Chief Directorate as an unqualified success.

Blackstone could not remember feeling like this before: couldn't put into so many words *exactly* how he did feel. He felt comfortable. And supremely confident, without those worrying dips into depression. But most of all there was relief at not having to worry any more. There'd never seemed to be a time in the past when part of his mind wasn't occupied with money, making calculations on scraps of paper, often virtually fingering the edges of the coins in his pocket to count how much he had. He didn't have to do that any longer, not any of it. Christ, it was a good feeling! Not something he wanted to lose, ever. So he was going to make bloody sure he didn't. The drawings so far had been easy. Not that he'd said so, of course. He hadn't made them look like a quick or simple job, either. He'd done them properly, top-quality stuff, giving good value for what he got.

And he hadn't flashed the money around, either. Not too much, anyway. The car, a second-hand Ford but a good one, nearly new, had cost more than he'd really planned to spend and he'd had to spread quite a lot on hire purchase, but there'd be no difficulty keeping up the payments, with his extra income guaranteed. And the separate holidays were booked, with Ruth and Ann. And it was good, being able to go into shops with either of them and say things like 'If you want it, it's yours' when they tried on a dress or something.

Blackstone thought back to another time, a time he was never going to know again, when he'd been worried as usual but cheered himself up, thinking of his luck in having both Ann and Ruth. Now everything *was* perfect, he decided: absolutely perfect.

12

Charlie's cubicle was on the fifth floor, overlooking an unused courtyard at the back. The corridor and other offices seemed much quieter than usual, with hardly anyone about, as if they'd all heard the air-raid siren and rushed off to the shelters before the bombs started to drop. At this door Charlie hesitated, looking through the fluted glass into the facing cubicle. It was nominally the office of Hubert Witherspoon, whom Charlie suspected of being the eager purveyor of his indiscretion to Harkness. It looked, as it always looked, like an entry for the Neat Office of the Year Award, but Witherspoon wasn't there. If there had been a rush for the air-raid shelters Witherspoon would have been way out in front to get the deepest, safest place with his sandwich pack and toilet deodorizer.

Charlie's quarters looked like the bomb had already scored a direct hit. The non-classified In-Traffic that Charlie was listed automatically to receive had continued uninterrupted while he had been away. It overflowed the provided tray, and messengers had made a pile beside, on the desk, and when that got high enough to topple over they had started stacking them on the floor. There was a second tray for signals advising Charlie in his absence that classified material was awaiting his signature and collection from Dispatch. It was empty, like it had been for months. On top of the two filing cabinets, in an empty milk bottle, drooped the skeleton of an atrophied tulip he'd stolen from St James' Park coming back from lunch one evening; he couldn't remember where he'd got the empty milk bottle. *The Times* still lay on his picked-at, clue-dotted blotter, folded as he'd left it at the crossword. Someone had filled in with a contrasting red pen the word that had baffled him – 'Idiot' – in response to the clue asking who told *Macbeth* that life was but a walking shadow. Witherspoon, guessed Charlie: the prick was always going on about Double-whatevers from Oxford and trying to prove how clever he was. Charlie didn't think the answer was right.

Charlie sat heavily in his chair, thrust sideways to get it going and managed a complete circle before the momentum stopped. The story of his recent existence, he thought; going around in circles getting nowhere. But not today. Today there was the confrontation with Harkness. Charlie was looking forward to it more than he'd looked forward to anything for a long time.

His move or Harkness'? His entry past the document check on the ground floor would have been tabbed, for instant notification. So Harkness, four floors above in that taken-over Director General's office, would know he was in the building. And protocol dictated that he wait in the rabbit hutch until he was summoned.

'Fuck that,' said Charlie to himself. He used the internal direct line which sometimes Sir Alistair Wilson had actually answered himself because that was what the line was for, immediate contact. It was Laura who replied.

'The prodigal returns!' announced Charlie. There was no immediate response and Charlie said: 'Hello?'

'We've been advised,' said Laura. Her voice was rehearsed-sad, the way people sympathize with death.

'How's Paul's prickly heat?'

Laura ignored the question. Instead she said: 'I thought you might have called in between.'

100

'Best I didn't,' assured Charlie.

'You any idea what you did!'

'Followed procedure,' recited Charlie. 'Now I've been ordered to report in. Shall I come on up?'

'Of course you can't come up just like that. I'll ask.'

'Shall I hang on?'

'I'll call you back.'

It was a full half hour before the call came. The outside corridors and office were as quiet as before and there was no one else in the lift. It took a further fifteen minutes to negotiate the top-floor security check before Charlie was admitted to the inner sanctum of squashy carpet and bewigged ancestors. They still clutched their globes and compasses and looked hopeful.

Laura was waiting at the door of her own office, through which he had to pass to reach Harkness. As he approached she felt out for his hand, a mourning gesture again, and said: 'I've been as worried as hell about you: I still am.'

'There's still a lot I don't understand,' lied Charlie.

'Be. . .' started the girl.

'. . .careful,' finished Charlie. 'Always. Trust me.'

Harkness was leaning forward oddly low against the Director General's desk, like a trench soldier who disbelieved the Armistice had been declared. The desk was completely clear, the man not bothering with the pretence of any previous or more important paper work: Harkness stared unblinkingly at Charlie as Charlie crossed the expansive office. The interior continued the style of the exterior, up-to-the-ankle carpet, yesteryear panelling and self-satisfied predecessors who'd always had butter on their bread. Once again there were no conveniently placed chairs, meaning that he had to stand: little cunt intent on little victories, Charlie thought. He was determined against the man achieving many more today.

Harkness cleared his throat and said: 'You caused a very great disturbance: a very great disturbance indeed.'

'Strictly adhering to laid-down regulations,' said Charlie. 'What's the result of the investigation, sir?' The respectful title was open contempt from a man who'd never before called Harkness sir and who'd never in his career observed any of the guidelines. And you know it and there's fuck all you can do about it, thought Charlie.

'You are not under surveillance,' said Harkness, matching formality with formality. The waistcoated suit was blue, the pastel accessories pale mauve.

Charlie let his shoulders fall, a man from whom a burden has been lifted. 'That's a relief!' he said.

'I would have liked prior discussion, before the full alarm was initiated,' blurted Harkness, just failing to stop the rise of anger in his voice.

I bet you would, you little shit, thought Charlie; so you could have contained everything. He said: 'Your specific orders are to react without any delay, sir.'

'Stop reminding me of regulations!'

Temper, temper, thought Charlie: I've hardly started yet. He said : 'So what was it all about, sir?'

Colour was increasingly suffusing Harkness' face, so that he looked like someone who'd fallen asleep in the sun. He said: 'It would appear to have been a false alarm.'

No you don't, decided Charlie. He said: 'I don't see how that could be, sir. Two men interrogated my mother and I categorically established that they were imposters.'

There was a prolonged silence and Charlie guessed the other man was trying to find the escape words and phrases. Stumble and thrash about, Charlie thought contentedly: there aren't any.

'There was an internal mistake,' managed Harkness finally. 'Men exceeded instructions.'

Charlie dropped his head to one side. 'I'm afraid I don't understand, sir.'

'A routine check that was taken too far.'

Now it was Charlie who let the quiet build up between them, conscious of Harkness' discomfort rising with it. When the silence was on the point of going on too long Charlie said: 'Routine check? By our own internal security, you mean?'

Harkness swallowed, nodding. 'Yes.'

'Are you telling me my mother was interrogated by members of *this* department!'

'Questioned,' Harkness tried to qualify. 'Questioned, not interrogated.'

'She's seventy-seven years old,' said Charlie, very softly, very controlled. 'Seventy-seven years old and senile.'

Harkness looked away, unable to meet Charlie's look. The man mumbled: 'Internal mistake, like I said.'

'There are operational memoranda,' reminded Charlie. Still soft, still controlled: You're going to roast until every little bit is cooked, ready to eat, Charlie promised himself.

'Overlooked, I'm afraid.'

'Overlooked by whom!'

'Impossible case-load, trying to fulfil two functions during the Director General's illness.'

That explanation had a said-before ring about it, isolated Charlie triumphantly. Determined to get a direct admission, Charlie said: 'MI5's involvement would automatically have brought the matter to the attention of the Joint Intelligence Committee, wouldn't it?' And the Prime Minister, who chairs it, Charlie concluded mentally.

In a life filled with more dislike and antagonism

103

than a mongoose on a snake farm, Charlie had been subjected to a great many hate-filled stares but few equal to the one that came at that moment from Richard Harkness. The man said: 'I think it right that I should extend to you the proper apology.'

Charlie tried to gauge how difficult, practically verging on the super-human, it would have been for Harkness to say that. And still I'm not satisfied, Charlie thought, relentlessly vindictive. He said: 'I'll pass that apology on to my mother, shall I? She was very unsettled by the episode.'

'If you would,' muttered Harkness. There was growing around the man an attitude of distraction, as if he found it difficult completely to concentrate.

Charlie felt neither pity nor sympathy. Neither was an easy attitude for him at the best of times and they were never likely to be extended to Harkness. Charlie made up rules, far less verbose and convoluted than those created by Harkness. One of the foremost was always shaft first the bastard trying to shaft you and with a blunter, hotter shafting machine. He said: 'I gave permission at the spy school for you to access my personal file. The one that includes the medical records. You did get it, did you?'

Harkness nodded his head, awkwardly, as if he were punch drunk. 'A further misunderstanding. I've returned it, of course.'

'This routine investigation to which I have been subjected?' persisted Charlie. 'Is it concluded now?'

'Yes,' said Harkness.

'I do have the right officially to be informed of that, don't I?' said Charlie.

'I'll let you have a memorandum today.'

'My personnel record should also have an attachment to that effect too, shouldn't it?'

'I'll ensure that it's done,' promised the other man.

104

'Thank you, sir,' said Charlie. 'I'm very glad everything has been settled so satisfactorily.' Enough, Charlie told himself; a time to shaft and a time to stop, enjoyable though it had been.

Laura was waiting apprehensively in the outer office, standing beside her desk. 'He's fired you, hasn't he?' she said.

'Of course not,' said Charlie, grinning. There's inside knowledge here, my son, he reminded himself. He said: 'Any chance of our getting together some time?'

'I'd like that,' said the girl.

Blackstone looked with disbelief at the other man, not immediately able to speak. Then he realized how stupid he must look and tried to recover, swallowing heavily. 'I see,' he said.

'I thought you'd realize it would have to come to an end some time,' said Losev.

'I didn't,' admitted Blackstone. Desperately he said: 'There's nothing at all?'

Losev shook his head. 'I can understand how awkward that is going to be for you, with two homes to support. That can't be easy.'

Blackstone stood more open mouthed than before, his tongue moving over his bottom lip. He said: 'Who are you?'

'Your friend, Henry. Still your friend. You mustn't worry.'

'I don't understand.'

'You will, when we've had a little chat.'

13

Natalia had been away on the Australian visit when Eduard became eligible for leave, which therefore had to be postponed, so it had been almost six months since they were last together. Natalia was relieved that another overseas trip had not intruded to make this visit impossible. And pleased at how quickly permission had been granted for her to take leave herself, a Friday and a Monday, giving them a long weekend together.

Natalia tried hard to make everything right for her son's homecoming. She planned a Saturday-night outing and shopped widely at the concessionary stores, where she hesitated uncertainly at the alcohol counter. Natalia hardly drank but believed, although she was not sure, there was a half bottle of vodka somewhere in the Mytninskaya apartment. Eduard was nineteen, living in an all-male, military environment, she reminded herself: a man, which had been a strangely abrupt realization when he'd been home for the last time. He'd expect her to have something in: consider it odd if she hadn't. Still hesitant Natalia bought whisky, vodka and some imported Danish beers. As an afterthought she added four bottles of French wine, two white and two red. In a final touch Natalia displayed flowers in the hallway and the living room: she knew Eduard wouldn't appreciate them – probably wouldn't be aware of them – but Natalia thought flowers in a home were welcoming so it was really a gesture for her own benefit.

His letter had guessed at his reaching Moscow some time in the afternoon but she knew the risk of delay was too great for her to start preparing the homecoming meal in advance of his arrival. Natalia wandered about the flat, touching and moving things that didn't need to be touched and spent time in Eduard's bedroom, tidying things already tidied. Why – or of what – was she nervous? Natalia couldn't decide. Just that she was nervous, which was ridiculous. What on earth was there to be nervous of, receiving home a soldier-son whom she had not seen for half a year? Nothing. Ridiculous, she told herself again.

It was gone seven when Eduard telephoned and she was glad she had not started to prepare because he still had to go through some leave formalities at the military post at the Kursk station. An hour, Eduard guessed: an hour and a half at the outside. It was more than two hours from the time of the call before he got there.

Natalia was unaccountably disoriented by Eduard's entrance into her home. He appeared to be bigger, filling more space and making everything correspondingly smaller. The army boots looked huge and the uniform was rough when he held her to him and kissed her, quickly as if he were embarrassed by the gesture. There was a smell to his clothing, a stale, unclean impression mingled with the odour of his own body. There was another, more obvious smell on his breath and Natalia wondered if it really had taken more than two hours for him to get through the railway station formalities.

The hallway greetings over, he stumped directly into his room with his bag and topcoat but reappeared immediately, looking around as if he hadn't seen the apartment before.

'It's good to see you, Eduard.'

'Good to be back.'

'I'm cooking beef: I'm afraid it might be a little overdone.'

'I'm starving!'

'Would you like a bath first? There's time.'

Eduard frowned but started a smile at the same time, as if he suspected her of making a joke. 'Bath! What for?'

Natalia raised and lowered her shoulders. 'I thought you might have felt like one after all the travelling.'

'No,' he said positively. He looked inquiringly around the apartment again as if looking for something.

'I got some drink in. Beer: vodka and whisky, too.'

Eduard allowed the grin to register. 'Bloody good!' he said.

Natalia couldn't remember his swearing even minimally in front of her before. He appeared unaware of having done so. She said: 'It's all in the kitchen. Why don't you get it yourself?'

'You want anything?'

'No thank you.' Natalia became aware that she had remained standing since his entry. While he was out of the room she sat down on one of the two easy chairs: he'd trodden something black, like oil, across the room and into his bedroom.

Eduard returned with a glass of vodka in one hand and a beer in the other. He gestured with the beer can from which he was drinking direct and said: 'Imported beer and beef in the oven! Still all the privileges! You should try the beer we get at the camps: just like horse pi. . .' He stopped just in time, but remained smiling. 'Absolutely filthy,' he finished.

'What's it like there?' There hadn't been any reports of nationalistic protests between the Armenians and Azerbaijanis for a long time, but she wished his officer-cadet field course had not been somewhere so active.

'Boring,' said Eduard at once. 'I don't know why we don't make our minds up: either shoot the idiots when they riot or stand back and let them kill each other. Perfect solution, one way or the other.' He slumped in the opposing chair and thrust both legs out towards her. The boots really did look huge: she couldn't see whatever had caused the marks he'd trodden through the apartment.

'How about your grades?'

'I'll graduate easily,' said Eduard.

He'd always found easy anything academic, always the perfect student, remembered Natalia. Like Igor had always had a quick and receptive mind. The recollection of the husband who had deserted them surprised Natalia: she couldn't think of the last time he'd come to mind. At once she decided it was not surprising at all. There had always been a strong facial resemblance between father and son, even in unconscious mannerisms like the way each flicked back the straying, coal-black hair and smiled crookedly, one mouth edge up, the other down, but Natalia was caught now by how much stronger the similarities seemed to her. Imagination, she dismissed. How could any of Igor's behaviour or attitudes have washed off on a son he'd abandoned when the child was three? She said: 'How much longer will you be attached to an active field unit?'

The boy shrugged, making a noise as he drank from the can. 'You know what the army's like. They don't have any idea where their ass is most of the time.'

There was no apology for the expression, which Natalia did not really understand. 'You don't know?'

'Shouldn't be more than another two or three months but there's no way of telling.'

Eduard helped himself to another vodka before she served the meal, for which he opened one of the bottles of red wine and for which he sat down without washing his hands. The boy ate bent low over the table, head close to his food, practically spooning it into his mouth in a hand-circling, conveyor-belt fashion. He finished long before her and helped himself to a further complete plateful. He gulped at the wine with food still in his mouth, swallowing and chewing at the same time. Natalia forced the conversation throughout, telling him as much as she felt able about her new job and explaining the overseas travel and how different it was from anything to which she'd been accustomed before. Eduard grunted acknowledgement sounds from time to time but she didn't get the impression he was listening fully to what she said.

Eduard allowed her to clear away without offering to help, settling with his legs outstretched once more, another glass of vodka resting upon his stomach between cupped hands. He'd undone his tunic and shirt collar and Natalia thought he looked very scruffy, a conscripted soldier instead of a would-be officer.

'There's some laundry,' he announced.

'I'll do it tomorrow.'

'Some of it is pretty disgusting. There's been a lot of moving about. Not much time to change.'

'That's all right,' accepted Natalia. 'You seem to be drinking a lot.' He'd had the majority of the wine, too.

Eduard examined the vodka glass as if he were surprised to find it in his hand. 'You should see the officers' mess at the weekend!' he said with bombastic teenage bravado. 'I can drink the rest of them unconscious: actually done it!'

The ability to drink more than anyone else, and never suffer a hangover, had been one of Igor's boasts, thought Natalia, isolating other similarity.

She said: 'You're not in an officers' mess now.'

Eduard grimaced, not appearing to regard it as the rebuke she intended. 'Good life, the military,' he said. 'I'm enjoying it.'

Another thing Igor had often said. It had taken her a long time to realize it was because of the freedom it gave him, to whore and impress women at air shows and exhibitions by flying faster or lower than anyone else. She guessed her ex-husband would have by now gained a substantive promotion in the Air Force. Igor would like that, insignias of rank on a fine uniform, medals and ribbons arrayed in lines. She wished it were not proving so easy to think of the man today. She reckoned the last time she had consistently done so was when she'd been with Charlie, here in Moscow, the reflections then those of persistent comparison, good against bad. Which, she supposed, was what they were again. She still wished it weren't so. She said: 'I've managed to get tickets for Saturday for the State Circus! It's a new season: quite a lot of fresh acts.'

Eduard stared at her with that frowning, about-to-laugh expression again. 'The circus!'

'It's hardly children's entertainment!'

Belatedly he realized her disappointment. 'It's just. . .well, I wish you'd mentioned it before.'

'I didn't think of it until about a week ago, when it was too late to write. And I wasn't sure I could get tickets anyway. They're not easy to come by, you know!'

'I made plans, that's all.'

'Plans!' exclaimed Natalia, genuinely upset at the flippancy with which he was discarding her proposed treat.

'With some of the other cadet-officers I came up from Baku with.'

'For Saturday night?'

'You don't mind, do you?'

'Of course not.'

'It's our first time off base for months.'

'I understand.'

'One of them says he knows some good places here where we can enjoy ourselves. Have a few drinks. . .a few laughs.'

And more, thought Natalia. The unchanged pattern: drink, whore, boast, exaggerate. 'I said I understood.'

'I knew you would.'

Eduard slept late, snoring loudly. His bedroom was redolent of him when Natalia crept in to collect up the laundry and she wondered how long the windows would have to be left open to air the place after he'd gone. The washing was filthy, a lot personally stained, and she doubted her son always emerged the victor in the drinking contests, as he claimed. If Eduard could handle his drink intake one way he did not appear to be able to do so in another. She pressed him to bathe when he finally arose and he said he supposed he should, though there was little enthusiasm. He had his first drink before noon, although only a beer. Eduard kept prowling around the apartment and Natalia guessed he was bored or felt restricted or both. She suggested an ice-hockey game that afternoon and he said OK without much interest although when they got to the stadium his demeanour changed. He yelled and shouted and swore uncaringly, although not obscenely, and when it ended said he'd enjoyed himself.

Afterwards Eduard said there didn't seem any point in his returning to Mytninskaya and then having to come out again so soon, so why didn't they have a drink to fill in the time before he had to meet friends. Because it was convenient they used the bar in the Berlin Hotel, on Zhdanova. Eduard ordered vodka with a beer chaser again, telling his mother to get more than one purchase ticket to save time when they wanted refills.

'There's no real reason for me to go back to the apartment, either,' said Natalia when they were seated. 'I might as well go on to the show straight from here.'

'Show?' queried Eduard blankly.

'The circus,' reminded Natalia sadly. 'It would be silly to waste both tickets.'

'Right!' agreed Eduard, with surprising eagerness. 'You'll have fun.'

Natalia moved to make the obvious reply but then stopped, saying nothing. Eduard took the tickets which lay between them and returned with more vodka and beer. 'You didn't want another juice, did you?'

'No,' said Natalia.

'I didn't think you would. That's why I got the beer, instead.'

'That's fine.' Natalia had no real interest in going to the circus on Vernadskovo by herself, but the alternative was to go home by herself which wasn't really an alternative at all. She realized that quite apart from wanting to see Eduard again she had been looking forward to some brief hours of simple companionship.

'So you won't need the car?' demanded Eduard, smiling.

'What?' she said, confused by the question.

'The car. You won't really need it if you're going to the circus, will you?'

'I've got to get home, afterwards.'

'Oh, yes,' said Eduard, waiting expectantly.

'Why?' she asked in weary resignation.

'I just thought. . .well. . .' shrugged Eduard. 'I mean it might have been useful if I could have

113

borrowed it. . .' He smiled, a little-boy-misunderstood expression. 'Silly idea.'

'I suppose I could always get a taxi.'

'Sure you wouldn't mind?' said Eduard, eager again and too impatient to bother with the charade of protesting that it would cause his mother too much inconvenience.

'I'd be upset if it were damaged.'

'You can trust me.'

It had never before occurred to Natalia to doubt that she could but she did now and was disturbed by the ease with which the uncertainty came to her. She recalled her reflection in the concessionary store: Eduard was a man living in a rough, even brutal, all-male environment of an army camp. She should be more understanding of how difficult it must be for him to make in minutes, at the snap of his fingers, the transition from one existence to another. She was letting her emotions become jumbled and convoluted, fashioning images where none existed. Natalia handed over the car keys and then, reminded, said: 'What about a key to get back into the flat?'

'You haven't a spare?'

'Not with me. I'll wait up.'

'I might be late,' said Eduard in quick warning.

'If it gets too late I'll go to bed and you can wake me up with the bell when you get home.'

'Sure you don't mind?'

There was a lot she was being asked not to mind tonight, thought Natalia. 'No,' she said.

The State Circus was spectacular, some of the acts so good that Natalia genuinely forgot the disappointment of not having Eduard with her. During an interval a woman on the far side of the empty place said how could people be so selfish as not to bother to use a seat that was so difficult to get, and Natalia said she couldn't imagine.

114

She stayed up at Mytninskaya until almost one o'clock in the morning and guessed she managed to remain awake for nearly an hour after she got into bed. She jerked awake in the morning, aware at once of not having let Eduard in. His bed had not been slept in although it was possible to detect a trace of his having occupied it the previous day: unthinkingly Natalia opened a window.

She sat tensed at the kitchen table, hands held tightly before her, unsure what immediately to do. The emergency services, she supposed. But in what order? She'd use her KGB rank and position to get the proper response: she'd never experienced it herself but the civilian militia were legendary for uncaring disregard. So who first, police or hospital services? Hospital services, she decided. There were other things that could have happened to him, beyond a traffic accident. He could have become involved in a fight or got so drunk he'd fallen down and hurt himself. Be in a sobering-up station, in fact. She wasn't sure but she didn't think such places, necessary to get fall-down drunks off the Moscow streets to prevent their freezing to death in the winter, were administered by either the police or medical authorities. Definitely try hospitals first.

Because of being in the KGB Natalia possessed that rarest of Moscow commodities, a telephone directory, and was actually looking up the numbers when the doorbell shrilled.

She ran to the door, hesitating for the briefest second to compose herself before opening it, expecting some official conveyor of bad news. Eduard stood with one hand outstretched against the frame, as if he needed its support. His uniform and shirt collar were undone again, sagging, and his face was red and bloated and his eyes red-veined.

'Didn't wake you up after all,' he avoided.

115

Eduard was still drunk Natalia decided: if not drunk then very close to it. 'Where have you been?'

'Decided not to disturb you. Slept in the car,' he said, grinning, making the lie obvious.

Were mothers supposed to hope quite so quickly that their sons didn't become infected by the whores they slept with? She said: 'You look dreadful. Come in and clean yourself up.'

'Little sleep first,' insisted Eduard, giving the lopsided smile of his father. He stayed grinning. 'Not very comfortable, sleeping in a car.'

It was past noon when he emerged from his bedroom, and once more Natalia had to insist upon his bathing. She tried to keep any distaste from showing in her voice when she asked if he'd enjoyed himself the previous night and pretended to believe the haphazard account of what he'd done. Throughout the rest of the day there were long silences between them, neither with anything left to say, and on the Monday, their last day together, Natalia took him out into Moscow again, trying to use up the time with constant activity in restaurants and bars and among the stalls in the GUM store.

Eduard had to leave very early on the Tuesday morning and Natalia got up to see him off. He said he had had a wonderful leave and Natalia said she had enjoyed it too. He wasn't sure when he would get his next furlough but he would let her know and Natalia said that would be fine and that she hoped the new job wouldn't clash with it, taking her out of the country. Eduard said he hoped that too. The farewell kiss was as clumsy and embarrassed as the greeting gesture had been. Each was relieved at the parting.

Natalia stripped the bed and washed the blankets as well as the sheets and opened all the bedroom windows to their fullest extent. As an afterthought she put both sets of flowers in the room, although they did not seem particularly scented. Afterwards, still with time to spare before having to get to the First Chief Directorate building, she sat at the same kitchen table and with the same tenseness in which she'd been held imagining Eduard lying injured or dead somewhere on the Sunday morning. It had been an appalling weekend: ugly and disgusting and awful. She didn't believe Eduard's behaviour had been the difficulty of adjusting from one environment to another. She believed he found it easy – easier than to conform any other way – to be brutal and coarse, like his father had been brutal and coarse. And in the end she'd come to hate his father.

Blackstone had been waiting when Losev arrived, getting quickly into the car but saying nothing as they drove to the seafront where Losev stopped intentionally in a car park from which it was possible to see the island, a distant grey outline beyond the dull sea.

'Well!' said Losev. 'You've had time to think.'

'It won't work,' insisted Blackstone. 'I told you, I've been refused on the project.'

The ambitious Losev hadn't told Moscow of the problem. 'Re-apply,' he insisted. He was determined to get Blackstone operational.

'There's no point,' shrugged Blackstone. 'They've got all they want.'

'It's worth a try,' persisted Losev.

Blackstone shrugged again, without replying. He was trapped whichever way he looked: and he considered he'd looked at every possible escape. He desperately wanted to continue receiving the money and felt no reluctance in getting it this way, although he knew precisely who this man calling himself Mr Stranger really was. What right did the company have to expect any loyalty, after the way they'd treated him! Served them right!

Losev said: 'I think you're being too easily beaten. You're an employee there, even if you're not part of the project. You can move around, can't you?'

'Not easily, in the restricted areas.'

'Have you tried?'

'I don't need to. I know.'

'Five hundred, every time you get me something,' bargained the balding KGB man. 'A bonus, for anything particularly good. Doesn't that appeal to you, five hundred pounds a week at least?'

'You know it does.'

'So do as I say.'

'How will I contact you?' capitulated Blackstone.

'I'll give you a phone number,' said Losev. 'It will always be manned.' He smiled across the car, offering an envelope. 'And didn't I tell you I was a friend?'

Blackstone looked at the envelope without taking it. 'What is it?'

'I don't want you to worry, about anything,' said the Russian. 'It's your first bonus, a sign of my good faith. Five hundred pounds for doing nothing.'

Blackstone took it eagerly. 'I'll do what I can,' he said.

'I knew you would,' said Losev.

14

There seemed to be a lull in the war. Charlie guessed that generals and brigadiers who fought real wars would have a technical phrase for it, like regrouping or retrenchment or reallocation of forces. Harkness was probably doing all of those things and working to invent more. But in the immediate days following the confrontation there was a respite, although Charlie was careful not to provide the acting chief with any excuse, no matter how inconsequential. He arrived at Westminster Bridge Road promptly on time and only took a measured hour for lunch and never left early. He was polite to Witherspoon, who returned soft-footed to his office the afternoon of Charlie's encounter with Harkness, and Witherspoon was polite back although Charlie got the impression of the man distancing himself, which was fine with Charlie who was fed up with the prick breathing constantly down his neck anyway. He made plans with Laura.

Charlie disposed of the atrophied flower and its milk bottle and paced himself to get through the huge backlog of official documentation and official publications and official and unofficial papers. He dealt first with the direct communications, putting his initials on forms and instructions that needed signed proof of his having read them. He responded with his own memoranda when required, reckoning the Brazilian rain forests were being destroyed solely to provide the paper necessary for Harkness' bureaucracy.

Charlie left the publications until last, although the daily inflow of newsprint meant the pile was constantly increasing, threatening to keep ahead of

119

his physical ability to read them before a fresh batch arrived. He tried to devise a system to clear it and win. He read initially everything printed in English and then, because it made the job easier, studied the analysts' translations and interpretations of the foreign material that was his responsibility before moving to the originals themselves.

So it was a long time after that first and those subsequently planted references in the Soviet media to Natalia Nikandrova Fedova before Charlie finally came upon them.

His recognition was instant although disbelieving and because the first reaction was disbelief he wanted to make sure and that only took seconds anyway, because that first reference, in a weeks-old edition of *Pravda*, clearly identified Natalia by name, as a delegate member on a visit to Australia. Charlie sat gazing at the photograph, wishing it were better. Natalia did not appear to have changed much: hardly at all, in fact. The picture showed her in civilian clothes, a businesslike, high-buttoned suit, and she was unsmiling in the official surroundings, hedged in by other stern-faced Russians. Her hair seemed shorter, though: when they had been together in Moscow Natalia had mostly worn it long, strained back and in a bun when she was working, loose and lustrously black when they were alone, more at her apartment in Mytninskaya than at his.

Charlie waited for a feeling, the sort of emotion he supposed he should experience, but there was nothing very much, not yet. Maybe there would be some reaction later. At the moment there was too much in the way, too many questions.

Charlie sectioned the newspaper and used its dating to scour every other Russian-language publication, a week either side. That produced a large photograph in *Izvestia* with a longer caption,

120

identifying Natalia for the first time as a translator. There was a subsequent story, again with a photograph, upon the delegation's return and although there were cross-checks he wanted to make at once, Charlie forced himself first to work to a pattern /and go completely through the backlog, unaware and uncaring of time. Which was how he located three more photographs and five further written accounts of Natalia's movements, through Canada and Washington. Satisfied at last that he had located every report in the publications for which he was responsible for monitoring, Charlie extended the search. Records maintained a Back Reference service of printed material. From it Charlie withdrew everything put out by Tass, the Soviet news agency, together with their entire picture issue, around the dates that corresponded with Natalia's overseas visits. He extended the inquiry, to include Australian, Canadian and American publications for the same period and found additional coverage and two more photographs for the dossier he began to collate.

By the time Charlie finally cleared his desk that dossier, which was personal, without any official classification or restriction and which therefore he carried back and forth from the Vauxhall apartment, was quite bulky although there was considerable repetition, which he weeded out.

So what, in total, did he have? Personal impressions first. Three of the Tass photographs were originals, not blurred newsprint reproductions. So he was able to be very sure that Natalia had not changed at all apart from wearing her hair much shorter, which he liked. He didn't recognize anything she wore but then it had been a long time since they'd been together, nearly two years, so it was natural she would have bought new clothes. And there would be an expectation – and a financial

121

would be an expectation – and a financial allowance to fulfil it – that she dress well as a representative of her government on overseas missions.

Which took him beyond personal reflections. What the hell was Natalia doing, flying around the world described as a translator? She was an exhaustively trained, highly qualified, very expert KGB debriefer: so highly trained and expert that in the end it had been Natalia who realized his flight from British imprisonment to the Soviet Union wasn't genuine but a complicated London espionage operation. But by which time, thank God, she'd felt more for him than about whatever it was he was doing. Dzerzhinsky Square didn't shift specialized people like Natalia around: no intelligence service did. So why? And not just reassigned to one department: Foreign Ministry in Australia, Trade Ministry in Canada and the United States. Something else that didn't make sense. Unanswerable, insoluble question after unanswerable, insoluble question. Which prompted another: Would he ever be able to find the answers?

A feeling came at last, an excitement of anticipation, but Charlie curbed it, refusing to fantasize, aware of an oversight and annoyed by it because keeping her safe was important and he didn't know if she still were. Charlie hadn't identified Natalia during his debriefing after the Moscow episode. If he had done, her name would have gone on to the general register and been shared with the CIA and maybe other Western intelligence agencies and exposed her to Christ knows how many hostile operations. She'd covered for him, in Russia. So he'd covered for her, back in the West. And for the same reason. And for that same reason he had to continue to make sure Natalia was still clean.

Charlie returned to the analysts' reports that had

accompanied what he had already studied, smiling that no 'KGB Known' tab had been set against Natalia's name; there was a comment upon the trade visit confirming continuing Soviet grain shortages, but that was all. It wasn't, however, absolute proof that Natalia had escaped positive identification because there were always other, separate analyses. Charlie had accessed computer records shortly after his repatriation, determined to protect her, so he only had to go back over the two immediate preceding years to discover if her name had been added to the register. Which he did. It hadn't.

Still safe, thought Charlie, back in his chicken-coop office. And how she'd stay. The publication-monitoring was designed precisely to achieve the sort of identification that Charlie had made: to add names to lists, Harkness' idea of intelligence-gathering. Fuck Harkness, Charlie decided, that most frequent of conclusions. He had not identified Natalia before and he was buggered if he would now.

Was that it then, an exercise in cleverness for his own personal satisfaction, like *The Times* crossword? For the moment, Charlie supposed. But only very much for the moment. He'd known the determination from that first sighting of her photograph and then her name, but hadn't bothered to confront it. But now he did, because it was time. The private, untidy file carefully locked in the bottom drawer of his tin desk contained three announcements of her intended trips in advance of Natalia making them. So what would he do if he came across another such announcement, alerting him to a forthcoming overseas visit? Charlie welcomed a question he could answer at last. And easily. Wherever, however, whatever, Charlie knew he'd try to get to her. Get to her. See her. Speak to her. Try to. . .Charlie stopped, braking the sudden rush of decisions. Too much, too quickly.

Were there to be the miracle — were they to meet again — how different was it likely to be from before, in Moscow? Another impossible question, with too many subsidiary queries and doubts and considerations. What about *the* consideration: the only thing that mattered. Whether this time she would stay with him.

Eduard had been the barrier before. How old would the boy be now? Eighteen: maybe nineteen, he wasn't sure because he couldn't remember the actual birthday. Whatever, no longer a boy: no longer the dependent barrier behind which she'd once hidden, frightened like it was understandable she should have been frightened.

Something else he would attempt, if there were ever a second chance. Beg her, plead with her, try to explain better and more convincingly than he had in Moscow. Anything, just to get her to stay.

Charlie finally let the fantasies, like the nostalgia, flow unchecked. They *could* be happy together, he knew. Not immediately, because that wasn't sensible to expect, but the difficulty wouldn't exactly be unhappiness. It would be uncertainty, while she adjusted and came to trust a new life: became accustomed to all the changes because it was Natalia who would be called upon to make more sacrifices than he would.

There was, though, one sacrifice that would be the same: maybe, even, greater in his case. He'd have to give up the service, the beloved existence in which he'd immersed himself and never imagined himself ever leaving, despite peripheral irritations like Harkness. He *would* have to give it up. It was unthinkable — quite inconceivable — for him to delude himself into thinking that if he and Natalia ever came together again he could somehow continue as he was.

Was he prepared to do that for her, like he would

124

be asking her do, for him: like he'd already, once, asked her to do for him? Yes, Charlie decided at once, without any lingering doubt or caveat. To have Natalia permanently with him, to marry her and live with her as naturally as they would ever be able to do anything naturally in their particular circumstances, Charlie knew he was prepared to give it all up. Everything. Without a moment's hesitation.

It was the weekend before the reflective Charlie completed his search for references to Natalia, the weekend he'd arranged the long-delayed date with Laura, after going down to Hampshire. Now he wished he hadn't. It was a reluctance he was quickly to put aside.

Charlie sat for almost half an hour holding the paper-skinned, unmoving hand and talking of whatever came into his head, trying for some shared reminiscence to lure her out from the private world into which she had retreated again, but his mother sat propped up in bed staring into emptiness, unaware he was there. He gave up, finally, leaving the chocolates with hard centres near where her hand lay on the bed, and made his way to the matron's office.

Ms Hewlett looked up as he entered and said at once: 'I'm sorry. It looked so promising, too.'

'When did it happen?'

'Quite soon after your last visit. She kept on about the pension inspectors but it became confused, of course. Twisted in her mind. She came to think she'd done something wrong and that they were going to punish her: that she was going to have to leave here. Kept saying she didn't want to go. I tried to explain it wasn't so, that they didn't mean any harm, but I don't think I really got through to her. . .' The woman paused, shaking her head. 'I was so hopeful.'

'I want to know something,' said Charlie, very slowly. 'Those inspectors. In your opinion was their visit responsible for my mother regressing, as she has?'

The matron adopted a doubtful expression, turning down the corners of her mouth. 'Impossible to say,' she said. 'Maybe. Then again, maybe not. People your mother's age, senile like she is, their minds fasten on the strangest things.'

'But if they *hadn't* come, there wouldn't have been the incident to fasten on to in the first place, would there?'

The matron frowned. 'You can go through life saying "if only. . ." but it doesn't get you very far,' she said philosophically.

'What are the chances of her coming out of it, like she did before?'

'There's always the possibility.'

'You don't sound as if you expect it to happen?'

'I never lose hope.'

'I left the chocolates on her bed.'

'I'll keep them safe here in the office, just in case.'

Charlie returned determinedly to London, glad after all he'd made the date for that evening. He got to the bar sufficiently ahead of Laura to have two drinks before she arrived. She offered herself to be kissed, so he did, and this time they went to a restaurant that had not been recommended in any food guide, and the meal was fine. He let Laura lead the conversation because he did not want to appear to do so in anything, agreeing it was fortunate the hospital had discovered Paul's infection to be caused by a virus and not by the heat, particularly as Paul had to spend a month in Brazil.

'Harkness is wary of you now,' she suddenly disclosed. 'There really was the most awful row, you know?'

'It *did* get to the Joint Intelligence Committee, didn't it?'

She nodded. 'He didn't even have me type up the memorandum of explanation. He insisted on doing it himself.'

Charlie smiled contentedly. 'Serves the bastard right.'

'I don't think he'll stop picking on you,' judged the girl. 'I think he's just waiting. . .catching his breath.'

'So am I,' said Charlie. 'And I've had more practice than he has.'

'I feel that I've been waiting for ever,' said Laura provocatively.

There were no messages this time on the answering machine at the Chelsea house. She poured brandy and wormed her way very close to him on the small couch and kept insisting that he kiss her, which Charlie did, wishing Paul didn't appear to be watching from the studio photograph.

'I'm so glad we're here like this at last,' she said.

'Would you do something for me?' asked Charlie, choosing his moment.

'I'll do whatever you want,' she said, misunderstanding.

'The two who went down to the nursing home to question my mother,' said Charlie. 'Do you think you could get their names, off the file? They would have submitted reports, wouldn't they?'

'What do you want to know that for?'

'Just curious,' said Charlie.

'Catching his breath?' queried Harkness.

'That's what he said,' confirmed Laura.

127

'Without any indication of what that meant?'

'None,' said the girl.

The acting Director General came around from behind his desk, so that he was closer to her. 'You really are doing remarkably well,' he said. 'I'm most grateful.'

15

It was an important conference, the first assessment session between the KGB chairman and Valeri Kalenin to consider the Star War material collected so far, and once again Berenkov travelled from the Moscow outskirts to wait for his friend at Dzerzhinsky Square.

Berenkov recalled the last occasion he had waited like this, standing before this same window overlooking the square, and decided he'd done very well obtaining what he had. Well enough, in fact, for headquarters etiquette to have been eased for him to be invited to the conference instead of being kept waiting cap-in-hand for the outcome to be relayed to him. Berenkov resented being kept out. It made no sense: it could actually be counterproductive always for there to be an intermediary despite that intermediary being someone he trusted as completely as Kalenin. Having spent so much of his operational life absolutely alone Berenkov felt difficulty in relying upon anyone else. It was all the more frustrating that he could do nothing about it, but to attempt to do so – suggest he should be included in the future, for instance – risked offending the other man. And worse, hinting that there was not complete trust between them. What about Kalenin's trust in him, he thought uneasily. There was no comparison: whatever happened, he wouldn't call upon Kalenin's protection.

It was the working of the electronic door that again warned Berenkov of his friend's return. The diminutive, bearded man stopped just inside, expressionless and momentarily unspeaking. Then Kalenin's face broke and he announced: 'We've done it!' and strode across to embrace Berenkov in a bear-hug of congratulation.

'There's sufficient for them to reach a conclusion?' queried Berenkov cautiously.

Kalenin nodded. 'There was a meeting of the Politburo this morning to consider the preliminary report of our space people at Baikonur on what we've so far got from America. Their view is that the American development is unquestionably the "garage" part of their Star Wars programme.'

'Garage?'

'The actual space facility to store the destructive missiles that would be triggered against any offensive rocket,' explained Kalenin simply.

It was obvious from the blueprints and drawings they'd already received from San Francisco that it was some sort of satellite but Berenkov hadn't guessed at this. He said: 'They're sure?'

'Convinced, according to the chairman,' said Kalenin. 'Which is as bad as it is good. It's good that we've told them what it is. But we've created our own burden to get all of it, so that Russia can win the race. . .' The man paused. 'Incidentally,' he said, smiling more broadly. 'You've been officially commended by name. There should be celebrations!'

Kalenin produced the vodka bottle from a drawer of his desk. Berenkov accepted the drink, feeling a stab of guilt at the way he was still keeping the Charlie Muffin pursuit from his friend. He said: 'Let's hope we can go on as we've started.'

'The technical instructions are that Britain is vitally important,' cautioned Kalenin. 'It's essential to know how their carbon fibre is being utilized. The guess is that it's a thermoplastic resin process but they need to do more than guess.'

'We're well established in America,' reflected

130

Berenkov. 'With the man Krogh we could hardly be better placed: within his own organization he can do virtually what he likes, demand access to whatever he wants, without challenge.'

'But what about England?'

'Untried, as yet,' admitted Berenkov honestly. 'We've got an employee desperate for money: a women situation again. But he hasn't anything like the access seniority that Krogh commands in America.'

'He can't be allowed to fail,' said Kalenin, the warning all the more ominous for its quiet simplicity. 'Everything *is* dependent upon us. We stand or fall by what happens now. Personally, I mean.'

'I know,' accepted Berenkov.

'You told the British *rezidentura* to be careful?'

Now was the opportunity to talk about Charlie Muffin and of baiting his trap with Natalia Nikandrova. At once came the barrier: it was still too soon to be sure that Kalenin would support him. And Berenkov was determined against being ordered to abort the idea. He said: 'I've taken every precaution.'

Blackstone thought excitedly that perhaps it was not going to be quite as difficult as he'd feared. He hadn't tried getting into the secure area yet, but there was the inevitable talk now that the project was under way. By listening instead of talking in the canteen and the social club he'd learned the basic matrix was going to be made by impregnating the carbon fibres with a polyetheretherketone petrol-based resin and that the sizing appeared quite large, although he couldn't risk asking actual dimensions or how many layers were being considered for the lamination. It was still enough, for a start. And to show he was trying. Blackstone considered it imperative that he appear to be trying, so that the money didn't dry up.

Blackstone found a public kiosk about three miles outside Newport and as Losev had promised the telephone was answered quickly, on the second ring, although not by the Russian he knew. Blackstone identified himself and said: 'I've got something.'

'We'll come to collect,' said the voice.

16

It was better now. He didn't feel good about it – he knew the enormity of what he was doing and the horrifying danger he faced in doing it – but as the days and then the weeks passed Emil Krogh lost the hollow-stomached terror of that first exchange encounter with Petrin on the San Francisco wharf. He was becoming accustomed to it, Krogh guessed. Or maybe it was because he could see an end to it: another month and it would be over. Christ, wouldn't that be a wonderful moment! Everything over. Finished. He'd be safe again. The Russian had been pretty reassuring about that: talked about their watching and monitoring the meeting places, checking it all out before making a move, every time. There'd been a lot of meeting places. The wharf, a couple of more times. Hotels, in the city and a motel, across in Berkeley. A roadside rest area, over the Golden Gate Bridge. Always the same, protective routine: he getting there first and waiting for Petrin's approach which wouldn't come until they were sure. Like today.

It was the wharf again, the pier-end restaurant with the view of the bay and the tourist helicopter fluttering over Alcatraz. Krogh got there right on time and said he'd wait at the table for his guest and ordered a martini with a lemon twist, very dry with no ice. It was good and he tasted the burn of the gin and felt the tension ease off slightly. Two helicopters passed each other, going to and from the island penitentiary no longer in use. Was it there that they'd sent people who did what he was doing, when it had been a prison? Krogh didn't think so but he

133

wasn't sure. Maybe there was a special place, all spies together. That's what he was, Krogh accepted. A spy against his own country, the sort of crime they'd executed people for, not so long ago. All because of the damned girls. Whores, both of them. Something else that had to end. Not yet, not until this business was well and truly over. One thing at a time. But certainly kiss them off. He hadn't seen either Barbara or Cindy much, since it had started: Cindy a couple of times, because he'd been in Los Angeles anyway, Barbara on two or three afternoons when she wasn't at art school. He thought Barbara was already getting the message, acting extra nice to him, eager to please. Barbara first, he decided. Then Cindy. No hassle, no hard feelings. Give them a few bucks, plenty of time to look around and find themselves somewhere else to live. He guessed there'd be crying scenes because that was the way it went, but that was all. They both knew the score: knew it had to happen some time. Krogh felt an odd relief at the decision to get rid of them. He didn't think he'd look around for anyone to replace them, either: pointless to get out of one blackmail situation and create another. Might as well go on as he was. Which he wouldn't, Krogh determined, positively. Time he straightened himself out, stopped acting like a jerk.

Petrin advanced easily through the restaurant, smiling slightly, very self-assured, and sat down in the facing chair.

'You've been lost in thought,' said the Russian, confirming at once the protective observation.

'I'd say I had a lot to think about, wouldn't you?' said Krogh.

'But not to worry about,' said Petrin.

'So you keep telling me,' said the American.

'I want you to believe it,' said Petrin sincerely. He'd heard from Moscow three days before of the official

134

commendation going on his KGB record and considered Krogh very important to his career. 'What is it today?'

'Gyro housings: the system is equipped with two sets, with a third for emergency. This is the first.'

'That's very good,' said Petrin.

Krogh believed he was being patronized and it irritated him. He said: 'It'll only take about another month: that was one of the things I was thinking about.'

'And it's gone as smoothly as I promised it would, hasn't it?'

'I want it to be over,' said Krogh.

There was a break while they ordered and it enabled Petrin time to reflect. Poor fool, thought the Russian, although without the slightest genuine sympathy. Krogh was theirs — more precisely *his* — to do with what they liked when they liked and how they liked. From now on Moscow had permanent access to every US classified document or defence contract with which Krogh and his company ever became associated, a forever-bubbling spring of secret information that Petrin was going to do his best to see never dried up. Because Petrin had already recognized the personal benefit that went way beyond the most recent commendation. That, he'd decided, was just the first of many that was going to come from each new disclosure he was going to get from this man, long after all Star Wars material. Which was not the end of that personal benefit. To remain Krogh's case officer would naturally entail his staying on in Los Angeles long after his expected tour of duty would normally have finished. Which Petrin, who liked America and the Californian climate and most of all the Californian girls, was more than happy to do. He said: 'I liked the cover article, in *Newsweek*.'

So had Krogh, despite what was happening to him. The photograph had been very good, making him look younger than he was, and the focus of the main article was of his epitomizing the American dream, the thrusting shopfloor worker rising to become the millionaire boss. With forced modesty Krogh shrugged and said: 'It was OK.'

'Help me with something beyond the drawings,' said Petrin. 'How's the actual construction work going?'

Krogh had wondered how long this sort of questioning would take: the bastard could go to hell. He said: 'Well enough.'

'That's not a direct answer, Emil.' The Russian had discarded the supposed politeness of surnames after the first meeting.

'That's the best there is,' insisted Krogh.

'No major snags or hold-ups?' persisted Petrin.

'No.'

'Not at all?'

'Not so far.'

Petrin stopped the impatience becoming obvious: he didn't want, this soon in their relationship, to have to let Krogh know he didn't have any independence any more. For the moment Krogh had to be allowed to retain some slight degree of self-respect. Petrin said: 'So what's the scheduled launch date?'

'It's too soon to be firm on that,' Krogh continued to evade. 'There still could too easily be hold-ups we can't anticipate. There's a lot of shopfloor testing to go through yet.'

'Provisionally then?' pressed Petrin.

'Maybe a year.'

'The Pentagon wouldn't go along with something as vague as that, Emil, would they?' said Petrin, finally deciding there had to be some correction after all. 'I know and you know that on a document or in a

136

letter I haven't seen yet there's a suggested date when this thing is going to be put into space. So what is it?'

The man *was* a bastard, slapping him down like some junior clerk. Miserably he said: 'September, next year.'

'How's Barbara?' said Petrin. 'And Cindy?'

'I don't want to talk about them,' refused Krogh.

'Well then I think it's important that you talk to me properly about other things when I ask,' said Petrin. 'I don't want to have to prise things out like that in future. You understand?'

Krogh flushed with anger but their food arrived, delaying the response. Krogh had only ordered Cobb salad and he pushed it aside almost at once. Lying, he said: 'I wasn't trying to be difficult.'

'It wouldn't benefit anyone for you to be, would it?' said Petrin. 'There's nothing to be gained by us falling out, is there?'

Patronizing again, thought Krogh. He said: 'What the hell do you expect! For us to be friends?'

'Why not?' said Petrin, open-faced. 'We've got to work together, haven't we?'

'Only for about another month, like I said.'

Now was as convenient a moment as any, thought the Russian. He said: 'We'll still have to meet regularly, won't we?'

'What do you mean!' demanded Krogh, fresh alarm flaring through him.

'I'll want to keep in touch,' said Petrin. 'Some of your testings might show the need for redesign, for instance. I'd need those redesign drawings, wouldn't I? I'm going to want the results of all the testings, too.'

'Nothing will go wrong,' insisted Krogh. 'Everything ends with the last drawing.'

Let the poor fool dream, thought Petrin, recalling his earlier thoughts. He said: 'Just as long as it takes,

He said: 'Just as long as it takes, that's all. That's why I don't want any antagonistic nonsense beween us. It doesn't achieve anything: gets in the way.'

Christ, how he'd like to teach this son-of-a-bitch a lesson, Krogh thought: physically beat the shit out of him, get the satisfaction of hurting him. He said: 'Suits me, I guess.'

Petrin smiled brightly, finishing his lobster. He said: 'Shouldn't I have the gyro drawing then?'

Krogh passed the package across the table and Petrin put it quickly into his briefcase. Krogh said: 'I'll have the drawings of the other two sets in a week.'

'You know that little park where the cable cars terminate on the other side of the hill, near Saks?' demanded Petrin.

'Yes.'

'That's where we'll meet, next Friday. You be there by noon.'

Just like a junior clerk, every time a finger-snapping command. He said: 'All right.'

'I'm glad we've had this little talk,' said Petrin. 'Cleared the air between us. I think that's a good thing, don't you?'

Krogh lifted and dropped his shoulders, wanting to get away from the other man. He said: 'I suppose so. I've got to get back to the plant.'

Petrin smiled again, signalling for the waiter. 'Let me settle the bill this time,' he said. 'After all, I'm the satisfied customer, aren't I?'

It was just the sort of luck that Henry Blackstone was seeking and he seized it at once, actually feeling more excited than guilty when it happened. There was scarcely guilt at all.

He never found out the reason but late one Thursday the request came from the secret project section to the general drawing office for some specimen

138

and no-longer-classified blueprints of a fin design for which the firm had unsuccessfully tendered during the European Ariane space programme. And Blackstone, who'd taken part in the European development, was deputed to be the intermediary. Which gave him temporary security accreditation to get inside the fenced-off area.

Blackstone carried more drawings than were necessary, all enclosed in cardboard storage tubes. Inside the secure building he intentionally took the wrong route along the wrong corridor, trawling for anything he could find. There were a number of small offices equipped with drawing boards, built around a larger, communal design and tracing area. He stopped at two on the pretext of getting directions for where he wanted to go, and saw the chance at once. Blackstone had timed his entry to be very close to clocking-off time, when everyone was packing up for the day, and at both small offices Blackstone identified the procedure being followed to protect what was being created. Each draughtsman and tracer was taking whatever was on his board into the larger, communal room to be logged and stored in a drawing locker sealed by a combination device. But *only* the top sheet design, leaving the impressed-upon backing paper still upon the board. Blackstone lingered in the corridor near the second office, supposedly checking the tubes he was carrying to decide which he had to hand over, until the occupant of the second office left to secure his day's work. It took Blackstone less than a minute to re-enter the room, roll up the unclipped backing paper and fit it into one of the superfluous tubes and regain the corridor again.

Heart hammering, Blackstone completed what he was officially there to do, apologized for bringing the unnecessary extra drawings and was back in his own office within the half hour. Done it! he thought euphorically: he'd done it and got away with it!

By working lightly over the paper with a soft-leaded pencil Blackstone was able to trace the outline of the blueprint that had been created on top of it – of a support arm and connecting rods – although some of the specification lettering was too indistinct for him to decipher. It was not important, he decided. He had sufficient to re-create the blueprint. And not just one. He'd divide it into two and deliver them separately, to get two payments. And the temporary security access lasted until he had to collect the Ariane designs! So he could go inside again, before he was summoned to make that collection!

17

When the summons came for Berenkov to meet
directly with scientific officials utilizing the American Star Wars information, without having everything filtered through Kalenin, the circumstances
emerged to be not at all what he wanted, in any respect. There was initially, however, no hint of what
was to come. The demand that he be prepared within two hours to leave Moscow, for the space centre
at Baikonur, was perhaps peremptory but there had
been such short-notice requests in the past, on other
things, so he felt no particular concern driving out to
Vnukovo airport. Rather, there was a satisfied anticipation: the first blueprint from England had arrived
three days before so they were receiving material
from the two sources at last. The likeliest explanation
could only be personal congratulation, although another commendation so soon was probably too much
to expect. His rank and position placed Berenkov beyond the airport formalities required even for internal travelling in the Soviet Union. That he expected.
He did not expect it to be a special military flight: it
was the first indication of an emergency suggested
by the two-hour departure limit. Kalenin was already
in a VIP lounge reserved for government officials,
serious-faced but calm, one of the Havana cigars he
so much enjoyed filling the room with its aroma.

'What is it?' demanded Berenkov at once.

Kalenin made an uncertain shoulder movement.
'I've not been told. Just to come, like you.'

Berenkov's customary ebullient confidence dip-
ped. He said: 'It has to be serious for us to be called
all the way to Baikonur.'

'That's pretty obvious,' said Kalenin.

'But what!' said Berenkov. 'We're getting it all now, from both sources!'

Kalenin shook his head. 'It's ludicrous, trying to speculate. We'll just have to wait.'

An airport official came hesitantly into the room, accompanied by a man in an undesignated military uniform to say their flight was ready. Berenkov hunched behind the other man out to the transporter, a shrouded grey-green shape in the darkness. There was no pretence at all about comfort. Only three sets of webbing seats had been rigged across the empty hull, which elsewhere remained cavernous and empty. The chemical toilet was behind a pull-round canvas curtain, the smell of its germicidal disinfectant quite heavy already. A coarse strap was looped across the seats to secure themselves for take-off. Neither Kalenin nor Berenkov bothered. A flight sergeant came to them almost at once after they cleared Moscow airspace to offer food but neither Kalenin nor Berenkov bothered about that, either. Fleetingly Berenkov considered asking if there were anything to drink but decided against it.

Kalenin shifted uncomfortably in his seat and said: 'It would have been good if we could have got some rest.'

'There's no point in trying,' said Berenkov. Could Kalenin really have slept, going towards so much uncertainty? The other man had lighted another cigar and Berenkov was grateful because it smelled better than the toilet chemicals. There appeared to be no heating and Berenkov thrust his hands into his topcoat pockets and burrowed his head down deeply into its collar. What! he demanded of himself. What could have gone wrong, so soon after the praise of the commendation? Kalenin was right about the stupidity of speculating, but Berenkov wanted *something*, some warning how to prepare himself for what was to come. He looked across the cold, vibrating aircraft to where Kalenin was huddled, like himself apart from the hand holding the cigar. It might be safer to follow Kalenin's lead, Berenkov thought, with rare modesty. The bearded man was a survivor of several previous regimes, adept at adjusting to headquarter circumstances and politics. One thought prompted another, this one disquieting. He'd been excluded from all such meetings until now, when it appeared there might be a problem. Was his inclusion the decision of the KGB chairman or the Politburo? Or of Kalenin, seeking a scapegoat?

A curtained limousine, a Zil, was already drawing towards the steps when the door swung back for their disembarkation. As he descended towards it Berenkov saw they were at neither a civilian nor a military airfield but at the facility for the space centre itself. It was far more extensive in ground area than a normal airport and there was none of the usual close-together cluster of administration buildings or hangars. What office quarters there were appeared very distant, to their left. There were at least three radar towers, each with static and revolving antennae, and a fenced-off expanse of various-sized storage tanks. Around the fencing were a lot of signs warning of the danger of highly inflammable contents: some of the bigger tanks had a shimmering aura of mist or steam, the sort of reaction Berenkov associated with something very cold being exposed to air.

It was thankfully warm inside the car. The vehicle set off towards the far-away office block and as they got nearer Berenkov saw quite close to it an odd assortment of crane-like structures which he assumed at once to be mobile support gantries, for rockets, but which to him looked more like the skeletal derricks of oil exploration equipment.

'You know what this looks like to me?' said Kalenin, beside him. 'This is how I'd imagine some moon station to be. You see how very few people there are about?'

The place *was* oddly deserted, acknowledged Berenkov. He said: 'I suppose it's a fitting appearance for the sort of work that goes on.'

At the main buildings, which turned out to be of two storeys with a glassed dome forming a third level, they were escorted by security personnel through a zig-zag of corridors before being ushered into a small conference room. Already waiting inside were four men, all civilians. They were grouped around a table set in front of a slightly elevated second section upon which there were two blackboards, on stands, with diagrams and charts already neatly pinned up. There were other papers strewn about the table and Berenkov believed he recognized some at least to be what had arrived from Petrin, in America. Kalenin pushed into the room ahead of Berenkov, nodding although not smiling to the assembled men, and Berenkov guessed there had been earlier meetings between them. Berenkov was only introduced formally to one of the four and assumed the man to be the senior of the group. His name was Nikolai Noskov. He was a stooped, carelessly dressed man with a difficult speech impediment: he had to struggle to get most words out, eyes closed with a combination of effort and frustration. It necessarily made him economical in everything he said, although another impression could have been that Noskov was rudely autocratic.

There were hand waves towards seats, almost impatient gestures of politeness. Noskov made several attempts and at last managed: 'Your coming here is very necessary.'

Berenkov waited for a response to come from

144

Kalenin, the senior officer, but the man said nothing so Berenkov didn't speak either.

Noskov shuffled through the disordered documents on the table, finally locating what he wanted. He pitched it slightly forwards, towards them, and said: 'Useless! Absolutely useless!'

Still Kalenin did not move so Berenkov reached for it, identifying it instantly as the blueprint that had arrived from England. It was of some type of armature. He said: 'Useless how?'

'Look at the side,' stuttered Noskov: the L was particularly difficult for him to pronounce.

'I don't understand,' said Berenkov.

'Each drawing has to have a specification instruction accompanying it,' said the scientist. 'A design drawing is no good without guidance to where it fits. Its function. Its component relationship to everything else.' He stopped, breathless, and from the discernible wheezing Berenkov guessed the man to be afflicted by asthma, as well.

'There are instructions,' insisted Berenkov, immediately abandoning the aircraft reflection to let Kalenin lead.

'Incomplete,' came back Noskov, just as insistent and without interruption on this one occasion. 'Impossible safely to incorporate.'

The problem, isolated Berenkov: at last! His mind moved immediately on from that realization, throwing up other, connected thoughts and there was, too, a surge of annoyance at being before this anonymous group of men in this fashion, paraded literally like some guilty incompetent. He didn't know the role of any of them, any more than he knew their names apart from Noskov, but he guessed they didn't have any more influence than he did. It was a protection exercise, he decided, guessing further. He didn't doubt there was something incomplete with the British drawing – they wouldn't risk being caught out on something so easily challenged – but whatever was missing was the excuse, not the reason, for this overly dramatic summons. This group – an inner committee, probably – were taking out insurance against any disasters in the future. The arguments at this meeting could be produced in future – which meant it was being witnessed or recorded – if anything went wrong, hopefully to show that the fault had been that of the information-gatherers, not of the technicians and specialists assigned to translate that information into viable space equipment. Time to provide lessons in practical, personal survival, thought Berenkov, feeling relaxed for the first time in hours. He said: 'I'm not at all surprised.' Everyone else was: even Kalenin, Berenkov suspected.

'What did you say!' demanded Noskov. His forced outrage overrode the impediment, so the words came out quite clearly again.

'I said that I am not at all surprised that information is coming incomplete,' elaborated Berenkov. 'How can it be otherwise, if I am expected to work as I am at present! I am a trained intelligence officer, controlling other trained intelligence officers. None of us are scientists. How can we be expected to know whether what we get is complete or otherwise, separated as we are? I need the facility every time to check and consult, guaranteeing you people here get everything you need properly to fulfil what you have to do.' Pedantically verbose, conceded Berenkov. But very necessary. The onus was now entirely reversed, switching the responsibility on to them, and from the expressions around the table they realized it.

'Which is an argument I have advanced from the very beginning,' came in Kalenin, further entangling the scientists. 'It is an objection I have firmly regis

146

tered in Moscow, although it was prior to our meetings there, Comrade Noskov. I would have advised you, of course, if I had been approached before this meeting instead of being simply instructed to attend it by the Politburo Secretariat.'

Noskov actually flushed. His mouth worked, desperately, but the words wouldn't come. He gave another hand gesture, a plea for help, and a studious, heavily moustached man to his left said: 'We were unaware of this.'

'We don't have the advantage of your name?' questioned Kalenin, with a cold smile.

'Guzins,' said the man. 'Yuri Ivanovich Guzins.'

'And you complained without any reference?' said Kalenin.

'This is regarded as extremely important,' tried Guzins in attempted explanation.

'All the more reason for proper liaison,' repeated Kalenin.

Relentlessly re-entering the conversation, Berenkov said: 'We've been shown one drawing: one out of forty-three I know so far to have been supplied. Is that the only one with which you find fault?'

'So far,' managed Noskov.

'The drawing you are rejecting was the last to be provided,' persisted Berenkov. 'You *must* have examined the others. Are they fully satisfactory! Or not!'

'They are satisfactory,' conceded the moustached Guzins.

'I consider this has been a very premature protest,' said Kalenin. 'Quite unnecessary at the level at which it was initiated, in fact.'

They'd won, decided Berenkov. Practically to the extent of it being no contest. He said: 'How do you know the British drawing has omissions?'

'We have the complete section of drawings from America to accommodate what arrived from Britain,' said Guzins. 'The British appear to be manufacturing the hinged arm to pivot the release doors, when an American destruct missile is fired upon any hostile attack rocket. There are no details of fitment, between one to the other.'

'What about another drawing which we don't yet have?'

'It should be upon this blueprint,' insisted Noskov.

'You were speaking with qualification,' picked out Berenkov, to the man with the moustache. 'You said the British *appear* to be constructing the release arm.'

Guzins looked briefly towards the man with the speech difficulty, who nodded. Guzins stoop up, going to the laid-out blackboards, and with a wooden pointer indicated two artist's impressions. The man said: 'Study carefully the armature drawn here. Each is identical to the other: it's the positioning that's different. It would accord it entirely different functions. One way it would literally operate the garage door. The other it could be forming part of a combined arm-device, to activate *two* doors.'

'What's the significance between the two?' asked Berenkov.

'The Americans have always insisted their Strategic Defence Initiative is entirely *defensive,*' lectured Guzins. 'One design makes this a comparatively simple, manoeuvrable container, conforming exactly to that insistence. The other gives it the combined capacity, to fire *offensive* missiles from space upon any target it chooses. You understand the importance of that difference?'

There were several moments of utter silence in the room. Then Berenkov said: 'Yes, we understand.'

On their way back to Moscow in the cold transporter, uncomfortable on their hard-ridged webbing seats, Kalenin announced: 'They'll be more cautious with complaints the next time.'

'I can understand the importance that's being attached to this if the apparatus has dual capacity.'

'There's no confirmation yet that it has.'

'What the hell went wrong, in Britain!'

'Something you've got to find out,' said Kalenin. 'And make sure it doesn't happen in the future.'

Laura demanded to arrange the evening and when he arrived to collect her from the Chelsea house Charlie found she'd prepared dinner in. The attempt at domesticity vaguely unsettled him, like her husband's photograph. She had cooked duck with black cherries and told him where to find the *grand cru* Margaux to go with it. Charlie opened the bottle to breathe, and said: 'so Paul's a wine connoisseur?'

Laura was at the separating doorway when he spoke, half turned towards the kitchen. She looked back into the room and then returned further into it, smiling and shaking her head. She stopped directly in front of him and said: 'Sit down, Charlie Muffin.'

He did as he was told, looking up at her questioningly.

'From everything I hear and from what I've read in reports I probably shouldn't have looked at, I'm prepared to accept you're a pretty shit-hot operative, hard as nails and twice as sharp,' said Laura. 'But you know something else that you are?'

He didn't want this conversation, Charlie decided. 'What?' he said.

'You're a romantic,' declared Laura. 'A genuine red roses, pink doves and violin-string romantic. Which you'll probably deny because you don't regard it as manly but which I think is lovely. But there's a risk of it getting in the way between us. I know you're uncomfortable being in another man's house and I'm sorry about that, although not as sorry as I was when I discovered how sweet-faced,

149

innocent-looking Paul was cheating on me, because I loved him very much. I suppose I still do, in a way: my problem. . .' She swept her arm around the room. 'He won't consider leaving me because I've got the inherited money to provide all this. And I won't risk telling him finally to get out because I've got this stupid fantasy that he might suddenly change and it'll be all right again. So at the moment we lead polite but separate lives. And I'm using you, Charlie Muffin. Like we both know you're using me, for what you want. If you like, we're both at the moment using each other for protection. So we're quits. I know this isn't love: that it won't be. I'm not even sure I'd want that encumbrance. OK?'

'Quite a speech,' said Charlie, nonplussed.

'I didn't set out to make one. It just happened.'

'There's a lot to discuss.'

'No there isn't,' rejected Laura. 'It's all said: no need for any more in-depth conversation. And I'm out of breath, anyway.'

'I. . .'

'. . .don't,' she stopped.

So he didn't.

The food was superb, the wine excellent and for the first time Charlie felt completely relaxed. When she poured the brandy, afterwards, Laura pointedly put Paul's photograph in a drawer and said: 'There! Better?'

'Much better,' he said, letting her fit herself against him on the couch as she liked to do.

'The person who interrogated your mother is named Smedley,' she announced, her head against his chest. 'David Smedley. The other one is Philip Abbott.'

'Thanks.'

'And Witherspoon is spending a lot of time with Harkness.'

'You think he was involved?'

'I don't know: just that he keeps being called into the office.'

'He's Harkness' protégé,' remembered Charlie.

'Don't do anything silly about it. Promise?'

'Never crossed my mind.'

Later – much later – in bed Charlie said: 'I don't think I'm a red roses, pink dove, violin-string romantic.'

'I knew you wouldn't, but you are,' insisted the girl.

'Rubbish.'

'How many times have you been in love?'

'You wouldn't believe me if I told you.'

'Paul's got a child, a little boy. By a girl he sees, on-and-off, in Fulham. I can't have children. That hurts me worst of all, that he's had a baby by someone else. He didn't have to do that, did he?'

'And you'd still try to make things work!'

'If Paul asked me to.'

Bloody incredible, thought Charlie. And she *was* wrong in her personal assessment of him: he wasn't really the romantic she thought him to be.

Some girls never understood men.

Harkness lived like a bachelor, although he was not. He had been married for twenty years to a woman as devout a Catholic as himself and although the marriage had irreparably collapsed into non-speaking acrimony there had never been any question of divorce. She lived in isolation on the top floor of the Hampstead house and he occupied the lower half: on Sunday mornings and evenings they attended different churches.

Harkness therefore ate at his club, which he did most evenings, and customarily alone. He did so that night angrily, frustrated that it was taking him so long to be confirmed as Director General. What

151

was necessary, he knew, was a success that could unquestionably be shown to be his: something that would stir the Joint Intelligence Committee into finally making the inevitable decision.

The problem was finding it.

18

The encounter was arranged for the seafront car park where they'd met before but which Losev hadn't used for a handover yet. It was perfect for today, a very large, open space which it was easy to keep under observation. Losev packed the area with operatives, but didn't approach it himself until well after the scheduled time and only then when one of his people reported Blackstone was there, quite alone.

The tracer was pacing nervously up near the entrance from the road, hands deep in his raincoat pockets, not visibly carrying anything. It was a hire car again, so Blackstone didn't recognize it and only came hurrying over when Losev sounded his horn. The Russian leaned across to open the passenger door and Blackstone came in gratefully out of the wind.

'Wondered where the hell you'd got to,' Blackstone complained. 'I've been waiting for hours.'

'Thirty minutes,' corrected Losev, taking the car on into the car park and stopping as he had on the first occasion, so they could see the island squatted on the horizon. 'And I had to be sure, didn't I?' The Russian's voice was tight in his fury.

'Sure of what?'

'That you'd be by yourself.'

'I don't understand what you're talking about.'

'Good,' said Losev. 'I wouldn't be very happy if you did.'

'What are you going on about!' Blackstone twisted in his seat so that he was looking across the car at the Russian, trying not to show the apprehension bubbling through him.

Losev didn't reply directly. Instead he said: 'You brought something for me today, Henry?' He would very much have liked to hit the man, slapped some sense into his stupid head.

'Of course,' said Blackstone, almost proudly. He took from inside his raincoat the envelope containing the second drawing he'd made from his tracing of the backing paper, eagerly handing it across the vehicle.

Losev took it but didn't open it. 'What about this one, Henry? Is it complete?'

'What sort of question is that!' Blackstone thought the outrage sounded genuine enough: inwardly he was numbed at being caught out and at the fear of losing the money he wanted so much.

'You know exactly what sort of question it is, Henry. The last drawing you gave me. . .the drawing for which you got five hundred pounds. . .didn't make sense to the experts,' said Losev calmly. 'There were some specification details missing.'

Blackstone reckoned there to be four lines he hadn't been able to read: five at the most. But he was sure he'd concealed the omission by the way he'd re-created the blueprint as an apparent original. He said: 'I thought it was all there! Believe me I did!'

'That's our problem, isn't it?' said Losev, still calm but finding it difficult because he'd lost personal credibility with Moscow over what had happened. 'How are we going to believe you in the future? Like now, for instance. Now I don't believe you.'

'Listen!' pleaded Blackstone. 'Please listen! I got a quick look at some blueprint material and I honestly thought I had everything. I wasn't trying to cheat.'

'That's exactly what we think you tried to do,' said Losev. 'Either that or set up some trap for me to fall into. Do you know what we had to do today: we had to bring a lot of men down here to make sure I was safe. Huge expenditure of manpower. All very inconvenient.'

'I'm sorry,' said Blackstone. 'I'm really very, very sorry.'

'That's what we are: very, very sorry. We thought we had an arrangement and it seems we don't have anything.'

'There's nothing missing from what you've got to-day,' said Blackstone, which was the truth. 'It's all there.'

'I hope so, Henry. You've no idea how much I hope so,' impressed Losev. Exaggerating, he said: 'If this one isn't right we're going to get very angry. We're going to think that our arrangement is over. You know what that means, don't you?'

'Don't do it!' said Blackstone, pleading again. 'Just wait and see.' Why had he taken such a chance: been so foolish!

'It'll need a lot now to convince me.'

And how in God's name was he going to get it! thought Blackstone desperately. He said hurriedly: 'I've got temporary access, into the secure section.'

'Where the work is actually being done!' seized Losev instantly. This was better, if it were true.

Blackstone nodded. 'And I've re-applied, like you told me. I haven't had a reply yet.'

'How long is this access going to last?'

'I don't know,' admitted Blackstone.

'So we've got to use it,' decided Losev, recognizing the chance to recover in Dzerzhinsky Square. 'I want the missing details for that first drawing. And what-ever else you can lay your hands on. Don't forget what I said. I want a lot.'

Blackstone realized at once that the demand was impossible, but knew it would be foolish to say so. 'Sure,' he said, instead. 'I'll do it. You'll see.'

The aerospace worker looked pointedly between

the just delivered envelope and Losev, who stared back, aware of the expectation. The Russian thought: You stupid, greedy bastard. He said: 'You can go now. Ruth will be home soon, won't she?'

'I thought. . .' started Blackstone, then stopped.

'What?'

Blackstone shook his head, understanding. 'Nothing,' he said.

'That's right, Henry. There is nothing: no more money, no more bonuses. Not until I'm sure. You please me, I'll please you. That clear?'

'I'll call you,' promised Blackstone, moving from the car.

'Make it soon,' urged Losev. 'I want it to be very soon.'

So did Blackstone. He wasn't broke, not by a long way yet, but he'd become accustomed to having money around and he wanted the security to go on, just knowing that it was *there*. Blackstone's constantly shifting emotions affected his reasoning: he was far more concerned to maintain the money supply than he was about being unmasked as a bigamist. Although that had begun the blackmail it had quickly ceased to matter in the way he thought. If only he could get the transfer he'd asked for! Praying for miracles, like he'd prayed for miracles before all this latest business began. But surely the fact that Springley hadn't replied yet indicated there was *some* consideration being given to his re-application! So there had to be a chance. Make sure the money kept coming, so he could go on feeling its comforting security.

Blackstone calculated his entry into the restricted work area the following evening around the same time as before, but on this occasion there was the benefit of his having the layout established in his mind. Unable to use the direction-seeking excuse again, he had to avoid the small office from which he'd stolen the original backing paper. He went along a corridor diametrically opposite from his first entry, which took him to the far side of the communal work room. As he walked Blackstone saw the end-of-the-day men shuffling from their separate sections to stow their blueprints in the same main drawing locker. But, more confident of his surroundings, Blackstone became aware of something else, too. The outer, bordering cubicles appeared to be where the prototype drawings were checked and refined, from their creation in the larger room. Which meant that the larger room was likely to contain a bigger selection of material, impressed upon backing paper or maybe discarded sketches in waste-paper baskets in advance of security collection. *I want a lot*, he remembered: like he remembered the threats that went with it.

Blackstone found the lavatory he was seeking half-way down the corridor and hurried in, tensed against there already being people inside. There weren't. He concealed himself in the furthest cubicle but did not turn the lock, to prevent the Engaged sign registering. Instead he sat on the pedestal with his legs stretched out in front of himself, keeping the door closed with his feet. The position also kept his feet and lower legs from being visible from outside. He reckoned at least four people came in and out: a far-away cubicle was used once. The conversations at the urinals covered the improbability of a previous night's soap opera on television, Italian food being better than French, and house prices going up on the island as fast as those on the mainland. Blackstone thought he recognized the voice of one of the men to be someone called Morton who'd joined the firm after him and without half as much experience, which just went to show how bloody unfair the whole selection for the secret project had been. His legs began to ache at the back, just behind his knees.

He let half an hour elapse before cautiously emerging. The building seemed quiet around him, some of the corridor and office lights already extinguished by their timeswitch. Blackstone remained stationary in the corridor, alert for movement or noise of people but hearing nothing. *I want a lot,* he thought again. There were a number of doors into the communal room. Blackstone chose one of the smaller, near a darkened corner. And was approaching a double drawing board when the voice said: 'What are you doing here!' Blackstone was so surprised he gave a muted cry of fright and dropped the drawing tube in which he'd hoped to sneak out whatever he could find.

The security drill was strictly adhered to, which meant the preliminary inquiry was immediate but it actually gave Blackstone an opportunity to compose himself and arrange his story because Springley had to be recalled, fortunately only from his usual early evening visit to the nearby sports and social club. Blackstone's own section chief was summoned back as well, along with the most senior director still on the premises and the head of security.

By the time the questioning began Blackstone was, incredibly, in one of his upswing moods, relaxed and relatively unworried. As he spoke he thought it was just like telling the truth. He produced his temporary security access authorization, which was agreed by them all to be valid. Blackstone's instruction to deliver the Ariane fin design was confirmed by his superior and Blackstone insisted his return that evening had been the action of a conscientious employee attempting to retrieve documents non-classified and

158

therefore insufficiently important to require a positive collection directive: if he were wrong about that then he was sorry. He'd only been trying to do his job. And here Blackstone introduced a further explanation he had mentally rehearsed while he waited for the examination to begin. He'd also hoped, he conceded in apparent admission, that he might personally encounter Robert Springley, from whom he still awaited a reply to his renewed application to be part of the project team. Again, Blackstone asserted, the action of a perhaps overly keen, conscientious worker. The absentminded, white-haired project leader at once confirmed such a reply was outstanding.

The drawings tubes he had been carrying were examined and found only to contain additional Ariane material, and a thorough check of the room in which he had been detained showed nothing interfered with and nothing missing.

Throughout Blackstone became increasingly aware that the examination was being conducted internally, without any outside police involvement, which had to be a good sign. And he didn't regard as ominous being told to hold himself in readiness for a fuller inquiry, pending which he would be formally upon suspension, because if they'd really believed him to be doing something wrong they wouldn't have allowed him off the premises in the first place. The most encouraging thing of all was the smiling farewell from Springley himself, who said when the inquiry had disbanded and they were getting ready to leave that he was sorry for the delay but that he hadn't made up his mind about the application yet.

He'd got away with it! decided Blackstone exultantly. And Springley *was* considering him. There certainly wasn't any cause to ring the emergency number in London and alert the man he knew as

Mr Stranger, which he further knew wasn't the man's real name at all.

There were other prescribed routines which automatically followed such a preliminary inquiry. One was that a report be sent to London, and because it involved the security of such a highly classified overseas project it was channelled to Westminster Bridge Road. The level of classification also required it to be personally studied by the acting Director General.

Richard Harkness decided at once it was an innocent, completely explained event of no importance whatsoever, which was already the conclusion of the inquiry group that had convened the night of the occurrence. But procedure dictated their own investigation be conducted, pointless though it would be in this case.

Harkness knew just the officer for pointless investigations.

The meeting that day was in Berkeley, near the university campus, the sort of crowded and jostled place that Petrin seemed to favour. Emil Krogh arrived on schedule and waited impatiently, moving from foot to foot and gazing up and down the pavement near the designated drug store, wishing the rendezvous were more secluded. The openness worried him and he said so when Petrin finally arrived.

'I like it this way,' said the Russian dismissively. He did not, of course, add that such locations made their every meeting and every handover that much easier for the positioned KGB officers to photograph.

19

The head of security at the aerospace factory was named Harry Slade. He had served in the British Army for twenty-five years, honourably retiring with the rank of sergeant major and a regimental photograph signed by all the officers. He wore two lines of campaign ribbons on an immaculate, rigidly pressed black uniform with a profusion of brightly shined buttons, and regarded Charlie Muffin with the distasteful regret of a missed parade-ground challenge. It was an effort, but he managed to avoid automatically calling Charlie 'sir'. The effort, like the attitude, was obvious but Charlie decided not to confront it: he was working away from Westminster Bridge Road for the first time in months, there would be expenses, the sun was shining and he was feeling generous. Slade confirmed that afternoon's appointment with Blackstone and showed Charlie the office that had been made available for him, the waiting room to a conference chamber. There were easy chairs as well as a more formal arrangement at a desk and there were fresh flowers in a proper vase and a view of the Medina river from the window. Charlie guessed the place to be three times the size of where he was accustomed to working at Westminster Bridge Road. At Charlie's insistence the security chief reviewed everything discussed at the inquiry and produced Blackstone's personnel record and then took Charlie on a tour of the fenced-off, secure section. There Charlie met the project manager, and Springley said he was sure it was all a fuss about nothing and Charlie truthfully said he didn't mind at all coming down from London

161

to check it out. Under Springley's guidance he was shown around the workrooms and the communal drawing area and saw how all the blueprints and drawing material were secured at the end of each evening.

'Personally checked every night by myself,' chipped in the escorting Slade. 'There's no danger of any classified information getting into the wrong hands from this building.'

'Glad to hear it,' said Charlie.

'I think the whole episode comes down to Blackstone's dedication to the job,' said the project manager. 'He's applied twice to join the team.'

'Are you taking him on?'

Springley shrugged. 'I might, if a vacancy occurs. There's no room at the moment, but I think there might be in a few weeks.'

Slade appeared surprised when Charlie asked to see where Blackstone normally worked, in the main building, but showed him anyway. Slade seemed affronted when Charlie said he didn't want the man to sit in on the afternoon's interview.

'I expected that you would,' said the security chief.

Charlie guessed the man would have kept Blackstone standing to attention throughout. He said: 'I prefer to be on my own.'

'I need to make a proper report to the company,' protested Slade. 'It's my job.'

'I'll tell you what happens,' promised Charlie. He'd never got on with sergeant majors and certainly didn't want the intrusion of this one with his judgement already made.

Blackstone was early. The tracer came inquiringly into the room after politely knocking, stopping in the doorway when he saw only Charlie there. He said: 'I was told to come here?'

'That's right,' said Charlie.

162

'Just you?'

'What did you expect?'

'I didn't. . .I don't know.' Which was true and the reason for Blackstone's vague confusion. He'd prepared himself to be confronted by a group of officials from London, maybe even some sort of panel but not just one person. And most certainly not by this tramp of a man who didn't look like an official of anything. Blackstone did not now have the confidence of the night he was caught – his feelings were actually on a downturn – but he was sure he didn't have anything to fear here.

Blackstone was a plump, quick-blinking man. He wore a well-pressed blue suit that Charlie guessed to be his Sunday best, with a crisp white shirt and with his hair combed carefully to cover the place where it was thinning, near his forehead. Charlie nodded across the desk at which he was already sitting and said: 'Why not take that chair there?'

Blackstone sat as he was told, his hands crossed in front of him in his lap. He said: 'This is all a silly misunderstanding.'

'Is it?' said Charlie mildly. 'Tell me about it.'

'I was just trying to be helpful.'

'Why don't you tell me about it?' invited Charlie.

'From when?' queried Blackstone.

'From whenever you like,' said Charlie.

Charlie listened, not looking fully at the other man but with his chair slightly turned, at times even gazing as if something had caught his attention on the river or further out, on the sea. Blackstone initially found the attitude unsettling. Then he decided there was nothing to be unsettled about: the man just wasn't very good, that was all. His self-assurance began its ascent.

'Drawing tubes?' stopped Charlie abruptly, swinging back from the window.

163

'What?' said Blackstone, off-balanced.

'When you went into the secure section on the second occasion you carried drawing tubes?'

'Yes.'

'Why?'

'It's the way blueprints are sometimes handled. Makes them easy to carry.'

'Surely the blueprints you'd delivered earlier were already in their own containers?'

Blackstone swallowed. 'I wasn't sure whether they still would be. Sometimes they get mislaid: I just decided to be sure.'

'So those you carried when you were challenged were empty?'

He wasn't going to be caught that easily, thought Blackstone. He said: 'No. They held drawings but there would have been room for more.'

'How far would you say it was, from where you work to the secure area?' asked Charlie, who'd carefully paced it out.

Blackstone shrugged. 'About a hundred yards; maybe more.'

'A little more, I'd say,' corrected Charlie. 'Nearer two hundred, in fact. Why walk two hundred yards from one building to another on the off-chance that the Ariane drawings would be ready for return? Why didn't you telephone to ask?'

Blackstone felt himself becoming hot. He gave another uncertain movement and said: 'I just didn't think of it. I knew the drawings were there and on the spur of the moment decided to call by.'

'Practically an hour after you should have gone home?'

Perspiration began on Blackstone's upper lip, making it itch and he wanted to wipe it off but it would have made him look nervous. He said: 'We can work flexi-hours here if we choose. Anyway, I

164

didn't really know what the time was. I was trying to see Mr Springley. I've applied for a transfer to the project.'

The reasonable explanation that had been produced before, remembered Charlie. He said: 'So it wasn't such a spur-of-the-moment decision after all?'

Unable to stand the itching any longer Blackstone moved his hand quickly across his face. He said: 'It began that way: it was only when I was at the section that the idea of trying to see Mr Springley occurred to me.'

'Spur of the moment yet you gave it sufficient thought to take along some spare drawing tubes in case the others had been mislaid?'

'I'd kept the unwanted ones by my desk. It was automatic to pick them up. I didn't positively think of it.'

Charlie was finding Blackstone a difficult person to assess. The man's demeanour had changed from the almost aggressive reassurance with which the interview had started to this sweated discomfort, but it would be wrong to read too much into that. He said: 'If you wanted to see the project head, why didn't you go to his office? Why were you in the main communal drawing area?'

'I wasn't sure where his office was.'

'You'd been in the section before, to deliver the Ariane blueprints.'

'But not to Mr Springley's office. It wasn't he who'd asked for them.' He'd been very wrong to imagine this was going to be an easy meeting, decided Blackstone. And more mistaken still to think that this unkempt man needn't be taken seriously.

'So what were you doing?'

'Looking for someone to direct me.'

'You must have known everyone would have gone home?'

'I told you, there's a flexi-hour system. Only no one was working that evening.'

'Crossing from one building to another, as you did, you must have seen a lot of people leaving?'

Blackstone tried to make a careless gesture. 'A few.'

Neither convincing nor unconvincing, thought Charlie. But then people more often than not did things without a completely logical explanation that could be examined later. Deciding to change the direction of the questioning to see if he could further disconcert the man, Charlie said: 'You've gone through security clearance?'

'Yes.'

'And signed the Official Secrets Act?'

'Yes,' agreed Blackstone again. What the hell was the man getting at now!

'I know of cases of people being jailed for twenty, even thirty years for contravening the Act.'

'What are you talking about!' Blackstone felt loose-stomached now, plunging into panicked depression and uncaring how he appeared to the other man.

'Penalties, for contravening the Official Secrets Act,' said Charlie quietly. Was Blackstone nervous enough to make a slip?

'I haven't contravened anything!' protested Blackstone. 'I told you how it happened! I didn't mean any harm!' Incredibly, for the first time, Blackstone's mind went properly beyond the money he'd been getting, fully to consider what could happen to him if he were found out. He remembered the inquiry the night he'd been caught not as an inquiry at all. Ridiculous though it now was to contemplate, it had all seemed like some sort of game, a contest between himself and men he knew and had worked with. But

166

that's all. Not once had he considered there being a *penalty*, at the end of it. But now he did. He thought about thirty years and didn't regard what was going on here as anything like a game. This was deadly serious: deadly, horrifyingly serious. Thirty years, he thought again.

Charlie's feet began to hurt, which he'd known they would when he'd walked from the ferry terminal to save the three-pound taxi fare. He crossed one leg over the other and slid his fingers inside his sagging shoe, massaging the ache. He said: 'What time did you enter the secure section?'

The bastard was going to pick on and on, wearing him down, until he made a mistake! Stick to what happened, Blackstone told himself: don't try to invent lies he might forget, under pressure. He said: 'I wasn't paying any particular attention to the time. Maybe five thirty. Maybe later.'

'That's funny,' said Charlie.

'What is?'

'According to the security report, you were challenged in the main drawing office at six thirty-five. You'd been there for a whole hour!'

Dear God, what was he going to do! The man obviously didn't believe him. He'd say so, soon: make some open accusation. Thirty years! Desperately Blackstone said: 'It could have been later than five thirty.'

'Let's give you the benefit of a lot of doubt,' said Charlie. 'Let's say you didn't go in until six. That's still half an hour. What were you doing alone in the building for half an hour?'

'I went to the lavatory.'

'The lavatory!'

'I had the need to go when I got to the building.'

'So you hid in the lavatory for thirty minutes?'

'I didn't *hide!*' denied Blackstone. 'I *went* to the lavatory.' Deflect him, thought Blackstone: he had to do something, say something, anything, to deflect the man to get the pressure off!

Blackstone was weakening, Charlie decided: on the ropes and weakening. But there still wasn't anything positively incriminating. Charlie said: 'Are you keen to get on the secret project?'

Blackstone groped for a handkerchief and made as if to blow his nose, using the pretext to wipe away the build-up of sweat and to delay his answer as long as possible. Stick to the truth as much as possible, he told himself. He said: 'I want very much to be part of it.'

'Why?' demanded Charlie.

'Secret work is always different: exciting. I like working on challenging projects.'

'What about the extra money?'

Careful! thought Blackstone. He said: 'It does carry a higher salary scale. And it's always nice to earn extra money.'

Charlie lowered his foot back to the floor, moving his toes inside the capacious Hush Puppies. His foot still ached. 'So!' he said briskly. 'You decide to show how conscientious you are. Around the time most other people were going home you enter a classified, secure working area hoping to see the project manager to talk about a transfer. But then you go into a toilet and stay there all the time, so that when you come out Springley has gone home, like everyone else. Making everything completely pointless.'

'I didn't have any alternative,' said Blackstone stubbornly. 'I was ill.'

'You didn't say that before.'

Blackstone's shirt was glued to his back by sweat and he had consciously to press one hand against the other in his lap to prevent the shake being noticeable.

168

He was gripped by despair, finding it difficult to hold in his mind which answers he'd given to which questions: difficult to get his mind to function at all. He said: 'It's not something you talk about, is it?'

'If you're asked to explain being on premises where you've no right to be I would think it's something you talk about,' insisted Charlie.

Blackstone shrugged, not knowing an answer. 'I didn't.' He knew he couldn't go on much longer. Soon he was going to say something, admit something, and it was all going to be over. Everything. Thirty years: he was going to go to prison for thirty years.

Time for a sharp confrontation, gauged Charlie. He said: 'You're very nervous, Henry. If this is all the innocent misunderstanding you say it is, why are you so nervous?'

Blackstone frantically thought he saw an escape. He was engulfed by fear and recognized it as desperate but it was a matter of the lesser against the greater and his mind was blocked by the thought of a lifetime sentence if he admitted what he'd done. He said: 'You're a policeman, aren't you?'

'Not really,' said Charlie. 'Why should that be important?'

'It's not, I don't suppose,' said Blackstone. 'But you don't believe me, do you? So you're going to go on digging and if you go on digging long enough you're going to find out, aren't you?' He was committed now. There was no going back: lesser against the greater, he tried to convince himself. Nothing could be greater than thirty years.

Here it comes! thought Charlie. He'd have to get Slade in to witness whatever the confession was when it came to be written down. Not time yet, though: the hurdle of the first admission was always the most difficult. Once they started talking they usually found it impossible to stop. He said: 'What is it I'm going to find out, Henry?'

'Two wives,' mumbled Blackstone. 'I've got two wives. Not legally allowed to do that, am I?'

Charlie held back from laughing out loud but it wasn't easy. 'Not my line of business,' he said. A reasonable enough explanation for the nervousness, he acknowledged.

'You're not interested in that!' An uncertain hope came through all the other switchbacking emotions. Surely he wasn't going to get away with it completely!

Charlie shook his head. 'Like I said, I'm not a policeman. That's nothing to do with me.'

'I thought it would be.' The man had accepted it! Blackstone decided hopefully.

A time to press hard and a time to behave softly, thought Charlie. Abruptly he announced: 'I think that's enough for today.'

'For today?'

'There are a few other things I'd like to cover but not today,' said Charlie. 'Why don't we break now? See each other again tomorrow morning.'

He *had* escaped, accepted Blackstone. Temporarily perhaps, but it was enough, just to get away from the back-and-forth questioning that had his head in a whirl, confusing him, so he couldn't think. He said: 'Of course. Whatever you say.'

'How about ten o'clock?'

Blackstone nodded agreement to the time and said: 'So you're not a policeman?'

'Nope.'

'Will you tell the police about me?'

'I told you, I'm not interested,' repeated Charlie.

For the first time there was a twitch of a smile, like a light clicking on and off. He'd well and truly deflected the other man, like he'd set out to do, determined Blackstone triumphantly. 'Appreciate it,'

170

he said. 'Not as if I'm hurting anyone, is it? I treat them both the same. They're both happy.'

'That's not why I'm here,' assured Charlie.

He'd won but only just, Blackstone realized objectively as he left the factory. And there was no telling for how long. He needed to talk to someone and there was only one person to whom he could talk. The urge was overwhelming to go to the first public kiosk he could find but Blackstone forced himself to stay calm, waiting until he'd crossed the river and was going inland before stopping at the telephone box he normally used, three miles outside of Newport. It wasn't Losev who took the call, of course, but Blackstone said at once there was an emergency and that he had to speak to the man with whom he personally dealt, refusing any explanation. It was arranged he should call back in fifteen minutes and when he did the Russian was there, waiting. The dam broke the moment Blackstone was connected. He babbled disjointedly and Losev stopped him and told him to relax, then demanded the account in a controlled, consecutive way. Blackstone managed it but not easily, pumping coins into the pay phone as one time period expired to run into another.

When Blackstone finished the Russian said: 'Why didn't you warn me when you were first caught?'

'I knew I'd got away with it that time.'

'And now you've admitted your bigamy?'

'I couldn't think of any other way to get him off my back: I couldn't think straight.'

'He's not going to do anything about it?'

'He said he wasn't.'

Losev was furious once more at the renewed difficulties Blackstone's detection posed for him personally, his mind far ahead of the immediate problems. It meant he couldn't recover with Moscow as he'd hoped over the incomplete drawing with which the

171

bastard had already tricked him. And that even if Blackstone got through the postponed interrogation he couldn't risk using the man for a long time. He said: 'You really think the project manager is looking favourably upon your re-application?'

'That's the impression I got. He was very friendly. I don't know what could happen now.'

So the man still had potential, acknowledged Losev, despite his anger. Too much for him to be disregarded or cast off, which was what Losev would have liked to do. As emphatically as possible he assured Blackstone there was nothing for him to worry about: that the only risk was in the man confessing. All Blackstone had to do was keep his head and he would be safe. 'Do you think you can do that?'

'I'll try,' said Blackstone, subdued.

'You've *got* to do it,' insisted Losev, as forcefully as possible. 'The only person who can put you in jail is yourself.'

'Should I keep in touch?'

'Not for a week or two. Don't do anything that might attract suspicion or attention,' ordered Losev.

'It frightens me to be questioned by someone I know to be an intelligence official, although he looks like a tramp.'

It worried Losev, too. Which was why the Soviet station chief rushed a surveillance squad to the Isle of Wight overnight, to be in position when Charlie went into the interrogation room that Blackstone had identified during his terrified call. They succeeded in getting a total of five photographs of Charlie. Losev was a very diligent as well as a very ambitious intelligence officer. He made the routine comparison at once with the dossier that Berenkov had sent from Moscow weeks before. And realized that while he might have encountered a setback with one assignment he had succeeded in another.

172

He'd identified the whereabouts of someone called Charlie Muffin.

Which an hour later, in Moscow, Berenkov regarded as very important indeed.

'This isn't like it used to be, is it?' asked Barbara. 'Not like it's supposed to be?'

'No,' agreed Krogh, glad she had initiated the conversation.

'I'm sorry.' She'd tried hard to make it work for him that night, but it hadn't. She sat at the side of the bed now, voluptuous and full breasted, wearing a diaphanous cover that secured at the neck with a tie and ended just short of her crotch. Her hair was unsecured, falling to her shoulders.

'One of those things, I guess,' said Krogh.

'I never think these sort of situations should end badly: people saying things that hurt.'

'I don't think that either,' agreed Krogh. It was all happening remarkably easily. Thank Christ something was, at last.

Barbara gestured around the San Francisco apartment. 'This is your place: I know that.'

'Take as long as you want. No hurry.'

'Thanks.'

'You need any money?'

'I guess the apartment agents will want a deposit. They often do.'

'Five thousand OK?'

'Thanks again.'

'I should be going.'

'Sure.'

'Take care.'

'You, too.'

'I will,' assured Krogh. 'I really will.'

20

There was a wariness about Blackstone but not the leaking nervousness of the previous day. He hadn't known what to expect then, but now he thought he did. He determined not to underestimate the other man because of the way he looked. And not to panic. Blackstone accepted that was what he'd done, blurting out the confession about Ann and Ruth like he had. He regretted that: regretted it bitterly. It had given a reason for his anxiety – he hoped – but he couldn't be sure what the man would do with the information, so he was vulnerable. But only from that, he tried to convince himself. The Russian had been right about the other business: without an open admission, they had no case against him. That's all he had to remember: no admission, no case. And not to panic.

Charlie, who'd found a very reasonable pub in which to stay just back from the seafront, savoured a bacon and two eggs breakfast and was enjoying being back in operation after his enforced hibernation, smiled up encouragingly at Blackstone's entry and said: 'Here we are again then!'

'Yes,' said Blackstone. The man seemed friendlier than the previous day but Blackstone wasn't going to be fooled by that.

'Where were we?' asked Charlie.

'I don't know,' said Blackstone, still cautious. 'You said you still had some questions.'

'I probably did,' said Charlie, as if he couldn't remember them any more. 'This is my first time on the Isle of Wight. I like it.'

'Some people find it claustrophobic,' allowed Blackstone.

'Do you?'

'No. I was born here. It's not a feeling you get if you're a born islander.'

'You got both your homes here?'

Careful! thought Blackstone at once: it appeared to be a way the man had, suddenly slipping in possibly tricky questions. He said: 'One here, one in Portsmouth, just across the water.'

'Best of both worlds then?'

'You're going to get me prosecuted for it, aren't you?'

Having jabbed at the man's weak point, to unsettle him, Charlie ignored the question. Instead he said: 'Something that I can't understand about the period you were inside the secure section that second time is how no one saw you. Out of twenty or so people in or around the building, no one saw you?'

No admission, no case, thought Blackstone. 'I don't know why either,' he shrugged.

'You any idea what the secret project is?'

Blackstone shook his head positively. 'How could I, if it's secret? The rumour is that it involves our carbon fibre process but that's rather obvious: that's what we specialize in.'

'Tell me about that,' invited Charlie.

Blackstone did, without difficulty, feeling quite relaxed with generalities and confident that here he was under no threat. He talked of reinforced resin systems and monoplastics and thermoset processes and guessed the other man was having trouble keeping up with him, which pleased Blackstone because it was good to feel superior for a change. Charlie interjected to ask which of the processes were being used on the secret project and Blackstone evaded the

175

trap easily, saying that he had no way of knowing. Blackstone saw another snare when Charlie asked what process he guessed it would be and actually laughed at the man, saying that he had no way of knowing that, either.

Blackstone's restored assurance faltered slightly when Charlie insisted on going back over the whole episode again but the hesitation was brief because he guessed the ploy was to jump on any variation from his first account. And he had that word perfect by now and knew when he finished he hadn't changed his story by a single word.

'Thanks for your time,' concluded Charlie politely.

'That's it?'

'Unless you've got anything else to tell me?'

'No,' said Blackstone at once. 'Nothing.'

'Then that's it,' agreed Charlie.

'What happens now?' asked Blackstone. 'Do I stay suspended?'

'I don't see why you should.'

No admission, no case, thought Blackstone: the feeling of satisfaction, of triumph, surged through him. He'd done it again! Not as easily as before, but he'd come through a second inquiry – with an intelligence officer this time – and got away with it again! He wished he could tell the Russian at once how well he'd done. Blackstone said: 'Thank you. I'm glad it's all over.'

'A silly misunderstanding, like you said,' suggested Charlie.

'It's good to be finally believed.'

'We've always got to be sure,' said Charlie.

'Oh, I understand,' allowed Blackstone generously, positively enjoying himself, genuinely knowing a feeling of superiority over Charlie. 'That's how it always should be.'

'So let's follow security procedures more closely in

the future, shall we?' grinned Charlie.

'Don't worry,' assured Blackstone, grinning back. 'I won't do anything like it again.'

'I'll tell the management and security that it's all settled,' promised Charlie.

Blackstone rose but stood uncertainly before the desk, wondering whether he should offer to shake hands. Deciding against it he said: 'I'll be going then?'

'Fine,' said Charlie.

After the man left the room Charlie sat for a long time looking out over the river and sea beyond, flecked with yacht sails and holiday ferries and motor craft, but seeing none of it. At last he shifted, finding his way to the office where the security chief sat strangely upright, as if trying not to wrinkle the immaculately maintained uniform, still hostile from being excluded from the encounters with Blackstone. Charlie patiently provided Slade with the promised report of the interviews and then crossed once more to the security area to speak, independently, with Springley.

Outside again, in the road between the two buildings, the former sergeant major said: 'So the suspension can be lifted right away?'

'From this moment,' agreed Charlie.

'You going to file a report when you get back to London?'

'Of course,' said Charlie. 'You know all about obeying orders, don't you?'

'Don't forget what I said, will you?' demanded the man. 'There's no danger of any classified information getting into the wrong hands from this establishment.'

'It's going to be one of the first points I make,' assured Charlie.

'Sorry you had a wasted trip,' said Slade, mollified

177

at last at the thought of his name featuring in a White-hall document.

'Happens all the time: think what a disaster it would be if they weren't wasted trips!'

But he didn't return immediately to London. Charlie Muffin was a man who reacted to hunches and instincts, which had invariably stood him in good stead in the past, although it would have been an exaggeration to describe his feeling quite so strongly on this occasion. At best, he felt a general unease. Whatever – hunch, instinct or unease – he considered it sufficient to stay on a while longer where the sun was still shining, the air was fresh and he got two fresh eggs for breakfast every morning, without even asking for them. And by so doing to impose upon Henry Blackstone, self-confessed bigamist and self-admitted security rule bender, a period of intense but undetected surveillance.

It proved a frustrating and even more unsettling exercise.

He followed Blackstone to and from his Newport home and he learned about the Monday night at the cinema and the darts night on Thursday. He decided Ann was an attractive-enough-looking housewife, although quite heavily overweight, who appeared content with her limited existence, which upon reflection the majority of housewives appeared to be. Using the authority of London headquarters he had Blackstone's bank statements and financial affairs accessed just as efficiently and thoroughly as the Russians before him, and uncovered the man's straitened circumstances. And was in a position to acknowledge – more quickly than the Russians at a comparable stage of their separate surveillance – that Blackstone's shortage of money was caused by the drain of maintaining the two admitted households. But there were no indicative, tell-tale deposits in any

178

financial account to show by as much as a penny the slightest additional, welcome income beyond that which the man received as a senior-grade tracer at an Isle of Wight aeronautics factory. Blackstone drank lager beer, on draught, not bottled. He preferred the colour blue, in the clothes he wore. He didn't smoke. He had an account at a betting shop. He didn't read a regular newspaper. He had no close male friends. He was, in fact, such a boring man that Charlie reckoned he had to have a prick like a baby's arm with an apple in its hand to keep one wife happy, let alone two, no matter how mundanely content they were.

But the sensation of unease wouldn't go. Rather, it increased and as the days passed Charlie encountered other feelings, like irritation and anger. Yet Blackstone did nothing nor behaved in the slightest way suspiciously, which worsened Charlie's irritation and anger.

Charlie allowed a full week to elapse before contacting Westminster Bridge Road. It was an open and therefore insecure telephone link, because it couldn't be anything else from where Charlie was operating and Charlie intended doing nothing beyond reporting an intention to return to the clerk whose sole function it was to receive inexplicable messages from people he could never ask to be more explicit. But there was a note against Charlie's code designation which meant he had to be routed through to the acting Director General.

'What in heaven's name do you imagine you've been doing!'

Charlie wondered if the man ever regretted the self-imposed discipline of not allowing himself to swear. Conscious of the restrictions of their communication method, Charlie said: 'Working. What else?'

'That's what I'd like to know. You've been gone a week.'

'I've been routed through to you,' reminded Charlie, not interested in Harkness' empty posturing, which was all it could be when they were speaking like this.

'Is there any cause for concern?'

Charlie hesitated, wondering how Harkness would react to a reply about uneasy, instinctive feelings. He said: 'No.'

'So your holiday is over!' said Harkness. 'Get back here!'

'The weather's been terrific,' said Charlie, indulging himself and careless of upsetting the other man. 'High seventies every day.'

'I said get back!'

'I've already logged the intention to do just that.'

Charlie managed the hydrofoil that left ahead of the evening rush hour, remembering as he sat down Blackstone's remark about people finding the island claustrophobic and deciding it was true. Pleasant though the visit had been, Charlie was looking forward to getting back to the mainland. Maybe there he wouldn't feel so hemmed in.

There were six seats available, after Charlie had taken his. Four were very quickly filled by part of the KGB squad that, upon Berenkov's adamant instructions from Moscow, had maintained an unremitting surveillance upon Charlie Muffin from the moment of his being indentified as Henry Blackstone's intelligence interrogator.

Like many men of supreme confidence Alexei Berenkov was also an emotional one, and briefly his eyes actually clouded at the cable from London announcing the detection of Charlie Muffin. It was all so perfect! So absolutely and completely perfect. It gave him Charlie Muffin, which was what he'd set out to accomplish. But of practically matching importance it had occurred in circumstances that provided the ideal opportunity at last to tell Kalenin. To stop deceiving the man. Not completely true, Berenkov qualified. There would still be minimal deception in the manner in which he presented the discovery, but very minimal. At least his friend would *know*. A further benefit from the circumstances was that Kalenin couldn't abort the pursuit, either.

Berenkov sought and gained a meeting with Kalenin in central Moscow that same day, late in the afternoon. The bearded First Deputy sat solemn-faced and unspeaking while Berenkov recounted the identification and then said: 'So we can't risk immediately using – even *trying* to use – the man Blackstone. And without the British material, we've failed.'

'I've already decided upon another way,' promised Berenkov.

'Charlie Muffin's involvement worries me,' said Kalenin, who knew the man from the Berenkov repatriation and from the later phoney defection to Russia. 'It worries me a lot.'

'I've decided how to resolve that, as well,' said Berenkov.

'Kill him, you mean?' said Kalenin dispassionately.

'Oh no,' said Berenkov at once. 'To kill him now would attract precisely the sort of attention we don't want. I've got something planned for Charlie Muffin that will be far worse than death.'

'This isn't a personal vendetta, is it?' queried Kalenin with sudden prescience.

'Of course not!' denied Berenkov.

21

Alexei Berenkov had no false illusions about what he
was trying to do in moving against Charlie Muffin.
Objectively he recognized that one miscalculation
could bring about his own destruction rather than
that of the man he sought to destroy. But with
his typical self-assurance he was not frightened by
that awareness. If there were a feeling it was one
of anticipation at finally manoeuvring just such a
situation. Berenkov *wanted* to confront Charlie Muffin, like combatants in some medieval contest, which
was perhaps a rather grandiose imagery but never-
theless how Berenkov thought of it and had for so
long planned it. Which, objective again, Berenkov
acknowledged to be pride, although he would not
have gone so far as to admit to conceit, as well.
Just pride. Dangerous – even reckless – pride in the
shifting uncertainty of Moscow. But still a contest
he was determined to have. He'd knowingly mis-
led Kalenin by denying any personal importance
in removing Charlie Muffin. *Everything* about the
operation was personal: a personal, private matter
that had finally to be resolved between them. Charlie
Muffin. Or himself. One to end the ultimate victor,
the other the permanently vanquished. It was not,
however, that the Russian hated or despised Charlie.
Far from it. Berenkov admired the man: respected
him as a superb espionage professional. It was precisely *because* of that admiration and respect that
Berenkov had set out to manipulate the encounter-
by-proxy, as he had.

There'd already been two contests between them.

The first had been Charlie's pursuit in England

and throughout Europe, doggedly unrelenting, stubbornly refusing the false trails and deceptions that Berenkov had laid and which succeeded in fooling everyone else. No doubt that time who had emerged the victor: the sentence at London's Old Bailey for running the Soviet spy ring had been forty years. And Berenkov would still have had twenty-eight to go if he hadn't been exchanged for the British and American intelligence directors whom Charlie led into Soviet captivity in retribution for their willingness to sacrifice him, despite all that he had done.

And then there was the Moscow episode during which Charlie had met Natalia Nikandrova Fedova. Not such a clear victory there but dangerously close. Certainly under intensive, necessarily brutal interrogation the Englishman Edwin Sampson, with whom Charlie had supposedly escaped from English imprisonment, after their staged treason conviction, had confessed that his function after Soviet acceptance had been to infiltrate the KGB. But despite the chemical and then bone-crushing questioning Sampson had maintained he didn't know Charlie Muffin's purpose in coming to Russia: that they had not been working together. The incident had come near to bringing him down, Berenkov remembered. He'd believed Charlie Muffin's defection to be genuine and accepted the man into his home and sponsored his appointment as instructor at the Soviet spy school, and but for Kalenin's defence and protection after the man had fled back to England would probably have been replaced as a security threat.

So this, an ultimate confrontation, was justified. Justified personally and justified professionally. And it was the one that Berenkov was sure, without any eroding doubt, he was going to win.

Berenkov realized that the sequence with which

he made his moves was of vital importance. And the most vitally important action of all remained obtaining the complete specifications for the American satellite. So at first, frustrating though it was to do so, he ignored England completely. Instead, using the secure diplomatic bag as his route for communication, Berenkov issued a series of instructions to Alexandr Petrin at the San Francisco consulate.

Only when he was completely satisfied that the American was to be activated in the way he wished did Berenkov revert to England. Here again he issued a series of acknowledge-as-comprehended orders, some of which were bewildering to the receiving Losev because following established intelligence procedure they were compartmented, without explanation of apparent relevance. There was no elaboration, for instance, for Blackstone having to be humoured with the promise of a retainer. Or, not in those first messages, how alternative arrangements were being made to obtain the English information.

The first practical step was to have the increasingly resentful Losev open a safe-custody facility, operated by a two-key, photographic recognition access, at a particular private bank in London's King William Street. Berenkov was an expert in tradecraft material and their uses from his period as a European field supervisor. He travelled personally to the KGB's Technical Directorate installation beyond the ring road, at Lyudertsy, to ensure he got exactly what he required, even though each of those requirements was a very normal tool of the espionage profession.

It was essential that Charlie ultimately realize there *had* been a confrontation between them and that he'd been utterly defeated. So Berenkov had the King William Street facility identified by name and access number in the micro-dot created for him by the Technical Directorate scientists as the site of the 'dead letter' drop, sure its significance would register with Charlie: it was the location and the method Berenkov himself had used all those years ago in London to exchange information with the Soviet embassy there. And which Charlie had been the officer to isolate and then to penetrate. In addition to the micro-dot Berenkov obtained a one-time-message cipher pad and had the experts further evolve for him a comparatively basic transposed letter-for-number communication code, which by being comparatively simple would make it matchingly easy for British cryptologists to break.

Berenkov shipped everything to London, again in the secure diplomatic bag. Once more there were detailed instructions to each of which the London station chief had to respond individually, guaranteeing complete understanding.

There were blueprints still outstanding from Emil Krogh's factory in California, which meant a delay to everything being set into motion (but the hindrance had its benefits.) The order needed authority greater than his, which meant discussing the majority of the intended operation with Kalenin. Berenkov accepted when he did so the perceptible reservation of the other man, wondering if, when it became the spectacular coup he knew it was undoubtedly going to be, Kalenin would move to rebuild the bridges between them.

'As a complete espionage proposal it's very fragile, Alexei,' cautioned Kalenin.

'I've built in many safeguards,' insisted Berenkov.

'It's what can't be foreseen that concerns me,' said Kalenin, unimpressed.

'The two can be separated,' argued Berenkov. 'The entrapment of Charlie Muffin won't conflict with our getting the space technology we want.'

185

'I don't see how we can ensure one doesn't impinge upon the other,' rebuked Kalenin. 'At some stage they have to become inextricably linked, according to your proposals.'

'Only when I know the space material is safe,' insisted Berenkov with his customary enthusiasm.

'When you were imprisoned in England I personally involved myself in the operation to get you freed,' reminded Kalenin. 'There was a faction within the government of the time that criticized your being arrested in the first place: described it as culpable carelessness. I defended you, against accusations like that. And became the bait to entice the British and American directors to Vienna where we seized them. Which, if it had gone wrong, could have exposed me to the same accusation.'

'I know all this,' said Berenkov, guessing the path the conversation was taking. He supposed it was inevitable, sooner or later.

'I would not welcome being called upon again to defend you against culpable carelessness,' announced Kalenin flatly. 'We none of us can afford to become involved in debates where charges like that can be levelled.'

Berenkov sighed, saddened but not surprised. It was, he supposed, a mark of the friendship still between them that Kalenin was warning him in advance how he would react if mistakes were made. He said: 'I would not like to put you into such a position.'

'May your saint be at your shoulder, Alexei.'

Berenkov swallowed, at the traditional Georgian invocation for good luck. 'I wish I knew how to reply,' he apologized. 'I don't know your folklore sufficiently well.'

Kalenin shook his head. 'There isn't a reply,' he said. 'After that there's usually nothing left to say.'

186

Berenkov refused to be depressed by the encounter with Kalenin. The other man had always been a headquarters planner immersed in headquarters politics, never an active overseas operative having to decide on the ground whether to take great risks to achieve even greater success. He might not know Georgian folklore but there was an axiom from his once adoptive Britain which appealed to him and by which he had ruled most of his operational life: *Chance governs all*. Berenkov saw no significance in it being from Milton's *Paradise Lost*.

Berenkov had one last piece to fit into his intricate jigsaw, a piece so important that without it there would be no final picture at all. Natalia entered Berenkov's office with her customary polite reserve, not sitting until she was invited and deferring always to her controller's authority.

'Another overseas assignment, Comrade Major,' announced Berenkov. 'This time we want you to go to England.'

Natalia was glad she was sitting because for the briefest moment there was a sweep of dizziness and she was unsure whether it would have showed if she had been standing. Without sufficient thought she said: 'I will look forward to that, Comrade General.'

'Will you!' seized Berenkov.

'I look forward to every assignment involving my new function,' said Natalia, recovering. Dear God, could it ever be possible!

The convenient event chosen by Berenkov to get Natalia to England was the country's premier aeronautical display, the Farnborough Air Show, which in itself was something of a coincidence considering the parallel operation to obtain space technology. There was a further coincidence in that Berenkov made his arrangements to publish the names and a communal photograph of the attending delegation

of which Natalia was to form part on the day that
Charlie Muffin returned from his investigation at
the Isle of Wight aerospace factory.

Charlie Muffin was still uneasy.

'I find it difficult to accept there was sufficient reason
to stay as long as you did,' declared Harkness.

As always there was nowhere for Charlie to sit,
but Charlie had gone beyond being annoyed by the
man's petty childishness. Far away, over Harkness'
shoulder, Charlie saw an advertising air balloon
making its stately progress above the wavering line of
the Thames: the distance was too great to make out
the name of the product being promoted. He said:
'In my judgement there was.'

'What?' demanded the acting Director General.

No, thought Charlie, positively. He was taking a
risk but that was nothing new and at the moment
he didn't quite know the new game Harkness was
playing. With stiff formality he said: 'I considered
there was reasonable enough suspicion to maintain
a period of surveillance upon someone who had
contravened security procedure.'

'And what did you find?'

'During the time I observed him he did not behave
in a suspicious manner,' said Charlie.

'So you had a holiday!'

Maybe he should have taken off his shoes and
socks and paddled, thought Charlie: wasn't seawater
supposed to be good for painful feet? He said: 'It was
not a holiday.'

'I shall require a full, written report.'

'I know the regulation.'

'And the fullest receipted support for all
expenses.'

'Actually I was surprised how expensive everything was,' said Charlie, just to antagonize the other

188

man. The air balloon was closer now and Charlie saw it was advertising what was described as a revolutionary new chocolate bar. He wondered if the centre would be hard, like his mother always demanded.

'Everything is to be receipted,' repeated Harkness.

'What's the latest medical report on Sir Alistair Wilson?' asked Charlie, with open disrespect.

'I don't consider it proper to engage in that sort of conversation with you,' refused Harkness.

Asshole, thought Charlie.

'He was openly insolent! Challenging me!' complained the acting Director General.

'He's arrogant,' concurred Witherspoon. 'And it's going to be his arrogance that will be his undoing.'

'One slip,' Harkness promised himself vehemently. 'That's all he needs to make. Just one slip.'

22

Today it would all be over. After today he could put
it all behind him: try to forget about it. That it ever
happened. Emil Krogh stopped the run of thought,
physically shaking his head as he took the sliproad
off the Bay Shore Freeway and started negotiating
the narrow streets towards the final meeting with the
Russian. Krogh knew he'd never be able to imagine it
hadn't happened. It would always be with him, somewhere in his mind. How people would have laughed
at him, sneering, calling him things like a horny old
goat if it had ever come out about the girls: getting
dumped from the company and dumped by Peggy.
Krogh shuddered at the horror of what might have
been. He'd done the only sensible, possible thing.
Thank God it was all over at last: the end of a
bad dream. Now it was clearing up time, Krogh
determined, positively. Barbara would be out of
the apartment in a week or two, so he could sell
that. Sell her car, too. Soon – next week maybe –
he'd kiss off Cindy and dispose of everything in Los
Angeles. Stop being a stupid son-of-a-bitch and settle
down with Peggy. He'd come damned close to falling
right off the edge of the cliff and it wasn't going to
happen again.

Krogh detected the green of McLaren Park ahead
and started looking for a parking meter. He tried
on Burrows, which would have put him close to the
entrance he wanted, but there were no spaces so he
had to make the turn on to Felton, where he was
lucky. He hesitated, putting the money in, unsure
how much time he needed. Not long, he decided:
there was nothing he had to say to Petrin except

goodbye and it would only take a second to do that and part with the last of the blueprints. Over, he thought again: finished. Krogh paid for half an hour and walked back towards the park, entering through the gate Petrin had designated and finding the bench where he had been told to sit. He did so, staring around, wondering who or where the watchers were who always ensured the meetings were safe. There were a lot of people about, strolling or walking dogs or jogging. There were a group of kids playing bad baseball on a makeshift diamond over to his right and Krogh thought he heard the crack of an iron against a golf ball but guessed he must have been mistaken because the municipal course was some way away, too far for the sound to have carried.

When Petrin approached it was from the direction of the course. Krogh saw the man early, walking without any apparent urgency or recognition, not even when he got quite close. When Petrin reached the bench he sat with his legs thrust out and head tilted slightly back, so that his face was to the sun.

'This is the sort of day that makes you feel good to be alive, isn't it?' clichéd the Russian.

'I guess so,' said Krogh. It *was* a good day but Krogh knew the way he felt came more from this being the last meeting between them. He hadn't warned the other man and was looking forward to making the announcement.

'So how are things?' said Petrin conversationally.

'From today they're going to be terrific,' said Krogh.

Petrin straightened slightly, looking sideways at the American. 'How's that?'

Instead of replying Krogh took the package from inside his jacket and handed it along the bench. He said: 'Here it is. The last one.' There was a feeling of satisfaction, but not as much as he'd expected.

Petrin came fully upright now. 'You mean I've got' it all! There's no more?'

'Nothing,' declared Krogh. 'We're through.' He had a sudden urge to give Petrin some idea of how he felt towards him, like telling the man to kiss his ass or go fuck himself or something.

'Ah!' exclaimed Petrin, a strange sound of contentment. He pocketed the envelope and said: 'I've been waiting for this moment.'

'Not as much as I have,' said Krogh. He wouldn't foul-mouth the man. He just wanted to get away, end it. He actually started to move but Petrin reached out, putting a restraining hand on his arm.

'Wait a moment, Emil,' said the Russian. 'There's something we have to talk about.'

'No there's not,' insisted Krogh. 'I've told you. You've got it all.'

'But that's the problem, you see? We haven't,' smiled Petrin.

Krogh settled back on the bench, looking nervously at the other man. 'What do you mean?'

'Exactly what you told me, all those weeks back. That we *don't* have it all, not without the British contribution.'

'I can't do anything about that: I gave you all that I had from Britain.'

'We've been thinking about that,' said Petrin easily. 'And we decided there is something you can do. Quite a lot, in fact. We want you to go to England and get all the stuff we're missing. You can do that for us, can't you, Emil?'

Krogh stared along the park bench, his mouth hanging open, unable to form any coherent thought. When he spoke it was weakly, like a sick man still not recovered from his illness. 'No!' he said, a mixture of fear and incredulity in his voice. 'No, I can't do that! That's stupid! Impossible.'

'No it isn't,' soothed Petrin. 'We've worked it all out: decided exactly how it will be done. You're a trained draughtsman, so you can understand drawings. And you can reproduce them. You're the chairman of the major manufacturing company here, in America. So you've every right to ask to see whatever is being done in England. And you've got the highest security clearance, so there can't be any difficulty with access. It's really childishly simple. Perfect.'

'No,' said Krogh, a man backing away. 'Please, no.'

'There's no other way,' insisted Petrin.

'I won't do it!' said Krogh in a pitiful attempt at belated bravery. 'I've finished! Done all I'm going to do! Finished!'

'Let's not get into a dispute,' sighed Petrin.

'Go to hell.'

'You can't refuse, Emil. You know that.'

'I don't care about all you've got on the girls,' lied Krogh.

Petrin sighed again. 'You know something, Emil? I really don't want to go back to Russia: to leave California, where you get days like this, when you feel good to be alive.'

'What the hell are you talking about now?'

'Got something else to show you,' said Petrin, taking a wad of photographs from an outer pocket of his jacket. 'Good selection, don't you think?'

Krogh stared down, shuffling with shaking hands through the photographs of himself and Petrin at their various hand-over meetings in and around San Francisco. At every location there was at least one shot of Krogh clearly passing across a package, just like he had that morning. 'What's this?' he said, groping for understanding.

'What do you think it is?'

'I know *what* it is: what they show. What's the point you're trying to make?'

193

'Not trying, Emil. *Making*,' stressed Petrin. 'You really see what they show? These are photographs of one of America's leading defence contractors, a man who made the cover of *Newsweek*, passing to an identifiable KGB officer all the details of America's intended Strategic Defence Initiative. You any idea how embarrassing it could be, if the authorities ever had access to these! They make whatever there was with Barbara and Cindy look like kid's stuff. Think of it, Emil. Think of the arrest and the trial and being put into some jail for about a thousand years. And it would be about a thousand years, wouldn't you say? Because if Washington knew the Soviet Union had the details then the Strategic Defence Initiative would be dead, wouldn't it? They'd have to start all over again. And that just wouldn't cost *billions*: that would cost tens of billions. I'd bet you that the President and the Administration would be so mad their eyes would pop. I know all about the judiciary being independent of the government but don't you think a word would be dropped here and there to the judges, to make sure an example was made . . .'

'Stop it!' tried Krogh desperately.

'Not just yet,' refused Petrin. 'I want you to think it through very fully. Can you conceive what it would be like, in a jail? All the violence? The homosexuality: male rapes, things like that? The filth and the stink? Everything sub-human.'

'I said stop it!'

'That's what I mean about not wanting to go back to Russia,' carried on Petrin, as if the other man hadn't spoken. 'If we can't get what we want and decide to wreck the Star Wars programme a different way, letting Washington know what we've got and who we got it from, it means I'd have to be safely returned to Moscow ahead of the revelation, so I couldn't be arrested. . .' Artificially the Russian

194

stretched his legs and put his face to the sun again. 'You any idea what the Russian winters are like, Emil? It gets cold enough there to freeze the balls off a statue. Much nicer here.'

'It won't work!'

'Yes it will.'

'It's the whole point of splitting the project up: a part of the security, to avoid anyone knowing the full picture!'

'But not to keep it from you, because you're special: you're the man who negotiated everything with the Pentagon. Who's every right to know all that's going on.'

Krogh, a drowning man snatching for straws, imagined he saw a passing, drifting chance of survival. 'It won't be my fault if I make the approach and I'm refused.' He wouldn't even bother, he decided. He'd let some time pass and tell Petrin he'd been denied access.

'It would be sad though, wouldn't it?' suggested Petrin mildly. 'We wouldn't have any choice then, would we? We'd have to disclose these photographs anyway to ensure Washington knew the programme was compromised and force them to rethink the whole thing. Billions, like I said: tens of billions.'

'Oh Jesus!' said Krogh despairingly.

'So you will do it, won't you Emil?'

'I'll try.'

'No,' lectured Petrin. 'You won't try: you'll *do* it. You understand what I'm saying?'

'Yes,' said Krogh numbly.

'I knew you would,' said Petrin encouragingly. 'You want to take those photographs as a reminder, like the stuff involving Barbara and Cindy?'

'Get them away from me!'

'I've never been to England, although I hear the weather won't be like it is here.'

195

'What?'

'England,' said Petrin. 'I'll be coming with you. Not on the same aircraft or anything like that, but I'll be in England while you're there, so you'll have a friend all the time. We think it's best to keep liaison with someone you know: you'd like that, wouldn't you?'

'You're a shit!' erupted Krogh. 'A complete and utter shit.'

'No I'm not,' disputed Petrin unoffended. 'I'm a Soviet intelligence officer successfully carrying out an important assignment.'

'You know what I'd like to do to you!'

'Forget it, Emil,' cautioned Petrin, still unperturbed. 'You're too old and too slow. And what would it prove anyway? Stop trying to behave like someone in those old black and white movies they show on late-night television.'

'Bastard!'

'There's something else I've got to tell you,' said Petrin, proving the accusation. 'You certainly can pick a piece of ass. That Barbara was the best fuck I've had for ages. . .much better than Cindy, I thought. Did I ever tell you that Cindy calls you her Daddy?'

When Krogh returned to his car there was a parking ticket fluttering from the windscreen wiper. It was white, like a flag of surrender.

There was the backlog of In-Tray traffic, as there always was after an absence from the office, and it built up for a further two days while Charlie did what he considered necessary after the Isle of Wight investigation. Which involved invoking special friendships. The man's name was William French. He was an electronics expert in the department's Technical Division and he owed Charlie for covering up a bungled radio interception during a Soviet

Foreign Ministry visit to London a year before. The man complained it wasn't going to be easy, and Charlie said nothing was. Then he said that because of the personal approach he assumed it was unofficial and Charlie agreed that it was, for the moment. French said he would do his best and Charlie said he was grateful. Only then, with meticulous care, did Charlie get around to composing the report to comply with Harkness' regulations.

It was not until the third day of his return to the London office that Charlie began on the official publications, but because it was quite close to the top of the pile he found the reference to Natalia's forthcoming visit to England within the first hour. It was in the English-language *Morning Star*, with a photograph of the entire Soviet delegation. Natalia was wearing a suit she'd worn in an earlier photograph of the Canadian trip, severe and businesslike, with her hair different from the earlier photographs, lighter against her head this time. Charlie thought she looked wonderful.

Charlie knew at once what he was going to do. He was going to be with Natalia again!

23

Vitali Losev was a greatly disappointed man. From being at the very centre of a major assignment, with all the personal benefits emanating from it, he now believed himself shunted aside on to its periphery, relegated to the role of a messenger boy. Certainly there'd been the congratulatory cable from Berenkov in Moscow, praising him for locating someone called Charlie Muffin. And there seemed to be some importance attached to the identification, from the activity that had followed. But Losev knew that obtaining the space information had been what really mattered: that would have been the prize to earn the recorded commendations. The prize and commendations denied him because of the idiotic Blackstone, an idiot he still had to humour and befriend, according to the inexplicable instructions from Moscow.

Losev bitterly accepted he had lost out completely to Alexandr Petrin, who was flying in triumphantly from the United States to remain the case officer on everything: case officer on the American and case officer responsible for the missing material. Leaving him on the sidelines. *A support function.* Those were the precise words in the instructions from Dzerzhinsky Square. What did a support function and all the other chores accompanying it mean other than he was a messenger boy!

Losev felt a burn of frustration. A messenger boy, and there was nothing he could do to reverse or change the position. Worse, he guessed he could be relieved even of that menial role – although he was head of the London *rezidentura* – if he made the slightest mistake, because Moscow had made it frighteningly clear that no error or oversight would be permitted. So he had to continue obediently in his subsidiary support position, a bystander to others gaining the glory he'd once seen to be his. *Deserved* to be his.

Dismayed though he was by the twist of events, Losev remained too professional to allow his despair to affect what he had to do, peripheral or lowly though he considered it to be. He personally supervised the imposed surveillance upon Charlie Muffin, monitoring the Vauxhall apartment and the journeys to and from Westminster Bridge Road and to a pub on the Thames embankment called The Pheasant and to a mews house in Chelsea which the convenient Voters' Register showed to be owned by a Mr and Mrs Paul Nolan.

And when Berenkov's specific instructions arrived, Losev again took personal charge, rehearsing everything that had to be accomplished before moving.

The entry into the Vauxhall flat and what had to be deposited there was obviously the essential part of the operation so Losev decided that was where his presence had to be. He divided the operatives into two groups, himself with the KGB break-in team in one, six field officers in the other. They stayed together on the Thursday morning outside the Vauxhall block until Charlie left, to be picked up at once by the field officers. They, in turn, divided again. Three rotated foot surveillance on Charlie while the others followed to Westminster Bridge Road in a radio-transmitter-equipped car from which they could warn Losev, wearing an ear-piece receiver, if Charlie left the headquarters building with the possibility of returning to Vauxhall before the break-in squad completed what they had to do.

Such was the degree of caution Losev observed, although what had to be accomplished inside Charlie's flat was not going to take a great deal of time, because like everything else Losev had planned ahead.

Losev insisted his team remain in their cars until he got the message that Charlie had entered the office building. And then initially he dispatched only one lock-picking expert into the apartment block, unwilling to risk arousing the suspicion of another resident or a caretaker with the entry of any larger group. The rest entered at staged, five-minute intervals: Losev was the first, so he could supervise everything when they arrived inside the flat to ensure their entry and departure remained completely undetected.

Individual responsibilities had been assigned before they'd left the embassy. The locksmith's function finished with the actual entry, although the man remained just inside the door and alert for any outside activity, like an attempted entry by a cleaner or a services inspector, such as a meter reader. Against any such surprise the man began fitting rubber wedges beneath the door and rubber-cushioned clamps at the two top corners. Another positioned himself at once at the window overlooking the street, a guard against the unexpected return of Charlie Muffin if the man succeeded in leaving Westminster Bridge Road unseen by the observers in the radio car. The third man, Andrei Aistov, was to work with Losev. Before they began Losev warned the inside group not to touch or disturb anything that didn't need to be touched.

'Although it would hardly matter,' he said, gazing around the disordered room. 'This place is more like some sort of nest than a home.'

'What's so important about this man?' queried Aistov.

Losev shrugged. 'Something we haven't been told.' Messenger boy, he thought again bitterly. 'Let's get started.'

'Where?' asked Aistev.

'The bedroom,' said Losev at once. 'That's where people hide money they shouldn't have.'

The station chief followed Aistov from the living room. It was Aistov who found the place in the skirting board, a break in the panelling where an additional piece of wood had been inserted to complete the length running along the wall against which the bed and a small dressing table abutted.

'I don't want the slightest mark.'

Aistov looked up sourly. 'There aren't going to be any.'

The man lay full length on the floor, the bed eased carefully away to allow him room to work. The fill-in boarding was held in place by four screws. Aistov worked patiently but surely, testing the resistance of each fastening before unscrewing it, not wanting the screwdriver to slip and noticeably score the screwhead. He had trouble with only one screw but he was able to release it by gently tapping the screwdriver handle, jarring it loose. Behind, when the panel came free, there was a hollowed gap about six inches deep.

'Perfect,' assessed Aistov. From his pocket he took £1,000, all in £50 notes and all contained in a Russian-manufactured envelope, together with one of the keys to the safe-custody facility in King William Street. After feeling around, to guarantee there were no unseen holes or spaces down which the cache could drop and be lost, he placed everything carefully inside. He said: 'It could be a terrible waste of money.'

'Moscow's loss,' reminded Losev.

Aistov replaced the panelling with the care with which he'd taken it out and stood back for Losev's examination. The man lay as close as Aistov had, gazing intently not just at the metal screws but at the disturbed wood, finally straightening up and nodding. 'A good job,' he praised.

From the bedroom Losev and Aistov went directly into Charlie's cluttered kitchen. They found the electric meter in a cupboard alongside an overcrowded sink and Losev stood back while the other man squeezed in to dismantle a casing panel as gently as he'd worked earlier in the bedroom.

'Is there sufficient room?' asked Losev, unable from where he stood to see past the other KGB man.

'Just,' guessed Aistov. From his pocket the man took the one-time cipher pad and taped it tightly against the inside of the casing section, hefting it in his hand to gauge the additional thickness he had created. Satisfied, he inched it back into its housing, cautious to avoid the obstruction interfering with the working mechanism. It went home without any halting blockage and as he tightened the butterfly screws to secure it into position Aistov said to his supervisor: 'This will bring it even further from any moving parts.'

'Let's be sure,' insisted Losev. Still unable to squeeze into the meter cupboard himself, the *rezident* gazed around the kitchen, seeking a site for the third item to be left in Charlie's flat, smiling as the ideal spot presented itself.

'It's fine,' came a muffled voice. 'The dial arms are revolving exactly as they should.'

'Let me see,' insisted Losev.

The technician stood back to give Losev room. The *rezident* squinted at the unmarked meter, wrinkling his nose at the damp, undersink smells of the space into which he was jammed, offended by them. The arms spun around the faces of the dials, as the technician had assured him they did.

Losev backed out and said: 'It's all going remarkably easily.'

'Why shouldn't it?' asked Aistov. 'What about the micro-dot?'

Losev pointed to the calendar on the inside of the kitchen door: the illustration for this month was a nakedly splayed, hugely busted woman with a wisp of chiffon draped to conceal her sex.

Aistov said: 'I've never known a woman with a body like that.'

'Not many men have,' agreed Losev. 'You choose: what month?'

'August,' decided Aistov. He hesitated. Then he said: 'The second Friday: it's my mother's birthday.'

This time Losev did the work. He carried everything in a box that fitted easily into his jacket pocket. He extracted it and settled at the kitchen table for the initial preparation. He took the dot from its protective plastic container with the special pointed-arm tweezers which he held in his left hand to apply the adhesive with the single-fibre brush in his right. When he nodded that he was ready Aistov took down the calendar and turned to the month of August. His hand trembling slightly from the concentrated strain, Losev lowered the dot to fit in the spot designated by his companion: it did so perfectly. Losev tamped it firmly into position and Aistov hung it back on the door. Losev stood back about two yards and said: 'It's absolutely undetectable.'

The breasts of the August pin-up were less pendulous but her sex was quite visible. Aistov said: 'I prefer this one.'

'Could be mother and daughter,' said Losev. 'Let's put it back like it was.'

Aistov returned the calendar to its original reading and followed the *rezident* back into the main room. The locksmith was at his post near the door and the other man was at the window, as they had left him. To the locksmith Losev said: 'Free the door; it's time to go.'

They left as they'd arrived, one by one, Losev being the last to be sure everything was secured and left exactly as it has been when they entered.

The message and the time of the promised call-back were waiting for Losev when he reached the embassy. He responded at once, forcing the unavoidable anger back as he drove through Kensington to the 'safe' house and its telephone which Blackstone had as his contact point.

'Did he give any indication of what he wanted?' Losev demanded at once from the duty telephone clerk.

The man shook his head. 'Just that it had to be you. And that it was important.'

'I'll believe it when I hear it,' said Losev.

Blackstone came on to the line precisely on time. He insisted he had been completely re-accepted as a loyal employee. When Losev pressed, the man said he hadn't heard but that he was still confident of being taken on to the secret project: if he didn't hear in a week he was going directly to ask for a reply.

'So it's looking hopeful?' said Losev. The friendliness was difficult. There was nothing new or important in anything the man had said.

'I think so. Certainly,' said the eager Blackstone.

'I'm very pleased. So will other people be,' said Losev.

'I was wondering. . .' started Blackstone and then stopped. He was doubling his horse-racing bets now and hadn't won for weeks.

'Wondering what?'

'This is just a setback, right? We're still going to go on together?'

'Of course we are,' assured Losev. 'I've got some

news for you. There's consideration being given to some sort of basic retainer, on the weeks when there isn't anything positive.'

'You really mean that!' snatched Blackstone.

'I'm still awaiting the final approval.'

'I'd be so grateful! You can't imagine how grateful!'

'Just keep in touch,' ordered Losev, reciting the instructions he'd been ordered by Berenkov to relay. 'At the moment nothing is guaranteed but it looks promising.'

'I'll do my best for you,' said Blackstone anxiously. 'I promise I will.'

Whether or not the British had broken the entrapping Soviet code had to be conveniently monitored and witnessed, so Berenkov set both up for London.

The first genuine Soviet espionage emplacement to be sacrificed was a dead-letter drop in the no longer used part of Highgate cemetery. It was a split-apart and sagging vault less than two hundred yards from Karl Marx's tomb. For a year it had been the undiscovered depository for minimally useful ship movement memoranda leaked by an Admiralty clerk, whom Berenkov also judged to be dispensable. Berenkov identified Highgate by acknowledging in code to the Russian embassy in London the importance of what they were receiving through it. Within twenty-four hours, fully observed by an undetected Soviet squad, the British set up their surveillance and twenty-four hours after that arrested the unwitting Admiralty clerk who was much later to be sentenced to eight years' imprisonment.

The second test involved a supposed Cuban businessman who was, in fact, a courier for the Dirección General de Inteligencia. Berenkov knew the man would be carrying a terrorist-customer list for Czech arms on a flight from London's Heathrow airport to Havana because Berenkov had ensured the delivery of the list, which was out of date anyway, to the Cuban embassy in London. On this occasion, in the same code, Berenkov cabled London on the value of the information being carried and supposedly ordered that any assistance sought should be given. Once more the airport seizure was witnessed by the watching Russians. The courier was not technically carrying anything illegal, for which he could have been arrested, but the terrorist list was seized on the grounds that it constituted information potentially useful to an enemy.

The code used by Berenkov for the two exchanges was the simple letter-transposed-for-figure cipher that the KGB's Technical Division had devised specifically for Berenkov. And which had been faithfully recorded on the micro-dot now attached to the girlie calendar in Charlie's apartment.

In Moscow Berenkov, satisfied that his code had been intercepted and broken, insisted on celebratory champagne and when Valentina asked what they were celebrating he said the very successful progress of an operation that was going to prove the advantage of sometimes acting audaciously.

In London Richard Harkness was equally ecstatic at their having penetrated a new Russian communication system although he didn't consider champagne because he never touched alcohol of any sort.

Both of what Harkness believed to. be intelligence successes had been commanded by Hubert Witherspoon. He didn't drink, either, so his celebration went unmarked as well.

24

William French, the electronics expert in the Technical Division, returned the favour sooner than Charlie had expected and Charlie knew he should have felt satisfied and vindicated but he didn't because things weren't sitting neatly in his mind, like he wanted them to sit. And there was a further uncomfortable dichotomy, an intrusion into his professional life by what he wanted privately to achieve by a reunion with Natalia. Which he quickly accepted was hardly a dichotomy at all because in these circumstances it was virtually impossible to differentiate between professional and private considerations.

He still tried.

Harkness was suddenly and unexpectedly leaving him alone, but realistically Charlie knew he couldn't rely on that continuing throughout the time Natalia was scheduled to be in London. And that he had therefore to remove absolutely the possibility of Harkness imposing another meaningless chore which risked keeping him apart from her.

The answer appeared easy and Charlie wished everything else was. From the information already released from Moscow he knew that Natalia was part of the delegation attending the Farnborough Air Show. And the Farnborough Air Show ran for a prescribed week in September. Still with three weeks' official leave due to him, Charlie filed the memorandum to Personnel and to Harkness requesting the entire period, to run before and after the show, to provide him with contingency time at either end and keep the period she would be in England sacrosanct from any interruption.

It was not difficult, either, to discover the hotel at which the Russian support staff were staying. A Permanent Secretary at the Foreign Office had earlier in his career been a cultural attaché at the British embassy in Budapest, where Charlie had prevented the embarrassment of an injudicious involvement with an Hungarian secretary. The grateful diplomat returned Charlie's call within twenty-four hours and said why didn't he try the Blair, slightly off the Bayswater Road. Just to be sure Charlie checked with an Inspector in the Special Branch Protection Unit, who confirmed the hotel while Charlie was still on the telephone.

Again Charlie allowed himself time at either end of the air-show week, reserving a day ahead and two days after the planned duration of the Russian visit. He followed up the telephone booking with a letter of confirmation and asked for confirmation in return, determined against anything going wrong.

And with conscious cynicism he continued to date Laura. He chose the weekend and rented a car and initially considered driving with her down to the Hampshire nursing home. But then changed his mind because when he telephoned ahead the matron said his mother hadn't come out of the relapse and wouldn't know he was there anyway. Instead they drove into Sussex and found a pub with oak beams and no slot machines or piped music in the bar.

On the way down Laura said Harkness appeared excited by the first major coup since his appointment as acting Director General but admitted she didn't know what it was because at the moment it was restricted to verbal reports to the Joint Intelligence Committee with the Cabinet Secretary taking the formal, four-copy-only notation.

'It's got to be important then?' queried Charlie curiously.

'Harkness seems to think so. Oh, I forgot! Wither-spoon is involved somehow.'

Charlie waited until they got to the pub before trying to resolve an uncertainty that had grown worryingly in his mind since the investigation on the Isle of Wight, directly asking Laura if she thought Harkness was still targeting him.

Laura frowned and said: 'Not at this actual moment: he's too caught up in this other thing, whatever it is. Why?'

'I just wondered,' said Charlie uncomfortably. He didn't like making mistakes, ever.

'Why so serious all of a sudden? You don't normally let it depress you.'

'No reason,' lied Charlie. Shit, he thought: he wasn't getting the sort of feedback he wanted.

'This is all pretty solemn for a dirty weekend in the country!' Laura complained brightly. 'Can't we forget the department, just for a little while?'

Charlie made the effort, which wasn't easy, but Laura seemed content enough. They ate pheasant for dinner and drank their coffee in the chimney inglenook and the bed had an old-fashioned feather mattress into which they sank, like snow. There were fresh eggs for breakfast, which was a reminder of the Isle of Wight which Charlie didn't need.

Laura gave a mew of disappointment when Charlie suggested returning to London in the morning, so he compromised and stopped for lunch on the way. They still reached Chelsea by mid-afternoon and Laura said why didn't they lounge about for the rest of the day reading the Sunday papers and why didn't he stay the night. Charlie said that would have been fine but there were things he had to do, and they made arrangements to get together some time during the week.

Back at the Vauxhall flat Charlie sat thinking for a

long time, until it became night and grew completely dark inside the living room. He finally put on the light and said to himself: 'You're slipping, my son! And when you slip you end up flat on your ass.'

It was very late before Charlie went to bed because when he finished doing the things he had to do he spent a long time thinking again. In the morning he was late for work, because he stopped for an hour on the way, but Harkness wasn't looking for him so he was not called upon to explain.

The Soviet observation of Charlie was established as a twenty-four hour rotating duty, nominally under the supervision of a KGB officer named Viktor Nikov. The man was on duty that Sunday night outside Charlie's flat. He said to his companion: 'Jobs like this really piss me off.' He suspected Losev had appointed him because of some personal animosity, although he couldn't decide the reason.

'How much longer?' asked the other man.

'I wish I knew,' said Nikov, with feeling.

Because the Blair was the designated hotel for the Russian party there was official justification for Losev's request to the management for a list of other registrations for the same period.

And Alexei Berenkov felt another flush of euphoria at the news of Charlie's reservation. Everything was unfolding as he intended it should: absolutely everything!

25

The physical reaction to what he was being forced to do began with Emil Krogh more than a week before his London flight. Some nights he did not sleep at all and on others he was always awake by three in the morning to lie, sweating with unformed fears, until it became light enough for him to get up. And then he was invariably sick, retching over the toilet pan until he couldn't be sick any more and then dry heaving until his eyes ran and his stomach and chest ached from the empty convulsions. He and Peggy slept in different beds and had their own separate bathrooms, but he still expected his wife to notice something, to make some remark, but she didn't. She had half suggested that she travel to England with him but he pointedly refused to pick up on the idea and she didn't press it, which was a small relief, but so small he instantly forgot it.

At Petrin's insistence they met for a final briefing session in the park again, although nearer the golf course this time. For once the Russian was prompt, arriving practically as soon as Krogh sat down.

'You're not looking any better,' accused Petrin at once.

So today there wasn't going to be any legs-spread relaxation and patronizing crap about the Californian weather. Krogh said: 'I'm all right.' For weeks, long before the sleeplessness, he'd tried to imagine a way out, and the previous night, puddled in perspiration, he'd realized that suicide would be an escape: he'd had to get up earlier than usual to be sick.

'You break down and everything goes,' warned Petrin.

'I'm not going to break down. I said I'm OK.'

'I'm going to London ahead of you,' announced Petrin. 'Everything will be ready for you when you arrive.'

'How do we contact each other?' asked Krogh dully.

'Where's your hotel reservation?'

'The Connaught.'

'Just check in and wait. I'll already be there.'

'After making sure it's safe?' said Krogh, in an attempt at a sneer that failed.

'Of course after making sure it's safe: you should be grateful,' said Petrin. 'That's why the way you look concerns me: the only thing you've got to be frightened of is yourself.'

'I keep telling you I'm all right.' Dear God how he wished that were true: increasingly he felt suspended from reality, like he'd felt sometimes when he was very drunk or when he'd smoked one of the special joints that Cindy rolled. He hadn't bothered to contact her, not even a telephone call, for nearly three weeks now. He decided not to, before he went to England. Maybe he never would again, just walk away and leave her, forget about the condo and the car. That's what he wanted to do, walk away and forget about everything and everyone.

'What do the British say?'

'That they're looking forward to meeting me,' said Krogh reluctantly. That had been another straw he'd attempted to clutch, the hope that the British would refuse to cooperate with him. But the Russian had anticipated his trying to hide that way and warned he would want to see any rejection letter. Which there hadn't been anyway so Krogh hadn't tried to lie.

'What about here?'

212

Krogh shrugged. 'Here I make the rules,' he said. It sounded conceited but wasn't. He'd announced his intention at the last directors' meeting and his father-in-law had seized upon it at once and launched into a speech about devotion to work and to the company and he'd gone along with it, thinking: If only they knew, if only they knew.

'So!' said Petrin, forcefully. 'If I'm going to get everything ready I've got to know what you want.'

Krogh gave another listless shrug. 'I don't really know, until I get there.'

Petrin sighed. 'The basics,' he insisted. 'Tell me what you're bound to need.'

'A drawing office, I suppose,' said Krogh simply. 'A board. All instruments. . .' He turned to the Russian, on the bench beside him. 'I don't see how this is going to work!' he said in weak protest. 'I could need to make dozens of drawings: I'm not going to be able to absorb and memorize everything in one visit. Not enough to re-create it *all*!'

Petrin turned too, to stare back at him. 'You're going to have to, Emil. And if you can't memorize it in one visit you're going to have to go again. And keep going until you *do* get it all. There's no choice about this: no choice at all.'

Krogh felt sick again, the familiar sensation, and swallowed against it. He said: 'That's all I can think of needing, at the moment. Anything else will have to wait until I get there and see the sort of work involved.'

'You keep a grip on yourself, you hear?'

It was the tone of voice he'd used towards Joey and Peter when they'd played up as kids, Krogh recognized. But he didn't feel any resentment: he didn't feel anything at all. All those sorts of attitude towards the other man – resentment and hatred and

contempt – were past now. There was only an emptiness, like a vacuum. There *were* ways to kill yourself,
without pain. Sleeping pills. A length of hose from
an exhaust pipe. The idea this time didn't bring the
stomach jump like it had during the night. He said:
'I'll see you in London.'

Petrin drove straight from McLaren Park to the
airport. He was one of those lucky travellers who
found it easy to sleep on aircraft and he did so,
soundly. It was a polar flight that landed in England
by mid-morning and he arrived feeling completely
rested. Any visit to the Soviet embassy was precluded
by the known permanent, twenty-four-hour watch
maintained upon it by British counter-intelligence.
Petrin went instead to the hotel where Krogh was
booked, remaining only long enough to register in
and unpack. Professionally cautious, Petrin rejected
the idea of a taxi. Instead he indulged himself by
circling the block to go through Grosvenor Square
and past the US embassy to reach Hyde Park, walking its full width to the bisecting park road before
cutting up towards the restaurant overlooking the
Serpentine lake. He made several checks as he did
so, ensuring there were no followers.

In the restaurant he did not take a seat, although
confirming there was a table reservation. Instead he
stood at the bar until Losev entered, staying expressionless until the man reached him. Petrin thought
he detected a reserve in the other man's greeting, but
conceded at once it could have been a misconception.

'The beer's warm,' Petrin cautioned.

'It frequently is in England,' said Losev. 'You get
used to it. There wasn't any need for the precautions
you took getting here: you were protected.'

Petrin was curious at the other man's need to boast
of the guarding observation: annoyed, too, that he
hadn't detected it, which he should have done. He

214

said: 'That's comforting to know.'

'How's your man?'

'Shaky,' admitted Petrin. 'Showing signs of the strain, which is pretty considerable.'

'He's not going to collapse, is he?'

'I don't think so: he knows what would happen if he did. There's a lot to be done before he arrives.'

A support role, thought Losev at once, bitterly: the other man's attitude was very much superior to subordinate. He said: 'Like what?'

'I want the equivalent of a complete drawing office: all conceivable equipment and instruments and a place where he can work without interruption. Can you manage that?'

I want, isolated Losev. And *can you manage that*, like it was some junior initiative test. He said, with some exaggeration: 'Of course. We have a completely secure house unknown to the British authorities quite near here, in Kensington.'

'What about equipping it?'

'Do you know precisely what he'll need?'

Instead of replying Petrin handed over the list he had composed at the beginning of the overnight flight, before sleeping.

Losev glanced at it, hot with irritation. He thought: Run, little messenger boy, run. He said: 'I'll organize it today.'

'Any change in the situation of the man you've got inside the factory here?'

It was a gloating question, decided Losev. Exaggerating again, he said: 'Now he's been cleared there's the possibility of a transfer. Moscow consider him important.'

'How soon is the transfer to be?' punctured Petrin at once.

'There's no date,' Losev was forced to admit, discomfited.

'It would be good to have the insurance of a second source,' said Petrin objectively.

A waiter advised that their table was ready and both men sat and ordered before picking up the conversation. Petrin asked for the details of travelling to and from the Isle of Wight and what the factory was like, and asked Losev to inform Moscow of his arrival: everything really was politely requested but Losev inferred them as demands and felt further antagonism, giving short, clipped responses. They agreed to communicate daily through the number that Blackstone had, which was to a telephone in the safe house Losev intended setting up as Krogh's drawing office, and Losev said he would forward any queries from Moscow to Petrin's hotel using the same route.

Towards the end of the meal Petrin was sure he had not been mistaken about Losev's initial reserve or about the later hostility. Finally he said: 'Is something wrong?'

'Wrong?'

'I have the impression I've offended you in some way.'

'No,' denied Losev. 'I'm not offended about anything. How could I be?'

'That's what I couldn't understand.'

'Maybe you're tired after the flight.'

Petrin gazed steadily at the London station chief across the tiny, window-side table. 'Maybe I am,' he agreed. Then he said: 'I don't think anything should be allowed to endanger what we've got to achieve, do you?'

'That remark is incomprehensible to me.'

'It means that we should work together,' said Petrin.

'I don't imagine it being any other way,' said Losev stiffly.

216

'Good,' said Petrin. 'I wouldn't like it to be any other way.'

Charlie caught Laura on the pavement outside the office. As soon as she saw him her face opened into a smile but Charlie didn't smile back. Bluntly he said: 'I'm going to have to back out of the arrangement we made on Sunday. I'm sorry.'

Laura's expression faded. She said: 'Why don't we rearrange something for another evening?'

'Maybe not for a little while.'

'Oh,' she said. 'I see.'

'I think it would be best.'

'I told you a long time ago there wasn't any danger of it getting out of hand. Not on my part anyway.'

'I remember,' said Charlie.

'Is it anything I've done? Or said?'

'No.'

'So why?'

'I just think it's best, that's all.'

'I think I deserve an explanation at least.'

'I can't give you one, not yet. Maybe after I get back from holiday.'

'Or until you want to learn something you can't get from anyone else!'

He'd deserved that, Charlie accepted. He still wished she hadn't said it. 'I'm sorry,' he repeated.

'Me, too,' said Laura, turning abruptly and hurrying into the building.

Charlie gave her time to get the lift to the floor high above his office and then followed her in. *Would* he ever be able to give her an explanation, he wondered.

'He gave no reason?' demanded Harkness, who'd been disappointed for weeks with the titbits of gossip Laura passed on.

217

'None,' said the sad-faced girl.

'Maybe after he gets back from holiday,' repeated Harkness reflectively. 'What could that mean?'

'I don't know,' said Laura.

'But I'm going to try to find out,' said Harkness positively.

26

Natalia started to prepare herself for England a long time before the scheduled departure date, realizing practically at once the mistake she had made. She should have followed far more closely the lead of the other women on the previous overseas trips and better spent the allowance she received on Western clothes. She could have bought far more than she had that one shopping day in Washington and she hadn't bothered at all in Australia or Canada. And she was anxious to be chic all the time: chic and cosmopolitan, not insular and dowdy.

Like a child denying that a hoped-for event could ever occur in the fervent belief that the opposite would happen, Natalia told herself as she had since getting her new appointment that there was no chance of her encountering Charlie. All the old arguments paraded through her mind in the weeks leading up to the trip, the fors and the againsts, her own private search for a conclusion different from any she'd reached before. To start with Charlie was an overseas operative, not internal counter-intelligence, so it wouldn't be his department who monitored the Russian visit, as all Russian visits were monitored. So there was no way he could know of her presence in the country. Except that she had been an internally functioning officer and was now assigned overseas duties, so maybe he *would* have access. She told herself it would be too much to expect, if on the off-chance he *did* learn about her, that it would mean anything to him anyway. It had all seemed real – so *very* real – in Moscow but there was always the doubt that for him it had been anything more than an affair of the moment, a temporary refuge from loneliness. He had, after all, gone back, hadn't he? Gone back to whom? Charlie had talked of Edith and the way she'd died but there could have been another wife, a woman he *hadn't* talked about. Except, she balanced hopefully again, he *had* pleaded with her to run with him. He wouldn't have done that if there'd been another woman in England, would he? The pendulum swung back in the other direction, to another familiar reflection: there might not have been a woman then but what about now?

Whatever, Natalia still determined to make herself as attractive as possible, all the time she was there.

She spent days in the vast market place of the GUM store, picking over and rejecting and picking over once more. She went to the Western concessionary outlets available to her as a KGB officer, on Vernadskovo and Gertsana, and couldn't make up her mind about anything on the first visits so she went a second time. She finally bought another business suit and two dresses and two pairs of shoes. And when she modelled them for herself back at the Mytninskaya apartment Natalia decided she didn't really like any of them and wondered if she'd be able to shop in London early in the trip, rather than at the end which seemed to be the custom. She considered changing her hairstyle, taking it even shorter, but decided against it because she'd already shortened it from how it had been when she and Charlie were together and she didn't want to alter herself too much. She experimented in front of the mirror with different make-up, applying more than she customarily did, but rejected any change here and for the same reason.

A fortnight before the departure day she received a scrawled note from Eduard, nothing more than a notification of another leave allocated and that she

220

was to expect him home. The dates he gave clashed with those of her being in London and Natalia was relieved and ashamed at herself for the feeling. She wrote back immediately, saying that she was sorry but that she would be away for the entire period and got a response just as quickly from her son. He said it didn't matter but that he would still use Mytninskaya: if she were going away she wouldn't be needing the car, would she, so would she leave the keys somewhere prominent for him to pick up when he got there?

Natalia looked despairingly around her polished, pin-neat home and tried to imagine who Eduard might bring with him to an apartment he knew to be empty and what they would do once they got there. And physically shuddered at the thought. The day after receiving the second letter Natalia sat for an hour trying to compose a note to leave for Eduard, running the gamut from a mother disappointed to a mother pleading through to a mother demanding change. And then threw all the drafts away, guessing at best Eduard would laugh with his friends at her efforts or at worst do something stupid or disgusting or both, just to defy her.

A conference was called, for the last week, at which the delegation members were introduced to each other and they all had to sit through a lecture now familiar to Natalia on the expected behaviour of Russians engaged on overseas visits. The stress was upon absolute propriety, with no excessive drinking or exuberant, attention gaining embarrassments. At no time were they to forget they were representatives of the Union of Soviet Socialist Republics.

Natalia didn't count heads but it was clearly the largest contingent with which she had so far travelled. Idly she tried to isolate the KGB escorts appointed to impose the discipline about which they were being warned, and decided at once upon a fidgeting, hunch-shouldered little man who constantly chewed his fingernails and whose name she remembered to be Gennadi Redin. She guessed there would be two more, at least.

Although there would have been little reason for it, Natalia wondered throughout the build-up if there would be any summons from Berenkov, like before. But there wasn't and she felt relieved. There would have been nothing for them properly to discuss and the huge man made her feel uncomfortable.

Alexei Berenkov did consider a meeting with the woman. And it was because there was no valid reason for it – which would have been obvious to her – that he decided against it. With everything constructed just as he intended, an intricate house of matches with only two or three more tiny sticks to be added, the customarily irrepressible Berenkov was apprehensive now of anything happening to bring it all crashing down. It was absolutely essential that she remain the unknowing, unwitting bait, not someone allowed the slightest suspicion: he didn't want her protecting Charlie Muffin again, as he was convinced she had protected him once before.

He set out to create further protection, in fact, actually on the day Natalia attended her delegation meeting, going early into Dzerzhinsky Square to meet with Kalenin. Berenkov did not, however, come at once to the point. Characteristically he allowed himself the boast and announced the London confirmation of Charlie Muffin's reservation at the delegation hotel, adding at once their positive awareness of the British breaking the communication code. Wanting the concession from his doubting friend, Berenkov said: 'It is encouraging, don't you think?'

'Situations often look encouraging at the preliminary planning stage,' refused Kalenin. 'I would not say we were anywhere beyond preliminary planning at the moment, would you?'

'Yes!' came back Berenkov abruptly, his impatience with Kalenin finally spilling over. 'I consider we are a very long way past that stage.'

'You've combined the two operations, brought them too close together,' insisted the First Deputy. 'You've created a danger where there was no need for one to be created, Alexei. It worries me.'

'And you've made that obvious for a considerable time now,' said Berenkov. He realized that, incredibly, it was their first positive argument.

The awareness seemed to come to Kalenin at the same time. Sadly he said: 'This really does seem to be a period of great change, in everything, doesn't it?'

'I hope not in everything,' said Berenkov sincerely. He would regret losing the man's friendship absolutely: it was something to which he was accustomed, so accustomed that he took it for granted. Despite their increasing disagreements over this current assignment it came as a shock to think of any split between them being permanent.

'So do I, old friend,' said Kalenin, still sadly.

'I'm considering the safety of both of us today,' offered Berenkov, extending a threadbare olive branch.

'How?'

'Baikonur,' declared Berenkov simply. 'I think we should take out insurance against any more sniping from the scientists, like they tried to take out insurance against us by complaining over our heads to the Politburo Secretariat.'

'I'm interested,' said Kalenin, smiling slightly.

'Why don't we fully remove the threat of any attack from there?' suggested Berenkov. 'The fact they haven't complained since must mean they're satisifed with everything we got from America. Which we now know to be complete. And which only leaves what Krogh is due to get from England. Why don't we move Nikolai Noskov, who led the attack against us, and Guzins, who seemed a pretty enthusiastic and senior supporter, to England?'

'What!' exclaimed Kalenin, astonished.

'Send them to England,' repeated Berenkov. 'I could get them there easily enough, by circuitous routing and on false documentation. They could monitor and approve everything that Krogh produces, on the spot, before it gets here. That way – if anything is missed, if there is a problem we can't anticipate – the responsibility is theirs, as the experts. Not ours.'

'That's brilliant,' admired Kalenin, smiling more broadly and matching the other man's simplicity now. 'But Noskov is *the* Strategic Defence Initiative expert! We couldn't risk exposing him to Western detection. It would be unthinkable.'

'What's the greater risk, to ourselves?' demanded Berenkov, who had thought his argument through. 'Is it failing to get the Star Wars missile in its entirety? Or the minimal possibility of Noskov being detected?'

Kalenin shook his head doubtfully. 'It's an impossible equation,' he protested. 'Of course we can't risk failing to get everything. But the Politburo would never risk Noskov: minimal or not, the danger is too great.'

'Insurance!' insisted Berenkov, undeterred. 'Let the Politburo make the refusal, which affords us some lessening of responsibility. And then, if they do refuse, propose that Guzins, still an expert but of lesser importance, be sent instead. More insurance still.'

Kalenin shook his head but this time it was a

gesture continuing the earlier admiration. 'You've always frightened me with the chances you're prepared to take but sometimes you think like someone who's survived here in Dzerzhinsky Square and in Moscow all his life.'

'You're going to propose it?'

'Exactly as you've suggested it.'

'It's all going to work out fine: everything, I mean,' said Berenkov, sensing a slight reconciliation between them.

'I hope, Alexei,' said Kalenin, the doubt coming back up like a briefly lowered shield. 'I hope.'

Emil Krogh rationalized it all in his confused mind and it came out fine – well, nearly fine – and he was suffused by an enveloping calm, the first mental peace that he'd known since he couldn't remember when. Of course it wasn't perfect. There'd be the stigma of taking his own life when he was mentally disturbed but there'd be a lot of evidence about how hard he'd worked, and people sympathized with dedicated men who drove themselves over the edge like that, so there wasn't much to sneer about there. He worried for a while about the life insurance for Peggy, because that was negated by suicide. But he calculated that the insurance was really for the corporation anyway – for their loss of a dynamic chairman – rather than anything personal, for Peggy. With the Monterey estate paid for completely and the stock he owned on the open market, she'd be a millionairess twice over. And that before he took into account the stock options in the company itself, which totted up to another million and a half. He'd read carefully through the fine print of the pension agreement and was sure that would be unaffected, so the income would be more than enough for her to live on, without her having to cash in anything.

It would leave Cindy with the condo and the car, but he'd already said goodbye to that anyway: he didn't even think about Cindy or the property any more. Certainly there'd be no chance of what he'd done ever becoming public, because there was no gain in the Russians exposing the empty blackmail. And so he would have defeated them, after all. Finally fucked them like they'd fucked him, because without the British contribution they'd have nothing. And now they weren't going to get the British contribution.

Krogh considered for some time leaving a note, actually working out the rambling phrases in his mind, stuff about pressure of work and how he found it increasingly difficult to cope. But then he reckoned that made him appear weak and he didn't want any weakness being publicly discussed so he decided not to leave any message.

He took a lot of trouble, building up the stockpile of pills, driving for miles to different pharmacies to spread the purchases and avoid any challenge from a curious dispenser. And despite their separate sleeping arrangements he didn't set out to do it at home, where Peggy might have interrupted and screwed it all up by discovering him too quickly and getting medical help.

Instead he made the sort of overnight business trip excuse he'd used a hundred times before and Peggy accepted it without question, like she'd accepted it those hundred times before. Krogh set out without any positive direction, driving up from Monterey towards San Francisco. He found himself on the Bay View side so he crossed over the Oakland Bridge and recognized the surroundings because one of the meetings with Petrin had been this way, at a motel that really had had Hell's Angels motorcycles in the car park. And then Krogh thought: Why not? It would be his way of shoving up the middle finger to the Russians when they learned what had happened. He started to concentrate and found the motel again. This time there were no Hell's Angels bikes.

Krogh paid in full and in cash and the clerk asked with smiling expectancy if there were going to be anyone else joining him, and was clearly surprised when Krogh said there wasn't. From the earlier motorcycles and the question about company Krogh expected the cabins to be whorehouse dirty but they weren't. Everything was pressed-cardboard cheap but it was clean, the bedding fresh and with even an unbroken wrapper band over the toilet seat to prove it had been sanitized after the last occupant.

Krogh toured it all and looked at himself in the bathroom mirror, seeking something different in the image gazing back at him but finding nothing. Except that he *did* look like hell, as Petrin kept complaining: the carefully tucked skin seemed sagged, especially around his neck, and his eyes were watery and veined. Krogh wondered what sort of photograph the newspapers would use: he hoped it was one of the early ones from his publicity portfolio. They'd been a good set and he'd liked them.

Back in the bedroom Krogh looked about him uncertainly, not sure what to do next. How *did* you kill yourself? Just did it, he supposed. He unzipped the overnight bag and took out the pill bottles and stacked them neatly on the table beside the bed, like he'd stood his soldiers up as a kid. At the bottom of the bag there was the quart of Jack Daniels he'd brought as well, because he thought he remembered it was a more effective way to kill yourself, mixing pills and booze, and he figured he might need a little Dutch courage anyway. In fact he'd do just that: just a little nip by itself first, to relax him.

Krogh poured a stiff one in a wrapper-sealed bath-room glass, grimacing slightly as the liquor burned its way down, and thought he'd take a second by itself, because why not? He decided to undress, for no particular reason, neatly hanging his suit in the closet, and sitting on the edge of the crisp bed in his shorts, feeling quite calm about what he was going to do. Halfway through the second drink he began emptying the pills out on the side table, so that he wouldn't have to fumble with childproof stoppers when he got fuzzy-headed, and then thought what the hell was he waiting for? So he started taking them. He did it patiently, not shovelling handfuls into his mouth or anything silly like that; a pill, a sip of whisky, a positive swallow, then waiting a few seconds before taking another.

Soon after he started Krogh began to belch, as if he had indigestion. He stopped for a while, mouth clamped shut. He had expected to be feeling some effect by now, a drowsiness, but there was nothing. There appeared to be an enormous number of pills in front of him, a mountain range. He started again, slowly like before, but after two the whisky caught in his throat and he coughed and a lot came up, sour and bitter tasting. Krogh swallowed and got them down and waited longer this time. When he resumed again he was feeling something, nothing like positive sleep but a tingling numbness to the back of his hands and his cheeks.

He threw up just after that. Krogh tried desperately not to, biting his lips closed and cupping his hands in front of his face but he realized he couldn't hold it down and so he rushed to the bathroom. The damned wrapper-band got in the way and he didn't quite make it but didn't cause too much of a mess.

He didn't think he'd lost everything so there would still be some effect from the pills, and certainly the numbness hadn't gone. He'd clung to the toilet bowl in the end so he stayed on the floor, crawling back into the bedroom and propping himself against the bed edge. Had to start again; get it right on this attempt. He developed the same pattern as before, a pill, a sip, a pause, but there was no indigestion and he didn't feel nauseous and the heaviness came, his eyelids too full to keep open. Krogh fought against it, wanting to be sure, trying to maintain the routine, vaguely conscious of spilling the drink over himself and several times dropping a pill he couldn't find because it rolled away so that he had to fumble for another.

He wasn't aware of losing consciousness. His realization was rather of waking up, his head feeling as if it were stuffed with cotton wool, but knowing at once where he was and that he hadn't taken enough and had to do more. The whisky now was foul to taste and he gagged and it ran down his chin. On rubber legs he staggered into the bathroom to get water in a second glass and started swallowing the pills with that, which was better and although he was beyond counting he knew he'd taken a lot and then there was blackness again.

The retching brought him out of his unconsciousness once more, although that wasn't his immediate impression because there was a dream that he was ill, dying, and everyone was gathered around and people were saying what a wonderful man he had been and what a great loss it would be. He tried not to vomit in front of all the sympathetic visitors because it was disgusting but he couldn't stop himself and then he was somehow back in the bathroom, sprawled by the toilet which he hadn't reached soon enough. Krogh rolled over in his own filth, unable to move any more, unable to make his body do anything, drifting in and out of consciousness.

It was absolutely quiet when he finally awoke, nothing moving in the early morning stillness. Krogh was bitterly cold, shivering violently, and he felt like the death that he'd tried to achieve but knew he couldn't. He stayed lying where he was, tears sobbing from him at his complete, aching helplessness.

The men were clearly frightened to be called before him which was what Berenkov wanted because fear was a great guarantor of orders being strictly obeyed.

'Is it quite clear what you are to do?' he demanded.

The nervous Gennadi Redin, whose major's rank put him in charge of the KGB escorts accompanying the delegation to Britain, said: 'Whatever happens we are to do nothing whatsoever to interfere with Comrade Natalia Nikandrova? She is to be allowed to do whatever she chooses, without question or challenge.'

'Absolutely,' confirmed Berenkov. 'Whatever she chooses.'

27

It was three days after the failed suicide attempt –
almost four taking the overnight flight into account
– when Emil Krogh landed in London. He still felt
ghastly. And looked it, too. His face was grey and
even more sagged, his eyes rheumy and with an occasional apprehensive tic pulling at the right side of his
face, near his mouth, so that he seemed to be smiling,
but grotesquely. There was a tremble to his hands, as
well: there was an almost permanent shake and at
times a more profound jump, actually lifting his
hands in small convulsions. Again it was his right side.

He didn't sleep at all during the flight and arrived
gravel-eyed and sour mouthed, a throbbing ache
moving beyond his head to run down the back of his
neck into his shoulders. Although his eyes were open
and his body moving there kept being momentary
breaks in his awareness of his surroundings, so that
he kept twitching back in apprehension at finding
himself in a place – like the immigration check and
the Customs hall and outside the terminal building,
seeking a taxi – without knowing how he got there.

He sat with his head back against the seat on the
drive into London, oblivious and uncaring about
the route or anything on it. At the hotel he went
robot-like through the registration formalities: in his
suite he jerked up, like a man awakening, unable to
remember getting there from the downstairs lobby.
He slumped into a chair in the sitting room, not
bothering to unpack, drifting in and out of positive
awareness, dreaming but not dreaming and never a
proper dream at all. His mind was blocked by the
squalor of the Oakland motel, and that was all he

kept thinking of: the smell and the filth and how he'd scrabbled around on his hands and knees the following morning, trying to clean away the mess he'd caused and then to clean himself and after that sneaking out, still early, without being seen and then driving aimlessly around, trying to recover. Incredibly Peggy seemed to accept his explanation of some gastroenteritis bug and he'd stayed away from the plant that day and played out the charade with his concerned father-in-law that evening, insisting it was only a passing, twenty-four-hour thing and that there was no reason at all for him to cancel the trip to England.

And now he was here, Krogh realized, in a sudden, coherent moment. Here, like he'd been told to be: obedient and waiting for them to snap their fingers for him to do whatever they wanted done, like a dog performing tricks. He supposed that's what he was: their performing animal, here boy, good dog, fetch boy, fetch.

Krogh's right hand leapt high in fright at the sound of the telephone. He sat, transfixed by the strident sound but not responding to it for several moments. When he did, finally, he just lifted it from its cradle, not able to speak to identify himself.

'Emil?'

Krogh still couldn't make a proper response. He grunted, a guttural sound, and Petrin repeated: 'Emil?'

'Yes,' said Krogh, at last. The word croaked out.

'How was the flight?'

'I don't know,' said Krogh stupidly.

'You don't know!'

'All right, I guess.'

'You tired?'

Krogh almost said again that he didn't know, but stopped. He said: 'Sort of.'

'I thought you'd want to rest for a while. But now there are things to be done. You called the Isle of Wight factory yet?'

'No.'

'Things like that,' said Petrin. 'And I want you to look at what we've set up for you. Make sure you've got everything you want.'

Krogh grunted again.

'Telephone the factory at three. Make an appointment for tomorrow: they're expecting you so it'll be convenient enough. But don't tell them where you're staying, unless they press. I don't want them to have an address,' ordered the Russian. 'Be downstairs at three thirty. I'll take you to where you're going to work.'

Krogh gave a third grunt.

'What's the matter?' demanded Petrin.

'Nothing.'

'You understood what I've said?'

'Yes.'

'Repeat it back to me.'

Krogh did and Petrin said: 'I'll be waiting for you.'

Krogh stayed for several moments by the telephone but at last willed himself to move. He finally unpacked. Then he showered and shaved and felt marginally better, but only marginally. He was hungry and nauseous at the same time. Fleetingly he considered getting something on room service but discarded the idea. His suite overlooked the outer road. He stood at the window, gazing in the direction of the unseen Berkeley Square. Grosvenor Square was unseen, too, to his left, but still close, not more than three or four hundred yards. Krogh knew the American embassy was there: the American embassy where the CIA and the FBI would have station officers. *You don't know me but my name is Emil Krogh and I have leaked to the Soviets everything I so far know about the ultimate destruction weapon forming part of the Strategic Defence Initiative. I'd like you to kill me because I've tried to do it myself but I couldn't do it right. I'm utterly inadequate, you see.* He felt more hungry than sick and wished he'd ordered something. Too late now. Have to wait until tonight: maybe a steak then. He couldn't remember the last time he'd had a proper, full meal: certainly a proper, full meal that he'd managed to keep down. Krogh went into the bathroom, where the lighting was better than the bedroom, and examined himself. The shower and shave had helped and he didn't think he looked as bad as he had when he'd arrived that morning. Definitely the pallor was better, not so grey. His eyes were still awash, though, and not just wet but very red. Drops, if he'd had any with him, might have helped. Something else that was too late. Almost three, he thought. He tried to remember the name of the project chief at the factory and couldn't, his mind an impenetrable blank. There was a stomach-opening panic and he scrambled through the letters and addresses in his briefcase, closing his eyes in the prayer-like hope that it was there, then suddenly came upon it. Springley: Robert Springley. Quite unusual. Stupid of him to have forgotten it. Couldn't afford to forget anything in the coming days. Had to remember everything, difficult, technical detail, and make the drawings. Get rid of the bastards, once and for all.

Krogh gave a tiny cry of surprise, a sharp intake of breath, when the telephone sounded again. Nervously, as if the receiver were hot and he risked burning himself from contact with it, Krogh picked it up. Once more he didn't say anything.

'Emil?'

Krogh squeezed his eyes shut, another praying gesture, absurdly relieved to hear Petrin's voice. Even more absurd, he wanted very much to have the man with him, looking after him, telling him what to do. 'Yes?'

'I didn't want you to sleep on, if in fact you were asleep. It's close to three.'

'I was awake. I know what time it is.'

'Good. Just wanted to make sure. I'll be waiting downstairs.'

'Is that where you are now?'

'No. Make your call now, OK?'

The line went dead. Fetch boy, fetch, thought Krogh. Staging his own infantile protest he waited until a couple of minutes past three before dialling the number. He was connected at once to Robert Springley. The exchange was predictable: how was he, and thanks he was fine in return and it had been a pleasant enough flight and yes the English weather was a contrast with what he was used to in California and – lying – he didn't feel too bad at the moment but he guessed the jet-lag would hit him any time now. Springley insisted he was looking forward very much to the meeting and thoughtfully dictated the train times from Waterloo station that would connect with a hydrofoil service from the mainland to get him to the Isle of Wight by eleven the following morning, if that weren't too early. Krogh assured the Englishman the schedule was convenient, replaced the telephone and hunched forward on the chair, thinking how easy it had all been. His hands weren't moving as much as they had been, earlier: not really a discernible shake any more. Just the vaguest movement of uncertainty.

Krogh tried another protest, remaining unnecessarily in his suite until three thirty, which put him downstairs in the lobby five minutes late. Petrin was waiting in the smaller of the two drawing rooms, to the right of the doors, actually looking at a copy of *Country Life* as if he were studiously reading the magazine. As he usually did, Petrin appeared quite relaxed and at ease. The man didn't look up until Krogh was quite close. When he did so at last he smiled and stood and quite illogically extended his hand, as if they were friends meeting after a long period. Instinctively Krogh responded to the offered handshake, wishing too late to stop that he hadn't. He was aware of the Russian studying him and waited for the complaint about how rough he looked but Petrin said nothing about his appearance. He didn't seem aware of the lateness, either.

'You call the factory?'

'Of course.'

'Everything OK?'

'That're expecting me at eleven tomorrow.'

'That's good, Emil. I'm very pleased.'

Krogh remembered reading that dog owners got better performances from their animals by expressions of encouragement. Trying to sound dismissive, he said: 'Shall we get on with it?'

Petrin smiled and defeated him, as he always did. The Russian said: 'I like your enthusiasm.'

The Soviet safe house was just off Rutland Gardens, a comparatively small property among the imposing five- and six-storeyed Regency buildings which are no longer individual houses but split-up and divided apartment and sometimes office conversions, each occupied by anonymous and indifferent strangers content to remain anonymous and indifferent, which made the location ideal for the Russians' unobserved use.

Virtually an entire room had been set aside for Krogh, although the equipment by no means filled it. Krogh's impression was that the contents of a commercial or industrial drawing supplier's showroom had been emptied, which was almost what *had* happened. There was a large, flat table bisecting the room across its centre and stacked with cartons of original drawing film and trace paper running from size A1 to A4. There were several containers of pencils and drawing pens, in varying colours. The large drawing board was a traditional design, with top and bottom rollers connecting a complete foldaway parallelogram drawing machine which was adjustable, to move either up or down or across a drawing. In front of the assembly was a swivelling drawing chair and there were two large, anglepoise lights and a more elaborate third illumination, with a series of manoeuvrable lamps attached to a bar from which lamps could be set and positioned to direct light in any particular direction or spot.

'Well?' asked Petrin. For once there was not the automatic confidence with which the man usually spoke.

'It looks all right,' said Krogh.

'But is it enough!' demanded Petrin. 'Is there anything we haven't got!'

'It looks adequate. But I won't really know until I see what I've got to draw.'

'Was it Springley you talked with?'

'Yes.'

'What's he expect?'

'We did not discuss anything on the telephone.'

'String it out,' ordered Petrin, confidently back in a position of command. 'I'm not minimizing the difficulty of what you're trying to do: it's impossible to expect you to retain half, let alone all of it. So prepare him for your coming back.'

'What if he baulks at that?'

'Don't let him: remember always that you are the major stakeholder in this thing. They'll defer to you because they'll think you're their access to American defence orders worth a lot of money.'

'It's all thought out, isn't it?' said Krogh dully.

Petrin frowned at the remark. 'Of course it is,' he said. 'Wouldn't you expect it to be?'

The question touched a nerve. The problem, reflected Krogh, was that he didn't know what to expect, about anything. He had the feeling of being lost in a completely alien environment, which he supposed he was. He said: 'So this is where I have to work. What else?'

'Nothing,' said Petrin simply. 'You go to the English factory, spend as much time there as you need, and then come back here and make the drawings we want.'

Krogh shook his head disbelievingly, laughing at the same time. 'It doesn't work like that; can't work like that.'

Petrin sighed. 'Then make it work your way!' he said irritably. 'That's what I've been trying to tell you: establish whatever work pattern you consider necessary. There is only one consideration: getting it all and getting it right.'

'Will you travel with me?'

'Do you want me to?'

Yes, thought Krogh at once. He hated and despised and loathed this man. Yet he wanted the reassurance of his presence, the knowledge that Petrin would be somewhere close at hand, ready if the need – whatever the need *was* – were to arise. He said; 'I don't know. . .I didn't. . .' and trailed away, feeling ridiculous.

'Emil!' said Petrin with stretched patience. 'You came in overnight on flight one zero nine. The plane was fifteen minutes late. You occupied a first class seat, four B, on the aisle. The Hackney carriage licence number of the taxi that brought you in from the airport was eight zero eight nine two five. . .' The Russian smiled. '. . . And when you go to the Isle

238

of Wight tomorrow you'll be just as thoroughly protected.'

'But are you coming?' insisted Krogh.

There had been long psychological training periods at the spy schools, particularly the academy on the Prospekt Mira, on how a suborned agent could become dependent upon his case officer, and Petrin isolated the indication immediately. Knowing that the reliance had to be made complete in the mind of the agent, Petrin repeated: 'Do you want me to?'

'Yes,' conceded Krogh.

From that same spy school instruction Petrin realized that the man was completely his now, to be moulded and shaped entirely as he wanted, like a piece of modelling clay. He said: 'Then I will. We won't actually travel as companions but I'll be with you all the time, like others will be. You're not to worry, you understand?'

Once, recalled Krogh, a remark about not worrying had annoyed him and he'd shouted back and told the man not to be absurd. He didn't shout back today. Instead he said: 'All right. I know.'

'Did you get any sleep at the hotel?'

'No.'

'It doesn't look like it,' said Petrin. He took a phial from his pocket, offering it to the other man. 'Here!' he said.

'What is it?'

'Just sleeping pills,' said the Russian. 'They're quite mild, but from the man we had on board I know you didn't sleep at all on the flight coming over and I guessed you'd need them.'

Krogh stared at the phial and thought of an Oakland motel room and visibly shuddered.

'What's the matter?'

'I don't think I want them,' said Krogh. He felt his stomach move at the recollection.

'You do, Emil. I want you to take them.'

Hesitantly the American took the offered bottle, realizing that accepting the pills wasn't the same as *taking* them, which he was sure he couldn't physically manage.

There was a movement to their left and a man appeared at a door to another room. The man said something in Russian, briefly, and even more briefly Petrin replied in Russian. The man withdrew at once.

'Who was that?' asked Krogh.

It had, in fact, been the KGB duty change for the constantly monitored telephone, which was installed in the adjoining room. Petrin said: 'No one to concern you. There'll probably be quite a few people around when you start working here.'

'What do I have to do now?' asked Krogh, showing his increasing reliance.

'Do you want to eat?'

The belated hunger he'd felt at the hotel had gone now and Krogh said: 'Not really.'

'Then just rest. You've got a lot to accomplish in the coming days.'

'I will,' undertook Krogh. He wouldn't sleep, he knew: it would be impossible.

'And I'll take you back,' said Petrin.

Petrin accompanied him to his suite. Inside Krogh looked curiously at the other man and said: 'What's happening now?'

'Now you take the sleeping pills I gave you,' said Petrin. 'Which you weren't going to do, were you?'

'No,' miserably admitted Krogh at once.

It was Petrin who got water from the bathroom and stood in front of the American while he took the dosage, an adult guaranteeing a child swallowed its medication.

'I know practically everything you'll do or try not

240

to do,' said Petrin. Mould the clay into any shape, he thought.

'Yes,' said Krogh in further dull acceptance.

'Remember, Emil. I'm here with you in the same hotel. Looking after you. You're safe.'

'Yes,' said Krogh again. He wished he didn't need the comfort of that assurance.

The person who was going to be around the American most of all when he worked in Rutland Gardens was Yuri Guzins, and the man was terrified. The suggestion that a scientist go from Baikonur to London to oversee the drawing was met with the sort of frenzied protest that Berenkov and Kalenin had expected. And as they further expected the project chief, Nikolai Noskov, succeeded in arguing himself out of the responsibility, so anxious to avoid it that it was actually he and not Kalenin who put forward Guzins' name as an alternative candidate.

Guzins tried to protest just as forcibly but he lacked Noskov's seniority. More importantly he lacked Kalenin's seniority *and* authority and was ordered first from Baikonur and then from Moscow with only forty-eight hours to prepare himself.

One of the man's final, weak protests had been that he spoke no language but Russian, so Vitali Losev was sent from London to chaperon the man from the first moment of his arrival into Europe, at Amsterdam's Schipol airport.

Losev went with deepening bitterness, viewing it as another secondary role and deciding that it was dangerous, too, when he saw the obvious, attention-attracting apprehension with which Guzins emerged from the arrival hall on to the main concourse. Losev moved at once to minimize it, directly approaching the heavily moustached scientist with the immediate assurance that he was going to be escorted and that there was no need for concern.

They entered Britain by a roundabout route, driving all the way from Amsterdam to Calais by car and crossing to Dover by sea ferry. Guzins travelled on a Greek passport that had been freighted in the diplomatic bag from Moscow to London and which Losev had carried with him to Holland, for their meeting. It was a completely uneventful trip and they arrived at Rutland Gardens late on a Thursday night.

'What is this place?' demanded Guzins at once, nervously.

'Your home,' said Losev. 'Welcome to England.'

28

With his customary objectivity – which in matters
of personal safety could be brutal – Charlie Muffin
admitted to himself that he was taking the biggest
risk of a risk-burdened life. Additionally, he accepted that what he was doing was reprehensibly
unprofessional. That any unbiased observer would
judge it to be bloody daft. And that he thought so
too: worse than bloody daft, in fact. Insane was a
far better word. He tried to balance the assessment
by telling himself he was irrevocably committed, but
refused that excuse at once, knowing it not to be the
case: that he could still change his mind. And then,
in complete honesty, confronted the fact that he
didn't want to operate any differently from the way
he was doing right now, so he wouldn't. Besides, to
change his mind at this point would be to admit
a mistake and Charlie had an inherent dislike of
admitting mistakes and most certainly wouldn't contemplate such an admission to Harkness. Which, he
conceded, made him not just bloody daft but bloody
minded, as well. And still left him facing the biggest
risk he'd ever knowingly taken. Because if this went
wrong by one tiny iota those who ruled his existence –
not shithead Harkness but Intelligence Committees
and permanent civil servants – might be sufficiently
pissed off with him to think a hundred years in a rat-
infested jail cell was too good and remove Charles
Edward Muffin from circulation altogether. Charlie was convinced such an embarrassment-avoiding
course had been taken before, with other insubor-
dinate troublemakers: far less trouble, far less difficulty, all so much neater.

The problem, which always seemed to be the same problem, was watching his ass at the same time as looking straight in front to see all the approaching dangers. He'd taken all the precautions he could think of taking, which hardly rated as precautions at all, and he couldn't think of anything else he could do. Which was unsettling because Charlie never liked to be absolutely devoid of ideas like he was this time.

He completely tidied his apartment and conceived fresh snares, and before he officially took his leave he treated William French to a pub lunch (pie, pickles and beer perfectly kept in wood barrels) to thank the man for what he had already done and to ask if he could keep in touch while he was away from the office.

'I'm not going to regret this, am I, Charlie?' probed the Technical Division scientist cautiously. 'A favour's a favour but this is coming close to needing some proper authority.'

'It'll be all right,' assured Charlie. I hope, he thought: he was never comfortable endangering mates, no matter how justified the necessity might be.

'I've kept my name off everything,' warned French. 'If there *is* any sort of fuck-up followed by an inquiry I won't even know what they're talking about or who Charlie Muffin is.'

'That's precisely what I'd expect you to do,' said Charlie honestly. 'You don't think I'd point the finger, do you!'

'No,' agreed the man at once. 'I don't think you'd do that under any circumstances.'

Charlie didn't imagine he would either: he just wasn't sure. He said: 'So I'll keep in touch, OK?'

'You know how I feel about open telephone lines,' said the man whose expertise *was* telephones.

'I'll be circumspect.'

244

'That's not much of a safeguard.'

'It is when we both know what we're talking about.'

It was, of course, necessary for Charlie fully to reconnoitre the Soviet delegation hotel and he sketched the surveillance over two days. He explored all the roads immediately adjacent to the Blair hotel, like Gloucester Terrace and Bathrust Street and Westbourne Crescent, giving particular attention to any that had one-way traffic restrictions, and then spread the check as far north as the Paddington Basin and as far south as Hyde Park, although he did not go down as far as the restaurant in which Vitali Losev had made his first hostile meeting with Alexandr Petrin.

With just days to go before Natalia's arrival, Charlie had his hair cut and bought two new shirts and a new tie and briefly considered – and rejected – new shoes, and alternated his two suits so that he could have both cleaned and pressed.

And then, finally, Charlie decided he was ready: there was nothing left to be done that he hadn't already done. All he could do now was wait. He admitted to himself that he was nervous: more nervous than he could remember being on a lot of past assignments, which was virtually how he was regarding this, an assignment. He had some idea, from the photographs, but he still wondered if Natalia would be the same when he saw her again for the first time.

Throughout all the preparations, the Soviet observers maintained their twenty-four-hour watch.

At its most basic a number-for-letter code transliterates directly the letter of an alphabet for its corresponding number, in the case of English the letter A represented by the figure one and running consecutively through to Z, which is twenty-six. There are, however, mathematical variations which can be introduced to make unravelling the cipher difficult – and hopefully impossible – for the codebreakers. If the sender and recipient agree in advance to use a variable of two, for instance, then the transliteration can range over five choices of letter: the intended letter and two either side. It can be further complicated by changing the variable from day to day, from odd to even numbers. And compounded by mixing two languages, English with Russian for example: in cyrillic Russian there is no easy equivalent for H or J but there are two possible inflections for the letter K.

Having purposely provided the British with what he wanted them to recognize as a number-for-letter code Berenkov had the KGB Technical Division introduce random variations established in advance by a translation key sent to the London embassy in the diplomatic bag.

The intention remained always for the interceptors eventually to be able to read the messages, whatever the variation, but for them to believe the more difficult changes indicated an increasing importance of the contents.

Which was precisely what happened.

The transmission from Moscow on the day Krogh arrived in London was a mixture of English and Russian and had a variable range rising from one to four. It was to take the codebreakers a week to comprehend it and when he received it Richard Harkness ranked it as the most important interception and translation so far made.

It said: REACTIVATE PAYMASTER BY ONE THOUSAND.

He hurried Hubert Witherspoon to the ninth floor.

29

Emil Krogh felt better. Not well and certainly not relaxed but there was no longer the impression that the ground was yielding beneath his feet when he walked, and he could think clearly and logically. The sleep had a lot to do with it, he guessed. And he *had* slept, soundly and dreamlessly – a combination, he supposed, of Petrin's tranquillizers and utter exhaustion. He'd awoken ravenously hungry and eaten a large breakfast without any aftermath of nausea, and minutes after he settled into his train compartment at Waterloo he was aware of the Russian slowly passing along the platform outside. The man appeared to be by himself, although Krogh knew that not to be the case, and did not look in to where he was sitting. Krogh wished he hadn't had the relief at knowing of Petrin's presence, because he recognized it as a reaction of weakness to have about a man who had inveigled him and was treating him as Petrin was. He just couldn't help it.

The train was on schedule but Krogh could not see Petrin when he got off at Southampton, not even during the three or four minutes he had to wait in the taxi queue. There was a flicker of alarm, which the American regretted as much as the earlier sensation of relief, but he forced himself on. At the hydrofoil terminal he saw Petrin get from a taxi, still alone, two vehicles behind him. Krogh went to the front on the hydrofoil and Petrin to the rear, so they were separated by the central driving platform and control cockpit, and when they disembarked at Cowes again there was no sign of the Russian.

There was a chauffeur-driven limousine waiting

for him as promised on the taxi-packed jetty and when Krogh's approach to it became obvious a haphazardly dressed man with fly-away white hair came forward and introduced himself as Robert Springley. They shook hands and parroted how pleased they were to meet each other and on the way to the chain ferry Springley said that with the imposed traffic detour it was as quick to walk but they'd thought a car was more convenient. Throughout the journey to the factory the project chief maintained the conversation, hoping Krogh was not too jet-lagged and was this his first time in England and how was he enjoying it. Krogh only had to respond minimally to keep up his side of the exchange.

At the factory gate, with Springley apologizing in advance, they had to get out of the car to go through the security formalities of signing Krogh in and getting him a temporary authority badge, and for the first time Krogh felt the briefest dip of apprehension. It was here, for the first time, that Springley referred to the Star Wars project. Still apologizing, Springley said they had tightened security since being awarded the contract and Krogh said the precaution was essential, surprised how level his voice was as he mouthed the hypocrisy.

'Everyone's waiting in the boardroom,' announced Springley.

'Everyone?'

Springley was walking slightly ahead of him so the man was unaware of Krogh's frown. The project chief said: 'The chairman, managing director. Most of the other directors and the senior people in the project team.'

Krogh supposed he should have anticipated a social situation but stupidly – preoccupied, he excused himself – he hadn't. Confronting the thought for the first time Krogh conceded he hadn't known what to expect, at all, apart from some half-formed idea of being with Springley and getting to the drawings. There was nothing he could do but go along with whatever they had laid on. Krogh hoped it wouldn't last long. Although he hadn't prepared himself with expectations there was one positive intention: Krogh wanted to get it over with, in the same urgency with which he'd wanted to finish what the Russians had forced him to do with the material from his own plant. He said: 'We will get around to seeing the actual work, won't we?'

'Sure,' said Springley, vaguely.

The boardroom was on the top floor of the main, three-storey building, a pleasantly large room glassed on two sides for a panoramic view of the river and the yacht moorings at its mouth. Inside the room the elongated conference table had been moved to one side and some chairs removed, to enable more standing room, and Krogh guessed the two smaller tables, one for the canapés, another for an array of drinks, were an addition to the usual furniture. Krogh later put the number at about eight but his first impression on entering the room was that a crowed of people awaited him. He succeeded in getting the chairman's name as John Bishop and that of the managing director as James Spear or Dear but after that the introductions were too quick and the identities blurred. Krogh accepted a scotch and soda, needing it, but declined the frequently offered snacks because there was a faint suggestion of sickness. The conversation began almost as aimlessly general as it had been with the project leader on the way from the hydrofoil terminal, but then a positive direction did start to emerge, initiated by the chairman. Bishop talked of his company's awareness of the importance of the shared contract and the managing director, whose name turned out to be Spear, picked up the theme and smiled anxiously and said they hoped it became not only entirely satisfactory but the beginning of a long and mutually beneficial association. And Krogh realized that Petrin's surmise the previous day, that the British firm saw him as an essential conduit for further American defence contracts, was correct.

Krogh seized upon it, deciding the cocktail party was not the waste of time he'd initially considered it to be but a useful opportunity to make easier what he was being blackmailed into doing. Carefully ensuring that Springley was close enough at hand to hear the discussion, Krogh assured those grouped around him that he and his company were equally conscious of its importance. He disclosed, truthfully, that it was the most substantial order they had ever received from the Pentagon. And insisted it was because they were so determined that everything *would* be entirely satisfactory and create the confidence sufficient for new contracts in the future that he had come all the way from California, for this consultation.

Bishop responded precisely as Krogh wanted, turning to Springley when he said: 'I couldn't agree more; liaison is essential.'

'I want to guarantee the complete compatibility of what we're manufacturing over there and the work you're doing here,' said Krogh. 'I know we've individually got sets of master drawings which are supposed to connect, one to the other, and that in theory they should marry together but I've known split defence undertakings before where that hasn't happened. . .' He smiled, shaking his head in invitation to a common experience. '. . . And you know what happens every time? The mistake is never the

250

fault of the Pentagon designers or draughtsmen: always the buck is passed to the contractors' interpretation and the next contract goes to somebody else.'

The chairman smiled, taking Krogh's cue. 'Bureaucracy! It's the same the world over.'

'I'm glad you agree my visit is necessary,' said Krogh.

'I think it's imperative,' insisted Bishop. Again the man spoke half looking at Springley.

Krogh decided, satisfied, that it was practically an order to the project chief to share and disclose everything that was demanded of him. Protecting himself further Krogh said: 'I'll probably want to come more than once. . .' He paused, sweeping his hand to embrace the reception put on for his benefit '. . . and I don't mean to all this, for which I thank you: you've been most kind. I mean to come back to spend some time with Mr Springley here to make sure we've got the compatibility we want. . .' Krogh allowed another pause, to establish his argument. He concluded: '. . . to guarantee the re-orders and new contracts we want.'

There were smiles from everyone in the room and Krogh realized, astonished, that he was welcoming the attention and admiration. It made him feel good: important. Which was preposterous: preposterous and ridiculous, and Krogh was embarrassed even to think it.

Spear, the managing director, said: 'Mr Krogh, you're welcome at this establishment as many times and for as long as you like.'

There were more drinks, which Krogh enjoyed, and then a call to lunch in a small directors' dining room, which was another social extension the American hadn't foreseen. He sat between Bishop and Spear, and was content to let the two men dominate the conversation. The talk was of other

251

space developments with which their company had been associated in Europe and the surprisingly poor commitment to space technology shown by the British government which expected profit return upon investment within a year or two and was never prepared to wait any time beyond. Krogh sympathized and agreed it was small-minded and short-sighted, and allowed himself to be drawn about his own company and the previous spacework they had completed for the American government. Towards the end, when he was talking of those defence contracts, Krogh's fragile confidence began to slip at the spectre of what he had already done and was continuing to do that day and at what would happen to him if he were ever caught. The meal ended with a rather embarrassing formal speech which the chairman rose to give, concluding with a toast to Krogh who, unprepared for this as with everything else, groped to his feet and muttered how pleased he was to be there and how gratified he was by everything that had been said.

Throughout the meal Springley sat opposite, although contributing little to the discussion. After the speech Bishop leaned across the table to the man and said: 'It's going to be full cooperation and liaison, OK?'

'I understand,' said the project chief. 'I'm sure Mr Krogh and I are going to get along together just fine.'

It was approaching four o'clock before they left the dining room and finally made their way towards the secure division of the factory. As they walked Krogh said: 'That went on a bit, didn't it?'

Springley smiled in understanding but didn't openly criticize. Instead he said: 'This contract is regarded pretty highly here. And you with it.'

Moving to capitalize upon the promises from the

chairman, Krogh said: 'So how many drawings do I have to consider, in all?'

'Twenty-four,' said Springley at once. 'Some very simple, some not so simple.'

Not as many as he had feared, from the lunchtime talk, thought Krogh. But still enough. It wasn't possible, until he saw them, to estimate how long it would take him to reproduce them all. He said: 'There's insufficient time left today for me to get anything but the most general overview.'

'If that,' agreed Springley.

Inside the division Krogh was introduced to those in the project team he had not yet met and as he went through the ritual he decided against any attempt in the last hour to memorize the drawings he had come to see. Instead, rather than concentrate upon one blueprint, he scanned them all, mentally categorizing them to assess the degree of work involved and the amount of time that would be involved in doing it. It was still only a rough calculation but he divided the drawings into eleven that were comparatively easy, little more than links between one to another of the remaining, much more intricate and difficult thirteen: although separate, some of the drawings were enlarged and more detailed specifications of other, more general plans. Krogh calculated that working flat out he could reproduce the easier, linking designs in two days, three at the outside, but that the other thirteen would each take him the minimum of a day and in several cases even longer.

'How's it look?' asked Springley, at his shoulder.

Krogh shrugged. 'Impossible to say, from a quick look like this: naturally it's all familiar. . .' He paused, looking around the facility, determined upon every advantage. 'Is there a place I can work, out of everybody's way, when I come back?'

'Of course,' assured Springley, gesturing to one of the smaller offices at the side of the communal drawing room. 'There are two or three rooms that aren't being used.'

'Thank you, for everything,' said Krogh.

Springley smiled faintly. 'We haven't done anything yet.'

'But it's going to work out, isn't it?' said Krogh. 'Work out just like we want it to.'

By lunchtime that day the news of Krogh's presence – 'the head of the American company, he's actually here!' – had spread throughout the factory. Henry Blackstone heard about it in the canteen and spent the afternoon close to a convenient window, so he saw Krogh cross into the secret division with Springley after the boardroom greeting. For no positive reason Blackstone lingered after finishing work, not immediately outside where he would have been recognized and possibly aroused curiosity by hanging about but along the road by a pub named after Queen Victoria, who had favoured the island as a holiday home, and so he had a perfect view of Krogh as the limousine swept by, returning the man to the mainland ferry terminal. Blackstone decided, pleased, that it was definitely something to report to the London number he now knew by heart. It obviously wasn't important enough to earn him the sort of money he would have got for a blueprint but he was sure it deserved some payment. He hoped so: he was desperately short of money, back in the sort of position he'd thought he'd escaped for ever. Blackstone was actually humming to himself as he drove towards Newport in the car upon which he was already two months behind with the payments.

Krogh didn't locate Petrin on the return journey, not even on the hydrofoil where it should have been easy, which he found unsettling but not positively worrying after what he regarded as the encouraging success of the day. He first became aware of the Russian when the train reached Waterloo and then he did not see him. Krogh had an awareness of a presence, very close, and a voice he recognized to be Petrin's said: 'Are we going straight to the house?'

Krogh jumped, involuntarily, despite the concourse noise of the main-line station. He stopped, turning to face the other man, and said: 'I wondered where you were: I looked but couldn't find you.'

'I don't make a habit of being easily seen,' said Petrin arrogantly. 'I asked if we were going straight to the house.'

'There's nothing for me to draw,' said Krogh.

The American purposely phrased the declaration, trying to disturb the Russian, but Petrin gave no alarmed response. Quite controlled, he said: 'How's that, Emil?'

With passengers swirling around them and metal-voiced announcements of train movements and delays echoing overhead, Krogh recounted what had happened that day. Petrin listened with his head slightly bowed, not looking directly at him, but started nodding as Krogh finished. The Russian looked up then and smiled and said: 'That's good: that's very good indeed. You've done well.'

Satisfaction stirred through Krogh at the congratulation, despite his trying to prevent it: he was like a child anxious for praise from an adult he sought to impress. He said: 'From what I've seen it's going to take at least a fortnight, maybe longer.'

'Just as long as we get it all,' reminded the Russian.

Vitali Losev listened patiently to Blackstone, at the other end of the line, sighing at the length at which the man was talking in a blatantly obvious attempt

255

to increase the importance of what he was saying. When Blackstone eventually finished, the Russian said: 'Thank you. That's very interesting.'

'I thought you'd want to know right away,' said Blackstone hopefully. 'I thought you'd consider it important.'

'Like I told you, it's interesting,' qualified Losev. 'It'll help to get that permanent payment organized.'

There was a long pause between them, Losev waiting contemptuously. At last, desperately, Blackstone said: 'You haven't heard anything yet then?'

'Not yet,' said Losev. 'Soon, I hope.'

30

It was a hotel clinging by its fingertips to the middle range of the package-tour market, reconciled to the number of couples named Smith who booked in for one night and left earlier in the morning, and wary of a health inspection swoop on the kitchens because you couldn't keep cockroaches completely from hotel kitchens, could you?

The foyer was a brave attempt at something it was not. There was an imitation marble floor of yellowy amber and the motif was continued with two imitation marble pillars in a matching colour. At various strategic points there were tall plants with large leaves which went well with the marble effect and just got away with conveying an interior garden atmosphere. The reception area was quite small and to the right of the double-fronted glass doors: behind the reception clerk all the rooms were itemized by open cubbyholes into which the keys fitted with their number tags hanging down, to show whether they were occupied or not, and which Charlie marked right away as a burglar's dream. There was a sitting area to the left, a couch and a set of chairs with ornately carved legs and arms and with upholstery featuring French pastoral scenes of pomaded men and crinolined women unaware of the rumbling tumbrils of revolution. It was the sort of brocade material Charlie had seen on genuine antiques and looked quite good when slightly frayed, which this was.

The clerk, a smiling girl, wondered if he were on holiday and Charlie agreed he was and she asked if he knew London well and Charlie said well enough.

She gestured to some unseen desk behind a potted plant and said it was manned between ten and four every weekday to get theatre tickets or tour trips and Charlie promised to remember.

He was given room 35 and taken to it by an elderly porter whose false teeth didn't fit and who therefore lisped when he talked. On the way up in a hicupping, metal-grilled lift Charlie patiently went through the here-for-a-holiday, first-time-in-London ritual. The old man showed him how to operate the television and opened the bathroom door to prove the room had one and said if there were anything at all Charlie wanted he only had to ask. Charlie thanked the man and tipped him two pounds because he invariably found hotel porters useful allies to have.

The room was small but adequate. There was a double bed at one side of which was a tray with a kettle and a selection of tea, coffee and powdered milk sachets for a do-it-yourself breakfast drink, a built-in clothes closet, a low table bordered with two easy chairs and the already identified television had a dial device for in-house movies. One was described as adult viewing and didn't become available until after 10 p.m. Charlie guessed the management had got a job lot with the fake marble tiles because the bathroom was a replica of the lobby. The bath was clean, there were enough towels and there was a tray of soaps and shampoo and conditioner in their individual packets. He was going to be quite comfortable, Charlie decided.

He unpacked and with instinctive professionalism set out to explore his surroundings. He followed the signs and discovered his room was conveniently positioned near the fire escape. It was an internal system, a back-stairs spiral of bare concrete steps with a metal hand rail. Charlie pushed through the door on his floor and descended the three flights to find where it emerged, out into the open. It was on to a tiny rear car park, where the dustbins were kept as well as vehicles. There was an alley leading from the front of the hotel, towards the park, but another feeder road for service lorries ran at right angles, as well: Charlie guessed the feeder road supplied several other hotels in the area.

It would have been convenient to have emerged through the fire door on the ground level but it would have made the clerk or the porter curious, so Charlie limped back up the three flights to use the public, rickety lift: by the time he'd been up and then down his legs as well as his feet ached, and Charlie felt the need to restore himself.

The bar was on the same side as the reception area but further back into the hotel, past more plants and the theatre ticket desk he now located. Charlie, not only a man of quick impressions but a degree-holding judge of hostelries, liked it at once. The colour scheme was predominantly restful red, with hunting scenes and prints of eighteenth-century London around the walls. The bar itself looked as if it were made from aged and heavy wood, which was probably plastic imitation like the outside tiles but Charlie thought it worked well enough. It was along the inner wall and impressively stocked with little-known brand-name scotch, which Charlie always considered a good sign. There were a few bar stools, a spread of tables and some benched seats.

Charlie expertly chose the corner stool, right against the wall, from which he had an immediate view of anyone entering but from whom he would not be easily seen until they got their bearings. He ordered an Islay malt and the barman said he didn't want ice or water did he and Charlie agreed that he didn't and was further impressed. A barman who knew how properly to serve Islay malt and was

259

able instantly to discern someone else who did as well was no newcomer to his trade. And practised hotel barmen were even better allies than porters because as well as proficiency with drinks they were usually proficient with gossip. The barman, whose name emerged as John and who, from the bracelets and the neckchain, was a lover of gold, let Charlie lead the conversation, which was another indication of experience and which Charlie started to do after the second drink. The man started to volunteer what Charlie sought by the time of the third drink, prompted by Charlie disclosing how long he intended staying.

'It's going to be interesting for you then,' said the man.

'How's that?' asked Charlie ingenuously.

'Got a special party arriving.'

'Special?'

'A group of Russians. Here for the Farnborough Air Show.'

'In this very hotel!' exclaimed Charlie, suitably impressed.

The barman nodded and smiled, content with the reaction. 'Practically taken over an entire floor.'

'That must create a headache for you all, an important group like that?' lured Charlie.

There was another nod. 'We've had a lot of Russians from the embassy, making sure everything is going to be all right. All the staff have been checked.'

'You personally?'

'Sure.'

'You mind that?'

A shrug this time. 'Not really. Unusual experience, really.'

'Practically an entire floor, you say?'

The man responded as Charlie hoped he would. 'The sixth,' he confirmed. 'And those rooms that aren't occupied have to stay empty while the party is here.'

'All rather exciting,' said Charlie. Would the restrictions the Russians imposed mean the sealing of the entire floor?

'I suppose so,' said the barman, a seen-it-all-before remark. 'You'd better get here early at night if you want a place to sit.'

'I will,' assured Charlie.

In the Soviet car outside Viktor Nikov, whose tour of personal observation it was, said bitterly: 'Drinking! He sits in the bar drinking and we sit here, with nothing!'

It was almost two months from their last being together, that weekend at the dacha, when Valentina finally raised it. They were making plans to go again, during another of Georgi's college breaks, and Valentina asked if Kalenin were coming and Berenkov admitted that he had not invited the man.

'Are you going to?' she demanded. Throughout the years that Berenkov's overseas postings had kept them apart Valentina had developed a peremptory independence unusual for the wife of an intelligence officer.

'I don't think so,' shrugged Berenkov.

'Why not?' She was a big woman, blonde and strong-featured. Impatient and uninterested in dieting she was putting her faith in tight corsetry and accepted that it was not really working.

'I don't think he'd welcome an invitation, at the moment.'

'So there *is* a difficulty between you?' seized Valentina, recalling her impression of quietness from the last dacha visit.

'It's not serious,' said Berenkov. I hope, he thought.

261

'Can you talk about it?'

'No,' refused Berenkov shortly, retreating at last behind the expected security-consciousness of his job.

'Who's right?'

Berenkov laughed, unoffended at his wife's directness. 'It's not like that. It's just different viewpoints.'

'Nothing could ever happen to us, could it?' asked the woman, with sudden concern. 'Nothing to upset the life we now have, I mean.'

Berenkov laughed at her again, in reassurance this time. 'Of course not,' he said. 'Why do you ask a thing like that?'

Valentina shook her head, refusing the question. 'I wouldn't want anything to upset the way we are now,' she said.

31

A pattern quickly developed and Emil Krogh relaxed further as he became accustomed to the work
surroundings at the Isle of Wight factory. When he
returned the second day Robert Springley took him
on a tour of the moulding rooms and explained in
detail the difference between the British-evolved
thermoplastic resin process, which enabled the carbon fibre to be reshaped without any loss of strength,
and the more easily shattered and unchangeable
thermoset system that had been employed at Krogh's
plant in California. He watched the fibre and resin
matrix being created in a temperature- and climate-
controlled environment and even before studying
the waiting blueprints in detail was able to understand how this section was going to assemble with
what they were building in America to create the
missile housing for the defence system.

The promised side office was made available to
him and at first Springley stayed close at hand to take
him through the drawings, which was an intrusion
Krogh didn't want but could do nothing about. It was
well into the afternoon before the man left him alone
and Krogh was finally able to make the notes he considered necessary to reproduce the manufacturing
plans. He did so in a way to satisfy Petrin and take
the pressure off himself. He separated the drawings
according to Springley's definition and concentrated
first upon the eleven easy ones. It took him that day
and most of the following to make sufficient notes
and late that afternoon returned with Petrin to the
Kensington house to begin work.

Vitali Losev was already there with the frightened

Yuri Guzins, and in the first half hour other men entered and left the room which had been set up as Krogh's drawing office. The American prepared his board and clipped his notes to it and set his lights, all the while feeling like a laboratory experiment under the scrutiny of so many people.

The progress was slower than Krogh anticipated. As soon as the American started to draw, Guzins, to whom he was never introduced, came and stood at his elbow and practically at once began asking highly technical questions which had to be painstakingly translated back and forth between them by Petrin. When Krogh, exasperated, asked what the hell was going on Petrin said it was a precaution they believed worthwhile to prevent any mistake, to which Krogh complained that his constantly being interrupted risked mistakes being made instead of being guarded against. Petrin accepted the protest and told Guzins to wait until a drawing was finished before querying it, which was the method they adopted, but by midnight Krogh had produced only six copies and was aching with exhaustion. His announcement that he couldn't draw any more provided the catalyst for the row that had simmered between Petrin and Losev from the moment of their first meeting.

Krogh spoke to Petrin when he said he wanted to stop but it was the unidentified Losev who responded.

'Work on!' ordered Losev, brusquely and in English.

'I said I'm too tired,' repeated Krogh.

Losev went to speak but Petrin got in first. 'I'll decide how he works,' said Petrin. He spoke in Russian.

'He's got to do more!' insisted Losev, also speaking in Russian. 'Who gives a damn how he feels!'

'Idiot!' said Petrin. 'Didn't you hear the conversation about mistakes? Tired men make mistakes!'

Krogh couldn't understand what was being said but their tone was sufficient for him to realize it was an argument.

'You don't have the authority to overrule me!' said Losev.

'Nor you to supercede me,' Petrin shouted back. 'So let's get it ruled from Moscow. Until which time I decide what Krogh will do and what he won't: he's my responsibility.'

Guzins stood with nibbled fingers to his mouth, looking apprehensively between the two men, bewildered by the sudden eruption. Surprisingly trying the role of peacemaker, he said: 'What's an argument like this going to achieve?'

Ignoring the scientist Losev said: 'I am the *rezident* in this country. Mine is the ultimate authority.'

'Which I am refusing to recognize,' said Petrin. 'Moscow can decide.'

Losev regretted the dispute now, suspecting Dzerzhinsky Square would favour Petrin in the choice. Retreating, he said: 'OK. Let him finish for the night.'

'There was never a question of his not doing so,' persisted Petrin. 'I'll want to see the cable exchanges with Moscow.' That *was* an encroachment upon the local KGB chief and Petrin knew it but he decided to make the challenge anyway: he wasn't frightened of what Moscow might decide and he was curious how far Losev would take the dispute.

'You'll see what's appropriate,' said Losev.

Not a capitulation, judged Petrin: but not the outright rejection it should have been, either. So the other man wasn't sure of himself. Wanting the exchange to end on his terms Petrin said disparagingly: 'Be here the same time tomorrow night,' and hurried

Krogh from the room with his hand cupped to the American's elbow.

'What went on back there?' asked Krogh when they were out in the street.

'Nothing important,' said Petrin dismissively. 'A stupid difference of opinion.'

Berenkov was irritated by the message when it reached him from London. Passingly he had thought of the possibility of friction between the two equally ranked men but put it from his mind. Now he looked upon it as an unnecessarily distracting squabble between two prima donnas who should have known better. Berenkov's immediate reaction was to give Petrin overall command but he held back. Losev *was* the British station chief. For the man to have Petrin appointed over him would be a blatant demotion and exacerbate the ill feeling which clearly already existed between them. The counter-balance was that the control of Emil Krogh had to remain with Petrin, who had succeeded – and was continuing to succeed – brilliantly in suborning and manipulating the American industrialist. So there could be no question of his surrendering that role to someone else.

Berenkov attempted to resolve the clash of vanities by neither giving nor taking from either, which was no resolve at all. He replied that Vitali Losev was head of the KGB *rezidentura* in London and should be accorded that authority. But that in the unusual circumstances of the assignment Alexandr Petrin retained unchallengeable control of the American and that nothing would be permitted to affect that. In an effort at long-distance head-banging Berenkov reminded both of the importance of what they were doing and said he did not wish to referee any further demarcation disputes.

The effect was for Petrin to consider his attitude

266

vindicated and for Losev to believe his authority *had* been diminished.

'Satisfied?' demanded Losev when the reply came.

'Very,' said Petrin. That day Krogh completed the remaining drawings he considered easy and got more than halfway through the first of those he considered more difficult.

Natalia was allocated a window seat and Gennadi Redin, whom she had already decided to be one of the KGB escorts, sat next to her – which she regretted because his nervousness became even more apparent on an aeroplane. He fidgeted and sweated excessively and drank a lot of vodka, which appeared to do nothing to allay his fears. It didn't make him drunk, either.

'Have you been to London before?' he asked her.

Natalia shook her head. 'No.'

'Looking forward to it?'

More than she had anticipated anything for a very long time, reflected Natalia, even though she was trying to keep her hopes tightly controlled. 'It will be an interesting experience,' she said guardedly. She was anxious to identify the other KGB personnel: she did not consider she had a lot to fear from this man.

'Tweed and woollen wear,' announced the man. 'That's what my wife has told me to bring her back.'

Natalia wondered again if she would be able to get out to buy more clothes at the beginning of the trip. 'I'll take her advice.'

There was a pilot's announcement that they had crossed the English coast and Natalia stared down at the pocket handkerchieves of fields set out far below.

'It's a very small country,' volunteered Redin. 'It's

always difficult to imagine how important it once was.'

'Isn't it important any more?' asked Natalia mildly.

'Oh no,' said Redin, convinced. 'It's just one of the states of Europe now.'

'I suppose it depends upon what you hope to find there,' said Natalia, more to herself than to him.

32

Charlie considered carefully how to stage the recognition with Natalia, knowing how vital the timing and the circumstances were. He knew the scheduled arrival of the Moscow flight, and his initial idea was simply to be in the seating area of frayed brocade when she entered with the rest of the party. And then he decided against it. He had no way of knowing if she wanted to see him as much as he wanted to see her but it was logical she would have thought of the possibility. But for him to be openly in the foyer, practically making it a confrontation, was too abrupt. He had to guard against any startled reaction to his presence because she *would* be with the rest of the delegation on arrival, and among that delegation would be KGB watchers alert for any unusual response, to anything. It was better that he be nowhere around for whatever registration formalities were to be completed: that she had time to settle in and adjust, however slightly, to her surroundings.

Charlie debated with himself, waiting unobtrusively outside the hotel, just to *see* her, and actually repeated the reconnoitre of the previous days, seeking out vantage points. There were some – the doorway of a towering Regency house converted into offices and a tiny, centre-of-the-road coppice of trees preserved by a parks department – but Charlie was uncomfortable being outside the hotel after the Russians had entered. One or maybe more of those KGB watchers would inevitably establish a surveillance position in the foyer, noting who followed the party in. And over long years of experience Charlie had found it was human nature – certainly

269

the human nature of supposedly trained intelligence officers, which it shouldn't have been – to be more interested in people following behind than in people already established ahead. So he abandoned that intention as well.

Instead, for the Russian arrival, Charlie kept completely out of the way. He sat in his room and tried to read newspapers, which didn't work because his concentration wouldn't hold, and he tried to become interested in his flickering television, but that didn't work either although he managed an hour watching horse racing from Goodwood and was glad he wasn't there in person because every horse upon which he placed a mental bet got lost in the field. He considered dialling one of the in-house movies but abandoned that, too. At last, more than thirty minutes before the delegation should have got to the hotel, Charlie went to his window, which was at the side of the hotel with only the narrowest view of the main Bayswater road along which they would travel. He had to press very closely against it to see anything at all and there was a constant traffic stream of cars and coaches and buses from which it was impossible to distinguish one from another and Charlie quickly gave that up, like everything else.

He was downstairs in the bar within five minutes of its opening for the evening, the first in and able to get the previously chosen seat, the stool at the corner of the bar and the abutting wall. Unasked the barman poured the scotch and said: 'They've arrived.'

'Did it all go smoothly?'

The man gave a shrug, a gesture which seemed to be close to an affection with him. 'I gather it was a bit chaotic, but then it normally is when a big party checks in.'

'How many are there?' asked Charlie, immediately alert.

'Twenty-five,' reported the informative man, just as quickly. 'Quite a few women as well as men.'

Where, wondered Charlie, was the only one who mattered? He said: 'They going to be difficult to look after as guests? I mean are there any special requests, that sort of thing?'

The barman replenished Charlie's glass. 'Not that I know of. There's a few policemen about, in case there are any protests. There are sometimes, apparently.'

'So I've heard.'

The barman moved away to serve another arriving customer, a man. From the suit Charlie guessed he wasn't Russian and got the confirmation when the newcomer ordered in a heavy Scots accent. The first Russians entered soon afterwards, two men and a woman. Charlie was easily able to hear and understand the conversation, although he gave no indication of being able to do so. They were embarrassed at their uncertainty of whether to order at the bar or be seated for the barman to come to them. The difficulty was resolved when the man did go to them. The woman, who had urged that they be seated, said she'd known all along that she was right. The older of the two men stumbled out the order, for beer and scotch. The Soviet conversation ranged over the flight from Russia to how different London was from what the woman had expected – 'a lot of buildings as big as in Moscow, which I hadn't thought there would be' – to where Harrods was and how worthwhile the forthcoming air show was going to be.

Their conversation became increasingly difficult for Charlie clearly to eavesdrop as other Russians came into the bar and either joined the original group or established their own parties and set up a conflicting chatter of cross-talk.

Charlie's earlier friendliness paid dividends because increasingly busy though he became the barman didn't forget him. Charlie sat alert to every new customer, each time feeling the bubble of half expectation when it was a woman he couldn't at first properly see but none was Natalia. He was alert for other things, too. He watched for recognitions from the other already identified members of the delegation or listened for the recognizable language, to assure himself that each newcomer *was* Russian and not an independent, unassociated guest at the hotel. Having established from the barman the total number in the Soviet party Charlie kept count, so that he was constantly aware of how many were missing. And instinctively self-protective, he set about locating the KGB escorts. After half an hour he was convinced about two, an uncertain, hunch-shouldered man who tried to join two separate groups which closed against him and a younger, aloof person with rimless spectacles and fair, almost white hair, who didn't try to join in at all but who sat studying everyone over an untouched glass of mineral water. There would be more, Charlie knew. He wondered if they were travelling with the party or would be drafted in from the embassy less than a mile away.

Around seven thirty the first arrivals started to move and Charlie overheard several references to food and understood from the conversation that a section of the hotel dining room had been partitioned off for them. At no time had the number in the Soviet party amounted to more than fifteen, Natalia had never been among them and Charlie felt a sink of disappointment. Which he recognized to be unrealistic, because from their time together in Moscow Charlie knew that she scarcely drank at all and that a bar was not an automatic place for her to visit. But it had clearly been the assembly point and Charlie had built up a conviction in his mind that was where he would see her. He grew quickly impatient at his professional lapse. He was behaving like an immature, lovesick teenager instead of an experienced operative who had already risked too much by exposing himself to a great many unknowns where unknowns shouldn't have been allowed. It was time to stop. To reverse the situation, at least: professionalism first, personal involvement second. Which was how it should be. And always had been, even with Edith. Charlie felt something approaching shock at realizing how his priorities had got out of sequence. Thank Christ he'd become aware of it this soon.

'Another one?'

Charlie looked up at the barman, shaking his head in his newfound determination to start conducting himself properly. He knew the aloof Russian he'd guessed to be KGB had registered him in the bar and decided it would be careless to remain any longer in a position so openly to monitor the Soviet party. Just as it would be a mistake, desperate though he was to do it, to eat in the hotel dining room in the hope of still catching sight of Natalia. Working as closely as this – much too close to be sensible – he had to ease himself from people's consciousness, not positively attract their attention by always being around.

He ate a disappointing meal in a Lebanese restaurant in the Edgware Road, remained attentive and therefore satisfied with everything that happened about him, and when he returned to the Bayswater hotel used the pretext of reading theatre bills around the reservation desk to check the bar again. There was quite a lot of noise and audible snatches of Russian but Natalia still wasn't there so he went directly up to his room.

Lying in the darkness Charlie let the disappointment sweep over him once more but did not get angry at the emotion as he had in the bar, because there was no longer any danger in the indulgence. It hadn't gone at all how he'd wanted. He'd imagined a recognition being made and of a meeting somehow arranged and of telling her the things he never had in Moscow – that how very often he'd wished he'd stayed instead of running – and of her saying things back that he wanted to hear. Never this; never absolutely nothing, not so much as a snatched glance of anyone who just *might* have been Natalia.

What if she hadn't, in the end, been one of the delegates at all! What if for any one of a dozen reasons her participation had been cancelled! Or the announced composition of the Russian party had been wrong! Or changed! The doubts and the questions flooded in on Charlie, so quickly it was difficult for him to evaluate one before another demanded attention. And then he stopped bothering to try to evaluate any of them separately because he recognized each was a distinct possibility. He tried to think beyond, to its significance, and couldn't because there was still so much by which he was confused and found impossible to work out.

He snapped on the sidelight, near the tea-making things, and booked an early morning call from the hotel operator. Charlie did not sleep properly, despite the assurance of waking up on time. He didn't dream: Charlie was rarely aware of dreaming. Instead he remained in a half-awake state, always knowing where he was and why he was there and he was already fully awake when the telephone rang. He made himself some tea from a sachet on a string and wished he hadn't, so he left it, and was shaved and showered by seven. He guessed he was far too early, which he proved to be, but he didn't think there was another way of doing it. A vaguely detached night porter – not the attentive old man with the ill-fitting teeth – was still on duty when Charlie descended to the foyer, which bustled with a surprising number of maids with vacuum cleaners and floor polishers, maintaining the artificial marble. Charlie saw no one he identified as Russian.

He decided that the house of converted offices was the best spot but that to establish himself there at once would make him too obvious, so he walked fully out into the Bayswater Road. At the junction he considered he was concealed from the hotel. For almost thirty minutes he maintained observation from there and while he was doing so he located the convenient newsagent's shop. When he felt he could not stay so far away from the hotel any longer Charlie bought two newspapers to hide behind deep in the entrance porchway of the Regency house. It was better concealment than Charlie had believed it would be. There was a half-enclosing, pillared fronting wall and a porticoed roof and inside it was encouragingly dark, too dark, in fact, even to use the newspapers as he intended.

There was one false alarm, when four Russians Charlie recognized from the bar the previous evening emerged from the hotel, but they merely walked down to the main road, towards the park, and then back again. By the time they reached the entrance the nervous KGB escort was on the steps. Charlie first thought the man was checking for the wandering group but he ignored them and then relaxed at the arrival of the expected transport. There were two large limousines and a back-up minibus. The man fussed about the order in which they were parked, after which he took a list from his pocket and hurried back inside the foyer. The first party of Russians straggled from the hotel almost at once.

Natalia was among the second loose grouping.

Charlie felt a jolt deep in his stomach, a physical sensation almost like a kick. She was wearing a high-necked suit, grey he guessed from where he stood, and carried a briefcase. Her hair was definitely shorter than he remembered and he had the impression that she was taller, which was obviously absurd. She seemed quite assured, with none of the shuffling apprehension of some of the others around her. Charlie thought she looked beautiful and decided at that moment that whatever risk – even sacrifice – he'd taken was worth it, just to see her again.

There was the customary confusion that always arises getting a body of people into different vehicles and for a few moments there was a lot of disordered milling around in the forecourt, with none of the Russians going anywhere.

Which was the moment Charlie made his move and when Natalia saw him. Charlie knew at once that she had, although with superb control she gave not the slightest outward reaction apart from the briefest stiffening in the way she stood and Charlie was sure that only he was aware of it because for that fleeting moment he allowed himself to look directly at her. Then he looked away and continued on into the hotel and on up to his room without looking back or paying any attention whatsoever to the later-assembling Russians.

Charlie pressed against the door to close it behind him and remained there for a few moments, realizing that he was shaking very slightly. He wasn't concerned at the nervousness: a nervous tension was necessary, protective, in a lot of situations. It only became an embarrassment during hostile interrogation. Charlie smiled at the reflection, intrigued at the connection of thoughts: the last time he's undergone a hostile interrogation was facing Natalia

276

in a Moscow debriefing house after his supposed escape from British imprisonment and defection to Moscow.

The shaking went very quickly. Charlie sat on his still unmade bed and took off the Hush Puppies to free his feet from their minimal incarceration and smiled to himself in satisfaction. She knew he was here: here and waiting for her. And he was sure she'd know where to look for him, that night.

With time to kill now, Charlie had a leisurely breakfast with greatly improved tea and read the previously ignored newspapers before leaving the hotel again to walk unerringly to one of the several public telephone boxes he had marked during his earlier study of the area.

Charlie bypassed the main switchboard at West-minster Bridge Road, dialling the number he knew would connect him directly to William French in the Technical Division.

'Anything?' asked Charlie, without any greeting.

'Yes,' said French, not needing it.

'How many?'

'Two.'

'Same as before?'

'Yes.'

'You made a trace yet?'

There was a long hesitation from the technical expert. Then French said: 'That's going further than we agreed.'

'Not a lot of point in leaving a thing half finished, is it?' prodded Charlie.

'You're a bastard!'

'Actually,' said Charlie mildly. 'My mother says my father's name was William. But I don't think she's too sure.' He'd have to call the Hampshire nursing home, to find out how she was.

The drawings shipped from London in the overnight diplomatic bag brought the tally of those so far provided by the American up to nine. And there was the advice from the separately received *rezidentura* cable that there would be a further four in the next shipment. That news alone was sufficient to make Alexei Berenkov a very happy man but there had been other separate cables and what he'd learned from them made Berenkov's satisfaction complete.

There were a series of reports from the London surveillance teams permanently monitoring Charlie Muffin. There was the record of his arriving at the hotel and of his lingering in the bar in the obvious hope of seeing Natalia – who irritatingly had not appeared until dinner and then been late – but most important of all was the message of a few moments earlier, the report of the passing contact encounter between them that very morning, at the entrance to the hotel.

They were definitely his marionettes, Berenkov determined: his own puppets whose strings he could pull and jerk to make them dance to whatever tune he chose to play. He smiled at his metaphor and then continued it: dance they would be made to do and it was time to turn up the music.

The message was already prepared and waiting for transmission to London on the broken code, because Berenkov had the sequence well established in his mind now. The transmission was in the full and supposedly more difficult combination code, mixing cyrillic Russian with English with two numbers – three and five – introduced as variables. The message consisted of twenty-six digits.

It was instantly intercepted, which Berenkov was sure it would be, and partially deciphered within two hours by decoders now exclusively assigned to its transcription and therefore familiar with all the

278

permutations that the Russian Technical Division had designed.

Richard Harkness attached enormous personal importance to his service's ability to read the cipher transmission, believing his proper utilization of it to be the way to his permanent appointment as Director General. He had taken a risk, which was quite out of character, in so early bringing the code-breaking to the attention of the Joint Intelligence Committee – and could still remember their frowned surprise – but it had paid off brilliantly with the two quick successes. Now they no longer frowned, because they were impressed, which they should have been. And Harkness was determined to continue impressing the group upon which his future so closely depended.

Always the man of rules, Harkness had issued a written decree that he should be alerted at the moment of an interception – even before its successful translation – and by the time Hubert Witherspoon responded to the summons to the top floor of Westminster Bridge Road the decode and its original lay side by side on the expansive and meticulously tidy desk.

'Another one?' anticipated Witherspoon at once. He was enjoying the increased favouritism since Harkness had got the acting directorship and was convinced it could only get better.

'But incomplete,' qualified Harkness, swivelling the message, already in its file binder, so that the other man could read it. The latter part of the transmission was deciphered in full – King William Street – but it was preceded by a group of nine numbers, 759001150.

Witherspoon frowned up. 'I don't understand.'

'No one in the decoding division does, either,' said Harkness. 'It won't decipher. Whichever key the decoders try it still comes out gibberish. They're reprogramming the computer but they're not happy.' Neither was Harkness. So far there had not been any difficulty that hadn't been quickly overcome, and the hindrance made him uneasy: he wanted uninterrupted success, not setbacks.

Witherspoon had stood to read the message. He sat back now, pulling at his lower lip, which was a mannerism. He immediately saw a possible explanation and was glad he could so quickly prove his cleverness to the other man. 'So!' said Witherspoon. 'We've got to assume a connection between this and the other message that is so far meaningless to us: REACTIVATE PAYMENT BY ONE THOUSAND?'

'Yes,' said Harkness cautiously.

'Then it fits, doesn't it?' invited Witherspoon.

Harkness wished he wasn't being asked to give an opinion because at that stage he didn't have one, but he was unembarrassed in front of the younger man. Harkness decided he'd been wise in making himself Witherspoon's protector. He said: 'How do you see it fitting?'

'The first message is most likely a payment instruction?'

'Yes?' agreed Harkness, still doubtful.

Witherspoon was aware of his mentor's difficulty and decided to make the next question rhetorical to avoid worsening it. 'And what do we have in King William Street? The Moscow Narodny Bank!'

'Oh yes!' agreed Harkness at once. 'That fits: that fits very well indeed. We're getting the beginning of an operation.'

'Maybe not the beginning,' qualified Witherspoon at once. 'The first message says *re*activate. Something had been ongoing and was suspended. Now it looks as if it's being resumed.'

This was *enough*, calculated Harkness: enough to

make a preliminary report to the joint planners, which had more than one benefit but all to his advantage. It would continue to prove their – and by 'their' the unavoidable inference was *his* – exceptional access to a vital intelligence source. And at the same time it eased the ultimate responsibility if things went wrong or failed completely to be interpreted because all the other agencies were represented and would be ordered to contribute, so any failure would be a shared one. Overly theatrical Harkness, who was a devotee of American crime series on television, said: 'All we've got to do is find out what it was. And is.'

'We've got no access into the bank?'

Harkness shook his head. 'None. Nor are we likely to get it.' The man paused. 'Could those digits be something as simple as a bank account number?'

'Possible,' said Witherspoon. 'The grouping looks too large, though. And there are too many for it to be a telephone number.'

'We should impose surveillance at once,' determined Harkness, pleased with a decisive action that would make his report appear even more complete. 'It'll be an enormous job but I want photographs so that we can run a comparison upon all known Soviet bloc people in London.'

'That *will* be an enormous undertaking,' said Witherspoon, coming as near as he felt able to querying the order.

'I'm not expecting us to get everybody,' accepted Harkness. 'Our man might just be among the ones we do get. Once we've got a face and an identity we'll have a lead to follow.'

'What else can we do?' asked Witherspoon.

'Continue to rely upon the code interception,' said Harkness confidently. 'That's our best chance.'

33

That night Charlie was in the bar at the same time as the previous evening but there were some Russians ahead of him, all men, and three he did not recognize from twenty-four hours earlier. His corner stool was vacant, however, and his regular drink served as he took it. Charlie was tight with excited anticipation and was glad the shaking of the morning wasn't showing. He would not have been surprised if it had. All he could think about was how soon the reunion was going to be. Soon now. So very soon.

'How's it been?' said Charlie to the barman, wanting any useful gossip before it became too busy for the man to talk.

'They were at Farnborough so it was quiet at lunchtime, thank God,' said the barman. 'I needed the rest after yesterday.'

'Kept you busy then?'

'There were about eight who didn't want to go to bed. And wouldn't.'

'I've heard it said the Russians are big drinkers,' offered Charlie encouragingly. 'What happened in the end?'

'One of the party came down and ordered them all out: a quiet one who was in earlier, when I think you were here. Kept to himself and drank only mineral water. You remember him?'

'No,' lied Charlie. Confirmation of KGB, he thought contentedly: ten out of ten and go to the top of the class. He said: 'They all go to bed then?'

'Like lambs,' said the man. 'Which merely left me with another hour to clear up.'

'Good for business, though?'

'They don't seem to have heard much about gratuities,' the man complained heavily.

He moved away to serve some more of the Soviet group who entered and Charlie gazed with apparent indifference across the bar but in fact straining to pick up a comprehensive conversation. He got most of one, from the first four men, and it intrigued him. It was devoted to that day's show and they appeared to be making a critically open assessment of two of their Ilyushin airliner exhibits compared to a Boeing aircraft on display. Neither of the two KGB men were in the bar yet and Charlie supposed the speakers wouldn't expect an outsider to be able to understand Russian but it was still more outspoken than he would have expected, in front of other arriving colleagues. Charlie concluded that either they were senior aviation specialists confident of their unassailable positions or *glasnost* and *perestroika* were being more successful within the Soviet Union than he understood them to be.

Charlie accepted the second whisky but warned himself to be careful. He was light years away from his capacity even to be slightly affected by what he was drinking but he wasn't going to do anything to mar the reunion with Natalia. That afternoon he'd bathed again and shaved again and just before coming down to the bar put on one of the new shirts with the still-crisp suit he hadn't worn since getting it back from the cleaners. From his reflection in the bar mirror he saw that the tuft of hair which always stood up like a cornfield suddenly hit by a strong wind was still plastered into some degree of neatness by the water he'd splashed on but he didn't expect it to stay that way because it never did. Not bad though, considering. He was too far away where he was sitting properly to check out the eyes but he'd examined them upstairs in the bathroom mirror and seen, gratefully, that there wasn't any redness. One broken blood vessel was making a tiny red canal down the left-hand side of his nose, but it was hardly noticeable unless you looked hard. There was certainly no puffiness of neglect or excessive indulgence in his face. But then why should there be? He was careful to balance the take-away junk food with something substantial at least two or three times a week and the single malt whisky couldn't be considered neglectful or indulgent by the most critical doctor. What was it the medical director had said at the spy school assessment? That he was in remarkable shape: something like that. Charlie hoped that Natalia would think so. Soon now, he thought again: so very soon.

The bar seemed even more crowded than the previous evening. The two KGB men were there, the aloof, get-to-bed official by himself as usual, the untouched mineral water in front of him, the fidgety one being rebuffed from group to group, like before. There was a small but competing group of English tourists entrenched by the far window and some separate individuals as well, and the barman was really having to work. There was little danger of drinking too much: it would have been difficult to get too much if he'd wanted it.

Abruptly Natalia was there.

Intent though he'd been, concentrating upon nothing or no one else, Natalia was over the threshold and already on her way into the bar before he fully realized it was her. With one realization came another – that she was not alone but escorted by a sparse-haired, plump man who was actually holding her cupped elbow proprietorially – and Charlie felt an immediate stab of jealousy. There was only passing recognition with the other delegation members ahead of them and they made no effort to join anyone. Natalia turned along the bar, which brought her facing completely towards him, but as she did so she twisted to speak to the attentive man with her and didn't look at Charlie at all. There was one vacant stool, about five yards from where Charlie was hunched, and Natalia took it. The man stood close beside her and put his hand upon the low back, still proprietorial. Charlie's jealousy grew.

The barman returned behind the bar after a few moments to serve them – white wine for Natalia, beer for the man – and while he was there he refilled Charlie's glass and said: 'This looks like being twice as bad as last night.'

'Why not get some help?' Charlie's throat felt clogged and he had to force himself to speak normally.

'I've asked. The manager says it's an unusual situation that doesn't arise often enough.'

'I feel sorry for you.' It had been easier to get the words out that time.

'I remember when this country had unions!' bemoaned the man, hurrying away.

He was behaving ridiculously, Charlie thought: losing his professional priorities again. Why the hell shouldn't she come into a bar with someone else on the delegation! What conceivable significance need it have! If he were so frightened of what *might* be, why stop there? Why the hell couldn't she be married or involved or utterly uninterested in him, after so long! Charlie looked up from his drink, not at her but at her angled reflection in the bar mirror, and found she was looking at him in precisely the same way, avoiding any chance of anyone guessing a connection between them. She gave no facial reaction either, but Charlie, who remained completely expressionless as well, didn't need any. It could only have been seconds but it seemed much longer and then Natalia broke the gaze, turning to catch something her companion said.

Charlie straightened slightly on the stool, decisively finishing his drink, and looked around for the barman, who was some way away getting an order from the English group. Charlie put two pounds beside his empty glass and as he left the room paused almost directly behind Natalia's chair and made a miming gesture for the man to charge the drinks to his room.

'Thirty-five,' he called out and the barman nodded.

In his room Charlie experimented, closing the door just before the point of engaging the lock, frustrated that he hadn't practised earlier to ensure it was feasible. The first time he took his hand away the door swung too far inwards, making it obvious it was unlatched, but it was better on the second attempt.

Charlie retreated further into the room, slightly raising and then lowering his arms as if he did not know what to do with his hands, which he didn't. He stared around the room, for no particular reason, caught sight of his reflection in the mirror and saw that his hair was like a windswept cornfield again. He pushed an uncertain hand across it but it sprang back up so he stopped trying. Would she have heard? Understood? It had seemed perfectly natural – and more importantly, undetectable to anyone else – when she'd positioned herself so near to him at the bar but there was no absolute guarantee she would have picked up the room number because he hadn't been able to make it a positive shout and there'd been a lot of noise. What could she do if she'd missed it? If she didn't come he'd have to think of something else to try tomorrow. But what if... ? Charlie never reached the end of his own question because there was the softest sound against the door

286

and then tentatively it was pushed open and Natalia stood framed in the doorway, smiling nervously at him. Her hesitation was only brief, a second, before she slipped in and properly closed the door behind her. Having done so she stayed with her back against it, as if she were frightened to come any further, and Charlie remained where he was, as if he were frightened, too.

'Hello,' said Charlie.

'Hello.'

'I. . .' he started and stopped. Then he said: 'I should have thought of something better to say but I haven't. Christ, I've missed you!'

Natalia came to him then, in a rush, and they clung to each other and kissed – awkwardly in their eagerness, more colliding than kissing at first – and Natalia pulled away breathlessly and said: 'Oh my darling I've missed you too! I've missed you so much!'

Charlie looked around the small, inadequately furnished room and then, holding both her hands in his, started back towards the bed for them to sit. Natalia didn't move, resisting him. He shook his head at her and said: 'I didn't mean. . .'

'. . .I know,' stopped Natalia, putting her finger to his lips. 'I can't stay. I'll be missed.'

'When?'

'Later. Just wait for me.'

'The thin one who doesn't drink watches everyone,' warned Charlie, remembering the conversation with the barman.

'Bondarev,' she recognized. 'I can get away. Don't worry.'

'I love you,' blurted Charlie.

'And I love you,' said Natalia.

Charlie waited. He guessed it would be for several hours and that he could have gone out to eat but he didn't want to: he didn't feel like eating or drinking or doing anything. Just waiting, to be there when she returned. It had happened, he realized, with something approaching surprise. They were together again and it was like it had been before. No, not like it had been before: before in Moscow it had been quieter, not frenzied. But the anxiousness, the snatching out for each other, was just a disbelieving excitement, that it *had* happened. It would be like it was before, soon enough. *I love you.* Her words – the way she said them – echoed in his mind. So there was no new husband, no involvement, no impediment. *I love you.* How would they. . .Charlie started to think and then stopped. He wouldn't plan, *couldn't* plan, how they would do anything. They just had to take every minute – grab every minute! – as it came. No forethought, no speculation. Just be together.

It was past midnight when Natalia came back. There was the same soft sound, the door opening and closing in an instant, and he was holding her again but calmer this time, less hurried. They were still by the door and Charlie felt out and locked it.

Natalia smiled at the precaution and said: 'I won't try to get away.'

'I don't want you to, not again.'

Her face straightened. 'Not yet. Let's not talk about anything yet.'

At the beginning, horrified, Charlie did not think in his anxiety that he would be able to make love to her. Natalia realized it and was very patient, coaxing and soothing, and he finally did and it was as perfect as they both wanted it to be. They climaxed in complete harmony, Natalia making tiny, muffled pleasure sounds, and Charlie wanted to do it again almost at once and it was perfect the second time. Afterwards they remained locked tightly together, as if to part would break the mood, Charlie with his head against Natalia's neck, stroking her thigh and running his hand up to her breast and then back again, Natalia feeling his face in the darkness like someone without sight etching his features into her mind.

It was Charlie who finally spoke, still not moving from how he lay against her. 'There's a lot to say.'

'Not tonight,' said Natalia. 'Tonight I just want it to be like this.' Oddly, Natalia felt frightened of words. She was back with Charlie, in Charlie's arms, and it was wonderful and she didn't want to think about anything else.

'Did you guess I'd get to you?'

'I hoped.' She wished he'd stop.

'I meant it. About your not getting away again.'

Natalia moved her fingers just slightly on his face to put them against his mouth, in the quieting gesture she'd made when she'd first come to him. ' Later.'

'Why later?'

Because I know it's a decision I have to make and now I've got to make it I'm frightened, thought Natalia. 'Please!' she said.

'OK! All right!' said Charlie, hurriedly retreating. He was wrong to pressure and crowd her so soon. They were together, which neither had believed ever to be possible, and that should be enough for the first night.

'Don't be angry,' pleaded Natalia, concerned she was spoiling the moment.

'Don't be silly,' said Charlie. 'How long can you stay?'

He felt her shrug. 'Not too long. Bondarev is very diligent.'

'What's your room?'

'Six twenty. But don't try to come: it's a sealed floor.'

'I know,' said Charlie. 'What about tomorrow?'

289

'You'll have to wait for me, like tonight.'

'Be careful.'

'I'll be all right,' said Natalia. 'You want to know something?'

'What?'

'I didn't believe I could ever be this happy any more.'

The problem that developed was caused by Yuri Ivanovich Guzins and in a way no one had foreseen.

The scientist's nervousness had worsened, not improved, as the days passed in the Kensington house, not helped by his refusal ever to leave it, so unreasonably frightened was he of British counter-intelligence detection. Although it was of his own choosing Guzins felt increasingly imprisoned and like a lot of imprisoned men his objectivity distorted. His constant preoccupation became the responsibility imposed upon him by his having to approve each drawing before its dispatch to Moscow in the embassy diplomatic bag. The breaking point came with a query relayed back from Baikonur on a drawing he had already sanctioned and too brusquely put by Vitali Losev, himself preoccupied by the conflict with Alexandr Petrin. It was actually a misunderstanding by a junior technician at the Soviet space complex, with no reflection at all upon Guzins, and corrected in minutes. But Guzins misconceived criticism in Moscow and decided that if he were to protect himself in future he had to go exhaustively through every tracing, practically debating every line with the American, before releasing it.

The language difficulty meant each question and answer had to be put either through Losev or Petrin, and the insistence delayed Krogh so much that he was only managing to complete half instead of an entire drawing at each session.

By the night of the reunion between Charlie and Natalia, just three miles away across Hyde Park, the backlog of drawings for which Guzins was withholding permission had reached six and there hadn't been a shipment to Moscow for two days.

'It's impossible to go on like this!' protested Losev.

'Then get instructions from Moscow that I don't have to arbitrate any more,' said Guzins hopefully.

34

The next day Charlie walked all the way to Marble Arch, where he finally succumbed to the protests from his feet. From there, on impulse, he took a cab to his home territory and The Pheasant. There the landlord, who knew him, suggested it was a nice day and Charlie said he'd known better. He didn't eat, because he didn't feel like it, and back at the hotel he avoided the bar in the evening. Natalia slipped into his room before midnight.

Charlie said: 'I worried like hell, all day.'

Natalia kissed him and said: 'There was no need.'

'We've got to talk.'

'Yes.'

'You first,' urged Charlie.

'What?'

'Everything. From the day I left you.'

Natalia's shoulders rose and fell. 'The strange thing is there doesn't seem a lot to say. I thought there would be but there isn't.' There was another shrug. 'I know that's silly and there must be but I can't think of it. All I can think of is being with you again.'

Charlie pressed her into the only easy chair in the room, perched himself on the edge of the bed directly in front of her and said: 'Tell me what there is. What you can think of.'

Natalia started hesitantly, unprepared. She talked of being finally admitted by Kalenin the day Charlie fled and of recounting the story they had rehearsed and of how frightened she had been, but how she'd been believed. 'Actually congratulated,' she volunteered.

'What happened to Edwin Sampson?' interrupted Charlie.

'I don't know. I told Kalenin he was a plant to infiltrate the KGB, like you said I should, but I never learned the outcome.'

'Poor bastard,' said Charlie softly.

'I thought you despised him.'

'He *was* a plant,' disclosed Charlie, telling her because there was no further hurt the man could possibly suffer. 'I didn't know it. I really thought he was a traitor from the very heart of our service but he wasn't. He'd been prepared for years, built up his credibility by leaking a lot of good stuff to convince Dzerzhinsky Square he was genuine. The idea was to embed him deeply into your Moscow headquarters to be the best source we'd ever had.'

'He would have broken under interrogation,' said Natalia distantly. 'It's easier to understand now why my story was accepted so readily.'

'I hope he did confess quickly enough,' said Charlie. 'There wouldn't have been any point in his resisting: in suffering. But he wouldn't have known that, would he?'

'No,' agreed Natalia, conscious of Charlie's guilt. 'Like you said, poor man.'

'I didn't know,' repeated Charlie.

'What about you?' demanded Natalia quickly. 'What was your part in the operation if you didn't know about Sampson?'

Charlie hesitated, and wondered why he did. He said: 'My being there was nothing to do with Sampson at all. I'd trapped Berenkov here in England and we knew he had been promoted through the KGB after he was repatriated. Our Director General guessed Berenkov, being the sort of man he was, would befriend me in Moscow, which he did. The hope was that by my running back he'd come under suspicion in Dzerzhinsky Square: maybe even be discredited. That was something else I didn't know, until I returned. I was told to make a series of contact meetings with a source whose identity I didn't know but that if the source didn't turn up – which of course he didn't, because there wasn't one – to get back here.'

'Which you did,' reminded Natalia pointedly.

'I've wished I hadn't, a million times,' said Charlie, just as pointedly.

'Berenkov wasn't discredited,' she revealed. 'He's still head of the First Chief Directorate. It was he who transferred me from debriefing.'

Charlie's hesitancy now was from his uncertainty how to guide the conversation. He said: 'Berenkov appointed you personally?'

'When I was summoned I thought it was to do with us: that they'd found out something we hadn't thought of and that I was going to be punished, after all.'

'What *is* your function now?' demanded Charlie.

Natalia told him of Berenkov's appointment interview and of the overseas visits she had already made and of which Charlie was already aware. She said: 'Berenkov regards the move as worthwhile: my assessments have proved accurate so far.'

'Are there often department changes like this within your service?'

Natalia lifted and dropped her shoulders again. 'I don't know. I haven't heard of them.'

Neither had he, thought Charlie. He said: 'Weren't you surprised?'

'Very,' conceded Natalia at once. She smiled and added: 'Pleased, too. I never thought it possible but I prayed   for   this.'

Enough, thought Charlie. He said: 'Who's the man you were with?'

'Man?' frowned Natalia, puzzled.

'Last night, in the bar?'

Natalia smiled again, shaking her head this time. 'His name is Golovanov. He's the chief aeronautical engineer from the Ilyushin plant and I've only known him for two days and he gropes a lot. OK?'

Charlie smiled back at her, shamefaced. 'I wanted to know.'

'There isn't anyone, Charlie. There hasn't been, not at all.'

'Good.'

'And?'

'No,' assured Charlie in return. 'No one.' What about Laura? Not the same, he told himself: not the same at all.

'I wondered,' admitted Natalia. 'Worried, which was stupid. Not my business, I mean.' .

'Isn't it your business?'

'We've talked enough tonight.'

'Why avoid it?'

'I'm frightened.'

'That's ridiculous.'

'I know.'

'So?'

'Please, Charlie!'

'No,' he refused.

'Later.'

'You've got to decide.'

'I know.'

'You said you loved me.'

'I do.'

'So what's left to decide?'

'You decided: you came back. You wouldn't stay in Moscow.'

'I told you it was a mistake I've regretted, a million times.'

'And I've told you I'm frightened.'

'You don't have to be.'

'Of course I do!' said Natalia impatiently.

Charlie wished he had not been so glib. 'We can do it!' he implored.

'I don't want to talk any more, not tonight.'

'Or last night, either.'

'Please!' she said again.

'I want you to stay. I want you to stay and marry me,' he declared.

Natalia stared at him, knowing that was exactly what she wanted, too, but unable to bring herself to say the actual words. She said: 'Let me think.'

'There's nothing to think about!'

'Tomorrow.'

'What'll be different then from now?'

'Tomorrow,' she insisted.

'I. . .' started Charlie and then stopped. Enough again, he decided.

'What?'

'Nothing.'

'It's late; I should go back.'

'You were later going back last night,' he reminded her.

'I don't feel. . .'

'. . .that wasn't what I meant.'

Once more they stared at each other for several moments, neither speaking. Then Natalia said: 'It's been my fault.'

'Mine,' contradicted Charlie.

She made an impatient gesture. 'Both our faults then!'

'I don't want there to be another mistake, not like last   time.'

Natalia   stood,   impulsively.   'Tomorrow,'   she repeated.

'Tomorrow,' Charlie accepted.

There was a minuscule escalation, the requirement for the London embassy to reply on the same eavesdropped code. The message from Berenkov, in Moscow, said: HAS PAST VISITOR MET GUEST? Losev, obedient to his instructions, replied: ENCOUNTER CONFIRMED.

'It's building up!' insisted Harkness.

'A visitor *is* a guest,' pointed out Witherspoon.

'Legend identities?' queried Harkness.

'It's a possibility,' suggested Witherspoon.

'Work on the supposition,' said Harkness.

35

Emil Krogh believed it would be the last day he'd
need at the factory and he was glad because he
thought Springley had started to become suspicious.
On the last visit the man had hung around the tiny
temporary office like he had on the first occasion but
his attitude was different: then he had been solicitous
and eager to help but now he was querulous and towards the end had openly questioned why the American wanted access to a set of drawings he had already
studied. The true reason was that Krogh had tak-
en insufficient notes from his previous examination
and had two drawings unfinished at the Kensington
house, adding to the backlog that the finicky Russian
was creating. Krogh improvised, inventing a story of
possibly finding an incompatibility between what the
two factories were creating and needing absolutely to
check. He actually sketched the American companion piece to which the English part was to be joined,
supposedly to substantiate his query, and Springley
had eventually appeared satisfied – but only just.

Petrin kept pressing him for a completion date for
the drawings which Krogh at the moment was refusing to give, convinced that if he provided a deadline
the Russians would insist he meet it, and he didn't
want any more pressure than he was already under.
But in his own mind he had decided another
week. It was a foregone conclusion that the technical expert with the moustache would insist upon his
usual translated interrogations, so a positive return
to California was impossible to fix yet but Krogh
was hopeful the delay wouldn't extend for more
than three days beyond his own finishing estimation.

Then home. Home to Peggy, with all this settled and behind him.

He'd written to Peggy, two long letters which he'd never done on a trip away from home before, telling her how much he wanted to get back. Which he did. Desperately. Back to the safety of people and places he knew. To be treated properly, like a human being, not disparaged and sneered at, like they constantly sneered at him now. He'd told Peggy he loved her, too, which was something else he hadn't done for longer than he could remember. And he did. He was going to prove it when he got back: make it up to her for all the half-assed screwing about and the neglect. He'd written that he was tired and wanted to rest – which he did, aching from fatigue although Petrin's pills were giving him some sort of sleep at nights – and that he intended they should take a vacation together. That's what he needed. To get away, just he and Peggy. Somewhere they could just relax, sleep a lot. Eat good food. Get well. The reflection came quite naturally but it surprised Krogh and then he wondered why it should. That was how he *did* feel about what had happened in America and was continuing here: like he was suffering a debilitating illness during which he'd done things over which he did not have complete control and which therefore he couldn't be called upon to account for. A person couldn't be blamed – accused of anything – when they were ill. That wasn't fair. But it was going to be all right. He was going to get well again soon now.

He announced when he arrived at the Isle of Wight factory that he thought this would be his last visit and that maybe he should say goodbye to Bishop and the other directors who'd welcomed him, which had the effect Krogh wanted, of getting Springley away from constantly looking over his shoulder. The project chief returned to say the chairman wanted to give him a farewell lunch and Krogh said he thought he would be through in time and that he'd be happy to accept.

Because it was a last-minute arrangement it was not so stiffly formal as the day he arrived, with less people in the directors' dining room. The chairman wanted the assurance that he'd had access to everything he wanted, which Krogh gave the man, recounting his invented story of an unfounded incompatibility to make it seem his trip had been worthwhile and hoping further to satisfy Springley, who was at the lunch. Bishop said if there were any uncertainties that arose later in his mind he was always welcome to return and Krogh promised to remember that. There was small talk about how much longer he intended remaining in England, and Spear, the managing director, agreed that another week in London would be nice at this time of the year. Then Spear disclosed he hoped to visit the West Coast in the near future and Krogh responded as he knew he was expected, inviting the man to be his guest both in California and at the plant, and they exchanged contact cards.

Krogh – with Petrin as his constant travelling protector – was back in London by late afternoon, although as had become their custom there was no open contact between them until they got to Kensington and the usual reception committee of Russians. To whom, generally and without sufficient thought, Krogh announced he did not need to visit the British factory any more.

'Good!' said Petrin at once and ahead of Losev, his open satisfaction reminiscent of the moment Krogh wrongly declared he was finished, in San Francisco's McLaren Park. 'So what's the positive completion date?' The demand had arrived from Moscow overnight: there'd been no explanation but the request had the highest priority designation and was in Berenkov's name.

Krogh gestured towards Guzins, hunched at the large document table over the drawings already completed but still unreleased, scribbling reminder notes for later queries in a lined notebook. 'Shouldn't you be asking him?'

'I'm asking you!'

'I don't know,' refused Krogh, enjoying his flimsy superiority. 'The completion if I am allowed to work uninterrupted will be very different from when I can possibly finish if we have to endure the nonsense of these nightly question-and-answer sessions.'

Losev had officially received the completion date demand, as the London *rezident*, and was enjoying the difficulty of his American counterpart. Wanting to exacerbate it he used English to talk to Petrin, so that the American could understand. Losev said: 'Moscow was very insistent, remember?'

Petrin ignored the intrusion. 'I'll say. . .' he started and then hesitated, showing his uncertainty.

Krogh was immediately aware of it. Cutting in quickly he said: 'It doesn't really matter what you say, does it? I am the person doing the job and I say I can't give you a positive date yet.'

Guzins seemed to become aware of a dispute going on in the room, although he could not understand what was being said. The moustached space scientist blinked up from his drawings, eyes moving between each of the other men in the room. 'Is there a problem?' he asked mildly.

'Be quiet,' dismissed Petrin, exasperated at how he'd so easily lost control of the situation and knowing there was little he could do to recover. Capitulating, he said to the American: 'Give me your estimate, then?'

'I can't,' insisted Krogh adamantly, buoyed with

unexpected courage.

'That's going to irritate Moscow,' suggested Losev, again talking to the other Russian but still in English.

Petrin looked contemptuously at the man, groping for a necessarily crushing retort. 'But not as much, I'm sure, as your abysmal failure to get what was required from here in the first place,' he managed. It was not as good as he would have liked but it was good enough. Losev's face flared at once and Petrin thought, contentedly: More than good enough.

'I have a lot of questions,' said Guzins from the work table.

'Later,' ordered Petrin curtly.

'Do you want me to talk? Or draw?' demanded Krogh.

'Draw,' said Petrin. Heavily he added: 'Draw quickly.'

'There's Moscow's cable, which requires an answer,' said Losev, trying to fight back.

'Which I want to see before it is transmitted,' said Petrin.

Alexei Berenkov was displeased by the difficulties that appeared to be arising in England but not as seriously as either of the Russian *rezidents* in London imagined he would be.

Photographs of what was being stolen from Britain had always been an important part of the ensnarement Berenkov was plotting for Charlie Muffin. The abrupt and delaying insistences of Yuri Guzins merely required their being taken sooner and more extensively than he had originally intended, but in many respects that would be a useful rehearsal. The need for the introduction at all also showed that any delay was caused by the obstructiveness of the Baikonur scientists, not from any inability of the First Chief Directorate of the KGB, which was a positive bonus.

302

The impossibility yet to get a specific date when they could expect to have a full set of drawings for the Star Wars missile housing was slightly more aggravating, because Berenkov could not move against Charlie Muffin as he intended until the drawings were safely completed. But here again there was a lot more for Berenkov to establish before the trap could be effectively and destructively sprung, so the inconvenience was minimal.

Berenkov did not inform London of either easy reaction, however. He demanded that Krogh be constantly pressed, to provide a finishing date, and in the same batch of instructions – sent not through the intercepted channel but in the unread diplomatic bag – ordered Losev to re-establish contact with Henry Blackstone and advise the man to expect a new control under a new codename, Visitor. The same day as Berenkov dispatched those instructions he sent a message over the open channel. It read:
ALERT VISITOR SOUTHWARDS.

36

All she could do was apologize, decided Natalia: admit to Charlie she'd behaved ridiculously and that she didn't know why and ask him to forgive her and say of course she wanted to stay and be with him for ever. Which she'd always known she did and dreamed about and all she'd thought about from the day he'd left her in Moscow and made even more ridiculous what had happened the previous night. Of course she was frightened: would be, for weeks and months and years. But that wasn't sufficient reason for what she'd done and said. Or rather, *hadn't* said. Natalia hadn't known then and didn't know now why she'd been so stupid. Stupid and ridiculous and. . .her mind seized, trying to find words in either Russian or English brutal enough to fit her idiocy and self-anger and failing. Just apologize: hold him and love him and apologize.

Natalia was impatient for the day to be over, to put things right between them. She was distracted at the air show, which she didn't enjoy anyway because there was too much noise and too much technical discussion and because she couldn't really see the purpose of her being there at all. And unconsciously – but dangerously – dismissive to others in the Soviet delegation until Gennadi Redin asked if something were wrong or if she were unwell, and Natalia made a belatedly determined effort to show she was neither and take attention – and curiosity – away from herself. She was early in the hotel bar that night and among the last to leave for the dining room, and table-hopped in their enclosed section until she was sure she was no longer the focus of any particular interest from the KGB escorts.

But always, to the minute, aware of the time. She pleaded tiredness to free herself from the tactile Golovanov over coffee in the lounge and was back in her room by eleven, careful to travel up to the sixth floor with another female interpreter and be seen to enter her room. Inside she stayed close to the door, intent upon the sounds from the corridor. The lift arrived, forcing her to withdraw, the first time she tried to leave. Natalia allowed five minutes before attempting to leave again. This time the corridor was deserted. She locked her door and in seconds was at the central stairway which looped around the lift-shaft, pushing through the firedoors but stopping on the landing, listening now for the sound of anyone climbing up to confront her. She heard nothing and started down, walking quite openly, the explanation of changing her mind and deciding to rejoin the late-night group in the coffee lounge or the bar already prepared, as it had been every night she had descended like this. Natalia encountered no one going down to the third floor, where she stopped, listening once more. There was still no sound from below. And the corridor along the third floor was empty. Now she hurried, thrusting through the firedoors and scurrying the short distance to Charlie's door, which was ajar as it had always been.

He was half on the bed, his back against the headboard, the television on but with the volume low. He got up at once, coming to her, and Natalia reached out and clung to him, her head against his chest, and found herself crying – like so much else without knowing why.

Charlie smoothed her hair and she felt his lips against her forehead. He said: 'You're OK. You're safe. What is it?'

Natalia shook her head, still against his chest, and said: 'Nothing.'

'You're crying!'

'I could hardly wait to get here. I've been so miserable, so *angry*, with myself all day. I don't know. . .' Natalia foundered to a halt. *Why* were the words in her head at other times never there when she needed them!

'I don't. . .' started Charlie.

'I'm sorry,' Natalia interrupted, wanting to say it all. 'So very, very sorry. Last night was a nonsense — *I* was nonsensical — and I can't understand. . .' There was another momentary stumble. '. . .I'm ashamed and sorry and say you'll forgive me.' Babbling like a fool, Natalia thought: I'm babbling like a fool — I *am* a fool — and making myself appear a bigger idiot.

Charlie pushed her away, holding her at arm's length. Natalia was red-eyed and red-nosed and serious-faced. He said: 'That it?'

She jerked her head up and down, not speaking because she couldn't get the words in the correct order.

He smiled at her and said: 'You've got a dew-drop on the end of your nose.'

Natalia gave a cry and swivelled away from him, scrubbing her hand across her face and said: 'My god. . .I don't believe it!'

'Actually you didn't have.'

'But. . .'

'I had to do something to stop you cutting your wrists and bleeding to death.'

She smiled back at him shyly. 'Oh I love you so much!' And she did: utterly and completely. How could she have the previous night. . .she began to think and then stopped, because she didn't have to go on. He'd forgiven her, made a joke about it and he was the most wonderful man she'd ever known and she was going to be with him for the rest of her life. For ever and ever and ever.

He led her further into the room, to the only easy chair again, and said: 'Last night *was* a nonsense, wasn't it?'

Natalia gave a helpless shoulder lift. 'I don't know why. . .'

'. . . You already told me.'

'You haven't said you forgive me.'

'You haven't definitely said you're going to stay.'

'I'm going to stay, my darling,' assured Natalia fervently. 'Of course I am going to stay.'

'You haven't told me about Eduard,' Charlie reminded solemnly.

'Perhaps because I don't want to.'

'What happened!' demanded Charlie, misunderstanding.

Natalia told him of Eduard's last leave and of her son's coarseness and of how much the boy had reminded her of her abandoning husband. 'He was awful! Disgusting! I hated it!'

'He's still your son,' frowned Charlie, in another reminder.

'He doesn't want me, need me, any more,' insisted Natalia. 'I'm sure his only reaction to my not going back will be to worry about his career. And under Gorbachev I don't think that will be affected: that he'll be affected.'

'There's a lot to plan. To work out,' said Charlie. 'I'll do it all.'

'I won't defect,' Natalia announced.

Charlie stared at her, bewildered. 'What!'

'I'll run with you. Stay with you. But I won't go through the debriefing routine: tell your people things that will make me a traitor.' The determination had not been so positively formed in her

307

mind the previous night – she hadn't *had* such a determination the previous night – but Natalia abruptly wondered if subconsciously that hadn't been partially responsible for what she now considered an aberration. Maybe Charlie would understand. Maybe he wouldn't. It was, after all, illogical, although not at all to her. Technically she *would* be a defector, a traitor: fit the description of all the denunciations that might be made against her. But not in reality, according to her own definition. She was remaining in a foreign, alien country with the man she loved and who loved her, in return. But that was all. She didn't intend disclosing any details of her previous operational life, any secrets. She felt for the Soviet Union as only a Russian could feel: could understand, even. She wouldn't betray or disgrace it.

'I see,' said Charlie doubtfully.

'I hope you do.'

'There'll be pressure.'

'I won't need to apply for asylum, if I'm your wife,' pointed out Natalia.

'No,' Charlie agreed, but still doubtfully. Professional decision time for him as well, he realized. There was no point in discussing it with her now, overcrowding her with ideas of change and sacrifice.

'I can't avoid the way I feel,' offered the woman.

'I said I understood.'

'When?'

The decisive question surprised Charlie. Even more surprising – astonishing – he realized that although he'd been consumed with her staying with him he hadn't given any thought to the mechanics of achieving it. He said: 'I'll need to think. To sort it out.'

'It can work, can't it?' Natalia demanded, doubtful herself now.

'Of course it can,' said Charlie encouragingly.

'We are going to be happy, aren't we?'

Charlie leaned across the narrow space separating them and pulled her to him, on the bed. 'I don't have to tell you that.'

'I want to hear you say it.'

'We're going to be happy,' said Charlie obediently. 'It's going to be difficult and involve a lot of adjustments and there are going to be disputes and arguments but mostly we're going to be happy.'

'I know that,' said Natalia. 'I'm prepared for it: all of it.'

Was she, wondered Charlie. He said:'How closely are you watched?'

Natalia hesitated. 'Fairly closely,' she conceded. She felt enormous relief at having committed herself. And anxiety, too. Anxiousness to *do* it: positively to flee and set up home with him. For the first time Natalia realized that in Moscow she'd never thought of their relationship as being properly settled and established: that it was as transitory as it had proved to be.

'Is there the possibility of your getting away from the group to be completely by yourself?'

Again there was not an immediate reply. Then she said: 'I've never actually tried it, not here. On the other trips there were shopping expeditions but everyone had to go in parties of three or four. And there always seemed to be someone from the local embassy, ostensibly to help with any language difficulties.'

'When do you think you'll have most time?'

Natalia considered once more. Then she said: 'Towards the end, I suppose. The days we go to the air show are fairly regimented.'

'What about feigning illness? Staying behind one day?'

She shook her head at once. 'They'd call the embassy doctor. Even if I managed to fool him someone from the embassy would stay with me. I might attract attention to myself, trying to do that.'

'The end then,' agreed Charlie.

'How will we do it?'

Something else he had not properly formulated in his mind. 'The simpler the better,' said Charlie. 'I'll fix it.'

'Take me to bed, Charlie.'

He did and it was better than before because neither of them was as anxious to prove anything. Afterwards Charlie said: 'In a few days we'll be together all the time.'

Beside him he felt Natalia suddenly shiver, as if she were cold. She said: 'Make it happen: please make it happen.'

Richard Harkness' emotions were mixed. There was immense satisfaction, at being named controller of the special, inter-agency task force to combat whatever the Soviets were evolving, because he saw that as the surest indicator yet of his inevitably getting the permanent, more important appointment. But there was also some caution. There unquestionably *was* an operation under way and they had cable exchanges to prove it. But not the slightest evidence yet *what* it was. Which created the dilemma for Harkness. Precisely because his task force was inter-agency whatever he did now would make him the focus of those agencies, particularly M15 who would regard the matter rightfully theirs as internal counter-intelligence and resent his usurping their authority and responsibility. If he got it right – he *had* to get it right – the prestige and the accolades would be his. But if there were a mistake and things went wrong, the backbiting and sniping would start

310

at once, ridiculing and denigrating him. So as well as being a satisfied man Richard Harkness was a worried one.

Within an hour of his return from the Joint Intelligence Committee meeting at which the task force had been created with him in charge Harkness summoned Witherspoon, who immediately responded with congratulations, through which Harkness sat patiently, nodding and smiling. Then he said: 'But we haven't got one *definite* fact to guide us!'

'Yes we have,' challenged Witherspoon at once. 'And so far we've overlooked it.'

'What?' demanded Harkness. The other man was young, much younger than officers were normally considered for promotion, but Harkness was thinking increasingly of elevating Witherspoon when he himself got the full director generalship. These past few months Witherspoon had proven himself an invaluable sounding board.

'The embassy itself!' insisted Witherspoon. 'That's where the Moscow messages are going to. And from which they're being answered.'

'And upon which there is a permanent watch!' accepted Harkness.

'Recorded observation which you've now got authority to call for,' reminded Witherspoon. 'The surveillance reports could take us to the next link in the chain.'

'I'll demand them,' said Harkness at once. 'And I want you to take control of the search: it should be fairly concentrated because we've got the date of the first intercepted message. There wouldn't seem to be any point in going back further than that.'

'Thank you for the confidence,' said Witherspoon.

'Still nothing from King William Street?'

Witherspoon shook his head. 'At least we've now got more manpower to carry on the observation.'

'Visitor and guest,' mused Harkness. 'Who's the visitor and who's the guest?'

'And who or what has been reactivated!' added Witherspoon.

'That could be another pointer,' seized Harkness at once. 'Let's widen the search of the other agency files. Find out if there's been an inquiry that ended inconclusively, with no action taken.'

'What about our own records?' queried Witherspoon.

'Yes,' agreed Harkness, although doubtfully. 'I suppose we should.'

'It'll come,' said Witherspoon confidently. 'I'm sure the breakthrough will come.'

Five miles away, in the Kensington safe house, Vitali Losev held the telephone loosely, keeping any impatience from his voice at the repeated and obvious attempt by Henry Blackstone to protract what he was saying and make it sound important.

'I thought you'd like to know that the American has gone,' said Blackstone.

'I do,' said Losev, forcing the enthusiasm. 'That's very useful.'

'And I'm expecting to hear any day about my re-application,' lied Blackstone.

'I've got something to tell you at last,' announced Losev, following the newly arrived orders from Moscow. 'You're going to get your retainer. And soon someone other than myself to deal with. He'll be known to you as Visitor.'

'Thank you,' said Blackstone. 'For the retainer I mean. Thank you.'

'We regard you as important,' mouthed Losev.

'How will I recognize him, this new man?'

'I'm coming to explain it to you,' promised Losev. 'And you'll recognize him well enough.'

37

Hubert Witherspoon had begun that evening, within an hour of his briefing from Harkness. And very quickly found that with such extensive facilities at his instant disposal his role as overall coordinator was not going to be as difficult as he'd initially believed it would be. At no time, however, did he imagine the break coming as quickly as it did.

That first night he requisitioned a conference room on the ninth floor, deciding he needed more room than there was in his cramped offices adjoining Charlie's and because the move brought him closer, with immediate access, to Richard Harkness. He ordered the photographic surveillance in King William Street increased and called for the observation reports of all the other agencies – but particularly M15 – over the previous month upon every Soviet and Eastern bloc installation, not just embassies and consulates but trade missions, tourist offices and national airline buildings. He demanded, for comparison, all cable and radio traffic intercepts and asked for a squad of four cryptologists to do nothing but run those comparisons against what they had obtained via the Soviet number-for-letter code. To speed that process he overnight asked scientists at Britain's worldwide listening facility, the Government Communications Headquarters at Cheltenham in Gloucestershire, to programme a computer to respond to trigger words and to feed in each – and then a combination of each – from the cables they had been reading in the hope of some earlier recognition. Gathering together the cryptologists gave Witherspoon the idea and he extended it, ordering the formation of small groups of men – never more than four or five – specifically to monitor and backcheck every suspicious report or inexplicable event involving Eastern bloc activity over the period being investigated. Again, for speed, Witherspoon requested a computer be programmed to throw up any connection with the Soviet code. He further had a physiognomy programme created for tell-in-seconds computer analysis of all surveillance photographs against known or suspected Eastern bloc officers operating in Britain.

The intended organization was as comprehensive as Witherspoon could conceive, although issuing the encompassing orders for its creation by others was completed comparatively quickly, before midnight. Fuelled by adrenaline, Witherspoon was back in his elevated ninth-floor room, high above all the activity he had initiated, soon after dawn, running it all through his mind in a search for anything he might have forgotten. It *was* all-encompassing, he assured himself. Yet the need was for a positive target, a way forward, and he hadn't been able to isolate that. The Soviet embassy, he thought, remembering the previous day's conversation with the acting Director General. They had agreed that was the conduit so it was upon the embassy that he had to concentrate. Witherspoon reviewed the requests and instructions he had already sent out covering the Kensington Palace Gardens building, looking for gaps and not finding them. He was sure he had covered everything. He'd demanded biographies upon the entire diplomatic staff, with the known and therefore more easily monitored *rezidentura,* and all available details of movements in and out, and the Foreign Office were checking visa applications, to show up any changes in the last month. A new arrival could fit the cable words, reflected Witherspoon: visitor or guest. How ironic it could be if the lead came as easily as that, without the necessity of everything else he had set up. The reflection ran on. Visitor and guest, thought Witherspoon, actually writing the words down on a reminder pad in front of him. Who in God's name was Visitor and who was Guest! Who. . .he began again and then halted. Who indeed! *Were* there visitors: guests? Witherspoon felt a lurch of anxiety because it was obvious – blatantly, absurdly obvious – and he hadn't thought of it! *They* hadn't thought of it! Maybe he'd been wise, calling upon God in time. It wasn't too late to recover, to add this demand to all the rest. It wouldn't appear an oversight, even, because it could be argued that the orders he'd already given covered parties of visiting Russians. What he now had to do was *focus* the demand, with a direct reference and connection to the embassy.

The resentment was obvious from the counter-intelligence contingent now under his jurisdiction but Witherspoon was peremptory with it, insisting upon a quick response because it was an easily answered question. Which indeed it proved to be. Within an hour there was confirmation of a delegation of visiting Russians in the country – attending the Farnborough Air Show – that they were staying at a monitored hotel and that there had been reasonably continuous but entirely understandable contact between it and the Russian embassy, less than a mile away down the Bayswater Road.

It was still, at that stage, nothing to become unduly excited about although Witherspoon *was* excited, exaggerating in his mind a possible connection. The expression 'monitored' meant a photographic record had been maintained and Witherspoon instructed that a picture of every member of the Russian delegation be run through the now-established physiognomy check. He also extended the profile comparison to include every supposed diplomat who had maintained contact from the embassy. Additionally, with no conscious forethought and certainly with no scientific facility for comparison, Witherspoon asked for a complete set of the photographs to be sent up for him to examine on the ninth floor.

It formed a fairly bulky dossier and was not confined to the hotel. From the different backgrounds as he flicked through Witherspoon realized that some of the snatched, concealed-camera photographs had been taken not in London but at the air show itself, where a man – or several men – with a camera would not have aroused any suspicion.

Witherspoon almost missed it, although he was never to admit it. He'd put the picture aside and had finished considering another and was about to place that upon the discard pile when he hesitated, recognition coming belatedly, and returned to the earlier one. He gazed down, bringing his head close over the print in astonishment, and openly giggled, loudly, in incredulous disbelief. He started instinctively to move but stopped himself, wanting to be sure because it wasn't absolutely clear. Witherspoon went back to the very beginning and studied again all the photographs he had already examined, although not this time concentrating upon the obvious subject but upon the background and people in that background. The picture at which he'd initially stopped *was* the first shot of Charlie Muffin, partially obscured by the door of a van or minibus. But there was a much clearer photograph further on in the selection, probably taken on a different day because the van or bus wasn't there any more. It was full face and unmistakable and Witherspoon sat back in his chair positively trembling at a discovery he did not have the slightest idea how to interpret. Only that it was enormous: utterly staggering. And he'd been the man to make it!

The access to Harkness *was* immediate. The pastel-shirted acting Director General – the suit was brown today – smiled up at Witherspoon's entry and said inquiringly: 'I wasn't expecting to hear from you this soon?'

Witherspoon wanted very much to make the announcement dramatic but couldn't find the appropriate words. So without saying anything he laid the two prints on the desk in front of Harkness, deciding, relieved, that the gesture was fairly dramatic as it was.

The acting Director General remained staring down at them for several moments. When, finally, he raised his head his pink face was already flushing red as it did when he was excited or angry or both. 'Why are these important?' he demanded, his voice tightly controlled.

'They are taken at a Bayswater hotel at which an official Soviet delegation is staying. They're attending the Farnborough Air Show.'

Harkness could not curb the start of a smile. 'When?'

'Two days ago.'

Harkness nodded, as if he were receiving confirmation of an already known fact. 'Right,' he said, softly and to himself. 'I've always been right. *Known* I was right.'

'What are we going to do?' asked Witherspoon. This was too important for him to volunteer suggestions and ideas this early anyway.

'Guard against the slightest error,' warned Harkness cautiously. He sat back in his too-large chair, making a tower from his put-together fingertips.

'Our earlier investigations – the investigations he thought he'd turned back upon us – will show we were quite correct to be suspicious. But he's still a serving officer in this organization: some opprobrium is unavoidable.'

'He was not your appointee,' said Witherspoon sycophantically. 'Neither was it your decision to re-admit him into the service, after his apparently proving his loyalty in Moscow.'

Harkness nodded gratefully, and smiled more fully, 'All the more reason for taking care now, when we've got him in circumstances that are indefensible. He's got a gutter cunning: let's never forget that'.

'But what *is* it?' pressed Witherspoon. 'Is our finding him like this an entire coincidence? Or is there a connection, a link, to the other business? Some of the intercepted messages could seem to fit.'

Harkness shook his head positively.'Too soon for any conjecture,' he insisted. 'At the moment we proceed in the belief that it *is* a coincidence, one quite apart from the other.'

'A separate investigation then?' accepted Witherspoon.

'But which I want you to supervise,' insisted the acting Director General. 'You know all the facts, everything. It can only be you.'

'I understand,' said Witherspoon. There could be no explanation Charlie Muffin could make, so the outcome was inevitable. Just as, Witherspoon determined, his own gaining of further and increased credibility in Harkness' opinion was inevitable.

'It has to be as thorough as it's possible to be: I'm not having the confounded man slip off the hook again. I want every case he's ever been engaged upon examined. . .' Harkness smiled in recollection. 'Which will be easy because the arrogant swine gave me permission to access his personnel file at the assessment school. Tear his office apart. And the place where he lives. I want that stripped, taken apart by experts, by the best people we've got. And the maximum observation, of course. We're to know what he's doing, every minute of the day. And night.'

'Why wait?' demanded Witherspoon urgently. 'Why not arrest him immediately? He's a serving intelligence officer, like you said. In a hotel, without orders, containing a group of Russians! That's enough, surely!'

'No,' refused Harkness. 'It would be premature. I know it's a risk, perhaps a terrible risk and that I've just warned against risks. But I'm not being inconsistent. We've got to take the chance because when we arrest Charlie Muffin I want every piece of evidence assembled and ready. I want everything so ready and prepared there won't be an answer or an excuse he can even consider offering.'

'All right,' accepted Witherspoon doubtfully.

'We've got him, Hubert! This time we've really got him!'

'Yes,' agreed Witherspoon. It was the first time the man had called him by his christian name.

'And you're the person who's made it possible,' said Harkness, in apparent recollection. 'Well done! Very well done indeed.'

'Thank you, sir,' said Witherspoon.

'I'll see to it that credit is properly accorded.'

'Thank you sir,' said Witherspoon again.

Charlie made his now customary excursion from the hotel, reflecting how things and surroundings soon became predictable in people's minds, and how dangerous it was. The telephone he'd used before was unoccupied and unvandalized. He dialled the direct number, as before, and recognized William French when the man replied.

319

'Any luck?' asked Charlie at once, guarded on the open line.

'Luck doesn't come into science and mathematics,' rejected French.

'It did with my mathematics,' said Charlie. 'I was bloody lucky if I got anything right at all.'

'I've got it,' announced the expert.

'I've been thinking,' said Charlie. 'I've asked a lot from you.'

'I've been thinking that for days!'

'Why don't you let me have an official account? But keep it vague: no memo to or memo from. Just the number.'

'I thought this was *un*official.'

'It's always a problem, deciding the difference, isn't it?' said Charlie. 'If you let me have a report then you're covered against censure if anyone demands an explanation, aren't you?'

'Sometimes I can't understand you at all,' protested the man.

'It's a trick of the trade,' said Charlie.

'Enjoying the holiday?'

'Could be better,' said Charlie.

38

The Kensington house became a bearpit of snarling, teeth-bared Russians each biting and clawing at the other. Emil Krogh remained as aloof and separate from it as possible, although there was a satisfaction from their falling out despite his not being able to understand the arguments because when the bickering began they reverted to their own language. But mostly the American sealed himself off from his surroundings: like an exhausted and about-to-sink swimmer just able to make out dry land in the distance, Krogh fixed his mind solely upon the soon arriving day when the drawings would be finished. His only real contribution to the dissent – which he hope contributed to it – was to go on refusing to answer the daily repeated demand to know when that finishing day would be. Krogh thought it did contribute because rows frequently erupted between Petrin and Losev within minutes of the refusal conversation taking place. Like they invariably did later in the day, which became the set-aside time to stop drawing to go through the nitpicking queries assembled by the moustached space expert. Once more Krogh was not able to follow the constant disputes with the man but again he didn't have to. It was clear that Petrin and Losev considered the line-by-line review to be a completely time-wasting obstruction and again Krogh attempted to worsen it, taking longer than was truly necessary to answer some points.

Despite the constant antagonism – an antagonism that developed into a contempt towards him from his countrymen – Yuri Guzins persisted with the nervous insistence, uncaring that the backlog was increasing, hoping that it was causing problems for the huge intelligence official who'd out-argued them at Baikonur. Guzins was sure it was that man who was responsible for his being in England. His release of drawings dwindled to one a day for inclusion in the diplomatic bag. And sometimes not even one.

These frictions were peripheral, however. The constant, unremitting fury was between Alexandr Petrin and Vitali Losev, the near hatred growing foolishly – and worse, ridiculously unprofessionally – to the extent that there no longer needed to be an identifiable reason for them to clash. Just to be together in a room was sufficient: thrust together they circled and goaded each other, literally like snarling bears in a pit.

It got so that Losev snatched illogically at small things in an effort to prove his superiority and when Berenkov's easy resolution to the problem of Yuri Guzins' delays arrived from Moscow the London station chief saw it as just such an opportunity. He went to Kensington ahead of the KGB technicians and announced the moment he entered the room: 'Moscow's patience has been exhausted waiting for what they're supposed to be receiving from you. As from today I am going to get this operation working as it should do.'

'The delay isn't my fault!' protested Petrin and regretted it at once because it made him sound petulant.

Losev smiled, isolating the whine. 'If you want to protest to Moscow you can, through the embassy channels,' he offered in apparent generosity, furthering Petrin's regret.

'How, precisely, are you going to speed up delivery?' demanded Petrin.

'Yes, how?' came the demand from across the

room from the listening Guzins.

'Wait!' insisted Losev. The effect would have been better if he'd tried to time the technicians' arrival to coincide with this moment but he decided, gratefully, that he had recovered some of the earlier ground lost to Petrin.

Guzins abandoned his inspection and note-taking, crossing the room towards them. 'There is no way the delivery can be speeded up,' he insisted. 'I won't allow the system to be changed!'

'Moscow considers it can,' said Losev cursorily, looking not at the space expert but at the door through which he expected the other Russians to enter.

'I demand to know how!' insisted Guzins, with frail bravery built upon his detailed inspection so far remaining unchallenged.

Losev came back to the man, smiling in open contempt. 'I told you to wait,' he repeated.

'You're posturing again. . .' began Petrin irritably, but was halted by the arrival at last of the Soviet team.

The first to enter the room, looking around curiously, was Yevgenni Zazulin, the professionally trained photographer who had copied the contents of Robert Springley's briefcase on the Isle of Wight. The second was Andrei Aistov, one of the men who had entered Charlie Muffin's apartment and who was nominally attached to the *rezidentura's* technical section. Zazulin carried two briefcase-size camera boxes constructed from lightweight metal. Aistov brought the more easily recognized equipment, two extendable light tripods, a selection of fan-opening reflector shades and high-wattage lights.

'No!' said Guzins at once, too loudly, guessing what was going to happen without having to be told now.

323

'I won't allow it! It defeats the purpose of what I'm doing. . .!'

The two new arrivals looked questioningly between the arguing men, halting halfway towards Krogh's drawing board and the long drawing table.

Losev looked back at them, nodding. 'Go ahead and set your equipment up,' he ordered. Turning to Guzins, he said: 'You're not in a position to allow or disallow anything. Moscow want technical photographs of all the outstanding drawings and those that follow.'

'But they won't have been checked!' said Guzins, still too loudly. 'That's why I was sent in the first place!'

Losev was back centre stage and clearly in charge, which was how he liked to be but hadn't been for far too long. Petrin did not think this particular dispute involved him and had walked away, towards Krogh who had stopped drawing and was swivelled on his chair, watching.

Losev said: 'But which you're not doing fast enough. So now there have got to be changes. . .' He allowed a pause for the intended point to register. 'Why should it upset you? This way there is an added check. It'll be fully understood that the photographed drawings *aren't* approved by you: that they are, if you like, unauthorized until the confirmation comes from you. But this way there's the chance of an additional approval – queries too, if necessary – from your colleagues at Baikonur. Yours isn't the sole responsibility any more: and that's what you're shit scared about, isn't it?'

Guzins shook his head, unconvinced by the rationalization and ignoring the sneer. 'It's going to be confusing,' he insisted. 'It won't be possible to keep a proper check, working this far apart. We'll end up not knowing what I've approved or what

324

Baikonur has approved and whether we agree or disagree. And what, ultimately, is it intended we construct from? The original drawings or these new photographs! If something is put into production based on the photographs and I find a fault then it's a complete *waste* of time: absolutely counter-productive!'

Losev blinked at the flurry of objections, accepting that some had validity. None of the possible confusion Guzins had picked out could personally affect or be blamed on him, he analysed gratefully. They couldn't adversely affect Petrin, either, which was regrettable. Impatiently he said: 'A checking system is perfectly easy to evolve! You simply number the drawings you're holding back from release. And those numbers will be reproduced when they're photographed. They can be cleared by you, by quoting the reference number. And the reference number can be quoted again by Baikonur, if they need any further clarification.'

'I want a protest registered,' said Guzins, weakening but with little convincing argument left. 'The reasons for my objections, too.'

'As you wish,' sighed Losev, making his boredom very clear.

On the far side of the room Krogh looked to the approaching Petrin and then the two men assembling their photographic gear and said: 'What the hell's going on now!'

'We're going to photograph your drawings,' said Petrin, obviously.

'Why?'

'A quicker, alternative way of getting them to Moscow.'

'So you're doing away with the nightly question-and-answer sessions?' asked the American hopefully. He could be through very soon if that

325

delay were obviated: three or four days at the outside.

'No,' said Petrin. 'That's to continue. I guess that the masters will remain your original drawings. This merely gives our people an idea of the complete concept.'

At last Losev and Guzins crossed the room, bringing them all together. Zazulin straightened from positioning his lights and arranging his cameras to focus directly down over the commandeered drawing table. He smiled and said: 'I need an absolutely firm surface.'

'Use whatever you need,' said Losev, uncaring.

'How many are there?'

'Those,' said Guzins, gesturing to the pile at the end of the table furthest away from the newly erected equipment.

'*All* of them!' exclaimed the photographer, the smile going.

'What's the problem?' demanded Losev.

'No problem,' assured Zazulin. 'Just don't expect it done quickly, that's all.'

Losev looked apprehensively at Petrin, expecting a sneering resumption of their argument. The American *rezident* looked back but said nothing.

The prospect of a continuing delay took away some of Losev's earlier satisfaction of being in control, because he'd wanted to advise Moscow that night of a consignment of photographs already in the diplomatic bag, but it did not diminish the feeling by much.

It wavered further, however, when he did get back to the embassy in Kensington Palace Gardens to find the change-over shift of Charlie Muffin observers waiting to report the obviously significant build-up of British surveillance on the Soviet delegation hotel.

326

'More than it's normal to expect?' demanded Losev at once.

'Much greater,' declared Viktor Nikov, who hopefully saw a chance of getting off the boring surveillance duty. 'This isn't a customary counter-intelligence operation at all. This is intensive targeting.'

'Upon one of our people? Or something to do *with* Charlie Muffin?' wondered Losev.

'Maybe that's the reason for our being there all this time?' suggested the other man. 'Maybe he's been spotting one of our people. At the moment I think the risk of our being identified by them makes it dangerous for us to remain like we are. I think we should withdraw before we get swept up in whatever's going on.'

Why the hell hadn't Moscow better advised him what the observation of Charlie Muffin was all about in the first place, thought Losev, the temporarily subdued anger surging up again. He was being held back by unfair and unnecessary restrictions. There was only one course that he could take: the only course he ever seemed able to take these days.

He had to report to Moscow and seek guidance.

As Charlie trudged the street – actually shuffled better described his progress – he thought back to the hobby he'd had when he was young, collecting train engine numbers. Proper trains they'd been then: steam engines that spat out grit and embers so you had to be careful you didn't get bits in your eyes. They'd all been graded then, into classes and models, all with important-sounding names. Not like the diesel and electric rubbish today, all the same, like identical items on a supermarket shelf. Would train number collection still be a kids' hobby today? Maybe, he thought, although he couldn't remember seeing any youthful collectors during any trips he'd recently taken. Maybe not, then. Charlie didn't think it would be as much fun today, with trains like there were around.

Before he went back to the hotel he went to his bank.

39

'What was Edith like?'

'I told you, in Moscow.'

'Not really,' contradicted Natalia. 'Just that you'd had a wife and that she had been killed. Not *about* her: what she was like.'

In the darkness Charlie felt Natalia pull slightly away from his shoulder, against which she had been lying, and knew she was looking at him, waiting. He said: 'Blonde. Not very big: quite slight, actually. She had a funny way of changing expression, very quickly. One minute she could be laughing, the next very serious. When that happened her face changed, like she was two different people.'

'Pretty?'

Charlie hesitated, seeking the proper reply. 'Not pretty pretty, the way some women are: not cute or actress pretty. I thought she was beautiful.'

'Do you still miss her?' Natalia had been unsure about initiating the conversation, not wanting to offend him, but she told herself that they were going to be married and that she had the right to know. Charlie didn't sound upset, although she couldn't see his face, and she was glad now she'd asked.

Again Charlie hesitated. 'Yes, I suppose I do,' he said honestly.

'I don't miss Igor,' Natalia disclosed. 'I thought about him quite a lot just before I came here but that was because I was comparing him to Eduard. But I haven't missed him for a very long time: maybe I never did. I guess yours was a different sort of love.'

'Perhaps,' conceded Charlie. 'There's a lot of regrets.' He'd never admitted it before but didn't feel embarrassed to talk about it with Natalia.

'I don't understand what you've just said.'

'I didn't treat her like I should have done,' conceded Charlie, in further admission. 'Behaved badly. Took a lot – too much – for granted. I regret that now.'

'Is that a clumsy way of telling me you had affairs?'

'Some. Not a lot.'

'Are you going to have affairs when we're married?'

'No.'

'You'd have hardly confessed it in advance, would you?' It was a light remark, not accusing.

'Why'd you ask then?'

'Just wanted to hear what you'd say.'

'I won't,' said Charlie. 'Ever.'

'Did she know what you did?'

Charlie nodded in the darkness, momentarily forgetting she couldn't see the gesture. 'Yes,' he said. 'That's how we met, in the department.'

'How do your people feel about department romances?'

Charlie paused yet again. Then he said: 'I don't know that there's a department policy. It happens, but not a lot.' As far as Charlie was aware it wasn't a subject upon which Harkness had issued an edict: he supposed the man would get around to it, some time.

'It's practically encouraged in the KGB,' revealed Natalia. 'Particularly in the First Chief Directorate, if an officer is going to follow the diplomatic route by being assigned to embassies or to consulates. When they're posted abroad the husband or wife goes as well and it puts two operatives in place rather than one. Cuts down the chances of seduction by a counter-intelligence plant, too.'

'Very practical indeed,' agreed Charlie.

'Did she worry? Did Edith worry?'

'I suppose so. . .' started Charlie, and stopped. 'No, that's stupid. Of course she worried. She just didn't talk about it a lot.'

Natalia noticeably shuddered. 'It must have been horrible, having someone you love working God knows where and having the access to what was happening to him: not knowing when you arrived in the morning if there'd be a dry, cold message from some embassy station saying that your husband had been arrested. Or killed'

'Actually she was in a different section, so she didn't have access,' said Charlie. 'And I never got arrested: not on a department assignment, that is.'

'Do you mind talking about it?' asked Natalia belatedly.

'No,' said Charlie.

'Can I ask you something very personal?'

'If you like.'

'What about children?'

Charlie took several seconds to reply. He said: 'We decided against it, at first. It was Edith's decision, really. Because of what I did. She thought. . .well, that it wasn't a good idea. Then she changed her mind: she'd left the department by then, wasn't doing anything. Not working, I mean. She became pregnant about a year after she quit. She lost it, just beyond two months. It didn't happen again. Her becoming pregnant. There were tests and things and there was no reason why it shouldn't have done. Medical, I mean. It just didn't.'

'Would you have liked a baby?'

'I'm not sure,' said Charlie, again with complete honesty. 'It all seemed to be over before I'd become used to the idea of having one in the first place. I don't ever remember making up my mind.'

'I'm thirty-eight, Charlie. Nearly thirty-nine.'

'So?'

'The chances of our having one aren't good.'

He laughed. 'You thinking that far ahead!'

'I haven't been, not until now. But why not?'

'No reason,' conceded Charlie. 'I haven't, that's all.'

'Think about it now,' she demanded.

'That's not the way it's decided!' protested Charlie.

'How is it decided?'

'I don't know!' struggled Charlie. 'People talk about it. . .discuss it for a while. . .'

'You don't want one, do you?' challenged Natalia openly.

'Maybe not,' said Charlie.

'Why not?'

'Frightened, I suppose.'

'What's there to be frightened of?'

'Something happening. Going wrong.'

'I never imagined you'd feel like that.'

Charlie shifted impatiently. His arm was numb from the length of time Natalia had been lying on it. He said: 'Isn't this part of the conversation academic, anyway? There's a lot of other things to think about first.'

'Like what?'

'Like what I'm going to do.'

'Do?'

'Job,' said Charlie.

Now it was Natalia who did not speak for several moments. When she did she moved further away, off his arm, and said: 'Put a light on.'

'Why?'

'Put a light on!'

He did. Natalia sat up, careless of the covering falling, unembarrassed at her nakedness. Her body was very firm, a young girl's litheness, her breasts with hardly any sag, her stomach hard.

'So?' he said. Charlie came up in the bed too, propping himself on his tingling arm, hoping it would restore the circulation. He wondered how she was going to phrase it.

'So what are you talking about?'

'I'm talking about getting another job, of course.'

'Where does of course come into it?'

'Darling!' said Charlie, pleading for her understanding. 'You surely don't imagine I can stay on in the service if you cross over and we stay together. . .get married! It would be absurd. I'll have to resign.'

'No!' She had to convince him, Natalia thought desperately.

'There's no alternative.'

'No, Charlie,' she insisted. 'You've got to find a way!'

'There isn't one!' said Charlie, just as insistently.

'Find one!' she hissed, wanting to shout at him but unable to risk the noise in the sleeping hotel.

'Why must I find a way, Natalia?' asked Charlie solemnly.

'Because if you don't it will destroy us.'

'That doesn't make sense.'

'It does to me. It makes very good sense. I might not have known much about Edith from our time in Moscow but I learned a lot of other things. Chief of which was what the service and the department mean to you. It's ingrained into you, Charlie. You think it, live it, exist on it.'

'It's a job I'm good at,' Charlie tried to qualify. 'There'll be others.'

Natalia shook her head in refusal. 'It wouldn't happen at once,' she said. 'Maybe not for quite a few months. But then you'd start to miss it and think about it more and more and it would grow up into a barrier between us. We'd start to fight, blame each other, and then it wouldn't be perfect any more.' She was right, Natalia knew: she was more

333

convinced than she had been about anything in her life that she was right.

'The department isn't like it was, before I was in Moscow,' said Charlie. 'There have been changes. It isn't that important to me.'

'That's not true. I don't think you believe it even.'

Charlie remembered the long-ago determination to endure whatever shit Harkness dumped upon him and conceded that it wasn't true, not completely. It was inevitable he would miss the department and there would always be regrets at not being part of it but Natalia was exaggerating to consider it becoming a problem between them. He said: 'It's what I have to do.'

There had to be a persuasion, a threat even! She thought of it and momentarily held back but then said: 'I can't be part of it.'

'I want you to say that properly,' said Charlie, more solemn that before.

'I won't cross to you,' announced Natalia.

'That's nonsense.'

Dear God, let him believe the lie, thought Natalia. Because at that moment she knew it to be an empty threat, so much did she want him. Having started it she had to go on, to make it sound convincing. She said: 'In Moscow you said you loved me?'

'Yes.'

'Was it true?'

'Of course it was true!' said Charlie, unhappy at the impatience sounding in his voice.

'Yet you came back: you wouldn't cross to me.'

'That's not even logical,' rejected Charlie. 'Then I was on an assignment, although I didn't know fully what it was. And I've told you how many times I wished I'd stayed.'

It *had* been a convoluted argument and Natalia was sorry now she'd tried to make the equation. She said: 'I'm not trying to tell you I wouldn't regret it. I'd regret it every day for the rest of my life. But not as much as I would everything collapsing between us if I stayed.' She hoped that had sounded better, but she wasn't sure it had.

Charlie was about to say that the decision wouldn't be his to make anyway – that he'd be instantly dismissed if he didn't resign first – but he stopped. This was a fatuous dispute and it was even more fatuous to protract. It was important, though, to end it so that Natalia didn't do – or consider doing – anything he didn't want her to. Charlie shrugged in apparent capitulation and said: 'All right! I'll find a way.'

Her face broke into an immediate smile. 'You truly mean it!'

'I truly mean it,' lied Charlie. The moment she fled she was irrevocably committed: that was the time to discuss what little personal future he might have.

Natalia seized his face between both her hands to kiss him, pulling him close so their nakedness touched and said: 'Oh my darling! I love you, love you, love you!'

'No more talk of changing your mind?'

'No more talk of changing my mind.'

Charlie lay sleepless for a long time after Natalia had slipped out to go back to her own room, hands cupped behind his head, not even bothering at first to extinguish the light she had insisted should be put on.

The following morning Charlie went for his usual promenade in the vicinity of the hotel but was back soon after the bar opened, where he hadn't been for several days. The barman's face opened at his entry and the man said: 'Hello! Thought you'd changed your mind and booked out early.'

'Been busy,' said Charlie. 'But I might have to leave sooner than I thought.' He never had enjoyed

335

playing the fool for too long. It made him feel uneasy, like so much else.

'Unbelievable!' exclaimed Harkness, jagged voiced in genuine shock. 'Absolutely unbelievable.'

The product of Witherspoon's organized search of Charlie's office and Vauxhall flat, together with the swamping surveillance of the hotel, was set out on a narrow conference table that Harkness had had moved in specially to accommodate all the evidence. The dossier containing all the intercepted cable transmission was also there.

'It is, isn't it?' agreed Witherspoon. 'Absolutely unbelievable.'

'Give me the sequence,' demanded Harkness.

'The dossier on the woman, Natalia Fedova, was among the material we seized in his desk. . .'

'No official logging of it being created! No indication of who she is? Why she's important.'

Witherspoon shook his head. 'No. Nothing in Records, either.'

Harkness gestured towards a set of photographs of Natalia. 'When were these taken?'

'This morning,' said Witherspoon. 'We're trailing her to Farnborough, of course.'

'Go on!' urged the acting Director General.

'The rest of the stuff we located at his flat,' said Witherspoon. 'An indescribable mess, incidentally. It wasn't easy to find. Some of the stuff was behind a skirting board in the bedroom. Some more in the casing of an electricity meter.'

Harkness started to reach towards what was on the table and then stopped. 'Forensically examined yet?'

'Not   yet.'

Harkness withdrew his hand and said: 'A thousand pounds exactly?'

336

'To the penny,' confirmed Witherspoon, guessing the point of the question.

'Reactivate payment by one thousand,' quoted Harkness.

Witherspoon smiled at guessing correctly. 'Has past visitor met guest?' he recited back 'Charlie Muffin qualifies as a past visitor, from that episode in Moscow. And the woman is a guest.'

Harkness' head moved up and down jerkily in his eagerness to agree. Excitedly he said: 'It fits! It all damned well fits!' and then looked up uncomfortably at the other man, having used the word damn. Quickly, with his accountant's mind, he said: 'We can step down all the other activities and surveillance. There's nothing to be gained now by the unnecessary use of manpower. We've solved our mystery.'

'I don't think we should let him run much longer,' warned Witherspoon.

'Not yet,' said Harkness. 'Not just yet. I want to assemble the proper inquiry panel. I hope one particular man can be there. I want Sir Alistair Wilson there to learn how his preciously guarded operative has been a Soviet spy all along.' And members of the Joint Intelligence Committee, Harkness thought: properly conducted, a preliminary inquiry to get rid of two men, not just one.

40

Everything had so far unfolded strictly according to the schedule he'd dictated – each puppet dancing to the strings he chose to pull – and Alexei Berenkov was disconcerted by the London *rezident*'s warning of increased British surveillance on the delegation hotel, because it was not in response to anything he had initiated. Not yet. He had intended other moves, further ensnaring evidence. But this put the timing out: disrupted the carefully conceived pattern. Of course there could be other explanations for the sudden British interest. Several, in fact. But Berenkov, first a field professional before he'd become a headquarters planner, decided he couldn't take any chance, not at this stage. He had to assume it *was* a premature reaction to what he'd done so far: that it was to do with Charlie Muffin.

Berenkov stood abruptly, angrily, from his desk in the First Chief Directorate building and went to the window overlooking the multi-laned highway that circles Moscow: the windows were double glazed, so there was no sound, although the road streamed with vehicles. Berenkov saw none of it, his entire concentration elsewhere. Right to assume but wrong to behave prematurely himself, he thought. He had to reassess, to analyse. Although it was not as complete as he'd planned, the circumstantial evidence was well enough spread. And sufficient for any determined prosecutor to present conclusively. What was left undone? The positive, linking connection to Blackstone, but that could be created easily enough, within twenty-four hours. Which left the apparent crime itself. Which in turn was dependent upon Emil

Krogh. Surveillance, Berenkov thought, with a flood of relief. At the moment the British only appeared to be watching, not acting. He'd always planned to fill the supposed 'dead letter' drop in King William Street *before* triggering the arrest but in further realization Berenkov accepted that did not necessarily need to be the sequence. Providing he knew the moment any move was made against Charlie Muffin – which meant continuing their own observation, despite the concern that Losev had passed on – he could do it quickly *after*.

Berenkov turned away from the ignored window, hurrying back to his desk, excited by the resolve. He had to think it through, to guarantee there were no pitfalls, but it seemed to be the perfect answer, the way for him to pick up the puppet strings again. The essential requirement was to decide how much time he would have, following any seizure of Charlie Muffin, to complete everything in King William Street. Which was dictated by the length of the British interrogation. Berenkov smiled in continuing satisfaction, because he had the perfect guide to that from his own arrest and questioning. A month, he remembered: almost an entire month of morning till night inquisition from Charlie Muffin, the man he intended, with exquisite irony, to place in precisely the same position. Not that he would need a month to complete everything, Berenkov estimated. Two days, perhaps: three at the most. For the first two or three days of his own detention they'd hardly come near him. They'd followed the classic interrogation technique, leaving him absolutely alone in a cell to let his imagination build up the fears and uncertainties and panic. He couldn't rely upon whatever happened to Charlie Muffin being exactly the same as his own experience, of course. But it was more than enough for him to plan around.

What about Valeri Kalenin? It would be protocol to brief the man, now that everything was so close: certainly an act of friendship. But there could be dangers in his discussing it with the other man. Although Berenkov himself was completely satisfied he'd evolved a way to compensate for anything the British might do there was always the possibility that the more nervous Kalenin wouldn't agree. He might even use the unexpected London activity as an excuse to cancel the entrapment altogether, irrespective of how advanced it already was. And Berenkov knew he could not ignore a direct order. Better – safer – that he wait. There was, after all, a perfectly reasonable explanation, if one were later demanded, for his saying nothing. There was no *proof* that the British moves concerned Charlie Muffin. He was simply taking precautions if it did: there could be no criticism or censure in that.

Berenkov spent more than an hour drafting and redrafting his detailed orders to London, the most insistent of which was that the Soviet watch upon the Bayswater hotel be maintained and not lifted. And that he be alerted the moment something – anything – occured involving Charlie Muffin, be it day or night.

Which necessarily meant his remaining permanently at the First Chief Directorate building, Berenkov accepted. After ensuring the dispatch of the London instructions Berenkov had a cot moved into his office.

'What's happened?' asked Valentina when he telephoned to tell her he was not coming home.

'Nothing yet,' replied Berenkov. With his customary belief in himself he added: 'But something will, soon now.'

Vitali Losev was in a foul mood, in no way alleviated

by this being the last occasion he would have to deal with or even talk to a man he despised. It had started to rain after he left London and he didn't have a topcoat. The weather worsened the further south he travelled and although he managed to dodge from cover to cover after getting off the train he was still soaked when he reached the Portsmouth bar he'd established as their meeting place, his trouser cuffs clinging wetly to his ankles, his jacket soggy on his shoulders.

Blackstone was already there. The man smiled up hopefully when Losev entered and said, unwisely: 'Rotten day?'

Losev didn't bother to answer. Instead he slid an envelope along the bar top and said: 'Here it is: the retainer.'

'How much is it?' demanded Blackstone. His tongue edged out, wetting his lips, as if he were tasting something.

'Two hundred,' said Losev.

'You're not wasting your money, believe me,' said Blackstone, thrusting the envelope into his pocket. 'I still need to know the recognition procedure for this new man, Visitor.'

Losev smiled. 'He knows you.'

'Knows me!'

'Why do you think no action was taken against you after the interview with that British security man?'

'Him!' exclaimed Blackstone, incredulous.

'What better way to protect ourselves?' said Losev. 'He's been on our side for years.'

Fifteen of the notes in the envelope in Blackstone's pocket were numbered consecutively with the money that had been secreted in Charlie Muffin's flat.

41

Charlie failed: despite all Natalia's patience and coaxing tonight nothing happened, *would* happen, not like it finally had when the problem occurred before. Charlie said Oh Christ and he was sorry and Natalia kissed him and told him not to be silly, that it didn't matter and who said it had to work every time.

'I did,' insisted Charlie, making a weak effort to ease his embarrassment.

'Chauvinist pig!' she accused, trying to help him here, too.

'It won't be like this again.'

'It will and it won't matter then, either.'

Charlie gestured around the bedroom and said: 'I'm not making excuses but this has all been a bit unreal, hasn't it?'

'Completely,' Natalia agreed at once. 'Unreal and wonderful.'

'I've worried, at the risks you've had to take.'

Natalia kissed him again, on the cheek, and said: 'I've been lucky. And careful. And prepared.'

'How prepared?'

'Like you told me, the simpler the better. If there'd ever been a challenge I'd have said I'd changed my mind and decided to go to the bar for a final drink. But I haven't had to.'

He had to tell her tonight, remembered Charlie. He said: 'And now you won't.'

'What?' she frowned at him.

'I'm checking out tomorrow.'

'But I. . .oh. . .'

'I've got to, haven't I?' urged Charlie. 'You just can't run, without some planning in advance.'

'Of course,' accepted Natalia at once. 'I just hadn't thought.' Or wanted to, she acknowledged, to herself. She felt safe, cocooned, in this bedroom: locked away where no one could get to them, hurt them. And more. His moving out, to make positive arrangements, finally committed her. And while she wanted to cross and was determined to cross she was still frightened. Frightened of being intercepted at the last minute and frightened of the unknowns of trying to live a new life in an environment and a country where she was a stranger and frightened of things she couldn't even conceive but feared would be ahead of her, lurking in dark corners.

'You don't sound sure?'

'Of course I'm sure: you know that. . .' Natalia trailed off. Then she said, hopefully. 'Can't you imagine how I feel?'

'I'm sorry,' said Charlie.

'What must I do?' she asked quietly.

'Do you know the rest of your itinerary?'

'Farnborough, for the remainder of the trade days. The afternoon of the last but one day here in London, for official receptions. The last day is packing up – the shopping I told you about – and then the plane back to Moscow in the late afternoon.'

Charlie sat nodding, not looking at her. 'The shopping expedition,' he decided. 'That creates the best opportunity: the safest. . .' he turned to her. 'Has there been any talk of groups being organized? Any arrangements made?'

'Loosely,' said Natalia. 'Everyone's talking about Harrods.'

'Make yourself part of it,' insisted Charlie. 'If your plane is going in the afternoon the outing will have to be in the morning. Just go with the group. It's a big store, usually crowded. Which is ideal. Let yourself become separated: it's got to appear completely accidental, to avoid any suspicion. There are a lot of exits and entrances. Make for the one directly opposite the underground – what you call metro – station. It's named Knightsbridge, after the district. Because it *is* a station it's busy, so there'll be a lot of cover from people using it.'

'What do I do then?'

'Just wait,' instructed Charlie. 'I'll be ready, whatever the time.'

'It all seems too. . .'

'. . .simple,' finished Charlie. 'It'll work.'

She smiled at the reminder. 'I'll learn,' she promised.

'Do you want me to go through it again?'

Natalia shook her head, serious-faced. 'No.'

'This is always the worst part, just before everything starts,' warned Charlie.

'I've never known it,' said Natalia. 'I wasn't trained as a field agent, like you. It's different for me: more difficult.'

'Just a few more days,' said Charlie. 'After that it'll all be over. We'll be settled.'

'Where?'

'I don't know, not yet.'

'I wish. . .' started Natalia, and stopped. Enough! she told herself, irritated. There was no other way – no safer way – and it was ridiculous to start saying she wished that there were. He was a professional who knew what he was doing. She had to trust him. There was surely no one else in whom she could better put that trust.

'What?'

'Nothing.'

'Let's not leave any uncertainty about anything,' pressed Charlie. 'We won't get second chances: neither of us expected this one.'

'No, really.' She didn't want to – she *wouldn't* –

show any weakness, let him know how really frightened she was. She was behaving like a child.

'You sure?' said Charlie, still pressing.

'Quite sure.'

Charlie looked at her, waiting, but Natalia didn't continue. He said: 'I'll be waiting.'

'I'll be there.'

The following morning Charlie telephoned reception from his room, apologizing for ending his booking early, but didn't go down into the foyer to settle his account until he was sure the Russian delegation would have left for Farnborough. When he got there the porter who'd greeted him the first day was behind his cubbyhole desk and Charlie smiled and said he was leaving and the porter said he was sorry he hadn't been able to be of more assistance.

'Not that it would have been easy,' said the man, his ill-fitting teeth moving as if they had a life of their own. 'Been a right work-up with all these Russians.'

'Other people have told me,' commiserated Charlie.

'Had to send out for more bar-stock two days ago,' disclosed the man. 'Some of them really *did* need minders!'

Charlie paid his bill and assured the reception clerk and the cashier that he'd enjoyed his stay and walked out into the forecourt towards the road and its taxi stand.

They got him just at its edge. There were three men, one very large, who emerged from a blue Ford. The large one waved a piece of paper towards Charlie but too quickly for him to read it. The man said: 'Charles Edward Muffin. This is a warrant for your arrest, issued under the necessary section of the Official Secrets Act.'

'Hands against the car roof, sunshine,' ordered his

immediate companion. 'It's always wise to give bastards like you a pat-down.'

Charlie did as he was told, unprotesting. The man ran his hands expertly over Charlie's body, seeking a weapon, finishing with further expertise by running the search finally down Charlie's right arm and snapping a handcuff around his wrist before Charlie guessed it was going to be done.

'Hey! What's going on!'

They all turned at the shout. The friendly, gold-loving barman named John was hurrying along the pavement, on his way to open up for the day.

The big arresting officer sighed and took a small folding wallet from his jacket pocket, holding it in front of the man to halt the approach. 'Smedley, Special Branch,' he said to the barman. 'Piss off!'

Charlie said apologetically to the barman: 'They've got to speak like that all the time otherwise they don't get the job.'

The man who had attached himself to the other end of the handcuff twisted in, thrusting Charlie into the rear of the car, and the big man got in on the other side, so that Charlie was crushed between them. The third man got in behind the driver's seat.

'You're nicked, you are!' insisted the large man. 'You're in the shit right up to your scruffy bloody neck.'

'I often am,' confided Charlie mildly. He looked at the man and said: 'So if you're Smedley. . .' He paused, turning to the man to whom he was tethered. '. . .then I suppose your name will be Abbott? You people normally stay together as partners, don't you?'

'What the fuck are you talking about!' demanded Smedley.

'Bullied any senile old ladies lately?' asked Charlie, in a very personal question of his own.

From that first alert, which came from the Soviet observers still in the hotel before Charlie was properly in the Special Branch car to be driven away, Vitali Losev had to do everything personally, specifically refused authority to delegate anything to any other Soviet intelligence officer and by so doing diminish or spread his own responsibility. Which was, he accepted, an open, threatening warning against his making the slightest error. He was not, however, unduly worried: identifiable responsibility against mistakes carried corresponding credit for success. And he did not consider what he had to do as particularly difficult. His predominant consideration, in fact, was that it put him very much in a position of superiority over everyone in the Kensington safe house but most importantly over Alexandr Petrin.

Losev approached the Kensington house by a circuitous, carefully checked route and did not hurry his final entry until he was completely sure that he was alone.

It was oddly quiet inside the large room where the drawing and the photographing were continuing, the atmosphere practically somnolent: Petrin was actually slumped in a chair, a discarded newspaper over his knees, heavy-eyed with boredom. There was a perceptible change when Losev entered the room, something like a stiffening going through the people in it, and Losev felt a flicker of satisfaction that the most discernible change came from Petrin.

'All very restful,' Losev jeered.

'Why not?' sighed Petrin. 'What some of us are doing is more tiring than for others.'

'Quite so,' said Losev. 'If it's too much for you I can always draft in some help.'

Petrin looked away, uninterested in the childish exchange. He said: 'I suppose there *is* some purpose in your coming here?'

'More than you'll ever know: or be permitted to know,' said Losev, turning away himself. Generally, to the other Russians, he said: 'I want an original drawing. And not one dated from several days ago because it's got to comply with a schedule of events. Has anything been finished today?'

'What's going on now!' demanded Guzins, in immediate protest.

'Something that does not concern you,' rejected Losev arrogantly. 'Answer the question. Is there a finished drawing from today?'

'I haven't even been able to consider it yet!' said Guzins.

'And I haven't photographed it, either,' said Zazulin.

'Do it now!' ordered Losev. 'Break off whatever you're doing. Change the film. Take whatever pictures you want of today's work and then let me have the drawing.'

'But that's going to confuse everything!' argued Zazulin. 'We're trying to maintain some sort of order about what we're doing.'

'Do as I say!' insisted Losev, exasperated.

'This is preposterous! Ludicrous!' said Guzins. 'When I get back to Moscow I shall complain.'

'Of course you will,' said Losev. In a pained voice he said: 'Now let's get on and start doing what I want, shall we?'

To comply Guzins had to abandon what he was doing, sort through the unapproved and therefore unnumbered drawings and then insert the number, so the sequence would correspond, before handing it over to Zazulin. The photographer had to unload and reload his camera and transfer from its

348

restraining frame the half-copied drawing for that upon which he now had to start working. Both men did so truculently, resentful of both the order and Losev's attitude.

As they worked Petrin left his chair and came alongside. He said to Losev, 'What *is* going on?'

'Something that you have no right to know,' rejected Losev again, haughtily. He spoiled it by adding carelessly: 'Nothing that affects what you're doing here.'

'Don't be ridiculous!' came back Petrin at once. 'Of course it affects what we're doing here! It involves one of the drawings!'

'*Separate* from what is being done here,' qualified Losev, regretting the lapse. 'Therefore none of your business.'

'I want your assurance of that,' insisted Petrin.

Losev smiled at the other *rezident* patronizingly. 'Then you have it. Just stay here and go on as you were. Doze, if you wish.'

Fortunately the drawing was of the final moulding process and not as detailed as some of the others had been, and Zazulin completed the copying in two hours. Losev thanked them with elaborate, taunting courtesy and was still out in the street again slightly after midday. Aware of the traffic congestion there would be travelling right across central London to the City by road Losev took the quicker underground, ironically using the line that took him through Knightsbridge station, where Charlie Muffin had arranged to meet Natalia.

Losev was received politely at the safe-custody facility in King William Street and escorted to the vault and to the box listed in Charlie Muffin's name, the second key to which had been left in Charlie's Vauxhall apartment. Losev deposited the drawing in seconds and, convinced of a good job well done, treated himself to an excellent fish lunch at Sweetings. A day or two before, his presence might have been recorded by the observation upon King William Street, although the safe-custody facility was not at the Narodny Bank. But that surveillance had been withdrawn, of course, in Harkness' belief that he and Witherspoon had solved their mystery.

No one ate in the safe house in Kensington, through a combination of anger and the need to restore the work routine as it had been before Losev's interruption.

'The man is insufferable,' complained Guzins.

'It's going to take me two hours at least to set up and check where I was, to make sure I don't miss out a frame,' supported Zazulin.

'It'll cause complete chaos in Baikonur,' said Guzins. 'They are going to get a set of photographs completely out of sequence and now there isn't a supporting drawing.'

Petrin glanced at Krogh, who was working on unaware of what they were discussing in Russian. 'That's easily solved,' he said. 'When Emil has finished everything he can go back and work out a duplicate.'

'What about the sequence in which the photographs are arriving?' demanded Guzins. 'That's still going to be confusing.'

Petrin considered the question, thinking back to the facile bickering with Losev. 'No it's not,' he said. 'You heard what was said: whatever the drawing was wanted for, it had no relevance to what we're doing here. We'll simply hold the photographs here until the intervening drawings are copied and everything will arrive in Moscow and at Baikonur in their correct order. That way no one get's confused.'

Guzins smiled shyly at the solution. 'Vasili Palvovich Losev is still insufferable,' he insisted.

Later, when he'd finished drawing for the day, Krogh said: 'What was all that commotion about?'

'Nothing,' dismissed Petrin. He decided against telling the American about the duplicate drawing: he'd leave that until the man imagined he'd finished, to avoid unnecessarily upsetting him. It would only require an extra day, anyway.

It was done, thought Berenkov in euphoric triumph: everything in place, and once today's waiting cable was dispatched from London in the code the British could read, it was done. Charlie Muffin would be destroyed far more effectively than by any bullet or bomb. Berenkov knew the man could never withstand any protracted period of imprisonment: Charlie Muffin was too independent, too rebellious. He'd crack. Become a vegetable or go insane. But before he did he'd know who did it to him. Know who'd been the ultimate victor.

There were twenty-three digits in the final message in that final arriving cable. It said: KING WILLIAM STREET FILLED.

42

The car went to Westminster Bridge Road, which was wrong because if the arrest had been proper he should have been taken to a police station with cells, and then Charlie realized how the arrest had been improper from the start. His first – startled – thought was about his theory on how some cases of people disgracing the department had been decisively handled, without recourse to a time-wasting trial. But Harkness wouldn't deny himself whatever official recognition were possible. Which left only one other explanation. He smiled at Smedley in the elevator sweeping up to the ninth floor and said: 'Nervous?'

Smedley said:'You don't impress me, prick!'

'You don't impress me, either,' said Charlie. 'I'd be nervous, if I were you.'

On this occasion there was no delaying security check and the office that Laura Noland normally occupied was empty. They didn't go to the Director General's suite anyway. With Smedley leading they marched towards the minor conference room which Witherspoon had taken over, because it was big enough to accommodate all the waiting people, and all the assembled evidence was there.

Charlie was not immediately interested in all the people there, only one. Sir Alistair Wilson, the Director General, was the only one standing. He did so minimally supported against a chair back: it was the most comfortable way for him because a permanently stiffened leg, badly set after a wartime polo accident, made it difficult for him to sit for any long period. He was whey-faced and much thinner than Charlie

352

remembered, the habitual check suit appearing too large for him.

'It's good to see you again, sir,' said Charlie.

Wilson stared at him across the half-moon table at which two men whom Charlie didn't know were sitting with Richard Harkness. Wilson did not reply and there was no facial expression whatsoever. Charlie was saddened but realistically accepted he couldn't expect anything else in the circumstances. At right angles to the half-moon table was another at which Hubert Witherspoon sat, behind several folders and binders. Adjoining him but at a separate table again there was a girl at a stenography machine and a male technician at elaborate but surprisingly old-fashioned tape-recording apparatus. Charlie looked at them both and decided that his guess at why he had been brought to Westminster Bridge Road was right. Smedley positioned himself at the door, like a guard, which Charlie supposed was how the man regarded himself. Abbott, the other interrogator of his mother, released Charlie from the handcuff and went to the door to join the other man.

'Here we all are then!' said Charlie brightly. His wrist hurt where the cuff had chafed it, but he refused the Special Branch men the satisfaction of massaging it.

The two unidentified men looked between each other, and Charlie wondered who they were. The obvious surmise was members of the Joint Intelligence Committee. One looked up at the standing Director General and said: 'Shall we get on then?'

Wilson sat at last, his left leg rigidly out-thrust beneath the table, and Charlie realized the man had been especially summoned to conduct the meeting. Harkness would have manoeuvred that, Charlie guessed: the deputy would want Wilson to supervise the destruction of someone he'd championed.

Wilson looked sideways to Harkness, nodded and said: 'Yes, let's get on with it.' Wilson's voice was frail, like the man.

Harkness jerked to his feet, moving from the table at which the committee sat towards Witherspoon and the neatly stacked folders. A pink shirt and handkerchief, worn with his school tie again, complemented Harkness' charcoal-grey suit, and the black brogues were brightly polished. Charlie looked at the shoes and was ready to bet they would hurt like a bugger.

'This department has been penetrated by an agent of the Soviet Union,' announced Harkness, dramatically. 'It will need further investigation accurately to say for how long that penetration has been but certainly it has existed since Charles Edward Muffin returned to this country from the Soviet Union and was quite wrongly allowed to remain in this organization. . .'

It wasn't just himself on shotgun trial, thought Charlie, looking at Sir Alistair Wilson. Harkness had to be very confident of himself to make such an open and direct attack on the Director General. Charlie was sure now that the other men at the half-moon table were from the Joint Intelligence Committee.

'. . . the damage will have been incalculable. Irreparable,' continued Harkness. 'The extent of that, too, will require further investigation. . .'

Charlie reckoned Harkness had waited years for this moment: mouthed the imagined words, maybe practised in front of a mirror.

'. . . I have always had the gravest doubts about Muffin's loyalty, as well as his ability,' went on Harkness. 'So much so that some months ago I authorized an internal investigation upon the man, which at the time proved inconclusive. It was not, however, mistaken. . .'

As rehearsed as he could be, calculated Charlie:

the man was even determined to get the apology over the harassment of his mother expunged from the record. Dig on, thought Charlie; dig a great big grave to bury yourself in, asshole.

'. . . some weeks ago this department was successful in breaking a new code with which Moscow was communicating with Russian intelligence officers – the KGB – in this country. . .' Harkness reached sideways and on cue Witherspoon handed him a piece of paper. 'The first message gave the location of a dead-letter drop in the Highgate area of London,' resumed the deputy Director General. 'It was placed under observation and a man who has subsequently admitted being an agent of the Soviet Union was arrested and is shortly to face trial. Another message led us to a terrorist courier, although unfortunately in that instance the opinion of the Attorney General was that no prosecution could successfully be initiated against the man. He has, however, been placed on the prohibited-aliens list at ports and airports of this country and his identity and photograph circulated to Western counter-intelligence agencies. . .' Harkness paused, sipping from a waiting glass of water on Witherspoon's table and Charlie thought: Television courtroom soap opera, circa 1960.

'. . . these two episodes are not connected to the matter being inquired into here. I mention them to establish the fact that the communication channel, which the Soviets are unaware of our being able to read, is undoubtedly genuine. . .'

Harkness continued the theatre by turning to look directly at Charlie at that moment and Charlie smiled and shook his head in a matchingly exaggerated gesture, for no other reason than to off-balance the man, which it did. Harkness blinked and coloured slightly and moved to speak but stopped and then started again. Charlie said: 'Sorry. Did I put you off?'

There was no flush of anger from Harkness this time. He actually smiled, indicating how assured he was, looking away in contempt. He said: 'Some weeks ago another message was decoded. . .' He looked down to the paper that Witherspoon had earlier handed him. '"Reactivate payment by one thousand",' he quoted. 'Please remember, particularly, the wording of that message. It's important. . .'

Charlie was inclined intently forward now, no longer complacent or mocking, learning things he didn't know.

'. . . that message was the first of several which initially meant nothing to us,' said Harkness. 'There was a reference to King William Street, in the City. . .'

'What!' demanded Charlie loudly.

Harkness was shocked into silence by the outburst. For several moments there was complete silence in the room, and still surprised Harkness repeated: 'King William Street,' and then clamped his mouth shut, not having intended to respond to the question.

'The bastard!' said Charlie, in quiet conversation with himself. 'The absolute bastard! But why?'

There was a further silence of which Charlie appeared briefly unaware and he seemed distracted when he looked up at last, to Wilson. He said: 'I'm sorry,' and shook his head, as if he were trying to clear it.

'You'll be given an opportunity to speak,' said Wilson.

'Yes, of course,' said Charlie, still distracted.

Harkness *was* uncertain now. He looked questioningly between Wilson and Charlie and then back to Wilson again. The Director General nodded but Harkness fumbled through various slips of paper before starting to talk. 'As I said, there was a reference to King William Street. An obvious operational instruction, involving something or someone to go south. And then to two equally obvious legend names. Visitor. And Guest. . .' Harkness paused, looking towards the group of men at the table. 'Please remember those words, too. They're also very material. . .'

The man took another drink of water. He said: 'You will be aware of the current Farnborough Air Show. In London at the moment, attending that show, is a Russian delegation. The majority – certainly one person who is extremely important in the context of this inquiry – are staying at the Blair Hotel, in Bayswater. An inter-agency task force, with myself as its head, was authorized to pursue as actively as possible the purpose and meaning of the messages we were intercepting but not understanding. That made available to us the counter-intelligence observations upon the Blair Hotel. . .' Harkness stopped again, turning once more directly to face Charlie. 'Those observations included the usual photographs and those phototgraphs showed the occupation in that hotel of Charles Edward Muffin, who was understood to be on leave from this department. . .'

There was a stir from among the men at the table which Harkness took as something like congratulation for work well done because he nodded his head in what looked like appreciation.

'As the result of that identification I again initiated a thorough investigation of the man. . .' He reached sideways without looking at Witherspoon, who placed in his hand a file that Charlie recognized. '. . . in his office in this very building this was discovered. A file – which was not listed on any register, which regulations I have introduced strictly require – upon one Natalia Nikandrova Fedova. She is a member of the Soviet delegation in this country. She is staying at the Blair Hotel. And it is my contention that she is clearly the person referred to by the legand name Guest. . . the control, I further contend, of Charles Edward Muffin, whom the records will show spent some time in the Soviet Union and who therefore fits the legend name Visitor. . .'

Harkness returned the folder and briefly leaned over the table in muffled conversation with Witherspoon. Turning back to the committee Harkness said: 'I make those contentions on the basis of further evidence. Convinced of an association between this woman and Muffin, I two days ago had a rummage search made of his flat, in Vauxhall. . .' Harkness extended his hand, so that the money was quite evident in its envelope. 'Extremely cleverly hidden, in a cavity behind a bedroom skirting board, was this envelope. It contains one thousand pounds. And I would remind you, gentlemen, of the first message I quoted to you in full: "Reactivate payment by one thousand".' Harkness felt out and was handed a key. 'This – obviously the key to some storage facility of which we are not at the moment sure – was also found in this hiding place. . .' There was another quick exchange and the key was traded by Witherspoon for the cipher pad. '. . . taped inside the casing of an electricity meter in the kitchen was this one-time cipher pad. It has been forensically tested and proven beyond doubt to be of Russian manufacture and was unquestionably the method by which Muffin communicated with Moscow . . .'

Harkness hesitated, looking triumphantly at Charlie, who gazed back at him but without any gesture on this occasion because he was intent upon how the deputy would continue. It was only when

Harkness did, saying: 'It is, I submit to you, the most damning incriminating evidence possible,' that Charlie smiled.

Harkness' voice was hoarse, being strained into a croak by the length of time he had been talking, but he pressed on, buoyed by the triumph of the moment and determined to omit nothing. 'I would have liked to pursue this investigation further before arresting the man,' he said. 'I felt, however, that this was impossible for two reasons. Two days from now the Soviet delegation, including Natalia Fedova – this man's control – returns to the Soviet Union...' The familiar demanding hand reached out and Witherspoon offered another slip of paper. '... and because of this, a message intercepted less than two hours ago. It reads: "King William Street filled".' Harkness gulped from his water-glass and said: 'I consider that this is overwhelmingly sufficient to justify the continued detention of Charles Edward Muffin, pending the further investigation I have intimated...an investigation for which I also seek the authority, on suspicion of activities detrimental to the State, of Natalia Nikandrova Fedova...'

Harkness finished, swallowing, but remained where he was in front of the evidence table for a few moments before walking back to join the men to whom he had been talking.

To Charlie, Harkness looked exhausted and probably was, but he was also flushed with elation. Charlie stood, waiting for permission from Wilson, feeling the throb developing in his feet, particularly the right one, near the ankle, and wished they'd let him sit. Another thing it was impossible to expect, he supposed, like getting any friendly reaction from the Director General.

'Well?' asked Wilson. There was a sad resignation in his voice.

359

'Is that it!' exclaimed Charlie. He made it intentionally discourteous, speaking not to the Director General but to Harkness.

The deputy director shifted uncomfortably, not expecting questioning, and looked to Wilson for guidance. Wilson said: 'Well, is it?' and Charlie guessed that Harkness regretted the earlier attack upon the older man.

'As I have made clear, the investigation is continuing,' maintained Harkness stiffly.

Charlie gave an exaggerated sigh, shook his head and said: 'Incredible! Absolutely incredible!'

'I'll not have play-acting,' warned Wilson. 'If you have something to say, hurry up and say it.'

'I have a lot to say, sir,' responded Charlie politely. 'And I ask you to bear with me because there is something going on that I don't fully understand, not yet. But which I've got to: *we've* got to.'

'You'll have all the time you want,' assured Wilson, the sadness still in his voice. 'I want to understand it, too.'

Charlie half turned, to look at the two Special Branch men by the door, and then back to Harkness. Charlie said: 'And it is going to be important that the investigation from now on is handled correctly and professionally. Not in the naive and amateurish way it appears to have been conducted so far. . .'

He hesitated, looking back to the guarded door where the two policemen were standing tight-faced and red with fury. There would have been an interruption anyway because from the table Harkness said: 'I must protest at this! I have presented what I consider sufficient evidence for this man to be detained in custody pending charge under the Official Secrets Act and I urge that this be done. And that this farce stop!'

'You've presented nothing!' challenged Charlie,

360

pleased at the way Harkness' protest enabled him to expose the man's obvious incompetence. Charlie glanced contemptuously back at the Special Branch couple and said: 'If I were an agent of a hostile power, which incidentally I am not nor have I ever been, do you know what I'd be doing now? Laughing at you. Laughing at you, like I would have been laughing all the way here in the car because I would have already known how weak your case was: how you didn't have one, in fact. Goliath over there made a big show at the hotel of waving a piece of paper and claiming it to be a warrant for my arrest. But cocked it up by referring to "the appropriate section" of the Official Secrets Act and not specifying the section, which he is required to do by law. A professionally trained agent, like I have been professionally trained but which some people here apparently haven't, although they should have been, would have realized at once what's happened. You've got a set of circumstances, most of which you haven't got a clue about, and you're hoping like hell for a confession, an explanation so that you'll at last understand. Right!'

'I refute that absolutely. . .' started Harkness but Charlie refused the man the escape: now, maybe not completeling today but certainly starting today, was the win-or-lose confrontation between himself and this carping, manoeuvring bastard. And Charlie didn't intend to lose. He said: 'So where's the warrant! Where's a proper warrant signed by a magistrate satisfied by evidence already laid before him that there is evidence to justify my arrest?'

Harkness shifted, looking to Witherspoon and then the two men by the door as if expecting rescue from them, and said: 'Under internal regulations governing the conduct of this department I have every authority to seize and detain an officer I suspect of being an agent of a hostile power.'

Got him, thought Charlie, satisfied at the admission. He said 'But we weren't talking about internal regulations governing the department, were we? We were talking about claims of legal warrants and hopes of full confessions and of hostile agents laughing at you.'

'There *is* authority under internal regulations,' came in Wilson. 'An exaggeration may have been made, but isn't it rather academic?'

'I don't think so, sir,' argued Charlie relentlessly. 'I think it indicates the slapdash, inefficient way this inquiry has been conducted: the sort of slapdash, inefficient way that can't be allowed to continue.'

Wilson's head dropped over the table, so that it was impossible to see the expression on his face: Charlie regretted that he couldn't. Wilson said: 'Point noted. Proceed.'

In what order should he proceed? wondered Charlie. The overriding essential was to prove his innocence. And there could still be a hitch in the way he'd set out to establish that. He said: 'What was the date of transmission of the message about reactivating by payment of one thousand?'

Harkness hesitated, looking across the room to Witherspoon and his dossier-cluttered table. The deputy director said: 'Mr Witherspoon, upon my instructions, was nominally in charge of the day-to-day running of the investigation and has the evidence before him. Could I suggest to the committee that Mr Witherspoon responds to the questions?'

The asshole! thought Charlie. Already Harkness was trying to back away from the responsibility and off-load the mistakes and oversights on to someone else. Charlie looked at the angularly tall man. He wasn't languid and self-assured today. Witherspoon was red-faced, like the policemen, moving his hands nervously among the files, not able to find what he

362

wanted and becoming more flustered. At last he said: 'The twenty-sixth.'

The relief warmed through Charlie. 'You're sure of that?' he insisted.

'Positive,' replied Witherspoon. 'I had already been appointed case officer of the communication intercepts. I logged the date personally.'

'Transmitted from Moscow to the Soviet embassy here in Kensington Palace Gardens?'

'That was where our technical division located the receiver.'

Charlie went back to Harkness, determined against the man evading any culpability. 'And it is your contention that the message was a signal for me to receive, somewhen between the twenty-sixth and your rummage search of my apartment three or four days ago, a payment of one thousand pounds from some KGB officer at the Soviet embassy? The thousand pounds subsequently discovered in a hiding place in my apartment?'

'It's the only possible, damning conclusion,' said Harkness.

'It's damning, all right,' agreed Charlie. Looking at Witherspoon he said: 'The cipher pad concealed elsewhere was subjected to forensic examination?'

'Which proved it to be of Russian manufacture,' confirmed the man.

'What about the money?'

'Of course.'

'What did that show?'

'A substantial number of fingerprints which, when compared to yours on your service and personnel file, proved to be identical.'

Harkness smiled sideways along the table at the other men and said: 'I'm sorry. That was a fact I omitted earlier.'

Still addressing Witherspoon, Charlie said: 'Anything else?'

'There was another set of fingerprints. It has so far been impossible to match them with anyone in our existing files of hostile East bloc personnel...' Wanting to impress with his thoroughness, Witherspoon added: 'Every record upon our files is being checked: those of friendly Allied countries as well. You'll understand it is a very large undertaking.'

'Staggering, I would imagine,' said Charlie. 'But I wouldn't think she works for any hostile East bloc government. I thought she was a nice little girl.'

'What!' asked Harkness, dry-throated again.

'Sally Dickenson,' said Charlie. 'That was what was on the name-plate, at least. Like I said, nice little girl. Bites her fingernails, though.'

'Charlie, you're not making sense,' protested Wilson.

'I will, sir. I will,' promised Charlie. Wilson had used his first name, he isolated. 'Nothing else?' he demanded from Witherspoon.

Witherspoon's confusion was increasing. He stared imploringly towards Harkness and then down at his files and then back up at Charlie. He shook his head and said unevenly: 'No. No, nothing.'

'Let's try some letters and figures,' suggested Charlie. 'How about B77 345113 and B78 345114 and B79 235115 and so on.'

Witherspoon shook his head, baffled. 'I don't understand,' he said.

'Then look at the forensic report!' said Charlie remorselessly. 'They're experts. They don't make the sort of mistakes that you do. There *is* something else, isn't there? There's got to be because it's standard procedure when any sum of money likely to be used as evidence is counted. It's got to be counted. And each note recorded by number, hasn't it!'

'Oh yes. Yes, I'm sorry,' agreed Witherspoon at once. 'I didn't think you meant that. . .I didn't. . .'

'No,' seized Charlie. 'You didn't think, did you! No one's thought, from the very beginning.'

'What's this proving, except your undeniable guilt?' intruded Harkness in a weak attempt to help his protégé.

Charlie chose to ignore the question, openly showing his contempt. 'So!' he pressed on. 'The numbers of the notes are listed, aren't they? And they're consecutive, aren't they?'

'Yes,' said Witherspoon. 'Yes, they are.'

'Are we soon getting to the point of this?' sighed Wilson.

'Please, sir!' pleaded Charlie. 'Not long now. Just let me have a few more minutes.'

'A very few more minutes,' cautioned Wilson.

Charlie turned back to Harkness. 'Some time ago – months ago, in fact – you made me the subject of an official internal inquiry?'

'I have already referred to that. And given my reasons for initiating it.'

'There was a period of surveillance?'

'Naturally.'

Charlie had to turn, to encompass Smedley and Abbott, before coming back to the deputy director. 'My mother, who is senile and confined to a nursing home, was even subjected to interrogation?'

Harkness couldn't withstand Charlie's unblinking stare. The deputy director looked away and said: 'There was considered proper reason.'

'Considered by whom?'

'Do I really have to undergo this sort of questioning!' protested Harkness.

'I'd appreciate your cooperation,' said Wilson. 'There appears to be a great deal here that needs explanation.'

'Considered by me,' admitted Harkness.

'Why?' persisted Charlie.

'I have always been suspicious of your time in Moscow, although you were supposed to be on assignment on behalf of this department, and you were subsequently allowed to return to it. To which I have already made reference. It was conceivable you might have discussed something of that visit – something incriminating – with your mother.'

'What!' exclaimed Charlie, genuinely astonished. 'The possibility of my discussing anything – incriminating or otherwise – with a mentally confused person is utterly *in*conceivable!'

'I subsequently acknowledged that it was perhaps excessive,' reminded Harkness. 'Very little else has proved to be.'

Charlie was conscious of Wilson's shift of impatience. Quickly he said to Witherspoon, 'You have among those folders the results of my most recent assessment examinations?'

'Yes.'

'Pull out just one marking for me,' asked Charlie. 'What was the adjudication for surveillance and observation, both detected and performed?'

'Really!' Wilson protested.

'In a very few moments I will be talking about a Soviet agent who *does* exist,' stopped Charlie.

'Reply to the question,' the Director General ordered Witherspoon urgently.

'Your rating for both is graded as excellent. Ninety-five per cent for detected surveillance, ninety-four for that which you conducted.'

Had he missed anything? wondered Charlie. He didn't think so, not at this stage. There would always be time to pick up and elaborate later. He faced the committee and the frowning Director General and said: 'When I finished the assessment course I was almost at once assigned to an inquiry upon the Isle of Wight, at a factory engaged on a joint development project with a Californian firm. The work is connected with the American Strategic Defence Initiative, Star Wars. A man named Blackstone, who is officially employed as a tracer although not on the secret project, had been found in suspicious circumstances. A company inquiry had already dismissed the matter as having no security risk. I was not satisfied, for reasons I shall make clear at the eventual prosecution. . .'

'. . . Prosecution!' broke in Harkness. 'You told me – your report says – that the man was beyond suspicion.'

'No I did not,' corrected Charlie. 'Read the file. I said that during the time I observed him he did not behave in a suspicious manner. There were things that made me curious, however. His attitude swung between extremes. He confessed to being a bigamist – which I admit did initially throw me in the wrong direction – but then, when I'd apparently accepted it as an explanation for his nervousness, never mentioned it again. He should have kept on about my reporting him to the police, for the crime. But he didn't. I even protracted the interview on the last day, to give him the opportunity. He didn't take it. And that second day he was much more confident. There were small discrepancies, too. He said he didn't know the sort of work going on, for instance, when it had been generally reported. . .' Charlie paused, smiling but in mockery towards Harkness. 'That's why I decided to stay on. I got to thinking: What is the most important thing a bigamist needs? And decided it was money. Which would make him an ideal target in a situation where there were secrets that the Russians might be interested in. So I watched. Like I said, there was nothing positively suspicious. But there was an episode with a telephone. It was a public kiosk, quite close to his home, yet he used it and not his own, so very close. I could not get near enough to identify the number he called but I could certainly see that he started from the bottom and the very top of the dial, so it had to be a London number prefixed by zero one. He followed by seven more digits, which further indicates it was a London connection. . .'

'. . . There is no log, no file note of this whatsoever. That is directly contrary to procedure,' cut in Harkness. 'How much more self-admission are we going to need from this man!'

'I agree with you,' said Charlie, before Wilson could speak. 'I contravened regulations, which I concede was wrong. But by this time other strange things were happening and I considered the course I took justified. As I said, Blackstone clearly called a London number. He spoke briefly, because I saw him. And then hung around the kiosk for about fifteen minutes – when his own house and his own telephone were less than five minutes away – to call again. That was all. I kept him under the closest surveillance for the remainder of a week and at no time did he do anything to arouse the slightest suspicion. . .'

It was Harkness who broke in again. Intent across the table, believing he was improving his accusations, the deputy Director said: 'Are you telling us that you've let a man you believe to be an agent continue working at an installation where the highest classified work is being carried out? And done nothing about it!'

'No,' said Charlie. 'I emphatically impressed upon the English project leader that Blackstone under no circumstances should be considered for employment, nor allowed within the restricted area at any time or under any circumstances whatsoever. But never to let him know that he was under any ban: rather that he might be seconded in response to an application he'd made. I also had our Technical Division impose a trace upon the Isle of Wight public kiosk to isolate all London calls made from it. . .' He looked across at Witherspoon: 'If you searched my office you should have come across the report.'

Witherspoon shook his head but to Harkness, who was staring at him furiously. 'There was just a number. It didn't mean anything.'

'Strange things,' prompted the Director General. 'You said there were other strange things happening.'

'I found myself under surveillance,' announced Charlie. 'It was very expert – more expert than it had been before – and it was unquestionably professional observation. . .' Charlie paused and said: 'And here I made a serious mistake, the only one I consider a I have made. And from which I hope to recover. . .' He looked, pointedly, from Harkness to Witherspoon and then to the Special Branch men. 'I had been, as you have heard, under constant internal harassment from this department. . .harassment I had identified and which had been openly acknowledged – an acknowledgement which is on file – to me by the deputy Director General prior to anything he has said here today. I inferred, quite wrongly, that what I had detected was a continuation of that harassment. I decided to run hare to the hounds, to see what more stupidity there was going to be. It was some time before I discovered it wasn't internal at all. That it was Soviet. . .'

'. . . You didn't report being targeted by a hostile foreign agency . . .!' broke in Harkness.

Charlie virtually ignored the question again, continuing to talk directly to Wilson. 'I didn't make the discovery immediately. It was some days after I returned from the Isle of Wight inquiry. I am extremely careful how I leave my flat: setting things that will alert me to an entry. I knew there *was* an entry – again I thought it was part of the internal investigation – because my door has several locks, one a Yale. But I never set it, because the others compensate: it's always latched. When I tried to enter my flat one evening the Yale lock had been dropped. There were other things – cabinet and room doors closed which I had left ajar or in positions from which I could recognize if they had been touched, the slight disarrangement of magazines that had been left in a particular order. But I couldn't, at first, discover why. It was a Sunday when I made a determined search. . .' Charlie paused, going to Witherspoon. 'You might like to take a note of the date, although of course it will be recorded by the official stenographers here. It was August 6. . .'

Witherspoon hesitated, frowning, and briefly made a notation on a pad in front of him.

'. . . I found the cipher pad first,' resumed Charlie. 'The door of the cupboard housing the electricity meter was one I had left slightly open and it had been closed when I first discovered the entry. It was much more difficult finding the money: I thought I'd covered the bedroom until I noticed the slight variation between the indentations in the carpet that the leg castors had made. The bed had been put back just a fraction out of alignment to where it had been before. . .'

Charlie paused, wishing he had water, like Harkness earlier. He said: 'That's when I realized who had really established the surveillance which had by now been in place for a considerable amount of time. And realized, too, that it was being directed very personally against me and was not some wider operation. So I decided to go on running hare . . .'

'. . . that would have been entirely wrong: against every regulation,' interjected the determined Harkness. 'If it were true – and I do not believe this absurdly concocted story for a minute – it should have been immediately reported to me!'

He'd already concluded that if he handled this confrontation wrongly he was lost, Charlie remembered: that it was all or nothing. Staring straight at Harkness, Charlie said: 'I did not have then – nor do I have now – any confidence whatsoever in this department properly to investigate what was or is happening. I was the obvious target: I decided to let it continue to run, to try to see at least if a direction or a purpose emerged, before reporting it officially.'

'That action, like that remark, was quite wrong,' said Wilson, and Harkness snatched a sideways look of gratitude to the Director General he had earlier criticized.

Shit, thought Charlie. And then another reflection: All or nothing. He said: 'It would not have been one I would have taken had different circumstances prevailed in this department.'

'The innuendo in that remark is even more improper,' said Wilson angrily, turning perceptibly towards a blazing-faced Harkness. 'I think it calls for an apology to certain people in this room.'

There were several moments of absolute silence, with everyone's concentration entirely upon Charlie. He swallowed and shuffled slightly on aching feet. Then he said: 'With respect to yourself, sir, I decline to make any apology to anyone in this room for anything I have so far said or implied.' There! he thought. Not just irrevocably committed: he'd put the noose around his own neck and had the do-it-yourself trapdoor lever in his hand.

'We have been very patient. . .' began Wilson, but

for the first time ever Charlie risked talking over the man: 'Please!' he said, knowing he had only the briefest chance to hold them. 'Just another few minutes. . .!' and when Wilson stopped talking, more in further anger than permission, Charlie hurried on: 'That money over there, the thousand pounds by which such great store is being set as being a Soviet payment to me, is *my* money.'

'What!' demanded Wilson, no longer angry.

He'd saved himself but he was still hanging on by his fingertips, Charlie calculated. 'There *was* a thousand pounds in that cavity, when I discovered it,' explained Charlie. 'A plant, like everything else has been planted. Not knowing – still not knowing even now – why it was being done, it was blatantly obvious I had to take what precautions I could to avoid any further mistakes. I made the discovery, as I have said, on August 6th, a Sunday. On the morning of Monday, August 7th, I took the thousand pounds and three of the top sheets off the cipher pad to my bank. It's the Barclays branch just across Vauxhall Bridge, on Millbank. I deposited it with an assistant manager, named Frederick Snelgrove, with written authority that it should be released upon demand to Sir Alistair Wilson. I then withdrew, in consecutively numbered notes from the cashier Sally Dickenson, whose fingerprints are on those notes, one thousand pounds from my own account. I had those numbers recorded and that record is also part of the provably dated deposit.'

Charlie stopped, hopefully, Nobody spoke. He said: 'No one seems to have realized the significance! All this was done on August 7th. The message – "Reactivate payment by one thousand" – was not sent from Moscow until August 26th, according to your evidence: *after*, nineteen days after, I had already found the thousand pounds, switched

372

it and made arrangements that any investigation – any *proper* investigation – would lead to its being eventually released to the Director General of this department.'

The reactions were mixed, throughout the room. The two unidentified men – who looked like clones of all the Whitehall mandarins Charlie had ever encountered – were bent sideways towards each other in whispered conversation. Sir Alistair Wilson was staring at him with obvious curiosity but with no other indication of what he was thinking. Harkness had a finger sideways to his mouth, gnawing at it in concentration, trying to absorb what Charlie had said. Witherspoon was scurrying through his documentation, seeking something. It was time to finish, while he was marginally ahead, decided Charlie. He said: 'There have been other things added to the bank deposit since that initial date. There is a long list of vehicle registration numbers, which I believe to have been used by various Soviet observation teams, particularly since I moved into the delegation hotel in Bayswater. I have not had the facility, away from this department, to check out the ownership for those registrations. I would suspect they are hired. Tracing the hiring back will, I hope, give us the names of some Soviet front companies which we might not at the moment be aware are being used by the KGB. . .'

He smiled back towards the rigid-faced Smedley. '. . . And there are also the numbers of our own people who have been in such painfully obvious position over the past three or four days. Three Fords, a Vauxhall and a Fiat. . .As I have already suggested, the investigation has been appallingly amateurish. . .'

'Anything else?' cut off Wilson. There was no longer any anger in the frail voice.

'I hope there will be when I know what was in the King William Street drop,' said Charlie. He turned to Harkness. 'So what was it?'

Harkness' hand came only partially away from his mouth. 'There still needs to be further investigation to discover its whereabouts,' the man conceded.

'What!' said Charlie. Confident now, he slightly overstressed the incredulity. 'You mean you don't even know where it is yet!'

'It will be found,' insisted Harkness.

'And I thought it was something else you'd just omitted to say,' said Charlie in disbelief. He turned to Witherspoon but with a positive body movement to include Smedley and Abbott. 'Who tossed my flat?'

There was no immediate response. Then Witherspoon breathed in heavily and squared his shoulders and said: 'It was done under my supervision.'

Charlie gestured to the other two men. 'By those two.'

Witherspoon nodded.

'And what did you find?'

'You have already heard what we found.'

'Jesus!' exclaimed Charlie. He hadn't imagined it was going to be this easy to exact the retribution for the harm he believed Smedley and Abott had caused his mother. He said: 'So you missed the micro-dot!'

There was a throat movement from Witherspoon, and Smedley's colour heightened. There was what might have been a groan from Wilson, but the sound was hardly audible and Charlie might have been mistaken.

Charlie began to look back to the assembled inquiry team but then hesitated. He said: 'No one has yet said here, in this room, what sort of code it is. it's a variable number-for-letter system: that's what the micro-dot says. That's right, isn't it?'

'Yes,' mumbled Witherspoon.

374

'And that message, the one that identifies King William Street. Was that all it said?'

From the look that passed between Harkness and Witherspoon Charlie didn't need the answer, but it came anyway. 'No,' said the man.

'What's missing?'

It was Harkness who spoke, once more trying to take the pressure off his protégé. 'Some numbers which, at the moment, the cryptologists cannot decipher.'

'They didn't need to,' sighed Charlie. He wouldn't allow them any respite, any let-up on their exposure: they'd sought utterly to destroy him, *were* still intent upon destroying him. He said: 'The key was already there if you'd correctly looked for it. Somewhere in the grouping the figures one and five and zero feature, don't they?'

Witherspoon hurried back to his message folder. 'At the end.'

'Three digits, out of a grouping of nine?' demanded Charlie. To Wilson he said: 'The grouping of nine was on the micro-dot: it's listed in the bank package for you. Could I ask you to cast your mind back to King William Street, sir?'

'Good God!' said Wilson, in recollection at last.

'Yes,' said Charlie. 'Berenkov wanted me to know he'd planned whatever it is that's going on. Which is arrogant, but then he always was an arrogant man. It was probably his only failing.'

'I can't follow this,' protested one of the unidentified men. He had a pronounced Welsh accent.

'A number of years ago,' said Charlie. 'I was responsible for the arrest and jailing of an extremely successful Soviet illegal, a trained KGB officer who was infiltrated into this country and who for several years ran a series of spy cells throughout Europe. At 150 King William Street, in the City of London, there is a privately owned safe-custody facility: clearing banks used to offer the service as a safe deposit box but very few do now. A number of private firms have filled the gap. Quite unknown by the company who own it, he used King William Street as a safe cut-out, a dead letter box to pass material between himself and KGB officers attached to the embassy here in London, without there ever being a requirement for them openly – or incriminatingly – to meet. . .' He glanced at Witherspoon. 'This investigation of me that you masterminded? Didn't you check my operational file: everything I'd ever done?'

There was a despairing head movement of confirmation and Charlie felt not a jot of pity for the man. Charlie said: 'It's all there, in the Berenkov case file. And if you'd worked out that 150 King William Street was the address then I would have hoped that even you could have guessed at the other numbers not being part of the code at all. But the number of the facility itself.'

There was a new briskness to Wilson's voice when he said: 'It's just past six o'clock: it'll be closed.'

'Which just might be to our benefit,' suggested Charlie. 'They'll have monitored the drop, after filling it. Because they'll want to know we've understood what they want us to. At the moment they'll think we haven't understood. . .' Charlie allowed the glance towards Harkness. 'Which until now we haven't, have we?'

'You think the company will cooperate?' asked Wilson.

'They did with Berenkov: they allowed us after-hours access then.'

It had suddenly become a planning discussion between two men, Charlie and the Director General, and Harkness flustered to intervene.

'There are other considerations!' he insisted. 'What

about this man form the Isle of Wight factory? Blackstone? He should be arrested immediately.'

'No!' said Charlie, practically shouting. 'I was picked up on the Isle of Wight: and Blackstone has an access telephone contact. For all we know there's a timed system: ana automatic alert if he does *not* call. Blackstone is neutralized: leave him.'

'I don't think you're in any position to say what will or will not be done!' rejected Harkness.

'He'll be left,' decided Wilson curtly.

Harkness actually flinched at being so obviously overruled. Trying to recover, he said: 'There's more I want explaining. What has Muffin been doing for almost a week at a hotel housing a Soviet delegation? And what is the connection between him and Natalia Nikandrova Fedova?'

It was Charlie's turn to create the awkward silence: although he should have been prepared, he wasn't, because he hadn't been able to think of any way *to* prepare himself. With absolute honesty he said: 'I went to the hotel for personal reasons, to make contact with the woman.'

'What's she got to do with all this other business?' demanded Harkness, not properly thinking out his question.

'At the moment I don't know,' admitted Charlie, in further honesty.

'That isn't a proper answer!' protested Harkness.

'I think the proper answers have got to come in the proper sequence,' intruded Wilson, urgent again. 'Which for far too long they haven't been doing. I want to find out – and find out quickly – what's in King William Street. Everything else can wait. We're going to recess but nobody goes anywhere. We're staying here, all of us, until this is completely resolved.'

No one actually did attempt to move anywhere in

those first few moments. Witherspoon was the first to stir, getting uncertainly to his feet and bringing his binders together in some sort of clearing up tidiness.

'Hubert!' said Charlie.

Witherspoon looked up, apprehensively questioning.

'The correct answer was "fools",' said Charlie.

'What?' gaped the man, in utter bewilderment.

'That crossword clue you filled in when you came poking around my office a long time ago: the one about life being a walking shadow, from *Macbeth*. You wrote "idiot" but the correct answer was "fools". . .either would have fitted perfectly here, though, don't you think?'

The atmosphere became much better inside the Kensington house and for obvious reason. It was Petrin who brought it about, his bored impatience finally coming to a head. He set out quietly, genuinely not wishing to foment a fresh dispute between himself and Losev, not because he was frightened of the man but because the perpetual arguments were very much part of his boredom. From apparently casual conversation with the photographer he learned there were only three outstanding drawings remaining to be copied in the absolute detail with which Zazulin was working. Continuing the query further, he discovered that Yuri Guzins had six drawings he still needed to go through with Krogh. And the American finally conceded that he was working on the last reproduction.

'So!' seized Petrin at once. 'We can finish!'

'What!' It was Zazulin who spoke, expressing the surprise of everyone.

'Finish,' repeated Petrin. 'If we work on now — don't stop — we could get everything done. End it.'

'I've got a lot. . .' started Guzins, but Petrin refused

him. 'Nothing that you couldn't get through with Emil if you stayed at it. He's practically completed the last of the original drawings: there's nothing to interrupt or distract the two of you now.'

'Maybe I could do it,' conceded Guzins reluctantly.

'What about you, Emil? You prepared to carry on, to clear everything up?'

'*Really* finish!'

Petrin paused. Still not the time to mention the one replacement drawing that was still needed. 'Really finish,' he said.

'I'll work for as long as is necessary,' guaranteed Krogh sincerely.

'I could certainly get all the photographs finished,' guaranteed Zazulin. 'I didn't know we were coming so near to the end of the original drawings.'

Predictably Losev felt cheated by being beaten to the suggestion by Petrin but even the London *rezident* was anxious for it to end now. To Zazulin he said: 'Could you finish in time to get a shipment to Moscow?'

'I think so.'

'Not the held-back cassette!' insisted Guzins at once. 'I must see an original: have an opportunity of discussing it with Krogh. The references on the photographs must accord to the drawings.'

'All right!' said Petrin. 'Don't worry! That's how it will be done.'

'Have you told Krogh yet there's a duplicate for him to complete?' asked Guzins. As always – as it always had to be for the monolingual Guzins – the conversation was in Russian.

'Not yet,' admitted Petrin. 'Let's wrap everything else up first.'

Which was what they did. There was a lot to occur elsewhere in an intervening period but in Kensington they worked on until everything was completed. And Zazulin did meet his commitment: he finished in time for all his photographic rolls to be included in that night's diplomatic pouch to Moscow. Only one cassette was held back in London, that of the drawing that the unknowing Krogh had still to make again.

43

There were varying degrees of shock from almost everyone in the room, the two unnamed men showing it most. Charlie, who'd caused it, wasn't shocked: he'd half expected something like this and thought he was a long way towards comprehending what had happened or was happening. Most of it anyway.

'Sure?' demanded Wilson, still gazing down at the drawing around which they were all grouped, on Witherspoon's evidence table.

'No,' admitted Charlie, although for accuracy, not to reassure them. 'All I can say is that it resembles drawings I was shown by the project leader when I made the Isle of Wight investigation.'

It had taken four hours to get the official search warrant authorized by a magistrate, locate the after-hours address of the managing director of the safe deposit company, persuade the man of the urgency of cooperating at once and finally to retrieve the blueprint from King William Street. While they waited – Charlie finally being allowed to sit – there had been sandwiches and coffee but little conversation. No one had spoken at all to Charlie until the drawing was unrolled and Charlie had announced its possible source. A disjointed, competing babble erupted the moment Charlie responded to the Director General's question, with the Whitehall official with the Welsh accent fractionally in the lead. 'Good God!' said the man, aghast. 'Have you any idea of the implications of this! The Foreign Office must be told: the Foreign Secretary himself . . .!'

The persistent, determined Harkness was already

trying to make his point before the first man finished. '. . . The key!' he tried, in fresh triumph. 'The key found in Muffin's flat fitted the safe deposit facility. And Muffin investigated on the Isle of Wight!'

'. . . This is a disaster!' endorsed the second official. 'This will end any technological cooperation between us and the United States for years. . .a disaster. . .!'

'. . .I think. . .' began his colleague but Wilson cut him off, trying to restore some order. 'Please be quiet!' he said. He didn't shout but despite the frailty there was authority in his voice and everyone stopped talking at once. The Director General looked around the room and said, more forcefully: 'Let's stop behaving like a lot of frightened chickens with a fox in the henhouse! I want to understand what we've got here, not listen to a bunch of hysterics!'

There was some embarrassment in the silence that settled. Harkness said: 'I do not think the observation I made should be ignored.'

'Nothing is being ignored,' said Wilson, and on this occasion Charlie was convinced there was a note of weariness in the Director General's tone towards the other man. He was aware of Wilson looking at him 'Charlie?' he invited.

'Like you said,' supported Charlie. 'Don't panic. The first thing to do is confirm that it *is* something from the space project.'

'It means delay. . .' the Welshman began to protest.

'. . .no it doesn't,' corrected Charlie. 'The Isle of Wight is less than an hour away, by helicopter. The factory even has its own landing pad. We already know Springley's address: the local police can have him there waiting for us before the machine arrives. . .'

'Yes,' accepted Wilson at once, nodding towards Witherspoon. 'Organize that now.'

'Blackstone,' insisted Harkness. 'The man has to be arrested!'

'No, he doesn't!' said Charlie, as Witherspoon left the room accompanied by Abbott, the second Special Branch officer. 'And for the same reason as before: we don't know yet if there's a cut-off warning system in operation. We've got to take things in their proper order.'

'Your accomplice. . .' started Harkness, and Charlie exploded.

'For Christ's sake!' he shouted, so loudly that Harkness actually stepped back and Smedley started forward from his guard position at the door before stopping again.

'Listen!' implored Charlie, more controlled. 'Just listen and think. You want to argue that I received that drawing from Blackstone, put it in the safe deposit facility and then told Moscow, correct. . . ?'

Harkness blinked back at him, saying nothing.

'How?' demanded Charlie. 'Tell me – tell us all – how! And why! The bloody drawing is dated, isn't it! With what is almost yesterday's date. You know to the second where I've been for the past three, almost four days: that I haven't been anywhere near the Isle of Wight to make any pick-up. You now who I've met, so you're equally well aware that Blackstone hasn't come to London, to give me anything. According to what you've said in this very room, I was actually under arrest when the message was intercepted to Moscow saying King William Street had been filled. So it couldn't have been me who filled it, could it! Or sent the message, because you've also told us the transmission and receiving point is *inside* the Soviet embassy in Kensington Palace Gardens. And why was that message sent at all? Just to go on fooling you, like it's fooled you all along. Why should the Soviet embassy *receiving* material from a dead letter box in King William Street alert Moscow *before* they pick it up! Surely even you can see the nonsense in that. Standard procedure – the *only* procedure – is to empty a box and *then* advise what you've got, if you want to, although that doesn't make a lot of sense either. . .' Charlie had to stop, breathless. He said: 'You were fed the numbers-for-letter code, like you were fed everything else. . .the dead letter drop that got you an arrest. . .the courier against whom you couldn't move. What did they amount to, either of them? Think about it! They didn't matter a damn. It was just the bait, for you to swallow. Which you did. Moscow has sucked you up and blown you out in bubbles. That code is Boy Scouts' stuff: senior Boy Scouts, maybe, but little more. It should never have been relied upon. . .had importance attached to it.'

'I think that's enough,' halted the Director General. 'I will say, however, that at this stage I agree with what has been said. It would seem to me that we are dealing with two separate things here. And for the moment the overwhelmingly important one is the discovery of a British document carrying the highest security classification being where it has no right to be. I want that run to ground first: everything else can wait.'

Harkness discernibly sagged. His immediate, concerned concentration focused upon the Whitehall officials and Charlie became even surer that they were in some way connected to the all-important Joint Intelligence Committee.

Everyone settled down to another period of waiting, for the arrival of Robert Springley. Harkness returned to the evidence table – although to the folders, not the drawing. The two Whitehall men withdrew pointedly to a part of the room where they could not be overheard and at once started an intense, head-bent conversation. The stenographer and the recording operator sat back, stretching, grateful for the temporary rest. The stiff-legged Wilson was the first to stand. The Director General caught Charlie's eye, jerking his head, and Charlie crossed to where the man was, beyond the half-moon table.

Wilson said: 'I think you've publicly made your point with sufficient forcefulness for the moment. No more.'

'Yes, sir,' accepted Charlie.

'I still want a further explanation.'

'Yes, sir.'

'For Christ's sake stop parroting "yes, sir" at me!'

'I'm pretty sure the drawing is from the Isle of Wight.'

'You're in deep trouble if it came from a man you let run.'

'I accept that.'

'Why the hell did you let it go on!'

'I thought I'd closed him off: that the risk was justified.'

Wilson snorted, in impatient anger, nodding in the direction of the intensely talking government officials. 'They're right, you know. If something involving America's Strategic Defence Initiative has reached the Russians from one of our places the shutters are going to come down with a sound we'll hear all the way from Washington. The Americans would actually have to consider abandoning it: starting all over again.'

'I realize that, too.'

'Christ!' said Wilson again but more to himself than to Charlie. 'I can't think of a comparable disaster! Nothing!'

They both turned, at movement from the door.

Witherspoon entered first, followed by Springley. The white-haired project chief had had time during the flight to recover from being roused from his bed but he was still blinking in bewilderment. He was wearing a carelessly put on tweed jacket over a roll-neck sweater. The man frowned around the room in continuing confusion, his face breaking slightly at recognition of Charlie Muffin.

When he spoke it was to Charlie. He said, complaining: 'No one will tell me anything, except that there's some sort of crisis: that this is a security committee. What is it? What's happened?'

Wilson said to Charlie: 'You might as well take him through it. He knows you.'

Harkness didn't hear the exchange but his look was one of undisguised hatred – and without caring that it was undisguised – as Charlie went to the project chief, to lead him back to the table where Harkness still stood. Charlie ignored the deputy Director. He picked up the flimsy drawing, offered it to Springley and said: 'Can you identify that?'

Springley only looked at it briefly, for no more than seconds. After which his gaze came up, first to Charlie and then more widely, out into the room. He was smiling slightly, the smile of someone completely baffled but who imagines they are having some incomprehensible trick played upon them. He said: 'What is this?'

'That's what I am asking you, Mr Springley,' said Charlie, cautious against giving the man any lead or guidance.

'One of the drawings,' said the project chief, spacing the words in growing disbelief. 'The final drawing of the planned sidescreen moulding, with the process description. Where did it come from?'

There were several sounds of audible reaction throughout the room but Charlie didn't see who made them. He said: 'That's what we want you to tell us.'

'Blackstone!' interrupted Harkness foolishly. 'It was stolen by Blackstone, wasn't it!'

There was another audible sound, one of annoyance, and Charlie knew this time it was from the Director General.

'No,' said Springley, shaking his head. 'It's one of the drawings from the project but not *the* drawing. It's a completely accurate copy. . .'

'By Blackstone!' said Harkness again, but it was not the deputy's interjection that caused the project manager to stop in mid-sentence. Springley went back to the drawing, looked up and said: 'Dear God! Oh dear God what's happened?'

Charlie thought that if God responded on each occasion he'd been called upon already it was going to be a busy night for all concerned. Encouragingly he said: 'What?'

'Krogh!' said Springley weakly. He shook his head once more. 'It *has* to be. I even thought. . .it actually crossed my mind. . .not very strongly, you understand. . .but I *did*. . .I thought it was strange. . .'

'I'm not following you,' said Charlie. 'Who's Krogh?'

'The chairman of the main American manufacturing company,' said Springley. 'He approached us weeks ago: said he wanted to visit to ensure that what we were making and what his plant were constructing were compatible. . .' The man trailed off, lost.

'The American manufacturer came to you!' prompted Charlie.

'Over a fortnight ago now,' confirmed Springley. 'The company checked his bona fides, of course. He had the topmost clearance. He said he wanted to study our drawings and he did, for days. Told me

387

once that he was glad he did, because he'd thought for a while that there had been an incompatibility. There wasn't, it turned out. That's what he said, anyway. . . Oh God, what a mess!'

'He saw everything?' pressed Charlie.

'Everything there was. All of it.'

'How many drawings?'

'Twenty-four.'

'Shit!' said Charlie, not talking to anyone but looking at what the project chief still held in his hands, which were shaking now. Charlie said: 'When did he leave. . .the last day he was with you?'

Springley shrugged uncertainly. 'Over a week ago. Maybe nine or ten days.'

'It's important!' said Charlie. 'Be precise.'

'I can't be, not exactly,' apologized Springley. 'Eight days, I think: yes, eight days.'

'Where is this American firm based?' It was the Welshman, from behind.

'California,' said Springley at once.

'We've got to tell America now! At once!' said the Whitehall official. 'It's still only afternoon there. They can pick him up at once.'

'He's not there, is he!' said Charlie, not bothering to turn. 'We've already seen that the drawing's dated, with what is now yesterday's date. And it was found *here*, in England. So that's where he's working, somewhere here in England.' And I bet I know where, Charlie thought.

'This gets worse. . .appalling. . .' said the Welshman. 'We must alert the embassy here, then. They've got security secondment in Grosvenor Square. FBI as well as CIA.'

Charlie moved slightly away from the project chief, gazing down contemplatively. When he looked up it was to Wilson. 'It *is* a disaster,' he said. 'An unmitigated one. If this man Krogh has been here, copied

388

all twenty-four drawings, then it can only mean he's already passed over, long ago, everything there was to have from his plant in California.'

'Yes,' agreed the Director General at once. 'And it doesn't matter a damn, in the end, that strictly speaking it's not our leak, either.'

'But that drawing *is* our responsibility, isn't it!' demanded Charlie suddenly. 'I mean we could argue that we've got the right of decision over it?'

Wilson frowned, head to one side, then looked for guidance to the other two men: Harkness was not included. First the Welshman, then the other official shrugged. Wilson said: 'What's the question about, Charlie?'

'Desperation,' admitted Charlie. 'Absolute, utter desperation.' He went back to Springley, gesturing to the drawing. 'Explain that to me. Completely. Every detail.'

'Like I said, it's a drawing of the sidescreen moulding,' began Springley hesitantly. 'More to explain the process, really. We got the contract for our reinforced resin system because it's more resilient than monoset carbon fibre. It performs better in the atmospheric vacuum of space, too.'

'Performs better how?' queried Charlie, needing everything.

'It doesn't give off vapour, like monoset: lenses, mirrored reflective detection devices, surfaces like that won't get fogged.'

'What's resilience got to do with it?'

'If monoset carbon fibre is struck, by space debris for instance, it shatters. Thermoset – our system – might be penetrated but the overall structure remains intact.'

'You called it reinforced resin?'

'The resin is made from polyetheretherketone: it's an oil by-product of petrol distillation. We construct a laminated matrix of resin and carbon fibre: in this case the complete lamination is twelve sheets in thickness.'

It wasn't coming, realized Charlie. Maybe it had been naive – really desperate – to imagine that it would. He said: 'So you lay sheets of carbon fibre, interspersed with the oil-based resin, one on top of each other?'

Despite the seriousness of the situation Springley smiled at the simplicity of the question. 'No,' he said. 'It's got to be created quasi-isotropic: meaning that it can carry loads in all directions. So as each layer is added it is laid at a different angle to that of the sheet beneath it. . .' The man hesitated. 'We call it a weave and it's very much like that. A sheet of carbon fibre is composed of many fine threads, all running in the same direction: as each sheet is laid one on top of the other those threads criss and cross to provide the strength of the final, composite sheet, very similar to weaving cloth. Only hundreds of times stronger.'

'We need to follow this, Charlie,' cautioned Wilson.

'I haven't got it yet,' freely admitted Charlie. To Springley he said: 'What about *how* it's made?'

Springley shrugged once more. 'In a moulding bay. . .' He indicated the process specifications, alongside the drawing. 'There are temperature and cleanliness requirements, of course. . .'

'What!' seized Charlie abruptly.

Springley continued to take Charlie through the drawing itemizing the points as he got to them. 'Constantly maintained temperature, at twenty degrees centigrade. Fifty per cent humidity. . .'

'. . .what are all these?' demanded Charlie, going ahead of the man. 'Dimethicones. . .magnesium sulphate. . .lanolin. . .camphor. . .salicylic acid. . . phenol. . .what's the importance of these things. . .?'

'I don't really see the point of singling out those

particular ingredients,' conceded Springley. 'There are many more, after all. We might just as well say any cream.'

'For what?' said Charlie, beginning to feel a tingle of hope.

'Every two or three laminations have to be pressed down to consolidate the vacuum,' said Springley. 'We've obviously got to be careful of voids.'

Charlie smiled. It wasn't perfect by any means – desperate, in fact – but it was an effort, at least. And still all might be a waste of time and effort. 'Especially in an expanding vacuum,' he agreed. 'How long would it take you to redraw that drawing? Exactly as it is, with just two lines omitted? And one inserted in their place?'

Springley turned down the corners of his mouth. 'No time at all,' he said. 'It's already there, complete. All I'd need to do is a simple copying job.'

'And you could match the lettering, by tracing that already there?'

'Yes.'

'When are we going to get this, Charlie?' asked the patient Director General.

'Now,' said Charlie. And told them.

'Ridiculous!' rejected the Welsh official at once. 'Preposterous and ridiculous.'

'And do I need to remind you that a diplomatic bag is sacrosanct?' asked his companion.

'No,' said Charlie, unperturbed. 'Or that it could very well be preposterous and ridiculous and achieve nothing. But we've been sitting around here for hours, using words like disaster and catastrophe and bemoaning the demise of any future technological exchange with the United States of America. We've agreed the Russians must have everything from California and certainly twenty of the British plans. . .' He waved the blueprint they had, for

391

emphasis. '. . .because Krogh appears to have been numbering them and this is twenty-one. So what have we got to lose, apart from our time tonight and Mr Springley's time tonight, and one simple, diplomatically illegal act. . .?' He swivelled to the project chief. 'You prepared to give us that time, Mr Springley?'

'Of course I am,' said the man.

To the others in the room Charlie said: 'OK, let's have another idea better than the desperate, preposterous, ridiculous one that I've put forward?'

No one volunteered immediately. Then the Director General said: 'We're grateful for your cooperation, Mr Springley. Tell us what materials you want and we'll get them for you immediately.'

Determined not to misunderstand, Springley said to Charlie: 'Dermatitis?'

Charlie nodded in agreement: 'Severe dermatitis.'

'Mr Springley,' stopped the Director General. 'Where did this man Krogh stay in London? There must have been a hotel? A telephone number at least.'

'I don't know,' said the project chief. 'I don't remember his giving me one.'

It was approaching dawn, fingers of light already feeling through the darkness, before everything was completed, although the revised drawing of the moulding and the carbon-fibre preparation process was back in the safe deposit facility long before that because Springley worked remarkably quickly. When the project chief did finish there was a tired repeated objection from one of the Whitehall officials, which Harkness tried to support, but Wilson brusquely overrode both. Abruptly Charlie dropped his earlier objection to Blackstone's arrest, because there was a purpose now, and orders were given for the man's detention, initially by the local police to await the arrival, by helicopter again, of a Special Branch escort back to London: pointedly Wilson avoided giving the job to either Smedley or Abbott. Springley was still in the room, so he overheard the planning and asked that the company chairman be awakened and brought to London as well to be told what had happened, and Wilson agreed at once. The duty officer at the American embassy was contacted and arrangements made for a seven o'clock breakfast meeting with the local station chiefs of America's Federal Bureau of Investigation and the Central Intelligence Agency. While all the calls were being made Charlie wandered across to where the files lay, sorted through, and located the telephone number and address of the Kensington house that William French, from the Technical Division, had identified from it. No one tried to stop him: Witherspoon was flustering in and out of the room obeying the instructions of the Director General and Harkness remained dully at the half-moon table, staring down sightlessly and seemingly unaware of all the activity. Towards the end Wilson stumped over to Charlie and said: 'Well?'

'We've forgotten the Kensington house,' said Charlie.

'Fix it,' agreed Wilson at once. Suddenly, depressed, he said: 'I'm going along with everything but I don't think it'll achieve anything.'

'It's an attempt, at something,' offered Charlie.

'I'd like you to take the meeting with the Americans.'

He'd been yelled at and vilified by everyone else so why not them as well, thought Charlie. 'All right,' he said.

'Let's try to get some rest and put our thoughts

in order,' suggested Wilson. 'It's almost five in the morning.'

By then there had been some changes at the Kensington safe house. When they'd finished that night, much earlier than the English group, Losev had agreed to the dismantling of the photographic gear, because there only remained the last, duplicate drawing to be redone, and they already had the photograph of that. So only the drawing materials remained. And Yuri Guzins, on his makeshift cot in a small side room. He was awake that morning, at five, knowing that he was finally going home. Emil Krogh was also awake, with the same thought. And so was Natalia Fedova, thinking not of going home but of leaving it, for ever.

Outside the Kensington house the arrest squads began to assemble, with orders to await instructions.

44

Charlie didn't sleep. There was a small dormitory at Westminster Bridge Road, for the overnight duty officers, but Charlie didn't bother to use it because there was hardly time to justify it. He slumped instead in his own office chair, feet up on the desk, and imagined at first it would be quite comfortable but quickly realized that it wasn't, not at all. He doubted that he would have slept, anyway. His mind was too full: overcrowded, in fact. And not just with what they'd done throughout the night and were going to have to go on doing, during the day.

There was still Natalia. Was she part of it? Was she a knowing cog in some entrapment machinery he still didn't fully comprehend? Charlie shook his head in the half light of the office. She couldn't have been! He knew her: had loved her and lived with her in Moscow. *Really* knew her. She couldn't have maintained the artifice during the time they'd been together now, in the hotel. He was sure she couldn't. There would have been a slip, some mistake. And yet. . .?

Charlie straightened more fully in the chair, abandoning the idea of trying to get comfortable. How about approaching it from another way, from what he *could* think through? Berenkov had set out, knowingly and intentionally, to inveigle him: bury him under a welter of phoney facts and evidence which could so easily have destroyed him. Actually got him jailed. Could still harm him: *I still want a fuller explanation*, the Director General had said. But why! thought Charlie, mentally echoing his earlier outburst when Harkness had presented his

395

inept case. Why had Berenkov tried to bring him down? The only conclusion was revenge for what had happened in the past, and Charlie rejected that as ridiculous. The breaking of Berenkov's cells and his arrest and imprisonment hadn't been personal. It was business: professional, accepted, understood business. Maybe the Moscow episode had been slightly different: then Berenkov had been positively pursued, with himself as the unknowing pursuer, but from what Natalia had told him the whole thing had failed, so that hardly counted.

Could Berenkov regard what he'd attempted to do as business, as well? Thought of it with the professional detachment with which Charlie regarded their previous confrontations? It was a possibility: perhaps the only conclusion. But why connect it so closely with another operation, the stealing of the Strategic Defence Initiative drawings? *That* wasn't professional: not properly – even literally – detached. It was a cardinal rule, for every intelligence service, that an operation should never overlap another sufficiently to put one at risk and by so doing endanger both. Which led on to another logical conclusion: that one – obtaining the drawings – was so far advanced and already successful that it could *not* be endangered. In which case they had been wasting their time, staying up all night.

A full circle, without finding an answer, recognized Charlie: an answer to anything. One step at a time, he decided: he'd argued throughout the night for them to proceed in the proper order, so that's what *he* had to do. Keep the sequence right. And there was a lot he had to do before deciding about Natalia. The self-honesty refused him. He was dodging the issue, he knew. Wanting it to go away – be resolved for him – so that the decision wouldn't be his. He was only sure about one thing. That he loved her. Wanted her. That none of this – whatever *this* was – had changed or affected his feelings for Natalia at all. What then? Muddied the waters, he supposed, unhappy at the cliché. Made it difficult, certainly, for him to see – to think – clearly.

Charlie left his office long before the appointment time, descending to the basement cafeteria where the just-finished security-cleared cleaners were bunched at tables and who looked accusingly at his intrusion into their early morning domain, some – because of his unshaven and more than usually dishevelled appearance – even with suspicion. Charlie smiled a general good morning. No one said anything back. He bought grey-coloured coffee and a glazed bun with currants on top, which was stale and filled up his throat before finally going down in an uncomfortable lump. When he blinked it was like closing his eyes against sandpaper and he kept wanting to yawn. Charlie decided he felt like shit. It would be better soon, when he was calling up the adrenaline to work things out. At least he hoped it would be. He abandoned the bun and the coffee, guessing that for the refreshments the previous night – or was it strictly speaking the same night? – they must have sent out because everything had been a bloody sight better than this. It was no wonder all those blokes like Burgess and Maclean and Philby and Blunt had gone over to the other side: they were probably just trying to get away from the canteen food.

In the brief period they'd been away the furniture in the conference room had been rearranged. The half-moon table remained, to provide a focus, but there was only one chair behind it now. Some – but Charlie didn't think all, from his recollection of the bulk – of the folders and binders were stacked at one end of it. The table at which Witherspoon

had sat and upon which the evidence had previously rested had gone completely. There were a new
stenographer and a new recording technician at the
note-taking desk, which had been moved to a further
and less obtrusive side of the room. A series of chairs
had been set out in the room itself, possibly no more
than ten although Charlie didn't bother to count.

Wilson was already there, crumpled and unshaven
like Charlie. The Director General was in conversation with Springley, who turned and at once introduced Charlie to the third man, John Bishop. The
company chairman was putty-faced and clearly dis-
orientated, shaking his head for no particular reason,
just in general, all-encompassing horror.

The man said: 'I can't believe it! *Won't* believe it. It
just couldn't be. Impossible.'

'It isn't and it has,' said Charlie brutally. The basic
belief of man, he thought: Misfortune always befalls
someone else. *This* would have been the moment for
that remark about life being a bitch. Then again,
maybe not. He said: 'Have you any idea where Krogh
stayed, in London?'

'I already asked,' said Wilson.

Bishop answered anyway. He gave a helpless shrug
and said: 'My secretary might have kept a number. . .' He looked at his watch. 'She won't be at the
factory yet. I wasn't told what it was all about until I
got here.'

'We've got someone going to her home, to get her
there early,' said the Director General. He went on,
talking over the two men: 'I've had Blackstone put in
a police cell.'

Charlie nodded. 'Let him sweat. No conversation
with anyone, not even when he's served food or
drink. He folded up last time at the thought of long
imprisonment: let him get a taste of what it can really
be like inside a cell.'

There was the sound of further arrivals behind. The two Whitehall men entered first and remained anonymous because Wilson made no attempt to introduce them to the company chairman. He didn't introduce the following Harkness by name, either, just as his deputy. Charlie stared at Harkness in open surprise. The man had completely changed, into a brown suit with cream accessories, and was fresh and pinkly shaved: around him hung a miasma of cologne, with lemon the predominant aroma.

'Bloody hell!' Charlie muttered.

'Did you say something?' demanded Harkness.

'Nothing,' said Charlie.

'This isn't over, you know!' said Harkness. 'All this. It isn't over.'

Charlie gazed at him, innocent-faced. 'I know it's not over,' he said, intentionally misunderstanding. 'That's why we've all come back here.'

The Americans' arrival prevented the exchange continuing. The two men halted uncertainly just inside the door and then the one slightly in front, a plump man with a crewcut and rimless spectacles isolated the Director General and smiled in recognition. He said: 'Sir Alistair! It's good to see you!'

Wilson gestured the men further into the room and named the names. The crewcut man turned out to be the CIA station chief, Hank Bowley. The FBI liaison, a much thinner, unsmiling man but about the same height as the other American, was identified as Philip McDonald.

Charlie watched them while the handshakes were exchanged, aware of both men looking intently at everyone – particularly their appearance – and thought, hopefully, that they seemed professional. They were certainly crisply fresh. There was a further smell of cologne, too.

'So what's all this about!' demanded Bowley. 'Our

duty man said you put a fire-alarm and earthquake priority classification on this!'

'Yes,' accepted Wilson. 'I suppose that's about right. Why don't we sit down, first?'

The Director General went to the one chair behind the half-moon table and the rest spread themselves among the waiting chairs. Charlie sat in the front row, at one end of the line. No one tried to join him. At the table Wilson cleared his throat, sighed and said: 'There's no pleasant or easy way to put this. We've every reason to believe that details of your most recent Strategic Defence Initiative development are compromised.'

There was one of those complete silences to which Charlie was becoming so accustomed. It was McDonald who broke it. The man said: 'I'd like you to run that by us again, real slow.' He had a very broad Southern accent, Texas or perhaps Louisiana.

Wilson picked up from the table the drawing that had been removed from the King William Street deposit box, starting to offer it and then stopping. Because he was nearest Charlie got up and ferried it to the two American intelligence men.

'What is this?' asked Bowley at once. There was no longer any affability about the man.

Wilson indicated the white-haired Springley, separated from the Americans by two rows of seats. Formally the Director General said: 'It has been positively identified by the project leader involved as a genuine copy-drawing from one forming part of the British participation in a Star Wars defensive missile due to be put into permanent, geo-stationary orbit by American shuttle.'

The Americans *were* professionals, both of them. There were no theatrical I-don't-believe-it or it's-a-disaster or calls upon the Almighty. The questions snapped out, quiet-voiced, calmly: How? Where?

400

Why? When? Wilson tidied the account when he replied, not confusing it in any way by introducing Charlie's supposed involvement.

'Sure it's not your guy, Blackstone?' pressed Bowley anxiously. 'That it's not confined just to the British end?'

'Krogh spent practically a week at the factory,' reminded Wilson. 'Studying every single drawing. What other reason would he have for doing that? Blackstone was closed off, from everything, after that one instance.'

'Son of a bitch!' said Bowley, his first expression of anger.

'What have you done, so far?' asked the steadier McDonald.

'Do you want to take it, Charlie?' invited the Director General wearily.

Charlie swivelled in his front seat, the better to see everyone. He considered standing but remembered that despite his bad leg Wilson had remained seated on this occasion, so he decided to do the same. As he spoke Charlie was aware of the expressions of astonishment growing on the Americans' faces and when he finished Bowley said: 'That's the stupidest, most half-assed idea I've ever heard of in my entire life.'

'Something like that,' accepted Charlie, unmoved.

'But what's the point!' came in McDonald.

'To see what happens, at the deposit facility. It'll give us some sort of guide, maybe, how bad things are. And taking a desperate, hopeless chance because of the date on the drawing you've got there in your hands. Let's face the fact: you've lost it. We've both lost it. Anything, I don't care how stupid or how half-assed, is worth a try.'

'And this is the best you could come up with: giving the goddamned thing back!'

401

'What would you like to do!' came back Charlie, irritated. 'Call up Dzerzhinsky Square and say they've played dirty pool and ask for everything back? Or invade Russia? Krogh's your traitor, not ours. So *you* think of something better!'

'There's nothing to be gained by fighting among ourselves,' warned Wilson.

'You think Krogh's still in this country?' questioned the calmer McDonald.

'Now that it's daylight and the main computers are open we're checking all airline bookings over the past week,' said Charlie. 'But I think he's more likely still to be here than back in California. According to the date that drawing is hardly more than twenty-four hours old. And it's number twenty-one: there should be three more to go.'

'So we check every hotel in London,' announced Bowley.

Charlie nodded towards Springley and Bishop. 'We're trying to short-circuit the time it would take to do that by having the factory records checked. But there might be a quicker way. From the telephone check on Blackstone, we've located a safe house that's not on our records: a place just off Rutland Gardens, in Kensington.'

'Then why aren't we there!' demanded Bowley in fresh anger.

'We are,' assured Charlie quietly. 'It's sealed: it has been for some hours.'

'OK!' said Bowley urgently. 'I know it's your jurisdiction but he's our national. We want in. Joint operation.'

Charlie looked for the decision to the Director General, who nodded. Charlie said: 'We could do with a wire picture, from your people. There must be one of Krogh from his Pentagon clearance.'

'I've got a lot to ask Washington: a lot to tell them,

too,' said Bowley miserably. 'Is there an office here I could use? I don't want to waste time going back to the embassy.'

'Of course,' said Wilson. 'Advise your people that I'll make personal contact with your directors, both of them, later today. But tell them I'm sorry.'

'We're all sorry, Sir Alistair,' said Bowley. 'Sorry as hell.'

'Let's get it over with,' said McDonald to his CIA counterpart. 'I want to assign as many people as I can to that safe house. Including myself.'

Krogh looked at the Russian across the taxi taking them to Kensington and said: 'I still can't understand why I've got to do this.' Late the previous night, after everything else had been cleared up, he'd made a token protest when he was finally told he had to make a duplicate drawing but Petrin had told him curtly to shut up, and so he had.

'He wants it so let's get it done,' sighed Petrin.

'I'm making a reservation to go home tomorrow,' said Krogh, straining for a tiny gesture of defiant independence.

'Sure,' said Petrin, letting the American have it. There'd be no difficulty cancelling it – or even refusing to let the man make it in the first place – if something came up later that morning to make it inconvenient.

'What about you?'

Petrin had been gazing uninterestedly away from the American, through the taxi window. He answered the man's look now, seeing the need. If I threw a stick, he thought, this man would run after it and bring it back to me. He said: 'I'll be going back, too.'

'Tomorrow?'

'We won't be flying together, Emil,' he refused.

403

What about the future? An always leaking source, Petrin remembered. He said: 'But we'll keep in touch though, shall we?'

'No!' said Krogh weakly.

'We'll see,' said the Russian, edging forward on his seat as the taxi slowed to stop at the junction of Rutland Gardens with the Knightsbridge Road: it had become the habit, developed from Petrin's instinctive caution although with that caution dulled now from too much repetition, to walk the rest of the way, never positively identifying the house even to a casual cab driver.

The seizure went wrong because of a mistaken assumption, which was easy for the later inquiries to criticize and condemn but understandable in the heat and tension of the moment, because Washington's reaction had been outright panic. There had been President-to-Prime Minister telephone calls and news of more CIA and FBI men arriving on a shared Agency plane and nerves were stretched cheese-wire tight. The belief of the stake-out squads, particularly among the London-based Americans, was that Krogh was already *inside* the house, living there, and that if he did not emerge after a certain time orders would be given to storm it. Not that he would approach it, virtually from their rear upon which no one was concentrating.

It was one of the embassy CIA men who first recognized Emil Krogh from the photographs that had been wired from Washington and a copy of which was now in every observing vehicle. The man snatched up the open channel radio in the parked Ford and yelled urgently: 'Behind! Krogh's coming from behind, from the main road! Grey suit, blue shirt. Fifty yards from the target house on foot with another male. Caucasian. Brown sport coat. Tan slacks. . .'

The mistakes began to compound themselves.

The observation teams should have allowed Krogh and Petrin to continue on into the house, where they would have been trapped. But two separate groups wrongly interpreted the warning to mean that Krogh was escaping from it, not going towards it. Men burst, far too obviously, from both vehicles.

Petrin realized what was happening seconds ahead of Krogh. He snatched out, halting the American, automatically beginning to turn before seeing that a third squad had left their vehicle and had closed off any escape back towards the main road. So he stopped, waiting.

A cry wailed out of Krogh, a whimpering, sobbing sound. And then he tried to run. There was nowhere he could have gone, because there were men blocking the road on either side of them, but he tried to flee anyway. The squads were concentrated upon the pavement, of course, so Krogh dashed blindly into the road from between two parked cars directly into the path of an oncoming Post Office delivery van. The American saw it and the van was not travelling fast and the driver had a few seconds to brake, so the impact was not a severe one: Krogh had his hands outstretched, in a warding-off gesture, and actually appeared to push himself away from the vehicle. There was, however, sufficient force to throw him over. He fell back towards the pavement but short of it and the front and the left side of his head struck precisely against the sharp kerb edge, instantly causing a depressed fracture from the temple practically to the rear of the skull. Apart from that, the American suffered only superficial bruising.

Other squads did storm the house then, emerging in minutes with the cringing, babbling Yuri Guzins and another Russian, tight-lipped and calm, like Petrin.

'I am innocent! I haven't done anything! please. . .!' gabbled Guzins.

'Shut up!' barked Petrin, in matching Russian. 'Say absolutely nothing. You can only suffer if you talk: if you tell them what's happened.'

None of the British or American officers surrounding them understood the exchange, because not one of them spoke the language. It was a further error not to have foreseen the need, like not keeping the three Russians apart from each other.

Upstairs, in the room where Krogh had worked, the two intelligence supervisors surveyed the drawing equipment.

'Holy shit!' said Bowley.

45

Charlie finally slept: or rather collapsed through utter exhaustion. He did so at last in the duty officers' dormitory and showered and shaved in the tiny adjoining bathroom when he got up in the afternoon, grateful afterwards that waiting for him were the fresh clothes that had been brought in, on Wilson's orders, from the Vauxhall flat. Only when he was dressing did Charlie realize, surprised it had taken him so long, that he was effectively under house arrest. And then he modified the thought: the Russians would have seen the Special Branch seizure and *expect* him to be in custody. Which made it impossible for him to return to an apartment they might still be watching, as a precaution. It was in between accepted mealtimes in the basement cafeteria. Charlie asked for eggs on toast. The eggs tasted like a sample from a Brazilian rubber tree and the toast was as hard as the bark through which the rubber might have seeped.

Back in his office Charlie sat and couldn't decide what to do; what he was expected to do. He wondered about Hubert Witherspoon, who was nowhere around. And then he wondered about Laura Nolan and whether she knew that he was back in the building. And then, avoiding it no longer, he wondered about Natalia and what she was doing and what she was thinking and – again – whether she had any part in the things that were happening all around him.

The summons from the Director General came in the half light of late afternoon and Charlie was glad because he was fed up wondering about things he couldn't resolve. Charlie was curious about who else

407

would be in the conference room, and even more curious when he entered and found there was no one apart from Wilson. The Director General was shaved and changed, which was an improvement upon that morning although the old man still looked ill. Charlie doubted Wilson would have returned all the way to his country home, in Hampshire, and then remembered there was a London pied-à-terre, somewhere in Mayfair. South Audley Street, he thought.

'I think we've trawled everything in,' announced Wilson. He was standing, just slightly propped against the table edge.

'Sir?' queried Charlie.

'We've been to your bank. Everything was as you'd said it would be, properly authorized for my receipt. Even the fingerprints of the cashier Sally Dickenson matched those on the banknotes issued against your name. And we recovered the missed micro-dot from your flat, at the same time as collecting your clothes.'

'How about the car numbers?'

'Companies, like you guessed they would be. Two we certainly knew already to be used by the Soviet embassy. One's new to us. Well done.'

'And Blackstone?'

'It's coming, in bits and pieces. He identified Vitali Losev from one of the counter-intelligence snatch pictures. Said he knew him by the name Stranger: Mr Stranger. But that he was expecting to be taken over by someone else. . .' Wilson smiled. 'The recognition was to be Visitor. There was some money in the house when he was arrested. There's some consecutive numbering with what was originally planted at your place.'

'I thought he might take slightly longer to crack,' reflected Charlie.

'He was with wife number two, on the Isle of Wight, when we picked him up,' reminded Wilson.

'We brought in Ruth, his first choice, because wives have a right to know what's happening to their husbands. There was a lot of crying: one big sad family. Or rather his families. He didn't seem able to concentrate. '

Charlie smiled. 'Stranger. . .Visitor. . .Guest,' he mused. 'Berenkov tried hard, didn't he?'

'It could have been a very effective disinformation, if it had worked,' admired Wilson. 'We would have had to check back on everything you'd ever done. . .anyone you'd ever met. It would have taken years.'

Charlie shook his head in rejection. 'It was too flawed.'

'Only because you found the stuff in your flat ahead of the cable from Moscow and did what you did with it,' insisted Wilson. 'If everything had been intact when we rummaged I would have put it forward for a decision to prosecute to the Attorney General.'

Charlie swallowed. He hadn't realized, until now, that it had been that close. 'It would still have been defensible,' he said insistently.

'Even if you'd got off – and I'm still not sure you would have done – there would have been too much suspicion around you to keep you on,' said the Director General.

Maybe it *had* been personal, thought Charlie: either way he would have been wrecked. He said: 'How did it go in Kensington?'

'Badly,' conceded Wilson at once. Succinctly he outlined what had happened and said: 'I've had complaints from both American directors already. It's getting to be buck-passing time. There's a lot of opposition to what we're trying to do but I haven't yet had a positive prime ministerial instruction to abort.'

'Do you think it will come?'

'I don't know. Maybe.'

'What about the three Russians?'

'We've separated them, of course, although it's probably too late. One we've already identified from his photograph as attached to the embassy: name's Obyedkov. I guess the one picked up in the street to be professional, too. Neither's said a word. The third one is practically melting all over the floor: he'll break soon enough. There's no doubt about the house though. It was all there: drawing board, all the equipment.'

'And Krogh.'

Wilson glanced at his watch. 'By now he should already have undergone one operation, in an attempt to lift the bone depression away from the brain. The prognosis, before the operation, was that it's caused quite a lot of damage. He'll be in intensive care for quite a while. So we still don't know whether the Russians got the lot.'

'If they had everything there wouldn't have been any purpose in going to the house this morning, would there?' pointed out Charlie.

The Director General shrugged. 'There's been too much guessing already: I don't want to add any more.'

'What are you going to do with the Russians?'

Wilson gave a wintry smile. 'I haven't decided yet,' he said. 'If the fat one who's falling apart tells all then we could make a case against them: bring in Losev, too, on the basis of Blackstone's confession. At the moment we can hold those we've got on suspicion of espionage: two of them for entry into Britain on false passports. . .' The smile broadened, becoming warmer. 'Or they could have a better, practical use, if we wanted some misleading information conveyed back to Moscow.'

'Yes they could, couldn't they?' said Charlie, smiling back.

'I've been doing most of the talking, Charlie.'

'I'm sorry?' queried Charlie.

'I want to know about the hotel. And Natalia Nikandrova Fedova.'

Charlie told him. He held nothing back and was completely honest, from the affair in Moscow up to their last conversation, two nights before.

The Director General listened blank-faced and without any interruption until Charlie had obviously finished. Then he said at once: 'You did not make an identification file, when you returned from Moscow?'

'No.'

'You should have done.'

'Yes.'

'Neither did you when you recognized the media reports?'

'No.'

'Which means you knowingly allowed a KGB officer to enter this country as a Soviet delegation member without any notification or alert to counter-espionage?'

'Yes.'

'And then went and set yourself down right in the middle?'

'Yes.'

'You're a bloody fool!' declared the older man.

'I've explained my reasons,' said Charlie.

'Which don't change the fact that you're a bloody fool.'

Charlie said nothing because the assessment was the right one.

Wilson sighed. 'I've tolerated a lot from you, for all the reasons we both know,' he said. 'There's a limit.'

'I did not behave – did not intend – to cause any

411

embarrassment or to compromise this department.'

'Bullshit!' exploded the Director General. 'You were *there*: have been photographed and are now known to counter-espionage to have been there! *That* embarrasses and compromises this department!'

'I've honestly explained my personal reasons for doing what I did,' tried Charlie. 'But I also knew, by the time I went to the hotel, that some trap was being set. I wanted to spring it.'

'Weak, Muffin, weak,' dismissed the Director General.

He was no longer being called by his first name, acknowledged Charlie. 'The truth,' he insisted.

Wilson came slightly away from the table, bending forward for emphasis. 'All right!' he said. 'So tell me this. If there had not been any of the other business – no hostile surveillance, no phoney evidence planted at your flat – and you'd learned as you did learn that Natalia Nikandrova Fedova was coming under some guise into this country? Would you have still made contact with her?'

Charlie hesitated. 'Yes,' he admitted finally.

Wilson shook his head in dismay. 'And you believe it's innocent!'

'I still don't know.'

'Or want to decide?'

'Maybe.'

'Think, man! Think!'

'I've done little else, for weeks.'

'Then think some more!' urged the Director General. 'Naivety doesn't become you: it's got to be wrong!'

'I'll concede some. Not all.'

'You really believe she'll come over?'

'I don't know but I think so.'

'She'd have to go through the system.'

'I told you what she said about that.'

'Rubbish! She doesn't have a choice. You know that. She should know that. It would be a condition of her acceptance.'

'I decided to deal with it once she'd crossed.'

'And there'd be another condition, of course.'

Charlie hesitated again. Then he said: 'Yes, I know.'

'You prepared for that?'

'Yes.'

'I can't accept that!' disputed Wilson. 'I don't think you've properly considered it.'

'I believe I have.'

'What would you do?'

Charlie humped his shoulders. 'I don't know.'

'Then you haven't thought it through!' insisted the Director General, slapping his thigh in finality. 'Not to the extent that you should have done.'

'Nothing about this episode has been easy to think through to it's proper, logical conclusion,' said Charlie.

Berenkov was concerned but not panicked. Not yet. The moment he received the alert from Losev he began the damage limitation, calculating step by step and with ice-cold expertise how bad the situation was. Bad, he judged: bad but not catastrophic. Petrin and Obyedkov were professionals and professionals daily faced the risk of seizure. They were trained for it: knew that if they were ever tried and imprisoned in the West an exchange would be arranged – as an exchange was every time arranged if a Russian intelligence officer were incarcerated – even if it meant jailing in Russia a visiting or diplomatic national from the arresting country on a trumped-up charge. Yuri Guzins was the weakness, the one who could make it a catastrophe. The man wasn't trained: would have no confident expectation

413

of release, in the event of being sent to prison. He'd be sitting in some cell now, unable to speak a word of the language, horrors crowding in upon horrors all around him. If he broke, confessed everything, Britain would have what they needed for a trial, and working in collusion with America – and the two countries *would* be working in collusion – there'd be enough for an enormous propaganda accusation throughout the West. And it didn't end there: scarcely began, in fact. Guzins was a top Soviet space scientist. Under skilful interrogation – promises of leniency if he cooperated – the man could be tricked into disclosing hugely damaging secrets of genuine Soviet research at Baikonur. The burly Directorate chief shook his head, tempted to revise his judgement. Maybe it did go beyond being bad: come close to being catastrophic. Certainly the potential existed.

Emil Krogh was another dangerous uncertainty. Berenkov didn't know what had happened to the American. Before he'd been seized Obyedkov had managed to babble on the emergency line to the embassy that there'd been an ambush in the street and that he and Guzins were about to be taken and then the instrument had been snatched from him and Losev had protectively disconnected from the English voice demanding from the other end who was there. Krogh was as weak a link as Guzins, Berenkov calculated. The American would actually be able to identify Guzins' speciality to the interrogators and guide them on how to pressure the Russian scientist.

It *did* go beyond being simply bad, thought Berenkov, revising his opinion at last. So it was time for another damage assessment: a personal one now. Disastrous though it might be, no criticism – no accusation of himself having made a mistake – could be levelled at him for the British discovering the Kensington house. That, always, had had to be an accepted, recognized risk. What then? The remaining drawing, he isolated at once: the one remaining drawing which the idiot Guzins had insisted upon being duplicated, and before the receipt of which he had refused to release the photographic copies that already existed. No problem, balanced Berenkov at once, relieved. The photographic copies *did* exist. Safe and secure and awaiting shipment, upon Guzins' authority. Which he could no longer exercise. When they arrived he would have satisfactorily fulfilled his brief, Berenkov told himself. There'd been a cost – possibly a very high cost – but nothing for which he could be blamed.

And there had, in addition, been the other, private success. From the messages from London the previous day Berenkov knew Charlie Muffin was now behind bars somewhere, facing the inevitability of many more years in precisely that situation. The Russian wondered if the British had started the questioning yet, giving the man the clue to how it had all been manipulated.

Berenkov stirred at last, satisfied that he had worked everything out to its proper conclusion and in its proper order of importance. There only remained one thing to complete, to make himself absolutely secure. It only took him minutes to compose the cable, ordering that the retained cassette be included in that night's diplomatic shipment from London.

Which it was.

Losev, who was still working out his reaction to the Kensington arrests, had anticipated it anyway and had the spool ready. The diplomatic bag reached London airport with two hours to spare before the Moscow-bound flight and was receipted and guaranteed its protection under the Vienna convention by the senior Customs controller on duty.

It was placed in the Customs safe to await final loading and removed from it – without Customs awareness – within fifteen minutes by Special Branch technicians who peeled off the diplomatic seal in such a way that it could be undetectably relocked. When they opened the bag itself they used magnets to hold back the device they detected by X-ray, which was intended to destruct upon unauthorized entry. They took the film cassette they found inside to the Special Branch photographic facility permanently maintained at the airport. There – in protective darkroom conditions – it was viewed in negative, which showed the sort of drawing for which they were looking, although not at that stage precisely which drawing. Following the detailed instruction from the Director General, prints were made from every frame. The negative roll was then fogged sufficiently badly to prevent any further prints being made from that part necessarily developed – and to prevent that development being detected by the Russians – and then rewound into its original casing which was pressured to distort slightly. Finally it was replaced in the diplomatic bag, and the bag resealed.

Two hours later, at Westminster Bridge Road, Wilson looked up from the prints at Charlie and said: 'You incredibly lucky bugger!'

'About time,' said Charlie.

46

Natalia was there.

And conducting herself well, properly, not standing on the pavement edge, looking around hopefully in a way that might have attracted attention but back against the entry to a shop and gazing in as if she were window shopping, someone with plenty of time to spare. Charlie was actually inside the opposite store, on the first floor from the overlooking window of which he could gaze down and see everything, as he needed to see everything. He thought she was alone: certainly there was no one in close proximity, a watcher or a guard. The emotion, his feeling for her, lumped inside him, a positive physical sensation. So she'd done it. She'd come. Was waiting. Waiting for him. *I'll be ready.* His promise to her, Charlie remembered, the night they'd made their final plans. These plans. So was he? Was he going to keep the promise and go and get her and run with her? Charlie swayed – the start of a movement – but then didn't move, remaining where he was, watching. Why had she had to turn up at all! Why hadn't she just stayed away, so that he would have known at once that she'd been part of it, instead of this: being there so that he stayed confused. *Didn't* know.

Maybe she should be waiting around the corner, in the main road and not in the side street directly opposite the store, Natalia thought abruptly. She'd expected Charlie to be there, prepared, so that there wouldn't be any delay like this. That had to be it! Around the corner in the main road. She moved, casually, which was very difficult for her because she was so frightened she felt lightheaded, nerves so taut her skin itched. What she really wanted to do was run the few yards to the junction and yell for him, shout out his name to make him come to her and get her away. Natalia reached the main road and started down it, pretending to study the windows again but desperately seeking him, aching for him to emerge from some doorway, some car. Where was he! Dear God, where was he?

Was her moving a signal to someone, someone he *hadn't* spotted? Still using her cover well, judged Charlie: surprisingly expert. *I wasn't trained as a field agent, like you.* That's what she'd told him, that last night. All right, her movements weren't perfect – weren't how he or a professional with years of experience knew how virtually to disappear on a crowded street – but she was still very good. So had she been trained? Brought up to a minimum standard at least, for this operation? And it had to be an operation. Something. What else could it be? Professional, Charlie decided: he had to be brutally, clinically professional, subjugate every feeling for her and examine everything that had happened, from the very beginning. And the very beginning had been her transfer, from a specific, highly skilled position to a nebulous, untitled role that exposed her to the West. Not just exposed her, Charlie reasoned on. *Publicly* exposed her because every trip she'd made out of Russia had been reported, with photographs. Wrong, determined Charlie, forcing that brutal, clinical judgement. Wrong like Sir Alistair Wilson had again insisted it was before giving him permission at last to leave Westminster Bridge Road and done it sadly and said goodbye, an unspoken reminder that if she were there and she did cross then the department would be closed to him, for ever. Not just wrong, by their assessment, either. Surely Natalia – Natalia who had been vague and casual

418

when he'd tried to talk about it with her – knew
that no service switched people around like she'd
been switched around. She hadn't been assigned
to one particular ministry, even: the only essential
appeared to have been a delegation, any delegation,
crossing to the West. Another incongruity: like so
many others.

Where was he! thought Natalia again, desperation worsening. She turned, walking back towards
the store, jostled and pushed by oncoming people
but hardly aware of them. Charlie wasn't like this:
couldn't be like this. He'd know what it would be
like, how dangerous it was. In the end there had
only been eight of them who'd wanted to come and
Bondarev had appointed himself the escort as well
as an embassy official, and she'd been away from the
shopping party for five minutes at least. There'd be
the search for her soon, curious at first but then the
panic, the alarm. Charlie had said he would look after her always. So why wasn't he looking after her
now! She thought: Please Charlie! Please Charlie,
where are you?

The hotel had been the most incongruous of all,
Charlie reasoned. How *could* Natalia have moved
around so easily and so freely, unless she'd been
permitted to do so? He knew from the barman how
the KGB watchers had monitored and herded up the
late-night drinkers not in their rooms. Natalia had
told him herself of Bondarev's diligence. And her
supposed explanation for being discovered coming
to him didn't withstand examination. Those same
KGB escorts would have known she scarcely drank
because it would have been in her personal records,
so it would have been something at once to arouse
their suspicion. *I've been lucky.* Charlie found it easy
to remember that remark: the tone of voice in which
Natalia had made it. Luck hadn't come into it, he

419

knew sadly. He could remember everything about that last night. He recalled her hesitation when he'd announced he was booking out. *I'll learn*, she said. Learn what? Was there a pointer in another, earlier conversation, the discussion about his being in Moscow? Had she come across to get to him and discover what he'd really been doing there? It was a possibility. No service liked an unclosed file. And according to Natalia's own admission, Berenkov was still head of the First Chief Directorate, with the power to have orchestrated everything just to find out.

Natalia reached the corner again and turned into the side street to the shop windows she'd first pretended to study. Her stomach was in turmoil and briefly she folded her arms across herself, so that she could scratch the irritation on her arms. He loved her! She knew he loved her, like she loved him! It had been unreal – like some absurd dream – at the hotel but it had been wonderful and she was sure it could have been even more wonderful when they were together somewhere safe, just by themselves. So why hadn't he come! He wasn't cruel: not a bastard. He wouldn't have tricked her – deceived her – like this. It was inconceivable. What would have been the point? There wasn't one. So it *had* to be inconceivable. Then where was he? Something had to have happened to him! He was lying hurt, injured somewhere! The guess brought a surge of anxiety, then conflicting emotions. Her eyes filmed at the idea of his being hurt and then she realized that if he were physically prevented from getting to her none of it was going to work because there was no one else who could come for her. Natalia had to keep her lips tight, biting them closed with her teeth, to prevent the whimper of despair. Don't let it happen like this, she thought; don't let everything collapse and fail like this! It couldn't! It wasn't fair.

420

Everything was going to be so good, so perfect. She was going to be happy and it seemed such a long time since she'd been happy. Minutes, she calculated: she couldn't stay any longer than minutes. Why hadn't he come? Why! Why! Why!

The Director General had been right, accepted Charlie. Natalia would have known she'd have to go through a debriefing procedure: that her acceptance would have been impossible without it. So what reason had there been for her announcing that she wouldn't cooperate? It didn't make sense. *I'll learn*, he remembered again. And then he thought further, to other things she'd said that night: to her insistence – near shouted insistence – that he remain in the service. *You've got to find a way*, she'd said. And more, when he'd argued against her. *I won't cross.* Was that the true meaning of her saying that she'd learn? That she wanted him to stay on in the hope of picking up, over the weeks and months, as much as she could about the department and its ongoing operations? Possible, Charlie decided: extremely possible. Certainly, for Soviet intelligence and the grand-gestured Berenkov, worth the attempt to link him with Natalia again.

She could defect, Natalia realized suddenly. Properly defect, like other people had before her. Let herself be sucked into the system of debriefing and interrogation that she'd told Charlie she wouldn't do. But bargain, in return, demand to know what had happened to him and to be allowed to see him, to be with him again. She started to tremble and had to hold herself again. It had taken every ounce of courage she could find to get this far: she didn't think she could do any more, endure the suspicion and hostility there would be, until she got back to Charlie. And she *wasn't* a defector, Natalia told herself: couldn't be. Defectors were traitors, people who hated their country, and she wasn't that. And there was another bar, one she'd stopped herself so far considering. What if Charlie *had* changed his mind: decided from their brief time at the hotel that Moscow had been a mistake and that he couldn't go on with the charade? He hadn't been able to make love to her that last night, had he? Hadn't wanted to. She'd only defect properly if she were guaranteed to see him again. And there was no way she could get that guarantee: no way she could know – really *know* – that he wanted her.

I'll learn echoed in Charlie's mind again, like a mocking taunt. There was something else she could learn, by being there today. Charlie knew the Russians had seen his arrest: one of the vehicles he'd identified from its registration number had been parked further along the street, nearer the Bayswater Road, when it all happened. But they'd like to know what happened afterwards; get some idea whether their entrapment had been completely successful or whether it had failed – as it *had* failed – for some reason they had been unable to anticipate. His approaching Natalia would tell them that. All it needed was for there to be some continuing observation of Natalia, the knowing bait – observation that could be a long way off even and be impossible for him to isolate this time – and they'd know. It could be the simplest but surest indicator they could possibly have, the entire reason for her being there. Their absolute, final insurance.

He couldn't watch any longer, Charlie decided. Didn't want to watch any longer. There were too many incongruities, too much that didn't have a logical, acceptable explanation. He'd gone along with it like he'd run hare to the Soviet surveillance, always suspecting Natalia to be part of it but hoping she wasn't, letting himself be deluded for a while because he'd *wanted* to be deluded. Which hadn't been hard because their nights at the hotel had been perfect and it had seemed that she *did* love him. But he couldn't allow the delusion to continue any longer. It had to end. Now. All over. Charlie's last sight of Natalia Nikandrova Fedova was of her standing with her arms across her body, as if she were cold. He turned, walking across the store, towards a far exit.

Charlie wasn't going to come, Natalia finally accepted. She'd waited long enough – too long – and now she had to hurry to get back to the others, to protect herself. That was all that mattered now, just protecting herself. She'd have to concoct some story of becoming bewildered, lost: of being glad that she'd found them at last. Bondarev would probably be suspicious but she would have come back so that's all he could be, just suspicious. It was difficult for her to care – properly to care – anyway, Natalia thought, hurriedly re-entering the store. Why hadn't Charlie come! She'd never know, Natalia realized: never be able to find out. She'd been so sure, too. So very sure that Charlie had loved her.

Berenkov panicked now.

Blind panic initially, his mind refusing to function which had never happened before, not even in England when he'd realized his arrest had been inevitable. He'd refused at first to believe the Technical Division report that the film was fogged and insisted on crossing to the department himself to be shown it under darkroom conditions, ordering that they try to develop some prints off it before at last conceding it was useless. It was then that Berenkov started to think, forcing himself to calculate and consider because it was important that he understand. Yevgennie Zazulin was a professional, an expert and none of the other films had been spoiled, and

Berenkov's first demand was to know if the damage were accidental or whether the diplomatic bag had been tampered with. The technical experts showed him the slight distortion of the cassette and judged it sufficient to have admitted the erasing light. They also reminded Berenkov of the destruct device which prevented the unauthorized entry into the diplomatic bag and assured him the seal had been intact when it arrived.

Back in his office Berenkov had consciously to force himself to think rationally and not let the fears jumble his reasoning. The one drawing that mattered! The only one for which there was not a drawn or photographic duplicate! Yuri Guzins' responsibility, Berenkov thought bitterly: it had been the space scientist's decision to withhold it. Would it not have been so disastrous in every other way he'd have hoped the interfering bastard be put on trial and jailed for a hundred years, without any possibility of getting out. Stupid reflection, recognized Berenkov, self-critical. He had to survive: escape censure. And there would be censure – more than likely dismissal and the punishable accusation of unprofessional negligence – if it were ever discovered, suspected even, that he'd seeded a trap in a minor, personally motivated operation with the one drawing they were missing.

There was still a chance, Berenkov decided frantically. He knew the safe custody facility in King William Street hadn't yet been cleared by the investigating British, because of course he'd ordered the closest observation to tell him everything had succeeded against Charlie Muffin. Now that wasn't important any more. The operation – the attack – upon Charlie Muffin had to be abandoned, forgotten if necessary. Only one thing was important now: recovering the drawing.

Berenkov sent his instructions, specifically entrusting Vitali Losev with the task of emptying the King William Street box, within two hours of learning that the film cassette was useless.

Losev went nervously. He knew there had been no formal protest yet to the Soviet embassy but it was impossible to assess how fast or in what direction the British investigation was proceeding. What he did know was that King William Street had been set up for the British to discover and that there was a very real risk of his walking into a trap of his own creation.

He was extremely careful approaching the security firm's offices, scouring the street and overlooking buildings for the slightest indication of surveillance but not finding it. He entered at last and asked for the box, every moment expecting an authoritative challenge or an arresting hand upon his shoulder. It was as quick to empty the box as it had been earlier to fill it, a matter of seconds, and then he was outside again, still without any interception. Knowing it could still happen – that the British would most likely have waited for him to get something incriminating in his possession before moving at all – Losev remained twitchingly tense. He'd intended recrossing London by underground but when the time came he decided against it, wanting the security of being enclosed and alone rather than to be among a lot of other people. He hailed a taxi and asked for Notting Hill Gate, leaving himself with just a short walk into Kensington Palace Gardens and the embassy.

Losev travelled alert to every vehicle around them on the jammed London streets, only starting to relax when they came close to Hyde Park. He walked hurriedly into the diplomatic enclave after paying off the cab, letting the breath gush from him when he pushed closed the side door admitting him to the embassy and the protection of what was officially regarded as Russian territory, where his safety was guaranteed.

Throughout the visit to King William Street, the recovery of the drawing and his return across London, Losev had been constantly monitored by British intelligence officers.

47

It was a week before Charlie was called to the ninth
floor, a week during which he was forbidden to go
anywhere near his Vauxhall flat but had to live
in a department-owned house in Hampstead and was
required, each succeeding day, to build up in the
minutest detail a report upon everything he had
done from the moment he'd detected the Soviet surveillance on the Isle of Wight. There were two interviews with the executives from the department's internal security division, hostile, antagonistic encounters with men who considered Charlie had exposed
the inadequacies and failings of their colleagues and
were determined to catch him out and find cause
for some internal disciplining. Charlie didn't believe
they did, to any degree of seriousness, but was in
any case hardly concerned. He obeyed the instructions and endured the interrogations but existed
through it all in a slough of crushing desponden-
cy, his mind and feelings absorbed to the exclusion
of anything else by that morning at the department
store window, gazing down upon Natalia for the
last time. He'd hesitated that day, at the moment
of leaving the store, all the conflicting reasoning
and common-sense decisions wiped out, his sole,
overwhelming desire abruptly to run back and get
to her. For several moments he'd remained just inside one of the exit doors, almost literally pulled in
opposing directions. He'd fought against the yearn-
ing and carried on, quitting the place, but since then,
every day and every night, he'd thought about nothing else, mentally rearranging the arguments, trying
to reach – pointless though that would now be – a

resolve different from that he'd made.

During the week the office across the corridor normally occupied by Hubert Witherspoon had remained empty and there had been no contact or communication from Richard St John Harkness, which Charlie had half expected but did not regret failing to receive.

He was curious, when he received the ninth-floor demand, if at last it was to be confronted by Harkness: the interview request was illegibly signed *pour procurationem* on Director General notepaper but during Sir Alistair Wilson's absence Harkness had frequently used it, according himself the promotion that had never occurred in reality.

But it hadn't come from Harkness. At the re-established security counter on the ninth floor he was collected by the primly permed Miss Harriet Jameson–Gore, Wilson's personal secretary who had been in temporary charge of the typing pool during the Director General's illness and escorted by her to the old man's office, where Wilson was waiting. Wilson was by the window, where the sill was just the right height for him to perch and take the pressure off his leg without actually sitting down. There were two vases of pink parfait roses on the man's desk, filling the room with their scent. Growing roses at his Hampshire home was Wilson's overriding hobby: oddly it was the presence of the flowers, more than Wilson being there to receive him, that told Charlie the man was back permanently in control. Charlie still didn't think the older man looked completely fit.

Wilson gestured Charlie towards the sagging visitor's chair that had been absent during Harkness' tenure, a scored and stained leather thing with a seat that kept descending after a person sat in it. Without extending any invitation the Director General poured Islay malt into two tumblers, which he held before

428

him for examination and then added more whisky to both.

He handed one to Charlie and said: 'I've got the report from internal security. And their recommendations. They've itemized eight positive breaches and recommend your severe reprimand and that those reprimands be logged on your service record.'

They'd have been pissed off at that being the best – or rather the worst – that they could do, Charlie knew. He said: 'I suppose that's about right.'

'I'll say it again,' remarked Wilson. 'You behaved like a bloody fool. An absolute bloody fool.'

'Yes,' accepted Charlie meekly. He didn't accept it at all but now was not the time to argue, sitting there with a glass of the Director General's whisky in his hand.

Wilson propped himself at the window again, gazing into his drink. 'Did she turn up?'

'Yes.'

'Alone?'

'She appeared to be. It was impossible in surroundings like that to be absolutely sure.'

'Why didn't you make the contact?'

'It wasn't right,' said Charlie. 'She had to know.'

Wilson nodded, in agreement. 'I would have thought so. We could be wrong, of course, but I doubt it. . .' He looked up from his glass. 'Was it important to you?'

'Yes,' admitted Charlie at once. 'Very important.'

'Then I'm sorry. Personally sorry, I mean.'

Charlie shrugged, not immediately speaking. Then he said: 'Whatever the full story, I had to allow the doubt.'

'Let's move on,' said Wilson briskly. 'There are other things that need to be discussed. I've read your account. . .'

'Yes?' said Charlie inquiringly.

'My impression is that it is completely honest.'

'It is,' assured Charlie.

'Then be honest about something else.'

'What?'

'Did you intentionally embark, before the Isle of Wight business, to set up the deputy Director General or Hubert Witherspoon?' demanded Wilson. 'Create situations – aware as you were of certain personal feelings concerning you – that would lead them to overstep the mark perhaps?'

Charlie stared directly across at the other man, holding his eyes. 'No, sir,' he lied, 'I did not.'

Wilson gazed back, matching Charlie's look just as directly. There were several moments of silence. Wilson said: 'I want your assurance on this. You are being utterly truthful about that?'

'Yes I am,' said Charlie, feeling no discomfort.

Wilson nodded three or four times, quite slowly, and made a sound as if he were humming to himself. He said: 'There were some serious management mistakes. The credibility of the department has been called into question.'

'I'm sorry to hear that,' said Charlie. He still felt no discomfort. Remorse, either. The bastards wouldn't have felt anything for him, if they'd caught him out in the beginning or if the Soviet manipulation had turned out differently. They'd have been out somewhere celebrating by now, two glasses of lemonade and lots of self-satisfied back-slapping about how clever they'd been, ridding the department of an embarrassing oddity called Charlie Muffin.

'It's been decided there should be certain changes,' disclosed Wilson. 'Mr Harkness is being appointed Finance Director.'

It was difficult for Charlie to remain straight-faced. No longer deputy Director General! Charlie had never expected that: imagined trying to achieve

it, even, because he wouldn't have thought it possible. And it wouldn't have been, not from what he'd
done, he recognized objectively. Their overreaction,
their embarrassing mistakes, had been related to
what they were fed by Moscow. His part in their
downfall had been to expose the Soviet manoeuvre
for what it was. He said: 'Who is the new deputy Director General going to be?'

'That's still to be decided,' refused Wilson.

'And Witherspoon?'

'Administration,' said Wilson vaguely. 'He will no
longer be maintained on the active roster.'

Charlie supposed he should feel some satisfaction
– be grateful at least that his two most active critics in
the place had been dumped at the same time – but he
didn't. Somehow it now seemed quite unimportant.
He said: 'What about me? Is any change to be made
to my role here?'

Wilson's face relaxed, into something of a smile.
'No,' he said. 'Nothing at all. But I want you to listen,
very carefully. Don't you ever take so many chances
again: try to run everything like a one-man army. It's
an absolute bloody miracle that things did not turn
out to be a bigger disaster than they were: a miracle
that the whole Russian scheme didn't get you sent
away for more years than you've got left to live.'

'What *has* happened?' asked Charlie.

Wilson gave an uncertain movement with his hand.
'One of the many things we'll never know is why they
held back the film roll of the drawing they planted
in King William Street. We can only thank Christ
that they did and we were able to destroy it. We
know they retrieved what we put there because we
followed Losev every step of the way. Now all we
can do is sit and pray, which is hardly enough but
all there is. There's been a lot of direct telephone
conversations between the President and the Prime

431

Minister. Between the American directors and myself, as well. No one believes it's going to work; that it stands a chance in hell.'

'What about the people rounded up from the safe house?'

'There's a lot of squabbling over that. America is pressing for a full-blown spy trial: certainly they want to sweat every drop they can out of the scientist. His name turns out to be Yuri Guzins, incidentally: we traced him from some photographs taken at the Soviet installation at Baikonur.'

'What do you want to do?'

'Guzins is tempting: bloody tempting,' said Wilson. 'The other two don't matter. I'd prefer to have Obyedkov expelled: usual grounds about activities not in keeping with his supposed diplomatic status. The other one too, for entering on a false passport. The FBI have identified him as Alexandr Petrin. He's based in the Soviet consulate in San Francisco. Washington take that as positive confirmation that Krogh's leaked everything there is to tell about the work his company were doing.'

'What about Krogh?'

'That's what really angers the Americans,' disclosed Wilson. 'There's been a second operation and there doesn't seem to be any doubt there's permanent and severe brain damage. He can't talk even if he wanted to. Seems it'll never be possible to bring him to trial.'

'So who's going to get their way?' pressed Charlie.

Wilson sighed, shifting himself against the window sill. 'The trouble with staging a major trial is that restricted though it would be, actually in camera, there would have to be some revelation that America has lost its Star Wars supremacy. That would cause an enormous public outcry in America but for the wrong reasons: there would be a

432

huge loss of confidence, a fear that they were no longer in control but vulnerable instead, not outrage that Russia steals Western technology, because most people accept that already. I can't see any purpose in finger-pointing: it's closing the stable door after the horse has bolted.'

'Which leaves Blackstone?'

'Who didn't actually do anything,' reminded the Director General. 'We'll orchestrate the court hearing quietly enough. It will be a closed session again. The charge will be *attempting* to assist in a hostile act, so there'll be a term of imprisonment. Losev will be incriminated, so we can get rid of him, cause Moscow some little inconvenience.'

'The decision is ours, here in London, isn't it?' pointed out Charlie. 'There could only be an American prosecution if Krogh could be arraigned, which he can't.'

Wilson smiled, a teeth-baring expression. 'I've made the point,' he said. 'It'll all come down in the end to a political chess game between London and Washington. Who gains or loses more by making or winning concessions.'

'I can't go back to Vauxhall, can I?' guessed Charlie.

'Of course not,' said the Director at once. 'We know that flat's identified, just like we know you were definitely targeted.'

'Pity,' said Charlie sadly. 'There's a good pub there. The Pheasant.'

'That's precluded too,' announced Wilson. 'You can stay at the department place for as long as you want, until you find something else. We'll clear Vauxhall for you. And there'll be the phoney trial, of course.'

Charlie had wondered if Wilson would do it. 'On the stuff that was supposed to be found in the flat?'

The Director General nodded. 'In camera again,' he agreed. 'Charge can be something like receiving payment for unspecified acts of espionage. The Attorney General isn't going to like his courts being used like this but I think I can persuade him. We belong to the same club, you know.'

'I didn't know,' said Charlie. 'It's necessary, I suppose.'

'If Berenkov believes you're out of circulation he isn't going to have another try, is he?'

'No,' agreed Charlie. 'So it's extremely necessary.'

Wilson laughed, adding whisky to both their glasses. 'Just imagine!' he said. 'Officially it'll mean you'll cease to exist.'

'People have been treating me like that for years,' said Charlie.

'Don't ever forget what I've said, about how you operate in the future?'

'I won't,' promised Charlie. Let's cross each bridge when we come to it, he thought easily.

'I mean it,' warned Wilson. 'Any more wild independence and I'll have you out of this department so fast your feet will leave scorch marks!'

'Trust me,' invited Charlie.

'Always the trouble, Charlie. Always the trouble.'

'I wanted to see you,' said Laura.

'Been busy,' said Charlie. 'Sorry.' If she had not actually come to the fifth floor and physically confronted him he would still probably have made an excuse to avoid their meeting – which, he decided, now they were together, was ridiculous. Why shouldn't they have a drink together?

'I know bits,' said Laura. 'Not a lot. Just bits.'

'It's very complicated,' said Charlie, in attempted dismissal. 'What's the financial department like?'

'Better view,' said Laura. 'He's trying to redesign

434

the expenses claims forms. He wants much more detail.' The entire department Harkness now controlled was separate from Westminster Bridge Road, across the river and nearer to Whitehall. Refusing to be put off, Laura said: 'I want to ask you something.'

'What?'

'That day in the street, when you told me you didn't want to keep the date? Did you know then that the Russians had picked you up?'

'Yes,' said Charlie.

'So it was to protect me?'

'It was probably already too late by then,' apologized Charlie. 'I wanted to keep you out of it if I could.'

Laura smiled and reached across the wine-bar table, pressing his hand. 'Thanks,' she said.

'I wish I'd realized sooner,' said Charlie. 'I was slow.'

'I did what you wanted, you know,' offered Laura. 'Before that, I mean. I gossiped to Harkness, about you. He seemed to think it was very important.'

'I'm sorry about that, too,' said Charlie. 'Using you like that.'

'Are you!' she demanded quizzically.

Charlie smiled back at her. 'Sort of,' he said.

'They say there was a woman involved,' said the girl. 'Someone you knew?'

'Yes,' said Charlie. The rumour mill was very active, he thought.

'Can you tell me about it?'

Charlie topped up both their glasses from the Montrachet bottle between them. 'No,' he said positively. Over, he thought: finished.

'Oh,' said Laura, rebuffed.

'There's nothing to tell,' said Charlie.

'Paul's asked for a divorce,' she announced

435

abruptly. 'His girlfriend is pregnant again. They want to get married.'

'I'm. . .' started Charlie, and stopped. He said: 'No. It would sound trite.'

'Thanks anyway.' She was silent for a moment and then she said: 'That's not why I made contact. I mean I didn't think. . .' Her voice trailed off and she shrugged.

'I didn't think it was,' said Charlie.

She smiled at him hesitantly. 'I'd like to see you sometimes, though. If you'd like to, that is. Nothing serious. No commitment. Just a drink occasionally, like now.'

'Yes,' said Charlie doubtfully. They were two lonely people, he thought. Why not?

'I shouldn't have said that,' regretted Laura hurriedly.

'Don't be silly.'

'Was she beautiful?'

'I thought so.'

'Sure you don't want to talk about it?'

'Very.'

'I went over to Fulham last weekend, where Paul and the girl are living. Hung about. Actually saw them. They were taking the first baby out for a walk. One of those pushchairs with wheels that twist in every direction. It's a little boy, you know, their first baby. Peter. Can't think why I went there now. They seemed very happy. They were laughing. He had his arm around her.'

Charlie wished desperately he could think of something to say, to help. Maybe he was helping by not saying anything.

'Sorry,' she said.

'There's nothing to be sorry about, not to me.'

She smiled at him sadly. 'You know that photograph that used to upset you, the one of Paul?'

'Yes.'

'He took it with him.'

'Don't go to Fulham any more,' advised Charlie.

'I won't.'

The bottle between them was empty. Charlie said: 'Would you like some more?'

'No,' refused Laura. 'I should be getting home.' She looked directly at him and said: 'I don't want you to come back with me.'

'I wasn't going to suggest it,' said Charlie.

'Just a drink, occasionally.'

'That would be good.'

'Life *is* a bitch, isn't it!' She said with sudden vehemence.

'Every time,' agreed Charlie.

'I thought there *was* going to be improvement, a week ago,' said the nursing home matron. 'There were definitely signs of some emergence. But in the end nothing happened.'

Charlie put the chocolates on the woman's desk and said: 'Why don't you have these?'

'We mustn't lose hope,' insisted the woman.

'I don't,' said Charlie. 'Ever.' There was something else he was never going to lose, either. The doubt that by feeding things back to Harkness as he had, through Laura, he'd actually caused his mother to be interrogated as she had been: that her remission wasn't the fault of the Special Branch men but his.

48

'Exceptional!' said Valeri Kalenin. 'Absolutely exceptional!'

'Thank you,' said Berenkov. This wasn't the first praise. Berenkov was accustomed to it, so the attitude was practised, humble deference. But today was particularly important to him. Berenkov was glad their friendship had been restored, the suspicion between them – more Kalenin's suspicion than his – swept away. He'd been fortunate, Berenkov accepted: incredibly fortunate. But only he knew it: would ever know it. Luck comes to the daring, he thought. He didn't think he would attempt to be the daring again. To himself – but only to himself – Berenkov conceded that he'd been badly frightened until that last drawing arrived from England in the diplomatic bag.

'Not my words,' allowed Kalenin honestly. 'The opinion of the commendation from the Praesidium itself. We're secure, Alexei. Secure. And you made us so.'

'Everyone is being extremely generous,' said Berenkov, remaining modest. So Kalenin, who'd been prepared to avoid the responsibility, was happy to be sharing the credit. Berenkov felt no resentment.

'I did not expect Guzins simply to be deported as he was,' qualified Kalenin. 'The British made an incredible mistake there. Over the whole affair, in fact.'

Further luck, reflected Berenkov. He said: 'I expected him to break: make a full incriminating confession.'

'So all we've lost is Petrin.'

'Always an acceptable sacrifice, like Obyedkov,' pointed out Berenkov. 'We can repatriate them, in time.'

'And we're permanently rid of Charlie Muffin!'

Berenkov smiled. The newspaper reports of Charlie Muffin's trial had been brief, dictated by the restrictions of the hearing, but he'd had them all sent to him from London. He said: 'Ten years. He'll never be able to endure ten years.'

'It was still a very great risk, doing what you did,' said Kalenin soberly.

'*Calculated* risk,' insisted Berenkov.

'It worried me,' admitted Kalenin.

Not as much as it worried me, at the very end, thought Berenkov. 'It worked,' he said, the conceit creeping through.

'What are you going to do about the woman?'

'Nothing,' said Berenkov. 'The function she fulfils is useful. Maybe I'll transfer her back to debriefing, but not immediately.'

'Did it ever occur to you that she might have defected, to be with him?'

'It was a possibility,' admitted Berenkov. 'But we always had her son as a hostage. She would have known that.'

'It's unimportant now,' judged Kalenin.

'What's the missile schedule?' asked Berenkov.

'Extremely advanced,' said Kalenin. 'The Foreign Minister is to make an announcement of our capability at a meeting on conventional weapons in Geneva next week. When the uproar subsides – we're estimating a week – there'll be the invitation to the Western media to witness the actual launch. All the Western ambassadors are going to be invited to Baikonur, as well. . .' Kalenin smiled. 'The intention is to make a big spectacle of it.'

'We'll certainly achieve that,' said Berenkov.

439

'I want to apologize to you, personally,' declared Kalenin. 'I was quite wrong to doubt you as I did.'

'It is forgotten,' dismissed Berenkov. 'Friends can doubt each other occasionally, can't they?'

'Never again,' assured Kalenin. 'Never again.'

'We're going up to the dacha next weekend,' said Berenkov. 'Georgi is home. Valentina would like you to come up with us.'

'I'd enjoy that,' accepted Kalenin. 'I'd enjoy that very much indeed.'

It was better now than when she had first returned: no one but Natalia would have been aware of the remaining scars because she'd rearranged an easy chair to cover the carpet burn and paid an odd-job man in the Mytinskaya apartment block to replace the shattered cabinet door in the kitchen.

It had been appalling when she'd got back. Like an animal cage from which the beasts had escaped or been driven. There had even been an animal-like smell, a gagging stench of the crowded-together bodies of whoever Eduard had brought back with him for his leave while she had been away. Apart from the carpet burn – a large, through-to-the-floorboards hole where something had been allowed to smoulder for a long time – and the smashed cabinet there had been empty bottles strewn throughout the kitchen, the sink filled with unwashed crockery, and the toilet bowl blocked with unflushed faeces. But that wasn't what caused Natalia's greatest offence. That had been her own bedroom. Eduard had allowed someone to use her bed. And not merely someone – a single person – because it had really been used, the sheets marked and stained. Natalia had felt violated, abused. She'd stripped the bed, heaving with revulsion, but hadn't washed the sheets because she'd known she wouldn't ever be able to

440

sleep in them again, not even if they were clean: she'd rolled them up into a ball and thrown them out and scoured and scalded everything in the flat and finally scoured herself in the hottest bath in which she could bear to immerse herself, trying to wash away the feeling of being befouled.

And cried.

The state of the flat had been the excuse that night. And for some nights after, but she couldn't call upon it any more, not after all these weeks. Not that she wept so much, not any longer. Only when she let herself think back to those nights: remembered the tenderness and the words they'd said to each other, the promises made but not kept. Like now. Natalia felt her eyes begin to fill but didn't care because she was quite alone in the apartment, as she was resigned to being for ever.

'Why didn't you come, Charlie?' she sobbed aloud. 'Oh dear God why didn't you come!'

The Soviet publicity surrounding the launch was brilliantly engineered and manipulated. The Foreign Minister's announcement in Geneva created the furore that Moscow anticipated, although it continued longer than expected, with Western analysts and commentators concluding that Moscow was at least ten years further advanced in its space technology than had been previously imagined and that the gap was probably too great for the United States to catch up. The Kremlin capitalized upon the reaction, staging a press conference for the world media at which the Foreign Minister expanded upon his initial announcement, pressing the fact that the Soviet Star Wars platform was entirely defensive – as America had always insisted theirs to be – and that its being put into space in no way affected or reversed the scaling down of missiles and weaponry already agreed and undertaken by the Warsaw Pact nations.

There was a frenzied response to the invitation to attend the actual launch, which was organized to obtain the maximum international impact. Satellites enabled television pictures to be transmitted live and worldwide, and the lift-off of the shuttle to take the missile into its two-hundred-mile-high geostationary orbit timed specifically to coincide with peak viewing time, particularly in America. As well as permitting full photographic facilities at the lift-off gantry, complete access was also made available inside the space control centre, to enable the launch to be followed up to orbiting height, where television cameras aboard the shuttle were to show the moment of launch and the establishment of the missile into its planned position in space.

The lift-off went faultlessly on a brilliantly clear day.

The shuttle arced off into its trajectory, with simultaneous translations into English of the crew conversation and after a momentary, snow-like flicker of interference the television pictures beamed back from space became perfectly clear.

The missile housing being disgorged from the belly of the shuttle looked remarkably like some space animal giving birth, which was how at least two television commentators described it. For the first few seconds it was hard to differentiate the platform from the shuttle but then, as it floated free, its shape became obvious.

It was about twenty yards from the mother ship when the explosion happened. One moment the television screens were filled with the picture of a square-shaped, box-like structure, the next it burst apart into a thousand fragments but in complete silence, which heightened the shock of its destruction. Then the television screens went blank.

'Good God!' said Wilson. Although he'd been expecting it – hoping for it – he still sounded shocked.

Charlie, who was in the room at Westminster Bridge Road with the Director General, watching the Soviet transmission, slowly released the pent-up breath. 'It worked,' he said, relieved.

'It's difficult to believe that something as simple as the grease of ordinary hand cream could prevent the bonding of the carbon fibre sheets and create an air-bubble void that would expand and explode like that in the vacuum of space, isn't it?' said Wilson.

'But it did,' said Charlie gratefully. 'It did.'